THE ACCIDENTAL DUKE

Book One in the
Mad Matchmaking Men of Waterloo

By Barbara Devlin

#ownvoices

Dragonblade Publishing, Inc. is an imprint of Kathryn Le Veque Novels, Inc.
P.O. Box 7968
La Verne CA 91750
ceo@dragonbladepublishing.com

Produced in the United States of America

First Edition April 2021
Print Edition

#ownvoices

ARE YOU SIGNED UP FOR DRAGONBLADE'S BLOG?

You'll get the latest news and information on exclusive giveaways, exclusive excerpts, coming releases, sales, free books, cover reveals and more.

Check out our complete list of authors, too!

No spam, no junk. That's a promise!

Sign Up Here

www.dragonbladepublishing.com

Dearest Reader;

Thank you for your support of a small press. At Dragonblade Publishing, we strive to bring you the highest quality Historical Romance from the some of the best authors in the business. Without your support, there is no 'us', so we sincerely hope you adore these stories and find some new favorite authors along the way.

Happy Reading!

CEO, Dragonblade Publishing

Author's Note

Dear Reader,

I am a person with a disability. It has taken years for me to admit that to those who don't know me. I hid my disability because I couldn't bear the pity, condescension, and sometimes open disdain with which others treated me. I didn't want to be the injured woman. The inferior woman. Less than. Other. Since the life-altering accident and permanent injury that ended my law enforcement career and devastated my world as I knew it, I endured years of painful therapy and rehabilitation with a single goal in mind: to conceal my condition. To avoid the inevitable questions. To escape the memories, if only for a little while. Yet, more than twenty years later, I still struggle with paralyzing panic during bad weather. I lock myself in my home on the anniversary of the day a drunk driver plowed into the accident scene I was investigating, leaving me pinned between a car and a guardrail.

There is no training to prepare us for disability and the accompanying mental trauma. It's something that must be experienced, firsthand, to truly understand. The associated stigma only inflicts more suffering. That's why I wrote this series. To help others struggling with disability, that they might realize there's nothing wrong with them. We're only human. Unfortunately, the assumptions surrounding disability are nothing new.

Research for this book led me to Dominique Jean Larrey, Napoleon's personal physician. Larrey wrote extensively on what he referred to as nostalgia or irritable heart. Today, we call it Post-Traumatic Stress Disorder (PTSD). What I discovered was countless troops from the Peninsular Wars experienced lingering effects of battlefield trauma, and many were committed to asylums, where treatment incorporated an array of methods, including starvation, sleep deprivation, and torture.

The descriptions of the fictional Little Bethlem, including treatment and torture devices, are based on accounts from the final report of the 1815 Parliamentary Committee on Madhouses and narratives by Edward Wakefield, an advocate for asylum reform. The committee sought to change management of the insane from one of confinement and physical restraint to one of re-education and socialization. For the wealthy, involuntary commitment was a lucrative business exploited by medical professionals promising a variety of cures for the right price.

Perhaps the most astonishing aspect of my personal experience creating this series was realizing how little has changed in the way of attitudes toward those with physical and mental disabilities. As my agent shopped the first book, I met with an editor from a traditional publisher at a conference. With a smile on her face, she explained to me that, while she enjoyed the story and my prose, no one wanted to read my *sick lit*. That's right. *Sick lit*. With that one sentence, she threw me back to the past. Back to that cold December day when everything changed. When I became a shadow of my former self. I started over in that moment. I just didn't know it at the time. So, after the unfortunate exchange, I returned to my room, sat on the bed, and cried. Then I got up and emailed my agent, and we started over again. In the end, I found a publisher who believed in me and my work. An advocate.

Dragonblade is the latest in a long line of supporters who've helped me make it where I am today. Who believed in me when I didn't believe in myself. Not the least of which is my network of family and friends. Perhaps the most significant champion in my corner is my husband, Mike. We weren't married when I was injured, but he didn't let that stop him from loving me or making me his wife, a privilege I've enjoyed for more than twenty years. So, if you learn anything from me, please, know that disability is not the end. In some ways, it's a new beginning, filled with just as much promise as the past. If this series helps just one person, the fight will have been worth it.

Thank you.
Barb

CHAPTER ONE

London
April, 1816

*T*HE SWEET STENCH *of blood mixed with sweat and damp earth weighed heavy in the air, an acrid pall thick as evening fog on the Thames. Mangled bodies, some bearing no recognizable features, littered the once resplendent countryside, which now manifested a seemingly infinite makeshift gravesite. The remaining survivors, beaten and butchered, their cries merging to form a morbid audial tapestry of misery and pain, stumbled to their respective camps, oblivious to the herald's cry declaring the winner, as if anyone could claim victory amid such massive human devastation.*

Crawling along the verge, a lone soldier, a mere shadow of a man, confused and afraid, shook himself alert and dragged himself toward safety. At least, he thought he headed in the right direction, but he didn't understand why he failed to advance. Instead, he struggled in place. After rolling onto his back, he sat upright and wiped his brow. Shielding his eyes from the sun's rays, he peered down. It was then he discovered the lower half of his left arm missing, and he screamed.

Venting an unholy howl of horror, British Army Major Anthony Erasmus Hildebrand Bartlett, 7th marquess of Rockingham, woke with a lurch and glanced from side to side. With his eyes focused on the canopy of his four-poster bed, as his heartbeat hammered in his chest and his pulse pounded in his ears, he gasped for breath. At last, he realized he prevailed in London.

After a few minutes, he pushed from the mattress, and the fear wrenching his gut subsided. With questionable balance, he staggered to the washstand. At the basin, he fought with the heavy pitcher but managed to fill the porcelain bowl. Then he splashed his face with water. Studying his reflection in the mirror, he frowned and shook his head.

How long would the nightmares terrorize his sleep?

How many times would he venture to that awful place?

The Battle of Waterloo may have ended the war with France, but it left behind a trail of victims still engaged in conflicts, real and imagined, nonetheless brutal as the original skirmish. While England celebrated Napoleon's defeat and exile, and life returned to normal on the streets of London, full of frivolous balls, promenades, and musicales that marked the start of the Season, Anthony remained imprisoned in the past.

At the Mont Saint Jean escarpment where he lost his limb and so much more.

"Anthony, are you there?" Father knocked and then opened the door. "I thought I heard you." Without invitation, he strolled into the bedchamber. "Are you all right, son?"

"Aside from the fact that I have no left hand, I suppose I am fine." Summoning composure, Anthony buried his nose in a towel and braced for another lecture, a predictable succession of which occupied his daily routine and chipped away at the last vestiges of his patience. There was a time when he considered his father a friend, but that changed when Anthony became the heir to a dukedom he did not want. Second sons required no regular reprimands on the importance of honor and duty. Tossing aside the cloth, he stared at the empty sleeve pinned to his shirt, which reflected a far greater loss than the absent appendage. "And I apologize if I disturbed you."

"You nap as you did when you were a babe, and that is what concerns me." And so the familiar discourse commenced, as dependable as the sunset, and his father frowned. "You have been home these eight months, yet you do not resume your normal activities. The war is over, yet you maintain the fight. Why do you shut yourself away from the world? Why do you not go out with your friends?" he asked in a sharp tone. "You are a war hero, distinguished by your courage displayed under Wellington's command. Why do you not celebrate—"

"What is there to celebrate?" His rapier retort cut through his father's impossible hopes, because Anthony had no desire to rejoin the world. At least, not in his current state. "The very suggestion inspires naught but disgust, and my friends are similarly battered and impaired." With a huff of frustration, Anthony speared his fingers through his hair and stomped to the window. As the familiar clamor of war filled his ears, he flung open the drapes. Gazing at the sky, he mourned the many casualties. How could he go on, waltzing through the ton's ballrooms, as though nothing happened? "John is dead, or did you forget him, already?"

"I forget nothing about my firstborn and your elder brother, but he *is* gone, God rest his soul." Tugging at the lapels of his coat, Father stood tall with his usual pomposity. "What use is there to dwell on a future that no longer exists?" he asked, with nary a hint of emotion. "And you are here, to take up the reins and ensure the continuation of our legacy, so all is not lost."

"Ah, yes." At the prospect, Anthony swallowed hard, given he never desired the title and its myriad responsibilities. Indeed, he preferred the relative invisibility associated with the life of a second son, and he longed for the bygone simplicity. Could he not just be himself? "There is that, *Your Grace.*"

Yes, he deliberately goaded his father, as he did before the war, but his father didn't take the bait, much to Anthony's disappointment. Could they not return to the old days, marked by good-natured ribbing and morning horse races along Rotten Row?

"You will check your tone, sir, because I raised you better than that, and you will not speak to me thus." The formidable patriarch, unerring in his focus, emerged, and Anthony's knees buckled, because he would rather cut off his other arm than fail his father. In an instant, Father bent and drew Anthony into a reassuring hug. "Easy, my boy. I do not pretend to understand your obsession with what is done and cannot be undone, or the invisible scars you carry as a blockade, of a sort, to exclude those who would provide succor in times of heartache. While I am proud to have sacrificed my sons on the altar of freedom from Napoleon's tyranny, I know you cannot persist in this fashion. I will no longer permit you to linger in this pitiful state."

"What do you intend?" As Father brushed Anthony's hair from his forehead, he arched a brow. "A spanking?"

"Something much worse, but do not tempt me." Father chuckled, and Anthony walked to the armoire, in search of distraction, that he might gather his wits and counter whatever hair-brained scheme his father proposed next. Could he simply not let Anthony mourn the loss of his arm? "A missive is just arrived from Lord Ainsworth."

"What has that to do with me?" He retrieved a yard-length swathe of linen and sighed, because the item represented another in a series of tasks Anthony could not perform for himself, given he had only half a left arm. Instead of seizing a diversion, he only reminded himself of his deficiency, and he cursed his miserable hide. "Lord Ainsworth is *your* friend, is he not?"

"Indeed, Ainsworth is my oldest and dearest childhood chum, dating to my tenure at Eton, when I still wore shortcoats." Father flicked his fingers, and Anthony dragged his heels as a petulant child. While his father tied a perfect mathematical, he sniffed. "Tomorrow, you and I shall journey to Upper Brook Street and pay call on your fiancée, Lady Arabella, because it is past due for you to renew your acquaintance. By the by, I plan to announce your engagement at the ball, in a fortnight."

"I beg your pardon?" A shudder of pure dread gripped his spine, and the room seemed to pitch and turn. Anthony hobbled and tripped, and in the floor an imaginary, fiery chasm opened wide, threatening to consume him. He fell to the carpet. The resulting jolt thrust him, headlong and without warning, into the grip of a gruesome reverie he could not defend against.

A rapid salvo echoed in his ears, accompanied by the telltale caustic fetor of gunpowder, which permeated and burned his nostrils. In a delusory flash of cannon fire, he transported to the bloody field and the infamous day that destroyed so many lives and with them the dreams borne of youthful ignorance and naiveté. Amid the black vortex, which threatened to swallow him whole, a faint summons beckoned.

"Anthony." Father's voice came to Anthony, as if from afar. "Anthony, I am here, son. Please, don't do this to yourself. You must let go of the past."

Of course, his father would assume Anthony controlled the vicious, unrelenting memories that caught him in their unforgiving trap without notice. In truth, he had no command of the tortuous curse that plagued his consciousness. Slowly, Anthony emerged from the horror. His lungs screamed for air, and he discovered he remained in his room, in London. The instruments of war faded into the background, and he returned to the present.

That was the cruelest aspect of his disability—the loss that seemed never-ending. What no one understood was that he didn't lose his arm just once, on that hill. Indeed, he lost it in countless different times and ways. Again and again, he suffered the injury in a seemingly agonizing cycle of the everyday trivialities of life that he could no longer perform: the inability to cut his own food, the helplessness when he struggled to dress himself, and the half-empty sleeve forever pinned to his coat, which all but screamed impotence. Little, if anything, of his former confident self endured. As the tattered remnants of his world crumbled to the ground, he collapsed in his father's arms and vomited on his pristine coat.

"Shh." Sitting on the floor, Father rocked, to and fro, and patted Anthony's back. "I am with you, my son, and you have my solemn vow that, together, we will rally again and survive this terrible tragedy."

"How?" Anthony pondered the bleak revelation and snorted. While he wanted to heal, he knew not how to go about it, and no one offered help. "By shackling me to some poor, unfortunate creature I haven't seen in more than fifteen years and can scarcely recall? How old is she, now?"

"Lady Arabella is eight and ten, old enough to stand as your wife. She is of excellent stock and will bear you many healthy sons to carry on the dukedom." Father rested his cheek to Anthony's crown, and he savored the comforting support. "You are my only surviving child, and I will not allow you to continue on this sullen path to ruin, because your torment devastates your mother."

His torment devastated her?

"And you honestly believe that Lady Arabella is the answer, when she was promised to my brother?" The mere thought gave Anthony a wicked case of collywobbles, because he had no desire to wed in his condition, which inspired a fresh series of dry heaves. "How do you know the lady is willing, given she was promised to John? What if her affections are engaged?"

"Lady Arabella is bound to the marquessate of Rockingham, regardless of who holds the title. Her preference never entered the equation, and she will do as she is told," his father stated with characteristic arrogance. He offered his handkerchief, which Anthony used to daub his mouth as he shrugged free. Balancing on a knee, he steadied himself and then stood. "And love is of no consequence in contracted unions, but you know that."

"Is that how you feel about Mama?" he asked with more than a little sarcasm, because nothing about his parents' union struck Anthony as felicitous. Mulling the prospect, he supposed it would have been better to suffer an honorable death on the battlefield than endure the hollow prison of matrimony, with its protracted demise over the course of untold years, which his sire proposed. "Or would you have me believe you covet a genuine attachment for my mother, when I suspect otherwise?"

"Your impudence tests the limits of my patience, and our beginning was as nondescript as any other, I suppose." Stretching to full height, Father doffed his spoiled coat, as Anthony rolled his shoulders and inhaled a deep breath. "But over the years we have developed an understanding and an authentic friendship. I would never do anything to cause her shame or angst, yet neither of us brought any illusions of sentimental love to the altar. If you are wise, you will approach your nuptials with similar expectations and common sense."

Neither Lady Arabella nor marriage manifested the source of Anthony's concern. Indeed, he remained numb to the pedestrian pleasures of everyday life. Billiards, cards, chess, and evenings at White's, once favored pastimes, inspired naught but apathy. The simple truth was he found no joy in anything. If only he could escape what now resided in the annals of history, he just might find a way to cope with all the tomorrows. "Father, as much as it grieves me to defy you, I cannot marry Lady Arabella, because I am in no condition to care for a wife."

Silence weighed heavy in the room, and palpable tension hung in the air. Even the bright sunlight from the windows could not dispel the chill of doom.

"It is regrettable that you are so quick to throw away what could be a chance at regaining a measure of happiness." Given Father's statement, Anthony breathed a sigh of relief. "Be that as it may, you were born into a position of power and privilege, and you will fulfill your obligations to this family, as the next in line," his father stated with grim finality. After adjusting the folds of Anthony's cravat, Father strode to the door. With his hand on the knob, he peered over his shoulder, and his nostrils flared. "In the morning, you will present yourself, groomed and garbed as a gentleman, whereupon you will accompany me to Upper Brook Street and gift a betrothal ring to your bride-to-be, so you had best reconcile yourself to it."

In that moment, Anthony ran to the basin, bent, and retched.

DRESS, PRIMP, PREEN, and pose; such was the life of a proper English lady. After a series of seemingly endless days spent in study of scintillating topics that focused on the finer points of menu planning, ledger tallying, etiquette, posture, and embroidery, a debutante embarked on the second chapter of her existence as a wife and a mother, where the sum of her worth rested on her ability to be seen and not heard, her voice forever silenced, perforce yielding to her husband's commands.

For Lady Arabella Hortence Gibbs, only child of the earl of Ainsworth, that would never suffice.

Garbed in a modest morning dress of pale yellow sprigged muslin with long sleeves and a lace collar, she lounged on the *chaise* and awaited her doom—and it was her doom. Although she appeared calm and reserved on the outside, inside she wrestled with her prepared speech, because she would take no mate without issuing her terms. If the new Lord Rockingham did not agree with her conditions, she would not accept him. Yet, even as she made her silent declaration of independence, she had no real choice in the matter.

That was the harshest blow of all.

Defined by society as an object, as property, as a plaything for men, women measured their future in the lack of opportunity, given they could control nothing of their own fate. If Arabella acquiesced, she would exist as a reflection of her future husband's predilections. Like it or not, her name, her freedom, and her fortune belonged to her prospective husband, yet she reached for something more, if only to remind herself that she was a person with a mind and a will of her own.

"Arabella, are you ready?" Ever the consummate matriarch, Mama presented an elegant image of everything Arabella disdained: the obedient servant. "Lord Rockingham is just arrived with His Grace, and we cannot dally, because you should make a good first impression on your future husband."

"Of course, Mama." While Arabella dearly loved her mother, she never understood how anyone could willingly settle for the trifling world, comprised of naught more challenging than the daily selection of perfume and petticoats and a marriage brokered for financial gain and to strengthen political connections. With one last check of her appearance in the long mirror, she smoothed her skirts and squared her shoulders. "Let us commence the negotiations."

Riding a crest of high dudgeon, she skimmed her palm along the polished balustrade as she descended the staircase. In the foyer, her father lingered with another gentleman, tall and distinguished.

"Ah, here she is, my pride and joy." Papa drew her to his side. "Your Grace, may I present my daughter, Lady Arabella." Then he gazed on her with unveiled delight, and she basked in his approval, because she loved her father. "Arabella, this is His Grace, Walter Bartlett, the Duke of Swanborough."

"Your Grace." As she had practiced countless times, she executed a perfect curtsey, but she would have preferred to fall on her face.

"It is a pleasure, Lady Arabella." The duke smiled as he assessed her from top to toe. She swallowed the urge to bare her teeth, like a mare at Tattersalls, for his inspection. "My, but she is a pretty little thing, Arthur. Perhaps she will inspire my son to rejoin the world."

"Oh, no doubt, no doubt." Papa hugged his belly and laughed. "And to be that young again."

Arabella quickly lowered her eyes, clenching her fists in the folds of her skirt. How she hated being spoken about as if she were invisible, or worse yet, mindless. Of course, most men treated women as such, and she aimed to change that, starting with her prospective groom.

"Arabella." Mama snapped her fingers. "Stop dawdling, because Lord Rockingham awaits."

With determination as a shield, Arabella inhaled a calming breath. Summoning patience, she marched into the fray. In the drawing room, a lone figure manifested an ominous specter of an unwelcome fate, and he turned on a heel when she paused at center. Before Papa could make the introductions, the tall, brown-haired stranger bowed.

"Lady Arabella, it is an honor." She liked the sound of that. "I am Anthony, the Marquess of Rockingham."

Impressive in stature, garbed in black breeches, a burgundy waistcoat trimmed in old gold, and a stunning coat of grey Bath superfine, with a crisp cravat and polished Hessians completing the ensemble, Anthony possessed a handsome profile which bore patrician features similar to his father's. Any woman, except Arabella, would have been thrilled to call him hers.

But it was what he lacked that snared her attention, and she blurted, "Why, you are missing an arm."

"*Arabella.*" With a sharp expression of disapproval, Papa clapped once, and she flinched. "Apologize."

"I am so sorry, Lord Rockingham." In her unintended blunder, had she undermined her position of authority prior to declaring her stance? "I meant no offense, but you startled me."

"No apologies necessary, because you are very observant." He smiled, revealing the hint of a dimple to the left of his mouth. Then he glanced at Papa and the duke. "Given our fast approaching nuptials, might I beg a moment in private with my fiancée, because I have not seen her since she was a girl of five?"

"Not without a chaperone, Lord Rockingham." Mama wagged a finger, as if the marquess were a naughty child. "After all, we must preserve Arabella's reputation until the vows are secured."

"But I can occupy the chair, and Lord Rockingham can sit on the sofa, Mama," Arabella stated with confidence and peered at her adversary. To her surprise, he favored her with a mischievous grin. Perhaps she found an ally, and how she needed one. "You do not suspect His Lordship will accost me with a table situated between us." Then she glanced at her father, to make a second appeal. Rocking on her heels, she lowered her chin and pouted, given he never could deny her. "What say you, Papa, if I promise to be good?"

"In normal circumstances, I would agree with Helen." Father appeared to give the request due consideration. "However, inasmuch we are to be family, we can make an exception and dispense with the usual proprieties, because we are not in public. To satisfy the feminine sensibilities, we will leave the doors open, and Helen can sit in the foyer." To the duke, Papa said, "I trust Anthony will behave like a gentleman?"

"Of course." His Grace chucked Father on the shoulder in a surprising display of amity, and she realized that, with or without her consent, her path was set. "Let us adjourn to the study, fix a date for the ceremony, review the contracts, and enjoy a celebratory brandy."

Thus she marched to her demise.

Alone, to a degree, with her opponent, Arabella perched on her makeshift throne and girded her defenses. Recalling her rehearsed oratory, she cleared her throat. "Lord Rockingham, while I am grateful that you deem me worthy of—"

"Lady Arabella, I cannot marry you." And just like that, Anthony stole the wind from her sails, yet his interests aligned perfectly with hers.

"I b-beg your pardon?" The man was not what she expected. Was it possible her prayers had been heard, and fate delivered a supporter? "Am I dreaming, or did you just declare your opposition to our union?"

"Believe me, I have no wish to cause offense, but I simply cannot abide by the terms of the pact between our two houses." Nervousness apparent, his fingers shook as he wiped his brow and scooted to the edge of his seat. "Given my appearance, I think it obvious I am unfit to assume the responsibilities of a husband and a father."

"Given your appearance?" Repeating the phrase in her mind, she canted her head and scrutinized him for some additional deficiency. "I don't follow. What else is wrong with you?" Indeed, he retained two eyes, a nose, fascinating lips, and both legs. Stumped, she leaned close and whispered, "Are you missing something of importance?"

At first, he opened his mouth, and then he blinked. Blushing, which she found quite charming, he cast a smile and tugged at his collar. "Uh, no. I remain wholly intact, insofar as the rest of my anatomy is concerned."

"I see." Actually, she didn't quite understand his cryptic comment. "But I should put you at ease, given your candor, and express similar reservations, because I have no wish to wed you, or anyone, for that matter."

"Indeed?" Anthony arched his brows. "Forgive my boldness, but you are handsome. Do not all debutantes live for the day they slip the parson's noose about some poor, misguided sot's neck?"

"Such as yourself?" She stuck her tongue in her cheek. Let him choke on that response. "Or do you rebel, as do I, given I have never thought of myself as a debutante?"

"Ah, you must be one of *those* ladies." The marquess snickered, and she bristled at the inference. "Let me guess. You admire the blathering lunacy of Wollstonecraft and her ilk?"

"Mary Wollstonecraft is a genius, and *A Vindication of the Rights of Woman* is a masterpiece of logic." Angry in an instant, Arabella's temper got the best of her, and she shook her fist. "Despite assertions to the contrary, you are not my superior, and I shall go to my grave rebuking such ridiculous notions. As Wollstonecraft argues, quite correctly, I might add, men benefit from education, which increases their reasoning capability. When women are provided the same advantages, we are equally rational beings. Thus, it is a patriarchal society that first stifles our intelligence and then punishes us when we react according to our deficiency."

"Is that so?" Narrowing his stare, Anthony lowered his chin and rested his elbow to his knee. "You talk too much."

"How dare you." From the foyer, Mama coughed, and Arabella checked her tone. In a low voice, she said, "Without doubt, you are the most rude, ill-mannered, illiterate, and...and—"

"The word you are looking for is insufferable." He winked.

"Oh, you are a vast deal more than insufferable, sir." At her insult, she anticipated hellfire and damnation. Instead, he burst into laughter, and it was in that moment she realized he deliberately baited her, but she knew not why. "I should not have said that, but you can be quite provoking, Lord Rockingham."

"You speak the truth, and I forgot polite protocol, so no harm done, Lady Arabella. While I am not certain I support your overall conclusions, I can appreciate your passion, as you glow, my dear." A hint of sadness invested his countenance, and she pondered the wounds she could not see, because, much like an onion, he possessed so many layers. "It may be difficult to believe, but I once coveted such strong convictions."

"Before the war?" Again, she overstepped the limits of urbane decorum, and in silence she vowed to improve. "Please, forgive me, my lord. I am not usually so—"

"—Intrusive?" The unveiled amusement in his gaze negated disapproval, and she sighed in relief. "Something tells me otherwise."

"So, you are insufferable, and I am intrusive. In all honesty, it has always been my downfall." She tried to adopt an air of refined composure but settled for something not quite so clumsy, because she liked him. She genuinely liked him. "But I would love to hear your gallant tales of life on the battlefield, because you must be very proud to have served your country with such valor."

"You think I should be proud? Of what?" On the heels of his query, which struck her as a tad sarcastic, everything in his demeanor transformed into something altogether dark and alarming. Gone was the boyish charm. In its place, palpable tension marred his elegant features, and in an instant, she confronted a stranger. "Pray, explain yourself, because the entire experience remains a mystery to me, and in its wake I question everything about myself."

"You are hurting." While Arabella read the Waterloo accounts in *The Times*, which lauded Wellington's cunning strategy, heroism, and victory, the articles reduced the lives of those lost to numerical figures bereft of the emotional toll exacted on the survivors. The wounded were by and large ignored, yet they represented casualties, too. She studied the empty coat sleeve pinned to his lapel, in so many ways a harsh reflection of his altered personality, and wondered of the horrors he must have witnessed. "But I do not reference your most obvious injury."

"Do you presume to know me?" he snapped. Myriad emotions flashed in his expression, and he bared his teeth. Then he exhaled and slapped his thigh. To her dismay, she incited a reaction she didn't comprehend, and she sought some means to mollify him. "Do you possess powers of divination, that you can read my thoughts?"

Despite his outward aggression, which she likened to a barking dog, she sensed underlying fear. So much fear. And anguish.

"On the contrary, I presume nothing and claim no such abilities." In light of his much-changed attitude, she should have been afraid, yet he scared her not, because he exhibited telltale elements of vulnerability, in the subtle tic of his right brow and the gentle tremor of his lower lip, which called to her on some base level. It would have been fascinating to know him in some capacity, and she ached to offer reassurance. Did no one detect the evidence of his agony but her? "But

I have eyes, Lord Rockingham, and you wear your pain like one of your garments. Perhaps you could recount your tale of woe, because I have been told I am an excellent listener, and it might help to share your burden. While it would seem we are not to wed, and I am in complete agreement with you regarding your decision, I would be your friend, if you permit it."

Indeed, she could never have too many friends, and he offered her the opportunity to be of use, which always appealed to her. Indeed, the man posited a puzzle just waiting for her to solve.

"Lady Arabella, I will make you a bargain. If you can work with me to devise a means of ending our engagement, excepting a scandal, never again will I force upon you my odious company, so I have no need of your friendship. But until that time, we shall play our part as the happy couple." She had not a chance to respond before Anthony fished a box from his pocket and set the tiny parcel on the table. Standing, he frowned. "Your betrothal ring, which my father insisted I gift today. Thus I have fulfilled his requirement, and now I will take my leave."

With that, Lord Rockingham strode from the drawing room without so much as a fond farewell, and she wondered what went wrong. Ears ringing, and her heart pounding in her chest, Arabella snatched the box and leaped from the chair. For a few seconds, she stared at the floor and pondered her next move. Then she shook herself alert and ran to the front windows, to see what he did for an encore. Sheltering in the shadows of the drapery, she stared beyond the glass at her baffling but captivating fiancé.

No, he was nothing like what she anticipated.

On the sidewalk, Anthony paced and argued with himself. Then he bumped into some unlucky passerby, who tumbled to the ground but quickly scrambled to his feet. When the stranger noted the marquess' missing limb, the bystander tipped his hat and rushed to the corner, and she could just imagine what that outward expression of pity did to

Anthony's confidence.

Shoulders slumped, he studied the pavement for several minutes, and some peculiar but deep-seated intrigue tugged at her conscience. How she longed to comfort him, though she didn't understand her reaction to a man who was, for all intents and purposes, unknown to her. Perhaps an internal sense of humanity motivated her, because she could not decipher the emotions swirling inside her.

When he lifted his chin and met her stare, what she glimpsed in his crystal blue eyes—a lethal mix of discernible anguish, shame, and profound self-loathing—reached through the distance between them to clutch her throat, to ravage her gut, to wreak havoc on her confidence, and she whimpered and pressed her palm to the glass.

Yet she did not—would not founder, because he needed someone to stand for him. While she would not be his wife, she could be his champion in that moment.

Drawing on her inner strength, honed in the late hours when she read books by candlelight, she stood for Lord Rockingham and found purpose where she least expected it. Slowly, she mouthed, *I see you.* In response, he darted down the lane.

For a long while she lingered, replaying recent events, until her mother called, and Arabella exhaled. "I will be right there, Mama."

After wiping a tear from her cheek, which she hadn't noticed until then, she opened the box and discovered a beautiful diamond and sapphire halo ring resting on a bed of pristine cotton. Toying with the bauble, she envisioned Lord Rockingham in all his tragic glory, like some mythical Greek god. It would take a strong woman to marry the interesting but damaged man, and she hoped he would find peace and solace with his special lady.

CHAPTER TWO

F OR SOME REASON Anthony never could discern, London society dressed in their finery to tour Hyde Park during the fashionable hours known as the Promenade, if for no other purpose than to be seen. Indeed the entire ridiculous ritual, which mixed layer upon layer of frippery and the outdoors, confused him. Part of the pomp and pageantry that comprised the *ton*, with its frivolous rituals and myriad dictates, the organized walk served as an opportunity to solidify connections, mark future husbands, and target an accommodating wife or widow. Of course, before the war, he saddled his beloved stallion and raced along Rotten Row with his brother or his father, but those days were gone and with them so much joy.

Now, as a prisoner of another campaign, he prepared to walk in the park as the dutiful son and heir with his parents, while the family rig carried him down the streets of Mayfair. Overhead, the blue sky boasted a brilliant sun and nary a cloud. Birds flitted about, and red squirrels scampered between trees. He enjoyed none of it. In a sense, he already occupied half his grave. Too bad Waterloo didn't finish the job. Instead, the conflict left him to wander the earth as an empty shell.

"Did you remember to send Lady Arabella a bouquet of roses?" Mama inquired, as she adjusted the lace trim of her glove.

"Yes." Of course, he neglected to mention that on the accompanying card he wrote nothing but his name.

Sitting in the family landau, which bobbled down Park Lane, he reflected on the last exchange he shared with his older brother, who had a penchant for trouble. Although John never said as much, Anthony's promotion to major served as a source of irritation between them. But it came as no surprise, given the elder's appetite for mischief. As a cavalry captain John had earned three reprimands for dereliction of duty, disobeying a direct order, and abandoning his post without leave to visit a nearby farmer's daughter, which undermined his prospects for military advancement.

In the chaos of war, John's adventurous nature led to his ultimate undoing. While Wellington assigned the cavalry to the borders of La Haye Sainte, John decided to take a small compliment of men into town, whereupon they confronted a unit of approximately five hundred and fifty cuirassiers, which fired a canister shot with lethal accuracy. John fell amid a cloud of gun smoke and dirt.

"Anthony, I spy your lovely fiancée." Mother gave him a gentle nudge, which ripped him from his dark trance. "Is she not charming in her lavender pelisse and matching bonnet?"

"Yes, she is quite fetching," he replied, without so much as a casual glance, because neither Arabella nor her attire mattered to him.

When the driver slowed and brought the rig to a halt, Father descended. A footman handed Mama to the sidewalk and then turned to assist Anthony, which grated his last nerve. He was no invalid, and he required no special care.

"Shall we join our soon-to-be in-laws and your future bride?" Father uttered the one phrase guaranteed to evoke a vicious tremor of anxiety.

After brushing a speck of lint from his lapel, Anthony scanned the collective for any sign of a rogue cuirassier, because he could not help himself, and adjusted the empty sleeve pinned to his coat. The crowd shuffled in various directions, but the sea of elegantly dressed ladies and gentlemen parted to reveal his fiancée, sitting atop an Arabian mare, and he swayed as his ears rang when he glimpsed the horse. Biting back fast-rising bile, he forced a smile and followed in his parents' wake.

Hot and cold at once, Anthony focused on the simple task of breathing and fought for balance as he strolled. But the cold, steel grip of fear imprisoned him in the past, amid the cannon fire, the clash of metal against metal, and the ghoulish cacophony of the dying. By the time he reached Arabella, it was all he could do to acknowledge her presence with a mere nod.

"Lord Rockingham, it is delightful to see you." If she noticed anything odd about his demeanor, she said naught, and he was grateful. "But you do not ride?"

"No, I do not." Panic rolled in his belly, and his pulse pounded. Assailed by another surprise attack of violent memories, which he was powerless to evade, he daubed his temple with a handkerchief. When her mount shifted in Anthony's direction, he flinched. "Careful, Lady Arabella. I have no wish to be trampled."

"But you are in no such danger." As she slid from the sidesaddle, she giggled and settled her palm in the crook of his elbow. "Papa, will you return Astraea to the footman, because I should walk with Lord Rockingham?"

"Of course, my dear." Lord Ainsworth seized the reins.

"You named your horse for a Greek goddess?" Anthony asked, as he desperately sought a distraction, else he might swoon and embarrass himself.

"The star maiden and goddess of justice, to be exact." Arabella met his gaze and studied him for a minute, which seemed an eternity. He wondered what she thought of him, not that it mattered, as she drew him into the rotation, while their respective mothers lingered in the rear. "And why not, because it suits my girl, given she is a gentle soul." In that instant, she flexed her fingers. "Will you tell me of the horse you lost?"

Dagger to the heart, with savage precision.

"How did you know?" Her otherwise pedestrian query flung him, headlong, back into hell, and he halted. When he teetered perilously, she steadied him, and he leaned toward her for support before righting himself. "I never mentioned him."

"You didn't have to utter a word, because your reaction to Astraea spoke volumes, and you paled, Lord Rockingham." Focusing on the lace that framed her heart-shaped face and delicate features, which quite arrested him, he found sanctuary in her smile and her discretion, even as her disturbing ability to guess his unrest unnerved him. "I suppose he was rather spectacular, because I cannot imagine you settling for anything less."

"Oh, he was majestic." Opening the door to his memory, Anthony sifted through the jagged shards of a bygone era and his naïve self, hale, whole, and unmarred by artillery. As if by magic, the hedgerows, throng, and sidewalk yielded to a cherished vision, and he could have wept at the sight. "At just over seventeen hands, with a coat as black as a crow's feather, Hesperus stood tall on the battlefield as a most impressive animal. Friesland born, from his deep heart-girth to his robust haunches, with cannon bones like the trunks of a mighty oak, he was short coupled from his croup to his withers, and he never failed to answer the call of duty."

"I wish I had known him." As a graceful sylph, she stretched her neck when she stared at him. "I gather Hesperus was even-tempered, too."

"Ah, he was a proud beast, but he snored like a grown man when he slept, and he favored red apples, which he consumed in a single bite." Without thought, he tugged her closer to his side, because she presented a lifeline of sorts. "He lived for the fight, and in the heat of war, we were one entity charging the field. When I moved he responded. With a subtle tense of my thighs, or a gentle flick of my wrist, Hesperus shifted in unison with me, and never were two creatures so perfectly matched. Yet, inasmuch as he confronted peril with fearless tenacity, he trembled at the sight of a stable mouse."

"What a character," she said in a soft voice. "You must miss him, terribly."

"Such that I cannot convey the depths of my despair at his loss." For a second, he closed his eyes. Tears beckoned as he relived the savage blast that ripped Hesperus from Anthony. But he gained a measure of strength when she squeezed his arm, in reassurance, because she spoke to him without actually speaking to him. "But the ultimate cruelty and unfairness is that in a moment of incomparable violence for which I have no direct recollection, life as I knew it ended. I know not where or how to reclaim and organize the remnants of what remains, or if it is even possible to recover."

"I cannot begin to comprehend your pain, because I cannot fathom a world without my beloved Astraea, although I know she cannot live forever. But had I known her presence would provoke such painful memories, I should have left her in the stable." Lady Arabella paused to sit on a bench, as if nothing he shared shocked her, when almost everyone, save his fellow veterans, avoided him. She welcomed him, and he liked her, but he would never tell her, because nothing could come of a union with him. "Yet, you cannot allow your memories of war to ruin this lovely day." She lifted her chin and smiled, and he thought her rather appealing. "The sky is clear, and the sun shines, my lord, yet you see none of the natural splendor. You must retrench or risk diminishing all that you gave in service to the Crown. And I wager John would not want you to forever mourn his death. Whatever your wounds, you are still here, and you must go on, if only to honor your brother's sacrifice, my lord."

"You make it sound so simple." To his amazement, the tension twisting his insides into gnarled knots, at last, abated in her company. It was not the first time she pierced the somber veil of misery that encircled his wretched existence. Just as she did during their previous meeting, when he intentionally baited her, she relieved the anxiety imprisoning him in its grip, and he longed to know more about her. What power did the lovely lady possess over him? "You were right."

"About what?" Elegant in her carriage, something he failed to note in their prior encounter, because he scarcely looked at her, she rested her hands in her lap. She extended an offer of friendship, and only a fool would deny her, given her classical features and lilting voice.

For a while, he studied her blue eyes and her thick lashes, which he could contemplate for hours if she let him. And how had he missed the swanlike curve of her neck during their earlier exchange? In that instant, he faced her, committing his full attention, and saw her as if for the first time.

He noticed the pulse that beat at her throat and the way she focused on him, turning her entire body in his direction, as though he were the most important thing in her world. Blessed with a wealth of brown hair, which he would splay across his pillow if given the chance, and with an ample bosom, she displayed the sort of fire any man would kill to claim in his bed. But it was her full lips that held him enrapt until she cleared her throat, and he started.

"You are a good listener." To his dismay and gratitude, because he wanted to get better, Arabella worked on him, easing frazzled nerves and silencing the rage that ran unchecked beneath his flesh. Without his consent or cooperation, she soothed his uncontrollable inner beast, and he was not sure he appreciated her peculiar ability, yet he could not tear himself away from her, despite his best efforts, and he vowed to learn more about her. With a sigh, Anthony glanced over his shoulder and discovered their mothers dawdling at a discreet distance. Sitting, he prodded her in play. "So, what would you suggest I do, all-knowing Lady Arabella, given I am unable to dig myself out of the pit of anguish I've created?"

"My, but you lay a lot on a lady for our first public appearance. Shall I solve the world's problems while I'm at it?" The stoicism of her expression gave him pause, until she surrendered to mirth, and he exhaled his relief. "You are shameless, my lord, and you are baiting me, again, which I refuse to take. Has this charming tack worked for you in the past, or am I the lone beneficiary of your half-hearted insults? By the by, I am certain you can do better, but I am not all-knowing."

For Anthony, what began as a snicker soon grew into a full-blown belly laugh, and it felt so good as he contemplated the absurdity of his query. Still, she bested him, and he savored it. How long had it been since he enjoyed a carefree moment of levity? He could not remember. But perched alongside what was for all intents and purposes a stranger, he felt as if he had reclaimed a small part of himself thought long lost. Thanks to his very much unwanted, pretty little fiancée.

"Lady Arabella, were I not engaged to marry you, I could like you." Exhaling, he noted they had garnered the attention of several nosey nobles, and he stood. "Help me devise a plan of escape from the demands of my father and the rank, and I shall be forever in your debt." Not to mention the mental hell that imprisoned him. "And if your offer still stands, I would accept your friendship, even if I am not to be your husband, which I hope you know has naught to do with you. Were I not carrying the wounds of battle, I just might marry you."

"Upon my word, my fiancé is quite sentimental." Adjusting her gloves, she stretched her legs and rose from the bench. "And while I consider myself of above-average intelligence, I have yet to identify a means of avoiding the parson's noose, given I am defined as chattel, by law, and must abide my father's commands without prejudice. Have you pondered the fact that you might *have* to wed me?"

"No, and I have no wish to, because an arranged union would not bode well for either of us." The suggestion elicited a wicked shudder of revulsion, because he would never saddle the spirited young woman with the hollow shell of a man he had become. And the truth was, he lacked more than an arm. He lacked a will to live. As Anthony offered his escort, his mind raced, and he sought a polite rejoinder to make his point clear. "I am beginning to think it would have been much better to have met an honorable death on the battlefield."

"Must you insult me, in truth, when I have been the soul of charity?" she snapped. Without missing a step, she regained her composure and nodded to Lady Jersey, and he admired Arabella's confidence and poise, as she deflected unwanted scrutiny with a simple, standard acknowledgement. "Not that I desire a husband, be it you or anyone else," she hissed. "If I may inquire, what is wrong with me?"

"Would that the problem were so simple." Given her expression of hurt, he realized he chewed boot leather. Inasmuch as he didn't desire a union, Arabella was blameless, and he would not cause her pain. "My apologies, Lady Arabella. As I have tried to explain, you are not the issue. Rather, I believe you deserve a man worthy of you, and that could never be me."

"You are forgiven, and I would have you know I disagree with your personal assessment, despite our brief acquaintance, given I am an excellent judge of character. However, that is of little consequence, which brings us back to your original question." A velvety brown tendril slipped from beneath her bonnet and caught the sunlight, revealing amber shades that harkened a comparison to his brandy, and he longed to stroke her hair. "If you truly wish to learn to live again, I recommend you not rush into any social commitments. Do not force your hand. Instead, I encourage you to take your time."

"But time is a resource in limited supply, in light of our betrothal, and my father intends to announce our nuptials at my family's gala, within a fortnight." No amount of arguments dissuaded his sire from the original plan of action, which appeared to have been carved in stone since the Dark Ages, and Anthony could find no way out of the contract, even after his solicitor reviewed the documents. "Yet I do appreciate your advice. Tell me, how do you remain so calm in the face of such discomposing developments, because I cannot reconcile myself to what my father deems my natural fate?"

"Oh, that is quite easy, given I have known, all my life, that I was bound to the future Duke of Swanborough." Arabella shrugged. "The only surprise is that you now occupy that position of prominence, in place of John, and you share my aversion to marriage."

"Did you know him well?" Since he was a child, Anthony always looked up to his older brother, and it struck him as grossly unfair that she settled for the lesser Lord Rockingham. "He was popular in the social circles." And incredibly successful with the widows, but Anthony neglected to mention that.

"In truth, John was a stranger to me." As they neared the spot where they entered the rotation, Arabella waved to her father. "While he sent the occasional gift, he never visited me. Indeed, I have spent more time in your estimable company than his."

"My father seems quite pleased with our match and makes no secret he prefers a ceremony before the end of the Season." Anthony noticed a familiar gentleman had joined the sires. "We must make a concerted effort to postpone and delay the nuptials, until we can figure out how to break the engagement."

"I concur. Thus, you may rely on me." They approached the group, and Arabella's expression brightened, as she played the part of the smitten fiancée to perfection. "Your Grace, it is a beautiful day, is it not?"

"Lady Arabella, it is a wondrous occasion, because Lord Ainsworth and I have secured the services of Mr. Hartwell to procure a special license, that you may wed with all due haste. Instead of announcing an engagement, in a fortnight we shall mark your union with a fête to end all fêtes, in place of our usual ball." Father peered at Anthony and winked. "What say you, my boy? Is that not stupendous news?"

In that instant, Anthony stumbled and fainted.

AMID A SLEW of whispers and finger-pointing gawkers, Arabella supported Anthony's head as he reclined in his family's carriage, where her father and His Grace conveyed her fiancé. With her handkerchief, she fanned her prospective groom's face, when he mumbled, and his eyelids fluttered.

"Shh, Lord Rockingham." She patted his cheek, as she admired his handsome features, so boyish in repose, in sharp contrast to the angry Waterloo veteran. "You are safe."

"What happened?" With an inexpressibly sweet countenance of confusion, which transformed into sobering comprehension, he gazed at her, and she smiled. "Please, tell me I didn't swoon in front of the *ton*."

"Well, I could do so, but I would be lying, and I detest duplicity." Shadows danced in his stare, given polite society could be anything but polite, and she seized upon an excuse that might salvage his pride, despite her inklings regarding his spell. "Perhaps you were too quick to dismiss your aching belly, because I suspect something you consumed for breakfast did not agree with you, and we should summon a doctor."

"What's that?" He blinked, and she knew the precise moment recognition dawned, because he shifted and dipped his chin. Shielded by their position, and beyond sight of unwanted spectators, Anthony twined his fingers in hers and squeezed her hand. Warmth spread from his grip to hers, and gooseflesh covered her from top to toe, which she would mull, later. "An excellent notion, Lady Arabella."

"Are you ill, Anthony?" His Grace folded his arms. "Why the devil did you not say something before now, given we could have stayed home and spared ourselves a public spectacle?"

"Because I didn't wish to disappoint you, Father." Invested with unmasked shame, he averted his stare, and she struggled with the unquenchable urge to comfort Anthony. Indeed, she yearned to protect him, because he needed a champion just then. "But I see now that I was wrong."

"You are too modest and beyond chivalrous, Lord Rockingham." In turn, with a clear understanding of the minor sacrifice required to spare her fiancé, she grasped his fingers. To the duke, Arabella said, "Your Grace, I all but begged Lord Rockingham to attend the Promenade, in the note I sent to express my gratitude for the beautiful flowers he gifted me. The blame is mine." Of course, she sent no note, because his accompanying card contained no salutation. "And it is a testament to Your Grace's influence, and Lord Rockingham's benevolence, that he did not refuse my pedestrian request. Thus, I owe Lord Rockingham and Your Grace an apology, but I only thought of the unparalleled pleasure of his company."

"Oh?" The duke blinked and glanced at her father. In unison, they smiled. "You are getting on well, so soon?"

"You might be surprised, because we are two like-minded individuals of singular purpose, Your Grace." In that she didn't lie. With reluctance, she retreated to the sidewalk. Praying Anthony cooperated, she adjusted the chinstrap of her poke bonnet. "And I hope Lord Rockingham improves enough to keep our appointment, because he promised to accompany me to Gunter's for ices, and I am uncontrollably excited."

"Worry not, Lady Arabella." Anthony arched a brow and compressed his lips. "I will accommodate you."

"That is most welcome news." The duke waved to his footmen. "Let us return home, and summon the physician."

"Come along, Arabella." Mama clapped twice, a habit Arabella always found annoying. "We should depart, as well. Since you sent your horse to the stable, you can ride with me."

"Yes, Mother." Gritting her teeth, she clamped shut her mouth and mustered the poise expected of her, yet her mind was anything but composed or quiet. After she climbed into the carriage, she settled into the squabs and rested her gloved hands in her lap. With a lurch, the equipage turned into the lane, and she noted her father's intense perusal. "What is it, Papa? What troubles you?"

"Nothing, my dear." Despite his answer, she sensed something was wrong, especially when he furrowed his brow. "So, Lord Rockingham has been kind to you?"

"Of course, he has." With an unconvincing laugh, she attempted to deflect the odd question, because she knew not what to make of it. "Why does His Grace insist we marry now? I thought most society weddings occurred near the end of the Season. In fact, we have no time to post the banns, which no doubt will arouse suspicion that I am in a delicate condition. What is the urgency?"

"His Grace fears his son's mental capacity wanes, by the minute, and Swanborough must ensure the continuity of his line, else a cousin, twice removed, is to inherit the title." Father pressed a fist to his mouth and shook his head. "But you need not fret, because I secured His Grace's promise to shelter you beneath his roof, that he might safeguard you, after your nuptials."

"You cannot be serious." Reflecting on the brief moments spent in Anthony's company, Arabella deemed him harmless. "Lord Rockingham is the best of men, and he is a war hero."

"That may have been true, once." Papa offered a smile that did not fool her for an instant. To her dismay, he genuinely believed Anthony posed a threat. "Combat has a way of altering a man, forever distorting his concept of reality, but Swanborough has a plan to deal with his son."

"Oh?" Arabella came alert and recalled Anthony's tender story. "I am not sure anyone need *deal* with Lord Rockingham, because he is kind and gentle."

"But he is much changed, thus Swanborough feels the situation is grave." Father cleared his throat and unbuttoned his coat. "Given the unique predicament, His Grace is prepared to offer compensation."

"Indeed, you are fortunate, in that your commitment is minimal." With an expression of inexplicable delight, Mama lifted her chin. "His Grace broached the possibility of a substantial financial incentive, should you produce a healthy male babe within the first year of your union. Your child will receive the finest care and education, and he will be the future Duke of Swanborough, while you will be given a small estate in Kent, a townhouse in London, and a generous annual income."

"I beg your pardon? You speak as if any offspring I birth will not reside with me. Know that if I am to be a mother, I would know my child." As her ears pealed with a carillon of panic, Arabella feared she might swoon, and she sympathized with Anthony's earlier reaction. Then something nefarious occurred to her. "And what of Lord Rockingham? What is to become of him?"

"He is of no concern to you." Never had she thought her father cruel, but his response, flippantly uttered, gave her pause. "Just fulfill your duty and have done with it."

"How can you say that?" Anger sparked, and she stifled an undignified curse, lest she incurred her sire's wrath, and she needed an ally. But what could Arabella do to save her friend and possible husband-to-be from his own relation and an unknown fate? While she had no wish to marry Anthony, she wanted to help him. "Father, you taught me to honor my commitments, and the marriage sacrament is the most important promise I can pledge in my life. I cannot abandon my husband once the vows have been spoken, and never would I surrender my child, to the duke or anyone else."

"Arabella, we have no choice." For as long as she could remember, her father had been her protector, her hero, but now he looked so weak. "I signed the contracts, and you belong to Lord Rockingham. However, Swanborough intends to save you from his son, and for that I am grateful. Rest assured, His Grace will make certain his son receives the best mental care at a facility equipped to handle him."

"But I require no such service, and Lord Rockingham is misunderstood and does not deserve to be institutionalized." Horrified by the prospect of Anthony's imprisonment, given he was a good man, she had no real explanation for his strange behavior, and that was part of the problem. Perhaps, if she could account for his unpredictable moods, she could spare him a stay at an asylum. Not for an instant would she permit anyone to commit her fiancé, but how could she fight His Grace? Glancing at the passing storefronts, she pounced on an idea. "Papa, I am distressed by the revelations you shared, and I wonder if we might divert to Finsbury Square, because I would visit the Temple of the Muses and procure a new book." She scooted to the edge of her seat and deployed her dependable pout. "You know my fondness for reading, and it helps me relax."

"Oh, do let us patronize the bookseller, Richard." Mama patted his arm. "I would love to peruse the cookbooks."

"All right." Cupping a hand to his mouth, Papa shouted, "Oy. Take us to Finsbury Square."

In a matter of minutes, the driver drew the landau to a halt before the familiar domed establishment in which she had spent many a cherished afternoon. As usual, she did not wait for the footman, opting instead to leap to the sidewalk, to her mother's protestations, whereupon Arabella all but ran into the shop.

Inside, she rounded the massive circular counter and strolled down one of the main aisles, bypassing row upon row of fiction, until she located the appropriate topic to suit her purpose. Beneath a sign marking the medical section, she scanned scores of titles, searching for a clue amid a rather large collection of books, which focused on such tantalizing subjects as bloodletting, excess vapors, and constipation.

When so many promising volumes yielded naught but disappointment, she resorted to a random perusal of the inventory, yet she found only more frustration. Just when she prepared to cede the quest, her gaze lit upon an intriguing leather-bound tome labeled *Soldier's Nostalgia and Other Battlefield Maladies* by Dominique Jean Larrey.

"Could it be so simple?" Biting her lip, Arabella pulled the heavy treatise from the shelf and opened to the table of contents. Scanning the various chapter headings, she squealed with excitement and turned to the overview. "Oh, dear. The author is a French physician, which I suspect Anthony will not appreciate. Then again, I need not apprise him of my sources." Thus, she gave her attention to the journal and devoured the introduction.

According to Dr. Larrey, combat experiences often resulted in a mental disorder typified by anxiety, stupor, heart palpitations, fever, loss of appetite, disturbed sleep, interminable thoughts of home, and excess melancholia. Further, the condition progressed in three stages. First, the afflicted soldier suffered heightened excitement and imagination, followed by a period of fever and prominent gastrointestinal distress, succeeded by acute frustration and depression.

"Upon my word." She gulped. "No wonder Lord Rockingham is irritable."

While she had no knowledge of the initial two phases as they pertained to her reluctant fiancé, she had spent enough time in Anthony's company to form a considerable opinion on the final episode, which he possessed with a vengeance. Smiling, she slammed shut the book, tucked it under her arm, and hurried to the novels section.

After locating a sufficiently flowery title that would garner her father's immediate disdain, thus ensuring he would ignore her other pick, she met her parents at the counter.

"Ah, there you are, my dear." Papa glanced at the top selection, wrinkled his nose, and snorted. "Oh, no. 'A Most Noble Swain for Her Delicate Heart.' Sounds awful, but I suppose I should be delighted that you read, and I am glad you found something that interests you."

"Worry not, Papa." Arabella clucked her tongue. "I found exactly what I wanted."

CHAPTER THREE

N ESTLED IN BERKLEY Square, Gunter's Tea Shop boasted a large
selection of English, French, and Italian sweetmeats. On a warm
afternoon, Mayfair society gathered to partake of various confections
and the requisite accompanying gossip, in another superficial display of
opulence. Anthony enjoyed the former but loathed the latter, yet he
tolerated the outing for Arabella, although he understood not his
desire to make her happy, when any extended association with him
was bound to result in misery.

A server delivered their order, an assortment of ice creams and
sorbets arranged in a set of Sèvres *tasses à glace*, situated on a *plateau au
bouret*. More ridiculous pomp for naught more than dessert, when a
simple bowl would suffice. His always fetching fiancée chose a bombe
ice, the mold of which bore more than a passing resemblance to a
particularly proud part of his anatomy, and he clenched his gut as she
innocently licked the erotic shape.

In the blink of an eye, he surrendered to an altogether strange
sensation, as he envisioned the delicate lady, nestled between his
thighs, on her knees, and his body came alive for the first time since
before Waterloo. Gazing at him with her wide baby blues that saw far
more than he wished, she bent, parted her plump, rosy lips, and took
him deeper into the hot enclave of her mouth, and he—

"This *épine-vinette* is delicious." Trailing her little pink tongue
about the bulbous tip of her ice, she moaned, and he almost spilled his

seed in his breeches. "And how is the *neige de pistachio?*"

"Quite good." Reluctant to abandon the captivating reverie, he jolted to the present. With a small silver spoon, he sampled a healthy portion and noted her intense scrutiny. "What are you looking at?"

"I was wondering about your appetite, given we are to be married." She peered at their mothers, who turned their chairs and commenced discussing the latest *on-dit*, no doubt to encourage the couple. In a low voice, Arabella asked, "Do you suffer any gastrointestinal maladies of which I should be aware when planning menus? Likewise, do you have any favorite dishes I should insert into the regular rotation?"

"You presume our union a forgone conclusion." Beneath the pointed stares their presence garnered because he was the heir to the dukedom of Swanborough, acute melancholia blanketed him in a thick cloud of gloom, and he pushed aside the treat. He had to find a way out of the betrothal, if for no other reason than to spare the graceful lady, even though she remained undeterred. "Did we not agree to identify a suitable excuse to end our engagement, or does the title tempt you?"

"We did, but I am befuddled, Lord Rockingham." Elegant and sensuous, at once, she posed an irresistible lure, yet she remained ignorant of her charms, and that drew him to her as a bee to honey. If only he could escape the past and begin anew, they might have a chance at happiness, but nothing could erase the hideous recollections of Waterloo. He had to set her free. "And if you insult me again with your rude suggestions, which reflect worse on your reputation than mine, I shall be too happy to cooperate with my father and yours, and you will have to manage on your own, with no ally. See how far that gets you from the parson's noose."

"You are right, Lady Arabella, and I am ashamed of my behavior." Duly chastised, he savored another taste of the ice. How he adored her temper, which he surmised took everything within her to control, given her brief but glorious outburst in her drawing room. What he would give to unleash that raw power in another more intimate realm, to sample the fire within her, to let it warm him, to divert him from his ugly reality, if only for a little while. Indeed, she was a rare glimpse of sunshine on a cloudy day. "Please, accept my apology. I cannot afford to offend you, because you are my only friend."

"Am I?" After a quick glance about the room, she scooted closer. "I do so wish to be your friend. As such, I must be honest with you. Our fathers conspire to negotiate hasty nuptials, that I might give birth to your heir, and I know not how to circumvent their plan."

"I know, because I have been unable to seize upon any means to avoid the contractual obligation enacted by our sires, and I am aware of their aim." In fact, he had spent countless hours trying to devise a solution to their quandary, with no success. Short of a miracle, Arabella would be his wife, unless he resorted to drastic measures. "English law binds us to a fate not of our making, and we may be trapped. If we must wed, I will do everything I can to protect you."

"And I vouchsafe the same, my lord." Under cover of the table and its linens, she reached for his hand, and he calmed at her mere touch, which never failed to soothe him. "But I am surprised by your reaction, because I would rattle the rooftops from here to Brighton, were I informed of such a nefarious plot against me. Rest assured, I will never let anyone harm you."

"You think me in need of your defense?" That surprised him, because his was the stronger sex. Then again, she was not like most women. And her comments, forceful in nature, struck him as rather odd, given noblemen traded in flesh, with routine, to ensure the future of their lineage. "Trust me, Lady Arabella, I may be a lot of things, including an addlepated lack wit, according to my father, but there is still fight left in me. If all else fails, I can run away, where no one will ever find me, and I would do so to save you."

"If it comes to that, I shall be forever in your debt." Squeezing his fingers, she smiled, and in that elementary act he found refuge and courage, because his closest relations treated him with fear and the accompanying telltale distance. "However, I would have your promise to contact me, that I might know you are all right, and your pledge to find a measure of happiness, because you deserve it."

"You have my word." In truth, Anthony doubted he could stay away, because she seemed to be the only one interested in his wellbeing, and he had formed a genuine fondness for her in the brief tenure of their acquaintance. Indeed, he liked her. "May I state something rather forward?"

"When have you not?" She gasped when he drew imaginary circles on her palm, and he savored her response. Oh, what he would do with her, were she to grace his bed.

"Point taken." He chuckled, as he regarded her high cheekbones and ivory complexion. In another time, he would have pursued her with relish. "You would have made a very fine Duchess of Swanborough."

"Praise, indeed." In that instant, Arabella withdrew from his grip in what struck him as a farewell, of sorts. "Do you know where you will go?"

"Back to the Continent, I suppose." Gazing at the world beyond the window, he pondered the possibilities of his future, which no longer possessed the lure it once had, and he sighed. "In some respects, I feel as if I left the best part of myself at Waterloo, amid the mud and blood, and, with a little luck, I might be able to reclaim what I lost if I return to the site and stare down my demons."

"I would argue your assertion, because I consider you the best of men, but what I would give to stand at your side when you do," she whispered, and despite his plans, he ached to kiss her. "What of your parents? Will you not miss them?"

"No more than they will miss me, I suspect." Then a particular notion gave him pause, as a stylishly garbed couple entered the establishment. "What will happen to you, in my absence?"

"I gather my father will negotiate another union, and I shall marry, unless I devise a plot to avoid it." The resignation in her response struck him as a wicked blow to the cheek, yet she maintained her characteristic poise, and Anthony realized he had grossly underestimated her inner fortitude. Indeed, she was a diamond of the first water. "Thus, my fate remains the same, regardless of your machinations and flight to freedom. My options are few, and I must obey, but I will hold true to my beliefs that my sex is equal to yours, no matter who I call husband."

"No doubt." With a spoon, he scraped the last of the pistachio ice cream from the dish and marveled at his relaxed state. In her company, he always enjoyed tranquility. "I hope your father chooses wisely, because you deserve a match every bit your equivalent."

"Thank you, my lord." Biting her bottom lip, which fascinated him more than he anticipated, Arabella inclined her head, and he noted a spattering of adorable freckles about her nose. "The bergamot ice beckons, but I cannot consume the entirety of it, and I would hate to waste it. Will you share it with me?"

"You read my thoughts." For a scarce instant, Anthony second-guessed his plan, because she brought him unfettered joy and harkened to his old, unspoiled self, but he could never be that man, again. Not when he lacked half an arm. "I have not indulged in such simple pleasures since prior to departing Cork for Mondego Bay, with Wellington, in eighteen hundred and eight. I was but two and twenty."

"Oh, I wish I had known you before the war, because I have such grandiose notions of your personality." Shifting in her seat, she favored him with an unhindered view of her beauty, but her intelligence held pride of place as her best trait, in his opinion, and he hoped her future spouse valued her mind as much, if not more so, as her appearance. "I wager you were quite the idealist, ready to take on the French and rout Boney, all on your own."

"Beyond naïve, I was stupid and ignorant, and I possessed no real combat knowledge." It irked him that she characterized him with lethal accuracy, when he often hid his torment from those closest to him because it was the only way he could cope with his cruel reality. "In truth, I wanted to play soldier, and when I purchased my commission in the army, I boasted I would save the world, alongside my brother. We were convinced that, together, we were invincible."

"Yet, what you confronted was not what you expected." She averted her stare, and he admired her profile and the gentle curve of her neck, as he found himself relaying personal information he never planned to share with anyone. "I gather it was disappointing."

"More than disappointing, it was horrific." The cosmopolitan scene yielded to a memory of the Portuguese countryside, while illusory opposing forces postured amid the refined linens and lace doilies of Gunter's. In agony, given the unwelcomed reverie, he dug his fingers into his thigh, to remind himself that he was awake and alive. "An infantryman must surrender his humanity to kill without hesitation, but I do not pass judgment, because that is the nature of war." Cannon fire echoed in his ears, and Anthony flinched despite his efforts to remain composed. "And I suppose every man confronts the moment innocence is lost, when he realizes he is naught but a pawn in a much larger game, the primary players of which are nowhere near the battlefield."

"I am so sorry, Lord Rockingham." Tears glittered in her sorrowful gaze, and her display of sympathy touched him. "My heart bleeds for you, and I wish there was something I could do to ease your suffering, because I know you are distressed."

"Please, do not cry for me." From his coat pocket he retrieved a handkerchief, which he handed her. "My world is on fire, shrouding the sun in thick smoke, such that the once potent rays cannot penetrate the haze, and you are the only light in my dismal reality. But

I know not how to extinguish the blaze consuming my existence, and I will not risk destroying you in the process, so I am lost, Lady Arabella."

"No, you are not lost." She daubed her cheeks and sniffed. "You are the bravest man of my acquaintance, and I would argue that with my last breath."

"I know you would." It occurred to him then that, of all the things he would leave in London, Anthony would miss Arabella the most, despite their brief acquaintance. But her subtle yet nonetheless spectacular beauty would carry him through the storm, and he committed her features to memory, that she might comfort him when they were apart. "Then we shall combine our efforts to avoid the altar, and I shall be forever in your debt."

SURPRISE OFTEN FUNCTIONED as a double-edged sword for the intended recipient, because the rude awakening could inspire either joy or panic. It was the latter response Arabella endured, when her parents revealed they would host an impromptu dinner party for fifty of their closest friends and connections that very evening. Her parents were anything but spontaneous. Regardless of her mother's assurances, Arabella suspected there were games afoot.

Standing before the long mirror, she toyed with the seed pearls trimming the bodice of her pale green *eau di nil* silk gown and scrutinized her coif. In usual circumstances, she paid little attention to her appearance, other than to ensure she wore sufficient cover and caused no embarrassment. Since her reputation remained inextricably intertwined with Anthony's, she resolved to put her best foot forward.

"My dear, your fiancé and your in-laws just arrived, and we would form the receiving line to present a united front when we welcome our guests." Mama snapped her fingers. "Come along, Arabella. We do not want to keep His Grace waiting."

"Of course not." Yes, her tone carried more than a bit of sarcasm, because she cared not for Anthony's father in light of his scheme. Why did he not take an interest in Anthony's wellbeing? After four days of reading, she suspected she knew her fiancé better than those closest to him, and that saddened her. As she descended the stairs, she vowed to protect him.

"Lady Arabella, you are a vision." His Grace dipped his chin and scrutinized her from top to toe. Suddenly, she reconsidered the fashionable gown, with its low-cut bodice. "Is your fiancée not lovely, Anthony?"

"As always." Devastatingly handsome in his polished ensemble, the centerpiece of which was a black coat trimmed in old gold, Anthony adjusted his cravat and bowed. "Good evening, Lady Arabella."

"Lord Rockingham." She curtseyed and studied him for any signs of distress. "Shall we assume our respective positions, since I believe our first arrivals approach the threshold?"

A series of hushed whispers preceded the tour of the receiving line, when the invitees noted the significance of the arrangement, which included a rare sighting of Her Grace, and Mama gushed like a giddy debutante, while inside Arabella wept. Would it not have been easier and much less trouble to hire a herald?

"I contacted my solicitor about converting my assets into usable resources." Anthony paused to acknowledge another guest. Then he bent his head and said, in a low voice, "It could take a sennight, or more, to sell my properties, so I instructed him to begin the process, posthaste."

"Are you sure that is wise?" With a fake smile, she welcomed another interloper. "Our parents conspire against us, and this spontaneous celebration does not bode well for our plans."

"Then we must delay, by any means." He stiffened his spine, and she noted the fine sheen of perspiration on his brow and the subtle but growing pants as he fought to draw breath. Recalling their discussion at Gunter's, and what he braved at war, she pledged to support him in all enterprises. "Feign illness, if necessary."

"It will be fine, Lord Rockingham." As he fidgeted with his cravat, she recalled Dr. Larrey's advice and sought a distraction. "Cook serves delicious pork ribs, and there are four courses, including a mouth-watering cheesecake, so I hope you brought your appetite."

"I am not hungry," he replied with a frown.

All right, she required another diversion.

"Papa purchased an expensive box of cigars for the occasion." Grasping at threads, she employed pedestrian bits of minutiae to avoid disaster. According to Dr. Larrey, anxiety would only increase Anthony's torment, causing him to act in a disturbing manner, which would not aid their cause. If possible, she would spare him further shame and a trip to an asylum. "And there is fine Spanish brandy, too."

"I prefer French." Little by little, he calmed while they conversed. "But I will drink whatever the host provides."

"Perhaps the Shrewsbury cakes are more to your liking?" Her mind raced, when he offered a slight smile, and Arabella aimed to keep it there for the remains of the evening and beyond. "Or should I send a footman to Gunter's for a vast deal more than decent portion of the *neige de pistachio* you favor, because you all but licked the dish?"

"Now you have my attention." Ah, the boyish demeanor emerged, and Anthony winked. "How I enjoyed that afternoon in your company."

"Oh, I echo your sentiments, because I delight in talking to you." Indeed, she loved talking to him, because he treated her like an adult. Their parents followed the last of the guests into the grand dining room, which adjoined the ballroom and featured two long tables, and Papa waved a summons. "I suppose we must do our duty, Lord Rockingham." She settled her palm in the crook of his arm. "Shall we join the party?"

"I would rather surrender my other limb." When she gave him a nudge, he met her stare, and his unutterable helplessness called to her on some basic level which she could not ignore. "Will you stay with me?"

Something inside her melted.

"Boney, himself, could not drag me from your side." For a scarce second, Anthony simply stood there, and Arabella desperately wanted to hold him, to console him, to reassure him that she would allow no one to harm him. "And whatever happens, we will face it, together."

"Perhaps you should escape to the Continent with me?" He chuckled, even as she considered the offer. "I can compose a suitable story to satisfy the *ton's* thirst for gossip, shouldering the blame, because my family can bear the brunt of the scandal. What say you, Lady Arabella? Fancy a sail?"

"I would love nothing more, Lord Rockingham, but I cannot abandon my parents." In the dining room, she was shocked to discover the seating arrangements conflicted with social edicts, because she had been assigned a position of prominence to the left of His Grace, and Anthony occupied the chair beside her. Per the rules of polite decorum, her fiancé should have been placed opposite her, and she should have been located near the center of the table. Gooseflesh covered her. Leaning close, she whispered, "Anthony, I think we are in trouble, because our parents appear euphoric, and I can only guess at the reason."

"I would wager you are correct." He paled and flinched, when the butler opened a bottle of champagne, the first in a series. "It looks as if your father's domestics prepare for a toast."

"Oh, no." Along with the Sèvres porcelain and polished silver settings, Mama deployed the Baccarat crystal, and the walls seemed to collapse on Arabella. "Anthony, promise me something."

"Anything, my lady." Shielded by the expensive linens, he clasped her hand. "What is it, Arabella?"

Strange, he actually tried to comfort her, and she glanced at the tray of glasses filled with the bubbly intoxicant. "Whatever happens, you will pay attention to me, to my eyes, to the sound of my voice, as we proceed through the evening."

"Why?" The butler uncorked another bottle, and Anthony started.

"Because we can survive the awkward affair if we rely on each other and present a united front." To her relief, no one noticed his blanched complexion, the lines of stress etched about the corner of his eyes, or the rigid set of his lips. "Agreed?"

In that moment, Their Graces stood, and the crowd quieted. In silence, Anthony indicated the affirmative with a nod.

"My honored guests, it is my distinct pleasure to welcome you to this informal dinner, and I must begin the festivities by expressing my thanks to Lord Ainsworth, my longtime friend, for temporarily ceding hosting duties that I might share the reason for this little gathering and allay your curiosity." The duke stared at Arabella and Anthony, and she shifted, as she would wager her most cherished book she could recite the forthcoming report. "Her Grace and I are proud to announce the engagement of our son Anthony, the Marquess of Rockingham, to Lady Arabella Hortence Gibbs, daughter of Lord and Lady Ainsworth, in nuptials to be officiated by the Archbishop, at my home, eleven days hence."

The room erupted with applause, and she teetered on the brink of hysteria but mustered a glance of adoration at Anthony. "Smile."

Not for a minute did he fool her, because he offered what could best be described as a brittle, lopsided grin. Exposed and vulnerable, he cast a silent plea, and she prayed he didn't swoon or scream. It was at that very instant she lifted her glass, if only to break the grip of fear clawing at her throat, and the duke called to order the group.

"To Anthony and Arabella." Oblivious to the unrest he inflicted on his son, His Grace faced her. "May they be blessed with many strong sons."

Her knees tingled, and she gulped the champagne, while Anthony drained his glass and signaled for a refill. Despite their plan, she surmised they enjoyed no escape, and she reclaimed her seat as resignation set in with a vengeance, because the announcement was tantamount to a marriage, barring a massive scandal. As far as society was concerned, the ceremony was but a formality.

And so the meal commenced, but it passed in a blur, as an army of servants delivered course after course, yet she hardly tasted the food. Although numerous guests extended congratulations, the words did not penetrate the imaginary but impermeable fog that enveloped her in a cold and lonely prison, and Anthony, her unfortunate cellmate, fared no better.

Every time he carried his fork to his mouth, his hand shook, and more than once he dropped a morsel in his lap. The strain manifested in his jerky movements and habitual coughing, and she expected him to vomit at any minute. When the footman cleared the dishes, and the butler rolled in a trolley, bearing brandy and her father's cigar box, Papa stood.

"Gentlemen, let us bid farewell to our ladies, that they might enjoy their tea and gossip in the drawing room." Papa assumed an air of superiority. "And we shall remain here, to discuss the latest news from Parliament."

"Please, do not leave me," Anthony whispered. "Without you, I am lost."

"But I must." Numb, yet fighting her own demons, Arabella pushed from the table. Drawing on Dr. Larrey's expertise, she composed a suitable response to reassure him. "However, you are safe. And what of your friends? Whatever they discuss, keep reminding yourself that you sit in my home, in London, and I am just down the hall."

"All right." His strained expression did not inspire confidence. "I can do that. Although I suspect my fellow veterans will only make things worse."

Reluctant to part from her fiancé, because he needed her, and she feared His Grace might commit Anthony sooner than later, she dragged her feet and followed the women. In the drawing room, the requisite hounding almost drove her over the edge, until a familiar and much welcomed face beckoned.

"Arabella, it has been too long since our last luncheon." Patience Wallace, Arabella's longtime friend and co-conspirator in women's causes, provided much-appreciated succor in a hug and a reliable shoulder. With blonde hair and green eyes, Patience commanded a small army of admirers, but none paid suit given her father was but a general in the army, sans noble rank. Still, Arabella promised to help her trustworthy chum secure a good match. But first, she needed to save Anthony from his father. "And why did you not write me of your impending wedding? I should be angry with you, because we never keep secrets from each other. So, tell me about the tragic but inexpressibly beautiful Lord Rockingham, because he reminds me of one of Shakespeare's doomed heroes."

"Really?" Arabella wiped her brow and noted Her Grace occupied a lone chair in the corner. "I was thinking more of Odysseus. And all of this happened so suddenly that I had no time to write you, but I planned to visit and strategize, tomorrow. Believe me, I require your wise counsel."

"Oh, no. I supposed the previous Lord Rockingham's demise ended the contract between your family and His Grace." Patience wrinkled her nose and clasped Arabella's hand. "And the marquess is far too elegant for Homer."

In concert, they giggled.

"Oh, Patience, if I confessed everything, I should turn your hair white, but you are the only one I can trust with the entire ugly truth." With a sigh of relief, Arabella related the details, withholding naught from her closest confidante. "So, you see, it is not necessarily a match made in heaven."

"But you are contracted, thus love never entered the arrangement. Given your partiality for reason and logic, which I know well, I don't understand your reticence." Patience claimed the *chaise* and patted the spot beside her. As usual, she reduced the situation to bare facts bereft of emotion. "Your mother appears overjoyed."

"Indeed, she is thrilled and thrives on the attention." In the center of the room, Mama held court, and Arabella frowned. "But I cannot stop thinking of the duke's plot, and I don't get your meaning."

"The answer is simple." Patience shrugged. "If Lord Rockingham is as emotionally unbalanced as you describe, I do not presume His Grace has any other option, so why do you not give him a choice or an alternate solution? You are an intelligent and enterprising sort, and I know you can devise another course of action that suits your purpose." She wagged a finger. "But I caution you to remember His Grace must protect the future heir to the dukedom, even if that requires commitment to a mental institution, and the law supports him."

"I will not allow it, because Anthony deserves so much more." Arabella gnashed her teeth and then checked her tone, because Patience was not the enemy. "In moments of clarity, he is the kindest, gentlest man blessed with an enormous heart. Indeed, he is not mad. He is simply misunderstood, and if anyone tries to harm Lord Rockingham, there will be quite the wake in this house."

"Of that I have no doubt, but I would wager on you, every day of the sennight and twice on Sunday, and I am with you, come what may. Remember, together we are invincible, and I am always in your corner. Woe the poor soul that challenges us." Patience laughed and then sobered. "Oh, dear. I believe you are summoned."

Trailing her friend's gaze, Arabella discovered Anthony looming in the hall, just beyond the doorway. The raw terror in his eyes provoked an intense desire to protect him, and she acknowledged him with a surreptitious nod, checking to ensure no one else noted his presence, before he turned and trod toward the study.

"Walk with me." Adopting an air of calm, Arabella moved with purpose. "And follow my lead."

Strolling at a relaxed pace, with nary a hint of urgency, Arabella and Patience embarked on a well-played ruse, as if they shared the enthusiasm in regard to the forthcoming marriage.

"You know, I find it remarkable that you resist the union with Lord Rockingham, because you are always so quick to identify adventitious circumstances, which is one of the many reasons I hold you in high regard," Patience declared studiously and waved a greeting to Lady Breckham. "Hear me, my friend. If you employ the common sense for which you are renowned, you will admit he is your perfect match, because he already relies on your strength. The balance of power in your relationship shifts in your favor, which is what you have always wanted, is it not?"

Arabella came to a halt and then resumed her tour about the room.

"I never thought of it like that." Mulling the prospects, which had eluded her to that point, Arabella approached the entry, with a new attitude, and stopped. "But you make an excellent argument, as always. How could I not have seen the obvious?"

"You are too close to the situation, and you fail to recognize he is just the mate for you, given you must marry." Patience gave her attention to the guests, as Arabella occupied a position behind her friend. "Go, now."

As Arabella crossed the foyer, a booming crescendo of laughter echoed from the dining room, where the men remained, and she jumped. In seconds, she navigated the corridor that led to Papa's study. At the door, she glanced left and then right before entering the dimly lit chamber.

A fire in the hearth bathed the relatively small space in a soft saffron glow, and she secured the oak panel and set the bolt. Slumped forward, cradling his face in his hand, Anthony emitted a groan, and she rushed to provide aid.

"My lord, what is wrong?" Framing his jaw, she lifted his head, and a tear streamed down his cheek. "Oh, Anthony, it is all right. I'm here."

"Help me. Make it stop." He winced and jolted her. "The cannons—we are too close. *Too close.*"

He revisited the battlefield.

"No, my lord, we are not too close." With her thumbs, she caressed his heated flesh, and she recounted Dr. Larrey's counsel. "You are with me, in London, and you are safe. Do you hear me?" Pinning him with her gaze, she swallowed hard. "It is Arabella, and you are unharmed, because there are no cannons here."

"But I heard them." Closing his eyes, he shivered. "Even now, the piercing salvo echoes in my ears."

"No, my lord. You are mistaken." Her mind raced, as she sifted through the knowledge from Larrey's book, until it dawned on her what may have instigated her fiancé's unrest. "Look at me, Anthony. It was the champagne bottle and naught more. I swear, there are no guns in this house."

In a flash, he growled and charged, pushing her against the wall, grinding his hips to hers, and then he grabbed her at the nape of the neck and covered her mouth with his. Frenzied at the onset, he besieged her flesh in a punishing slip and slide that stole the breath from her lungs as she tried to keep pace.

Thus was Arabella's first kiss.

On the heels of the deed, the sensations, so many, lured her into the mesmerizing storm, and she plummeted, headlong, to her fate. Delicious heat seared her veins, and a deep-seated hunger unfurled in the pit of her belly, beckoning her to answer his call. A shiver of excitement sashayed over her flesh, suffused her nerves, and pulsed in her heart. When he plunged his tongue into her mouth, she welcomed the tender invasion and mimicked his movements, as she dug her fingernails into his shoulders.

Slowly, the tension eased, and he loosened his grip. To her shock, he skimmed her back and drew her from the wall. With his one arm, he hugged her about the waist. Angling his head, his ensuing exchange enticed her with his characteristic gentle tenor.

A thousand times more provocative than the prior clumsy, groping, urgent experience, he seduced her with playful nips and suckles that nurtured and intensified her appetite. In those treasured moments, she realized she was seeing him, the true Anthony, for the first time, and she yielded, of her own free will, to her scarred hero. Just as she gained her feet, everything halted.

Then he ended the tryst and retreated.

For a few minutes, they simply stood there and stared at each other, and she ached to hold him.

"I have taken liberties." Grazing her bottom lip with his thumb, he sighed. "I apologize, Arabella, and I promise it will not happen again."

"Don't bother." She closed the distance and perched on tiptoes. Winding her arms about his neck, she kissed him with all she had and for all she was worth.

CHAPTER FOUR

A RAY OF sunlight cut a path across the Aubusson rug as Anthony lounged in his sitting room, mulling the events of the previous night. On the mantel, the clock counted the minutes with a repetitive *tick-tock*, and breakfast sat untouched on a tray. Yet he remained rooted in the overstuffed chair where he reclined for the past several hours, pondering that kiss.

No, he did not refer to his clumsy exchanges after the terrors plagued him following his father's impromptu announcement at Lord Ainsworth's home. Rather, Anthony could not stop thinking about Arabella's untutored but fervent charge. Even now, if he closed his eyes, he could taste her as she clutched the lapels of his coat and launched the sweetest attempted seduction of his memory.

Delicate hands framed his face, sumptuous lips tempted him beyond the limits of his self-control, and a series of flirty hums and breathy sighs brought his body alive. Gritting his teeth, he tensed his loins and rubbed his aching erection, which he longed to unleash between Arabella's thighs.

When a knock interrupted the cherished reverie, he cursed. "Come."

"Are you dressed?" Father called from the hall.

"Aye." Well, that put an end to the sweet interlude. With a huff, Anthony rolled his eyes. "What do you want?"

"Don't use that tone with me." His father trod into the room, and

Anthony wondered what offense he committed. "Do you plan to sulk, all day?"

"I have not decided." Indeed, Arabella's kiss dangled before him, as a proverbial carrot, and he reconsidered his scheme because she possessed something every man desired in a wife: unbridled desire. "What business is it of yours?"

"Your friends pay call, and they await your presence in my study." Father drew an envelope from his coat pocket. "And this came for you, this morning."

"What friends?" Anthony stood too fast and splayed his lone arm for balance. With a sniff of annoyance, he snatched the opened missive from his father's grasp. "And what is this?"

After unfolding the letter, he read the contents, and his heart sank.

"Plan on going somewhere?" Father scowled, and Anthony realized his secret was not so secret. "And I refer to that motley crew of twisted and damaged soldiers you persist in entertaining. Why can you not socialize with whole men, instead of those dark souls?"

"Perhaps because I have much in common with those dark souls." After crumbling the parchment, which detailed the sum of his estate, as well as the sheer impossibility of a hasty settlement, from his solicitor, Anthony threw the message on the floor, along with the last fragments of hope for escape. Resigned to his situation, he slumped his shoulders. "In regard to my financial affairs, you leave me little choice in the matter, because you force me into a union I neither want nor need."

"Must I repeat the fact that you have no choice?" In the bedchamber, Father yanked a hacking jacket from the armoire and marched into the sitting room. "Here." He flung the garment at Anthony. "Make yourself presentable because you are the marquess of Rockingham, and I expect you to act like it. And there will be no more talk of running away, else I shall post guards at your side."

"You wouldn't dare." Although Anthony knew better, as he

shrugged into the jacket, because his father would not be denied. "I'm not a child."

"Then stop behaving like one." Father none too gently speared his fingers through Anthony's hair. "Be a man and do your duty, else I will ensure by any means necessary that you perform as you were taught."

"I am a man, but you persist in treating me like a babe suckling at its mother's teat." Anthony stepped into one Hessian and then another. Did no one see him? Did no one recognize his torment? "And I am trying to do the right thing by Lady Arabella, because I *am* genuinely fond of her, thus I would not burden her with a maimed beast that should have been put out of its misery on the field."

"Stop talking about yourself as though you no longer exist, and do you not understand that if you refuse to wed her and accept your position, the dukedom passes to Cousin Herschel?" Performing the responsibilities of a valet, Father fastened Anthony's shirt collar. "If you care for Lady Arabella, as you claim, do you believe she will fare better with him?"

"That buffoon?" Anthony snorted, when he envisioned the gentle but spirited lady with an idiot that would stifle her strength and intelligence. "He cannot tie a cravat even with two good hands and the assistance of his valet."

"Perhaps, now you comprehend the gravity of the situation." Father shook his head. "Would you entrust our legacy to his care?"

The real question was would Anthony entrust Arabella to his cousin.

"I would not give my best hound into Herschel's custody." And that was putting it mildly. Assessing his appearance in the long mirror, he considered his life with Arabella as a permanent fixture. Blessed with singular wit and enviable strength, she would pose something more than an ornament in his world.

She would be his partner.

One thing was certain; he would never be bored.

When Father arched a brow, Anthony sighed in exasperation. "All right. I give you my word I will not leave London, but I am not convinced that a wedding is necessary, at this time. Why must I marry, now? Can it not wait until Lady Arabella and I are better acquainted? Can we not delay until the end of the Season?"

"Make her your wife, and you can know her quite intimately. If she does not please you, then you can always take a mistress." Anthony grimaced at the mere suggestion, given that kiss, the effects of which he savored even then. As they walked into the hall, Father wagged a finger. "Until your ceremony, you will behave as a gentleman, and try not to bring shame upon this family."

"Of course." They descended the grand staircase, and Anthony seethed in silence and gritted his teeth against a biting retort, because he lacked an arm, not a brain. In the foyer, he sketched a mock salute, hoping to irritate his father, given he already returned the favor. "If you will excuse me, I should greet my guests."

Leashing his temper, he navigated the side hall and halted before the door to his father's study. As he rested his hand on the knob, the metal cooled his heated palm, and the tension investing his frame abated.

In the blink of an eye, the cavalry bugle blared, the infantry drummer beat the familiar *pa rum pum pum pum*, and he jolted to the past. To another involuntary, violent recollection. The mordant miasma of gunpowder burned his throat and eyes, and he gasped for air and wiped a stray tear, as he sank further into hell. A morose *cri de cœur* rose above the din of war, filling his ears with a sorrowful collection of pleas, none of which he could discharge, given his injury, and it was the helplessness amid so much agony that battered his conscience.

Somehow, through the fog, Arabella beckoned in a hushed voice, *Anthony.*

An alluring vision formed, and his lady reached for him with outstretched arms. The terrifying urgency yielded to the slow, intoxicating smolder of passion, as he recalled, in startling detail, their tryst in Lord Ainsworth's study. How she yanked his hair and bit his lip. How she pressed her feminine curves to him and uttered his name in a whispered plea, unmistakable in its meaning.

Shaking himself alert, Anthony opened the door and strolled into the study, whereupon he found four equally damaged Waterloo veterans. While they bore no blood relation, they were nonetheless his brothers in arms.

"Gentlemen, this is a surprise and a much-appreciated reunion." Anthony walked straight to his childhood chum, Lord Rawden Durrant, the Earl of Beaulieu, and shook his hand. "Beaulieu, it is always good to see you."

"Wish I could say the same of you, and I doubt it is much appreciated, given you avoided us like the plague at the dinner party." Ever the mischievous scamp, Beaulieu possessed a biting cleverness, which he honed at Anthony's expense, during their years at Eton. Although Beaulieu lost his left eye at Waterloo, he remained as sharp as ever. "You look like something that rolled in with the tide, after a shark's nasty mangling. What have you done to yourself?"

"Perhaps, impending marriage does that to a man, although I claim no direct knowledge, because I remain blissfully unattached." Lord Michael Donithorn, second son of the marquess of Landsdowne, snickered, as he hobbled on crutches, because Wellington's penultimate battle cost Lord Michael the lower half of his right leg. "But I would not protest, given the lady in question, because she is quite handsome, and you could do far worse."

"He *has* done worse." Lord Hunter Lee, the earl of Greyson, chuckled. As with the other military men, Greyson also suffered invisible wounds. After a year in solitary confinement as a prisoner of war, he struggled with a deep-seated fear of crowds, thus his appearance was a rarity. "Remember that bare-arsed jaunt through the library, at the Howard's, after Lord Beddington caught Anthony docking in Lady Beddington's honey harbor, amid Lord Howard's collection of atlases?"

"Perhaps he wanted to chart some new territory." Lord Arthur James, earl of Warrington, waggled his brows. Partially blinded by gunpowder burns, the once bold and bawdy nobleman had all but retreated from society, and his presence was not lost on Anthony. "And that is a ball I will never forget, especially when Rockingham escaped via the terrace, where I indulged in a little inappropriate behavior, with the widow Harrison, beneath the canopy of an oak. But I was not the only one he sent running for shelter in the shadows."

"That is why I always dally in the shrubbery." Beaulieu smirked. "Although I recommend avoiding the rose bushes, because I once tangled with a thorn where no one should get a thorn, such that I required the services, above and beyond the call of duty, of my valet to extricate it, given I was too embarrassed to summon a doctor."

"Did you have to go there?" Lord Michael winced. "I give thanks, every day, that I survived the savagery of battle with that part of my anatomy intact."

"Oh, I say." Greyson grimaced. "Take anything but that."

"Ah, how this reminds me of those nights spent gathered around the campfire, in La Haye Sainte." Anthony perched on the edge of his father's desk and reflected on the quiet, dark hours of the conflict, which contrasted with the hell of daylight. "Gentlemen, while I am grateful for your estimable company, I would know what brings you to my door?"

"Our leader announces his betrothal, and we are supposed to ignore the felicitous occasion?" Beaulieu eased to a high back chair near the hearth. "At the very least, this calls for a celebratory brandy, although I would also include a final wild night of wenching, if you are so inclined."

"Where are my manners?" Anthony slapped his thigh and stood.

At a side table, he lifted a crystal decanter and filled five glasses with the amber liquid. "As to the wenching, I have no interest in such games, but I appreciate the thought."

"What did I tell you?" Lord Michael glanced at Beaulieu, as Anthony played host and made the rounds. "Something is most definitely wrong in the world when a soldier declines a night of wenching."

"I hoped you were mistaken." Beaulieu rubbed his chin, which denoted intense scrutiny and was always dangerous where he was concerned. "But I noticed he appeared on the verge of vomiting when His Grace announced the impending nuptials, at Ainsworth's dinner."

"Please, don't talk about me as though I am not here." While Anthony chafed at Beaulieu's observation, he could not argue his friend's assertion. "I get enough of that from my father."

"But you are not here." Warrington averted his gaze and sighed. "We have not seen you since we departed the Continent. What returned to London is a puzzle I cannot solve."

"I rescind my previous statement, because I would prefer you ignore me." Anthony plopped into the leather chair behind his father's desk.

"Not a chance." Standing near the windows overlooking Berkley Square, Greyson stretched tall, and Anthony realized there was no escaping his friends, because they, too, suffered the same curse. "Now, why don't you tell us what troubles you, when you are bound to that pretty bit o' fluff? The Rockingham I know would be plotting all manner of salacious encroaches on her virginal territory, to plant your flag on her most intimate mound, yet you look like you just lost your best hound."

"Well done." Lord Michael saluted. "Could not have said it better, myself."

"Thank you." Greyson nodded.

"Must you really ask that question?" Anthony stretched his booted feet and considered his gentle lady. "Do you not comprehend that I am forced to the altar by a sire intent on securing an heir, at any price?" Then he met each man's stare. "Are you not plagued by the nightmares? Do the terrors not haunt you in crowded rooms? Have your injuries not rendered you less than what you were, prior to the war? Do people not yield the field, avoiding you whenever you make an appearance, as if you shed some invisible but potent infection?"

"Aye." Lord Michael lifted a brandy balloon to his lips, and his hand shook. "All the time."

"I refuse to attend most social events." Leaning forward, Greyson rested elbows to knees. "Else I fear I will run amok."

"As do I." Warrington cast a pained expression. "Owing to my impairment, I am spared the pitiful glances, yet there is naught wrong with my ears, and I cannot abide the condescension I detect."

"Not to mention, you wish to keep your distance from Lady Horatia." Lord Michael canted his head. "Although your decision to break off your engagement still baffles me, because it is well known that she loves you."

"You know bloody well why I ended the betrothal. I would not saddle her with a partially blind man, when she deserves much more." Warrington shifted his weight, and Anthony reflected on their similar arguments against marriage. For some reason, when considering his friend's predicament, the logic seemed flawed, because the lady wanted Warrington, injuries and all. "And we are not here to discuss my difficulties."

"At least your woman waited for you." Lord Michael snorted. "I returned home to find my supposedly devoted fiancée wed to my rival, who refused to defend our great nation, while I sacrificed myself on the battlefield."

"Yet we are outcasts in our own country." Anthony mulled the absurdity of the situation. "We fought to defend the world against Napoleon's oppression, but we are prisoners on our lands, and I am chained to a title and a woman I never wanted."

"I had no idea we were going to be honest, today. Had I known I would've stayed home." Beaulieu clenched his jaws. "And they call us mad. I'm not mad. I'm furious."

"As am I." Lord Michael slapped the armrest of his chair. "But we cannot blame all our troubles on society, because we are wounded, not dead. We are war heroes, yet we hide in our libraries and studies, bemoaning our treatment. How can we complain, when we do naught more than cower in the shadows? I, for one, refuse to surrender the future I covet, even though I lost my faithless fiancée."

"What do you suggest?" Curious, Anthony rested an elbow to the blotter and cradled his chin in his palm, because he could glean no solution. "Should I give my father what he wants?"

"Is that how you choose to look at the situation?" Lord Michael wrinkled his nose. "Because I see a man of rank and wealth betrothed to a woman of incomparable beauty, and the possibilities are endless, should you decide to dictate your fate. If you want, you can create a family. You can build a life and rejoin the world." He shrugged. "I suppose it is much easier to sit idle and let your father control your destiny."

"Have care how you speak to me." Despite Anthony's affinity for his lifelong friends, he would brook no insult from anyone. Tension weighed heavy, given he knew better than anyone his position. "Now, explain yourself, because you tread on dangerous ground. How am I to dictate my fate, given my father holds me to a contract negotiated for my brother, when I gained my title by John's death? The marquessate, the fortune, and the bride belonged to him. None of it is mine to own."

"I would think it obvious, provided you quit playing the victim." Lord Michael pinned Anthony with a lethal stare, and he hated when his chum posed decisive arguments. "John is gone, and you remain, thus Lady Arabella, Rockingham, and the entailments are yours, and I would give anything to walk in your boots. You need only seize what fate has bestowed upon you, and plot your own course. You complain that your father drags you to the altar, but you fail to mention that it is because you force him to do so. Stop fighting, take up the reins of your life, and charge, because that is who you are, or have you forgot yourself?"

Piercing silence reinforced Lord Michael's perspective, because Anthony could form no rebuke, and it was not for lack of trying. When he sought some sign of support from his comrades, they offered naught but sheepish grins. Yet, he would wager their reactions would be quite different were it their heads on the connubial chopping block. Still, from every angle he approached the disconcerting stance, he could contrive no decent rebuttal, and he excelled at counterattacks.

"Lord Michael is right." Beaulieu smacked his lips and glowered. "Well, that leaves a foul taste in the mouth."

"Very funny." Lord Michael rolled his eyes, even as the tension abated. "I'm trying to make a point, and you are making jokes."

"And making sense." Anthony could not believe what he was about to proclaim, but he had nothing to lose and, if Lord Michael was right, everything to gain. With renewed interest, Anthony eased back in his chair and revisited the memory of that kiss. "Just what do you propose?"

IT WAS LATE in the afternoon when Arabella hosted Patience for tea in the back parlor. While she tried to present an attentive posture, she could not stop thinking about last night, when she kissed her fiancé, in Papa's study. What had she been thinking, behaving in such a brazen manner? Of course, Anthony voiced no complaints when she ravished him. Rather, he encouraged her, as he—

"That is enough." Patience folded her arms, and Arabella snapped to attention. "What happened with the gorgeous but tortured Lord

Rockingham, because you have not stopped blushing since I got here, and I will have a full account."

"It was nothing." That was partly true, because it was nothing like Arabella had ever experienced. "I provided comfort, because he was tormented by his war service. Beyond that, there is naught more to tell."

"And pigs fly." Arching a brow, Patience frowned. "Now, give over, else I am not your friend, because you do not trust me with your deepest, darkest secrets."

"Oh, all right." Again, Arabella's cheeks burned. "We kissed."

"I knew it." Bouncing, Patience squealed. "And?"

"And that is all." Given the intimacy of the exchange, Arabella struggled to form the words to describe what she felt. And, oh, what she felt in his embrace. "Really, it was over before it began and hardly worth note."

"And if you tell yourself that enough, you just might convince yourself, but you could never fool me." As always, Patience exhibited profuse amounts of the trait for which she was named. "What was it like? I once heard that a good kiss could curl your toes. Did he curl your toes?"

"In truth, he curled everything." Reliving the moment, Arabella collapsed amid the throw pillows and sighed. "And then...and then..." She pressed a palm to her forehead and closed her eyes. "And then I returned the favor."

"You did what?" At Patience's outburst, Arabella started. "You kissed him?"

"Yes." Arabella lurched upright. "Believe me, I am just as shocked by the revelation. Bless my soul, I know not what came over me, but I could not help myself." In her mind, she replayed the events and sighed. "There we were, alone, in Papa's study. It was dark, save the light from the hearth, and Anthony was distraught. He was emotionally charged with a ferocity that could rival the sun, and I could not resist him. Indeed, I didn't want to resist him, but I found myself leading the charge, to my unutterable amazement, and I savored it."

"And that surprises you?" Patience tittered. "Given your propensity for exploration is well known, and the fact that Lord Rockingham poses new, fertile territory for inspection, I wonder what took you so long to venture forth, my friend."

"Trust me, I found my feet, given I am rather more than seven, but that is not the end of the rendezvous." Arabella glanced over her shoulder, to ensure she enjoyed the privacy of the back parlor. Then she leaned forward and whispered, "He caressed my breast, and I allowed it."

"You didn't." Patience blinked, as Arabella nodded. "Upon my word, you quite take my breath away."

"Believe me, it had the same effect on me." Exhaling, Arabella reflected on the sweet memory. "Even though he fondled me through my gown and my chemise, I swear his touch scorched my flesh, and I am in a quandary."

"How so, because I would think your tryst mollified your concerns?" Patience grinned. "Clearly, you two are compatible. Have we not always said that if we are to wed, we will do it right and marry for love?"

"We have, but we both know physical attraction does not equate love." And that nagging distinction kept Arabella from celebrating her impending union, given Anthony's protestations.

"But it is a very important start." Ever the strategist, Patience always identified the advantage of any given situation. "And it is not as if you have any choice, because you must take a husband. As I remarked, last night, you would do well to opt for the candidate who relies on you, and that is Lord Rockingham, in spades."

Even Arabella could not deny her friend's position.

Just then, Mama rushed into the room.

"Arabella, you have callers, and I put them in the drawing room, but I am meeting with the cook, concerning the menu for your wedding breakfast." To Patience, Mama said, "Miss Wallace, do you mind acting as chaperone, in my stead?"

"It would be my pleasure." Patience stood, and Arabella followed suit.

"Who is it, Mama?" Arabella smoothed the skirts of her pale blue morning dress. In the mirror, she adjusted the fichu about her bodice, which preserved her modesty. "As I am anticipating no other guests."

"I gather they are acquaintances of your fiancé." Mama snapped her fingers. "Now, don't dawdle, because I taught you better."

"Yes, Mama." In the hall, Arabella glanced at Patience. "This is a curious development. I wonder who it is and what they want?"

"Only one way to find out." Patience claimed Arabella's hand, and they veered left, in the foyer, to arrive at the double-door entry of the drawing room.

What they confronted bore more than a passing resemblance to a comedy of errors, because a group of imposing men she recognized from last night's receiving line argued amongst themselves.

"I cannot believe I let you talk me into this hair-brained scheme." One estimable specimen scowled. "We promised Rockingham our support. We said naught of enacting a plot to bring him to the altar."

That comment captured her attention.

"I must concur with Warrington." Another complained. "While I am more than willing to help Rockingham, I am no machinating mama, and I refuse to reduce myself to such humiliation, because there is only so much indignity a man can endure."

While the fascinating collective, some featuring obvious war injuries, squabbled, Arabella elbowed Patience. "What are we to make of this development?"

"I am not sure." Patience snickered. "But it appears our presence is not required, because they have not even acknowledged us, yet I would know the purpose of their visit, given their heated debate. At the very least, they put on a good show and are quite entertaining."

"Gentlemen, it is absolutely necessary, and he would do the same for us, were we in his predicament." A tall, blond Adonis, sporting a patch over his left eye, made an impassioned plea and then turned his gaze on Arabella. "Ah, the ladies are here." His demeanor transformed into something somewhat dangerous, as he bowed and favored her with a smile she didn't trust for a minute. "Lady Arabella, I am Rawden Durrant, Earl of Beaulieu."

"Yes, I remember, given we were formally introduced at my father's impromptu dinner, although we didn't speak beyond the customary greeting." To her recollection, Anthony considered Beaulieu a close friend, although they appeared to avoid each other at the event. Then again, nothing went as expected after His Grace announced the engagement, so she understood her fiancé's unusual behavior. With Patience firmly anchored alongside, Arabella led her friend to the *chaise*. "Please, be seated."

"Thank you." He perched at the edge of the sofa. "Allow me to present Lord Michael Donithorn, Hunter Lee, earl of Greyson, and Arthur James, earl of Warrington."

"Welcome." Arabella curtseyed. "Permit me to introduce my dearest companion, Miss Patience Wallace." Beneath the weight of their stares, she fidgeted with the lace trim of her sleeve. "Pray, to what do I owe this impressive gathering?"

"Wallace?" Lord Beaulieu arched a brow. "Are you any relation to General Wallace?"

"Yes, he is my father." Patience scooted closer to Arabella. "Did you serve with him at Waterloo?"

"Indeed, we all fought beside him at the great battle." Lord Beaulieu again smiled, which did nothing to inspire confidence. "Along with our mutual friend, Lord Rockingham, and he is why we seek an audience."

"Oh?" Arabella braced. "I am curious, my lord. What can I do for you, because any friend of my fiancé is a friend of mine?"

"Actually, it is what we would do for you that brings us here." At Lord Beaulieu's pronouncement, images of havoc flitted through her mind, though she knew not why. "To be specific, we would help you bring Lord Rockingham to the altar, given his reticence."

Beaulieu could have knocked her over with a feather.

"Fascinating." Patience tapped her chin. "Especially since Lady Arabella shares his reservations."

"Really?" Lord Beaulieu's gaze widened. "I thought all ladies lived for the auspicious occasion."

"Just as not all men are the same, we are not like all ladies, my lord." Patience cast a smug smile. "You would do well to remember that, Lord Beaulieu."

"Well then, I suppose that settles it." Lord Greyson stood. "What say we make for White's, because I am in serious need of a drink?"

"Not so fast." When Arabella expected Lord Beaulieu to cede the field, he stayed his friend with an upraised palm. "Apologies if I offended your delicate sensibilities, Miss Wallace." No doubt his unveiled condescension grated Patience's last nerve, and Arabella stifled a gurgle of mirth, because he knew just how to counter her friend. "But we are here to extend our assistance to Lady Arabella, that we might bring her hesitant beau to the church, on time, because Lord Rockingham is the best of men."

"I could not agree more." Curious, Arabella pondered his outrageous statement. Whoever heard of male matchmakers? "However, even the noblest of intentions cannot vanquish the trepidation of an ambivalent groom, and that is putting it mildly, because Lord Rockingham made it clear, in no uncertain terms, he does not wish to marry me. Given the delicacy of the matter, I require the utmost discretion."

"That goes without saying, Lady Arabella. It might interest you to know that Lord Rockingham has had a change of heart." Lord Michael huffed a breath and frowned, and his declaration echoed in her ears. "The question we face, in this moment, is whether or not *you* wish to marry Lord Rockingham."

How simple his query sounded, when her answer would shape the rest of her life. Perched on the precipice of her own Rubicon, her options were few. Given the kiss she could not ignore, she owed it to herself to contemplate the positive aspects of a union. She could support Anthony in his previous position and end up with someone far worse, or she could fight for him. Yet, everything came down to one incontrovertible truth. She liked Anthony. Her instincts, which she trusted, told her that, despite his sporadic peculiar behavior. He was a good man, but there was something else she could not deny.

As Patience so aptly pointed out, whether or not Anthony realized it, he already relied on Arabella. The tryst in Papa's study proved beyond all doubt that he needed her, and in some respects, she needed him. It was a rare opportunity to gain a husband who looked to his wife for strength, and theirs would function as a true partnership. Anthony was a man broken by the horrors of battle and still fighting a private war with himself, and she longed to help him. Not because she intended to rule him, but because she had developed tender feelings for the tormented soldier.

And then there was that kiss.

"Lord Beaulieu, just what do you propose?" Praying she was doing the right thing, in that instant, Arabella twined her fingers in Patience's. "I am amenable to your offer of assistance, provided I know the extent of our collaboration, although I am not entirely convinced we will succeed."

"Our aim is to act as matchmakers, of a sort." Lord Beaulieu compressed his lips, and the other three gentlemen groaned, in unison. "After all, who knows better how to attract a man than a man?"

"Is that so?" Patience remarked with a hint of sarcasm in her tone. "Have you any previous experience in such matters, Lord Beaulieu?"

"No, I do not." Beaulieu stared down his nose. "How difficult can it be, given women do it all the time?"

Arabella knew not how to respond. Then she peered at Patience. In concert, they burst into laughter.

"That does it." Lord Greyson stood. "I knew your plan was one of sheer lunacy, and I cannot believe I let you talk me into it."

"Wait, please." Arabella jumped to her feet. "I apologize, my lord, and I meant no offense, but you must admit the scheme is rather startling in its uniqueness, because never have I heard of such an enterprise undertaken by your sex."

"Of course, it is unheard of, and I know of no one who would embark on such insanity, present lunatic company excepted." Lord Greyson shrugged. "Society already believes we are adrift in a jolly boat sans an oar. Mark my words, they will call us the Mad Matchmakers of Waterloo."

"Surely, you jest." Just like that, Arabella gained four less than graceful but nonetheless chivalrous co-conspirators. "But, if all else fails, the name has a nice ring to it."

CHAPTER FIVE

G ARBED FOR DINNER, Anthony descended the grand staircase. In the foyer, he turned right and strolled into the drawing room, where his mother lingered. "Where is Father?"

"He dines out, tonight." The firm set of her jaw betrayed her air of serenity, belying the fact that she knew her husband spent the evening with his mistress. His father's propensity to keep a courtesan always confused Anthony, because he considered his mother a beautiful woman. Indeed, she was the envy of many society ladies, yet she spent much of her time alone. Even at Ainsworth's dinner, she kept to herself. "Would you care for a glass of sherry?"

"No, thank you, Mama." Sitting on the sofa, he adjusted the sleeve pinned to his lapel. "May I ask you a question?"

"Of course, my dear." Ever the lady, she glided to a chair and perched as if posing for a portrait, as was her way, and he admired her delicate features. "What troubles you? I gather it has something to do with your impending nuptials?"

"Am I that obvious?" When she nodded, he chuckled. "Mama, my objection to the union has naught to do with Lady Arabella, because she is a very fine woman. Rather, it is my physical fitness that is at issue."

"And you struggle with memories of the war." It should not have surprised him that she saw through his semblance of calm. With perfect posture, she clasped her hands in her lap. "How often I think of

John and his carefree nature. I suspect, had he survived, he would have come home and resumed his life, inasmuch as he left it. Yet, owing to his brash behavior, his demise did not so much shock as it saddened me. In some respects, I expected the regrettable news. But you, well, you were always a different sort. Whereas John was a boisterous, temperamental child, you were quiet and thoughtful, and I never doubted you would return to England."

"Do you believe I should marry Lady Arabella?" Yes, he still had reservations, despite his friends' encouragement. "Can I make her happy?"

"That you raise the question provides the answer." Hers was not the response he anticipated, and he scooted to the edge of his seat. "While I loved your brother, God rest him, I can admit, in all honesty, that John would not have made a devoted spouse. But you? You will care for her, as proven by your concerns for her welfare even now. You honor your commitments, and it is my hope you will also find love, although there are no guarantees, which you well know."

"Love?" His gut roiled at the suggestion. "I know naught of that emotion beyond the filial sort, Mama."

"But you will respect the vows, because such constancy of character is embedded in your disposition." Inclining her head, she smiled. "And love exists within you, whether or not you appreciate it, and it knows you. Yet, your steadfast heart is but one of the many reasons I love you, and you will make Lady Arabella a most loyal mate."

To his chagrin, he realized, too late, that he hurt his mother, because he forced her to confront all that she never enjoyed. Indeed, he promised he would never treat Arabella with the indifference to which his father subjected Mama, and he would never take a mistress.

"Why did you stay with him?" Anthony reflected on the past, on the years she spent nurturing her sons, only to be ignored for her efforts. "Why are you still here?"

"Because, like you, I keep my word. And where would I go?" Mama stood and strolled to the hearth, where she stared at the flames. Tall and slender, with a touch of grey in the hair about her temples, she personified elegance. "While I was but five and ten when I wed His Grace, my mother explained to me, in detail, what my new position involved and my part to play, and I obeyed. And there have been compensations, you and your brother. For good or ill, I am Her Grace, the Duchess of Swanborough, and I shall take the rank to my grave, because I earned it a thousand times over the years. In regard to your father's predilection for less than gracious company with the manners of a feral cat, I never had any illusions of fidelity when it came to His Grace, and he took no pains to disappoint me."

"Still, you must have wanted something more, Mama." As he studied the intricate print on the Aubusson carpet, he imaged a fanciful girl, full of hope, only to have her dreams dashed, and inside he wept for his mother. "What if I suffer the same fate or worse? What if I fail Lady Arabella in the same fashion, because I am hollow, Mama? I am an empty shell, and I would rather sever my other arm than cause Lady Arabella anguish, given she is but an innocent victim of Father's ambition."

"Only if you allow him to define your union." She turned and faced him, and never had he seen such determination in her expression. "But there is another way, my son, if you would consider it."

"And that is—what, Mama?" Curious, he stood and walked to her. "What would you have me do?"

"Fight." In a startling display of emotion, Mama clenched a fist. "Fight for your future. Fight for your wife. Fight for the life you were destined to lead. More important, fight for what you deserve, my darling boy."

"I'm afraid." No, Anthony was terrified. "I'm a coward, Mama."

"Of course, you are afraid. That you admit it speaks to the contrary, in terms of cowardice. Indeed, you are no milquetoast." She brushed aside a lock of hair from his forehead. "Fear is only natural, but you must not let it stop you from achieving all that is possible with Lady Arabella, as I daresay she covets the same goals."

"What if I am incapable of giving her what she wants?" In an instant, he reflected on the past, on the battlefield, on the countless casualties, and on those first waking hours in a medical tent, when he came alert in a panic. "In so many ways I remain trapped at the escarpment, at Mont Saint Jean, and I would argue I left the best part of myself at Waterloo, but I do not refer to the lower portion of my arm. What if my cooperation results in Lady Arabella's destruction?"

"I believe you underestimate yourself and your future bride." Mama cupped his cheek, as she often did when he was a boy, and even now the simple act comforted him. "You are stronger than you realize. You survived the hell of war, you are safe, and you returned home a hero. While I would never presume I know what you endured, I can say it is pointless to dwell on the horrors you confronted or define your life by what is done. Whatever you do, you must move forward.

"As for Lady Arabella, I know her mother quite well, because His Grace and Lord Ainsworth share a longstanding acquaintance. To your benefit, your fiancée is educated, and she is no prim miss, if I have judged her accurately. I thought she might have a positive influence on John, and I am even more certain she will succeed with you. Indeed, she is the sort of woman who can give you the chance at a love match, and I could not have picked a better bride, so I urge you not to take her for granted."

"I would never do that." In fact, his goal was just the opposite. And he never considered himself a hero. The true heroes of Waterloo remained in that mortar-scarred land, forever committed to the annals of history as a statistic. As a number, bereft of individual recognition. While those of the noble set were brought to England for internment, those with no money or prestige were reduced to naught but a faceless aggregate, in a mass grave with no headstone. "Can you not see that I am trying to protect her?"

"You like her." With the hint of amusement, Mama stepped back and appraised him. "Don't deny it."

"I'm not denying it, because I am quite fond of her. Although I cannot say why, there is something about her." A series of cherished vignettes played before him, as his fiancée offered unshakeable support and sweet kisses, and he clung to the reassurance Lady Arabella provided even when she was not with him. Somehow, she touched him without actually touching him, and in the short span of their renewed acquaintance, he had come to rely on her. "I need her, Mama. I cannot say why, but the prospect terrifies me, because, even though I survived Waterloo, I don't think I could withstand her rejection. That just might be the end of me."

"Then give her no reason to spurn you." Mama took his hand in hers. "Have the courage and strength to be a good and faithful husband. Share your world with her, and she will do the same for you. Give her your heart, and she will gift you hers. Hurt her, and she will serve you still. She may even forgive you, but she will never forget the pain you caused her."

"All right." He pondered her reasoning, but he could not escape the suspicion that Arabella was better off without him. Yet, he wanted her.

"Then there will be no more talk of leaving England." Mama arched a brow. "Your father told me about your plan, and I have to admit I was quite vexed that you would depart without saying goodbye."

"Is there no privacy in this household?" He cursed under his breath. "Sorry, Mama. And I would have composed a note."

"Yours would have been a failed enterprise." She compressed her lips. "Because your father would have found you, no matter where you fled, given his influence reaches far and wide."

"You speak as if from experience." And Anthony ruminated on the implication.

"We all have our secrets." Something in Mama's bearing struck him, and he contemplated the meaning of her declaration. "I would spare you the same regret."

"You left my father?" Stunned by the prospect, Anthony stumbled and almost fell, but she steadied him. "You tried to break free?"

"Once." She sighed. "A long time ago, when I was but seven and ten, and your father insisted I give him the heir for which I was contracted. I ran away, but he found me and brought me home. Confined to my bedchamber, I had no visitors save him, and we conceived John shortly thereafter. Three months after giving birth, I was pregnant with you. After that, he left me in peace and saw to it that I wanted for nothing."

"Can you really say that?" Anger spiked, given what she suffered. Her horrific revelation did much to explain his father's perspective of marriage, and Anthony gritted his teeth in disgust. "While I am well acquainted with our laws regarding women, I consider what he did an abomination, if not criminal. And what of you? Do you not want something more?"

"I beg your pardon, Your Grace." Walker, the longtime butler, loomed in the doorway and bowed. "But dinner is served, and Lord Beaulieu is just arrived for Lord Rockingham."

"Please, show him in, at once." Mama glanced at Anthony. "Were you expecting a guest?"

"No." Anthony made for the door to head off his fellow veteran, but Beaulieu charged forth. "What are you doing here?"

"I have an extra ticket for Vauxhall, and I have come to fetch you for a night of fun and music." Beaulieu rocked on his heels. "Tell me you have not eaten, because I would take dinner at my reserved supper-box."

"Had I known of your plans I would have accepted." Anthony stared at his mother. "However, we were just about to—"

"Oh, no." Mama waved and led him into the foyer. "I insist you venture out with your friends. It has been too long since you indulged in such felicitous exploits, and you are past due. And I shall dine in my sitting room and read a book."

"Mama, are you sure?" Given their conversation, Anthony didn't want to abandon her, as had his father. "I can go out some other time."

"Excuse me, Your Grace." A burly footman, one of Father's recent hires, stepped to the fore. "But His Grace left specific instructions that Lord Rockingham must remain in residence."

"Yes, I am sure His Grace did just that." Mama drew herself up with noble hauteur, and Anthony almost felt sorry for the manservant, because no one gainsaid his mother. "Since His Grace is not here, you will abide my directive, and I hereby discharge you of your duties, because we no longer require your services. If you will go with Walker, he will see that you are compensated."

The unfortunate blackguard shuffled his feet. "But His Grace—"

"Do you dare question my authority in my home?" Mama gave the poor soul a look that could wither the most stalwart adversary, and he retreated. "I thought not." Then she turned to Anthony. "Have a lovely evening, my son."

IN A PAINTING by Francis Hayman, two milkmaids clasped hands and danced, garbed in their best finery, while a porter hoisted a garland, comprised of a pyramid of silver plates, flagons, tankards, and flowers. Arabella scrutinized the masterpiece, which decorated the private supper-box Lord Beaulieu secured for the evening at Vauxhall Gardens, and she pondered the nobleman's scheme.

From the moment her father announced her amended betrothal, her world was on fire, as Anthony put it the afternoon they spent at Gunter's, and she knew not how to douse the flames. Instead, she fanned the blaze, igniting an inferno, because she contemplated marriage to a man who would own her, and she shuddered at the thought.

However, if she had to serve anyone, she would serve Anthony.

"Are you chilled, Lady Arabella?" Lord Greyson, one of the well-intentioned yet quixotic veterans determined to aid her campaign, stared at her and frowned. "May I be of assistance? Shall I send for a pot of tea, to warm you?"

"No, thank you, my lord, although it is kind of you to offer." She studied the interesting nobleman and could not ignore the tension emanating from him. Much like Anthony, Lord Greyson glanced back and forth, as if he anticipated an enemy combatant would spring forth and attack, at any moment. "It is a lovely evening, is it not?"

"Yes." He clenched his jaw.

"I understand Hook plays for us tonight." She tried again to distract him.

"Yes." Lord Greyson fidgeted with his cravat.

"Will you stop being rude and converse with the lady, as would a gentleman?" Lord Warrington shook his head. "Even I can see she is nervous, and that is not saying much, given I am half-blind. Talk to her and put her at ease, you ill-gotten tub of guts."

"Immature name calling aside, if you are so inclined, why don't you talk to her?" Lord Greyson started when a loud crash reverberated from an unknown source. "Apologies, Lady Arabella, because I meant no insult, but we share naught in common to encourage discussion, and it has been a long time since I attempted to entertain a lady."

"Entertain?" Warrington rolled his eyes. "Are you always such a half-wit, or is today a special occasion?"

"At least I'm trying." Lord Greyson slapped his thigh. "And calling you stupid would be an insult to stupid people."

"Gentlemen, please, don't quarrel. And you underestimate yourself, Lord Greyson." Despite his attempts to portray an air of nonchalance, she saw through his *faux bon vivant* disguise. "While I appreciate your efforts, you need not feel compelled to amuse me, because I am quite capable of occupying myself."

Beyond the colonnade, which boasted straight tablature and urn-topped finials, the fashionable set mingled in the grove, in the shadow of the Temple of Comus. In the past, whenever Papa brought Mama and Arabella to Vauxhall, Arabella thrilled to the experience. Yet, as she awaited Anthony's arrival, she wrung her fingers.

"What is wrong?" Patience, ever the reliable chaperone, elbowed Arabella. "I thought you welcomed the Mad Matchmakers and their unconventional assistance. Do you doubt them?"

"I'm not sure what I feel." And that was the problem, as Arabella always set clear, attainable goals, but her impending nuptials seemed anything but clear or attainable, given the duke's plot. What could she do to save Anthony, when His Grace held all the power? "From where I stand, the situation strikes me as impossible."

"But you will not let that dissuade you." Patience chucked Arabella's chin. "Because you love a challenge, and I wager Lord Rockingham is challenge personified."

"He is much more than that, and even I am unsure of my ability to assist him, given I am an amateur." Arabella reflected on the book and its contents, regarding nostalgia. "However, I am resolved to try, because he has no one else. Even the Mad Matchmakers carry invisible scars, though I doubt they know it."

"Then I suggest you smile, because your fiancé is just arrived." Patience nodded. "And you do not want to alarm him."

Alarm him?

Glancing over her shoulder, Arabella spied Anthony. When his gaze met hers, he smiled, and telltale warmth filled her cheeks. Just once, she wished she could control her reaction to him, but he reached through her defenses to touch her, despite her best efforts to contain him. Perhaps that was why she struggled with her decision to marry him.

There was a peculiar sort of intimacy to uncertainty.

Nestled deep in the dark recesses of her mind, like a foreign invasion, indecision took root, infecting and undermining her confidence in all other aspects of her life. Apprehension lingered, festered, and poisoned the otherwise innocuous facets of her existence, until persistent hesitation plagued every part of her world, such that she second-guessed something as simple as whether to eat strawberry jam or orange marmalade on her scone. In some respects, she scarcely knew herself, anymore, due to the disquieting emotions that wreaked havoc on her senses, and that frightened her most.

And it was all because of a man.

Her man.

"Lady Arabella, this is a welcome surprise." As always, Anthony greeted her with his customary charm, which put her at ease, and she rolled her shoulders. Then he arched a brow and peered at Lord Beaulieu. "Although something tells me our meeting is more by design than chance."

"I beg your pardon." With an angsty expression, which didn't fool her for an instant, Lord Beaulieu clutched a hand to his chest. "My only motive was to enjoy a relaxed night in the pleasure gardens of Vauxhall. And since when do I dictate the earl of Ainsworth's schedule? How could I have predicted Lady Arabella's attendance?"

"Me thinks thou dost protest too much." So handsome in a rich blue coat trimmed in old gold, Anthony smirked as he took her hand in his and kissed her gloved knuckles. "But you mistake my meaning, because mine is an observation, not a complaint." To Arabella, he said, "Shall we tour the grove, my lady?"

"I would like that above all things, my lord." Together, they stepped from the supper-box, and she clutched his arm. "Can we visit the acrobats?"

"Just a minute." Patience snapped her fingers. "You cannot venture forth without a chaperone."

"A chaperone?" Lord Beaulieu scowled. "Are they or are they not affianced? What good is a betrothal, if you cannot enjoy your bride-to-be's company, unreservedly?"

"They are, but until they speak the vows, Lady Arabella must be accompanied by an escort." Patience wrinkled her nose, and Arabella laughed. "Despite the engagement, we cannot risk her reputation."

"Upon my word, but what damage can Lord Rockingham do?" With an air of disgust mixed with arrogance, Lord Beaulieu shifted his weight. "The man has but one hand."

"And I suppose that is quite enough, for a rake of his stature and experience." Like a high-born debutante, Patience assumed a position that left Lord Beaulieu no choice but to abide her command, and Arabella admired her friend's strength. "Or do you claim Lord Rockingham suffers impotence, Lord Beaulieu?"

"How dare you cast aspersions on Lord Rockingham's abilities to satisfy his future bride." Beaulieu sniffed. "And I wager he remains as skilled as he was before the war."

"Thank you for the vote of confidence." Huffing a breath, Anthony shook his head. "Shall we?"

While Lord Beaulieu and Patience argued the finer but questionable points of male supremacy from a discreet distance, Lord Rockingham led Arabella toward the Grand South Walk, where they joined the promenade.

"It is a beautiful night, is it not?" As Arabella navigated the crush, she studied the tense lines about his eyes and the firm set of his jaw. When someone burst into laughter, Anthony flinched, and she squeezed his arm. "It is all right. Just a few rambunctious revelers. Do you often partake of Vauxhall?"

"How long have you been conspiring with my friends?" At his query, she drew up short and sought a response to placate him. "And don't insult me by feigning ignorance, because we both know you are anything but ignorant."

"Not long, but you are not supposed to know of their involvement, beyond what they discussed with you, however obvious it appears, and I would not for the life of me try to make sense of their logic. Indeed, I could not if I wanted to, because they are more than a little eccentric for matchmakers. However, for their sakes, I ask you not to apprise them that you are aware of their attempts at matchmaking, given they dearly want to support us." When they neared a tall hedgerow, he tugged her behind the shrubbery. While she should have been shocked by his behavior, she was not, given their previous assignation. And she wanted to be alone with him. "They care for you, a great deal, my lord. In some respects, I believe you give them hope, because if you succeed, they think they can too. And theirs is a harmless endeavor. What damage can they do?"

"You think this harmless?" he asked in a low voice, as he drew her near, which gave her a chill. "Because all manner of naughty thoughts occur to me, at the moment. And you might be surprised by what my band of brothers in arms can achieve, when they act in concert."

"They want you to be happy." She shivered, when his breath caressed the crest of her ear. "Is that so wrong?"

"If that is their aim and naught more, then I support their involvement." Given the setting sun, the dark, serpentine walk afforded privacy when he pulled her close, and his eyes flared. Just his touch warmed her from top to toes. "Because, although I am not entirely certain about our union, and I have not yielded the fight, I am leaning in your favor, my lady. I see no way to avoid our wedding."

"Well, at least you retain your usual charm." He chuckled, and she brushed the forever drooping lock of hair from his forehead. "And I share your position, given I have no real choice in the matter."

"I know that, and despite our mutual reservations, I would make you happy." Flames flickered in his heated stare as he tightened his hold about her waist, and she rested her palms to his lapels. "I would be a good husband and indulge your independent spirit, because I consider your strength a boon."

"Do you?" Perched on tiptoes, she studied his beautiful mouth and ached for him to kiss her. "Because I am my own person, and I cannot change, my lord. Not for you. Not for anyone."

"Oh, I'm counting on it." In that moment, he bent his head and kissed her.

And kept kissing her.

That was what she needed to quiet the doubts nagging her conscience. Reassurance in the form of what she heretofore would have described as a pedestrian physical expression, based on the books she read. But Anthony changed all that, because it was not so pedestrian given his aggressive flicks of his tongue, in concert with his bold fondling of her bottom through her skirts. Indeed, the fact that he had one hand did not in any way limit his abilities to tempt her, and nothing could mute the force of his touch. When he pressed his hips to hers, and she noted the telltale firmness of his erection, she grew dizzy with undeniable longing, but he held her, safe and sound, and she did not falter.

Passion rang a mighty salvo in her ears, blazing a trail from their point of contact to the pit of her belly, and she moaned when he ravished the curve of her neck. Beguiled by something she did not quite understand, she gripped his thick hair and stared at the starry sky, while desire tasted her. Then, to her unmitigated frustration, he halted his play, and she clung to him.

"My lord, what is happening to us?" Gasping for breath, and shivering from the power of their exchange, she nuzzled him. Patience was right. The man was plenty dangerous with a single hand. "What have you done to me?"

"I want you, sweet Arabella." He chuckled. "And no one is more surprised than I, because I have not felt this alive since before the war."

"I know what you mean." Shifting, she met his stare. "Because I feel it, too."

"Did I scare you?" To her disappointment, he removed his hand from her bottom and cupped her cheek. With infinite tenderness that melted her heart, he caressed her lips with the pad of his thumb. "Are you frightened?"

"Of you?" She gave vent to nervous laughter. "Never, my lord, because you will not hurt me."

"You are that sure?" Anthony brushed his mouth to hers. "You believe in me that much?"

For Arabella, it was a moment of unvarnished truth, and she did not hesitate. "Yes."

Nothing could have prepared her for the ensuing tryst, because Anthony again pulled her into his one-armed embrace and made more improper advances on her person. In a masterful opening sally, he let fly a barrage of inexpressibly intimate kisses that left her breathless, and his lone hand seemed to be everywhere at once. Indeed, she discovered he loosened the bodice of her gown when he took turns stroking her nipples, and she loved every minute of it—until Lord Beaulieu cleared his throat.

"Excuse me, because I am not one to interrupt a bloody good seduction—not that I was spying on your progress, which was commendable given the setting—but Lord Ainsworth seeks Lady Arabella. I suggest you right yourselves, because you don't want to be caught dallying in the bushes." Lord Beaulieu averted his gaze and snickered. "Upon my word, Greyson just launched a brilliant flanking maneuver, but even now Ainsworth approaches, so I suggest you make haste."

"Oh, dear." Panicking, in light of her unfamiliarity with such wanton circumstances, Arabella tucked in her chemise and retied the bow that sat at the center of her décolletage, given Anthony's enthusiastic encroachment on her breasts, and then she repaired the damage to his cravat and smoothed his hair. "Papa is here. What shall we do?"

"Just follow my lead." With the innocence of a babe, Anthony pointed at a tree. "And this is an excellent specimen of a deciduous elm, with its thick canopy of oval leaves with serrated edges. But it is the grayish-blue bark that sets the elm apart from other species—oh, Lord Ainsworth. How are you, this fine evening?"

"I am well, Lord Rockingham." Papa blinked and sputtered, and she bit her tongue against laughter. How she admired Anthony's resourcefulness. "But I grew alarmed when I did not locate my daughter in Lord Beaulieu's supper-box, given his promise to guard her."

"Papa, you worry for nothing, because I'm quite protected, and Lord Beaulieu and Miss Wallace stand as competent chaperones." Gaining her wits, Arabella rocked on her heels and glanced at Anthony. Did she just glimpse another side of the man unspoiled by war? "But Lord Rockingham offered a lesson in the mysteries of nature, and he is a vast deal more than knowledgeable in such matters." Of course, that was putting it mildly. "I would invite him to dine with us, Thursday next, if you are amenable."

"It should not surprise me that you enjoy the otherwise mundane topic, and Lord Rockingham is always welcome at our table." Papa drew a handkerchief from his coat pocket and daubed his forehead. "But the lamp-lighters shall assume their stations, at any minute, and I know you don't want to miss the spectacle."

"You are correct, and I thank you, given it is my favorite part of the evening." Like a proper lady, Arabella settled her hand in the crook of Anthony's arm, and he winked at her. The casual observer never would have suspected that only minutes ago, her fiancé slipped his fingers down her bodice to tweak her nipple. "Although I would never describe Lord Rockingham's impromptu tutelage as mundane, because I found it rather stimulating."

CHAPTER SIX

THE VALET TIED a precise mathematical, as Anthony scrutinized his black tailcoat, waistcoat, and trousers. Wondering how he let Beaulieu talk him into attending the Netherton's ball, when all Anthony wanted to do was climb into bed and crawl beneath the covers, he studied the empty sleeve pinned to his lapel and frowned. Would he never become accustomed to the sight?

"I beg your pardon, my lord." Standing in the entry from the sitting room, the butler bowed. "Lord Beaulieu is just arrived, and I installed him in the drawing room."

"Thank you, Walker. Tell him I will be down, posthaste." To the valet, Anthony said, "That will be all, Page."

In unison, the servants bowed and exited Anthony's chamber.

Alone, he walked to the windows and peered at the star-filled sky. So many nights he spent in quiet contemplation, gazing at the constellations on the eve of battle, but the habit had long since ceased to provide comfort. Then again, nothing could ease his current concerns, given the gravity of his predicament. Well, that was not exactly true, because one woman managed to cut through the misery to touch the man, and he simply could not continue without her.

Despite his reservations, and of that there were many, he would marry Lady Arabella.

Not out of some antiquated sense of duty. Not to fulfill a contract. Not even to make his father happy. No, Anthony would marry

Arabella because he wanted her. Because he needed her.

Resolved to persevere, he took one last glance at his reflection in the long mirror and saluted. Then he turned on a heel and marched downstairs. As expected, he found his friend dawdling in the drawing room.

"For a second, I thought you might not show for our adventure." Beaulieu clasped his hands. "What say you, old chum? Ready to woo your bride-to-be?"

"I must be insane to let you talk me into this, because she is already mine." Anthony rolled his eyes, and a queasy sensation roiled his belly. "But if you insist, I see no reason to delay the inevitable. Shall we depart?"

"Oh, come now." Ever the mischievous scoundrel, Beaulieu clucked his tongue and grabbed Anthony's arm. "This will be such fun, given my motives in pursuit of an unwed woman have never been so honorable."

"Wait." Anthony drew up short. "There is something you should know." When Beaulieu arched a brow, Anthony shuffled his feet and shifted his weight. "Lady Arabella does not wish to marry me, although her decision has naught to do with me, personally. Indeed, she would remain a spinster, if given the choice, and she is every bit as forced as am I."

"Really?" To Anthony's surprise, Beaulieu accepted the rather shocking pronouncement with unimpaired aplomb. "Shall we depart?"

"Did you hear what I said?" In the foyer, Anthony halted. He pondered the possibility of a rejection and swayed. Then he recalled Arabella's admission that Beaulieu conspired against Anthony. "Would you waste your time trying to bring a reluctant bride to the altar? The lady does not want me."

"Why so glum, when you have yet to court her? And don't even try to claim you find her unattractive, given you were not discussing the finer points of Vauxhall foliage when I interrupted your impressive advance the other night. Unless a wayward leaf somehow slipped down her bodice, not that I noticed, and she could not find the rogue frond, so you fished it out for her in a selfless act of chivalry. The lady made no protest that I detected, which bodes well for your wedding night." Beaulieu gave Anthony an abrupt shove out the door. "And when a man fondles a woman's bosom, not that I was watching, and she voices no objection, she is either a doxy or she is emotionally attached. Since Lady Arabella is no whore, we must presume she covets feelings for you. Trust me, once we deploy our powers of persuasion, she will fall into your arms—sorry, I mean your embrace, and consider herself a most fortunate wife."

"I had not thought of that." But Anthony's mind raced in all manner of salacious directions, because she made no attempt to forestall his ravishment. "But you are correct."

"When am I not?" Beaulieu skipped down the entrance stairs. "And you may name your firstborn for me, in a show of gratitude."

"I wish I shared your confidence, but I am not half so optimistic. Must have something to do with your unhinged personality." Distracted, Anthony caught his toe, tripped, and tumbled, face first, into the coach. "That does not portend well for our enterprise."

"Stop nagging, because that is a wife's occupation." With a none too gentle push, Beaulieu thrust Anthony into the squabs. "Although you do a rousing impersonation."

"Very funny." Secure in his seat, Anthony brushed a speck of lint from his coat and mulled the situation. If Arabella rejected him, he didn't think he could survive her refusal of his suit. "No matter what you say, this is a disaster in the making."

"All right." As the equipage lurched forward, Beaulieu crossed his legs and adopted a disgustingly sanguine air. "If you choose to view it that way, then so be it. Everything is dreadful. You are rich as Croesus, heir to one of the most prestigious dukedoms in England, and betrothed to a young, stunning debutante cursed with a strong sense of herself, her own opinions, and a wickedly tempting bosom. Would that I had your troubles."

"That is quite enough, because I get your meaning." It irritated Anthony that Beaulieu reduced a life-altering scenario to such elementary terms. Then again, given Arabella's response during their tryst at Vauxhall, Beaulieu had a point. "And do not let me catch you ogling my fiancée."

"Jealous?" Beaulieu waggled his brows. "Although I don't blame you, because there must be countless rakes just waiting to plow her fertile fields."

"Don't be ridiculous." Folding his arm, Anthony checked his fingernails, but he was jealous, all the same. "Lady Arabella is true of heart, and she honors her commitments."

"Still, she is a spirited filly. I wager she is apt to rush her fences, in the right circumstances, with the proper tutelage, which makes for delicious sport. And don't even try to convince me that you haven't noticed her figure." Beaulieu lowered his chin. "What say you, old friend? Ready to sample a taste of her honey pot? Want to sail her sweet harbor? Aching to pound her clam with your ham?"

"Will you stop talking about my bride-to-be as though she were naught more than a common doxy?" Indeed, Lady Arabella possessed immeasurable qualities Anthony was just beginning to explore, and she spoke to him on some enigmatic level that defied reason. If he were brutally honest with himself, he sincerely looked forward to his wedding night. "If you dare cast aspersions on her character, I will call you out, friend or no friend, and meet you on Paddington Green, at dawn."

"Now you speak like a husband." With a cat-that-ate-the-canary grin, Beaulieu leaned back in the cushions. "Practicing for the real thing?"

"Oh, shut up." When Anthony groaned, Beaulieu burst into laughter.

For the remains of the brief drive to the estimable London residence on Park Lane, Anthony brooded, yet his pulse raced when they arrived at the gate, because he anxiously anticipated another tryst with his lady. He needed to know she wanted him, in any capacity, but he would take his time and gauge her interest. When the coach drew to a halt before the main entrance, he yanked the latch and opened the door. With a sharp elbow to the ribs, he pushed past the footman.

In the foyer, he rushed through the receiving line, uttering arbitrary salutations, because he wanted to speak to Lady Arabella. At the arched access, he paused and handed the butler a card.

The manservant cleared his throat. "His lordship, the Marquess of Rockingham."

As usual, the crowd stared, and he shoved his way into the crush. He veered left and then right, searching for his fiancée, but he spied no sign of her. The chasmal ballroom opened to an equally impressive dining room, where a collection of tables welcomed revelers to linger, converse, and feast on a decadent array of dishes, and the cacophonous throng jolted him.

Anthony halted.

In the blink of an eye, he transported to the battlefield, to the huge encampment at the foot of a large escarpment in Le Haye Sainte, and to the tattered tents and the battered remnants of men who gathered to partake of a bit of soup or some horrid concoction that passed for food. Whatever the field cooks served, the soldiers ate, and he knew not the origins of some of the meals he consumed, but the less than elegant nourishment kept him going.

Kept him fighting.

"Are you all right?" When Beaulieu rested his palms to Anthony's shoulders, he flinched and returned to the present.

"I am fine." Anthony shrugged free, because he needed his fiancée now more than ever. Somehow, some way, he would propose. It probably wouldn't be sophisticated or particularly passionate, but it would be in earnest, and that was important to him. She had to know he chose her. "But I cannot find Lady Arabella."

"That is because you look in the wrong place." Adjusting the patch that concealed his injured eye, Beaulieu inclined his head and glanced at the dance floor.

To Anthony's amazement, he located his bride-to-be in the company of Lord Greyson, the former prisoner of war, as they made the rotations amid a sea of couples. "How did you manage to get Greyson here, given his disdain for public assemblies?"

"Believe me, it was not easy." Beaulieu compressed his lips. "But he would do anything for a case of my best brandy."

While Anthony was glad to see his chum out and about, he would rather Greyson sought alternative companionship. For some reason Anthony could not fathom, he did not appreciate his friend partnering Arabella, even for something so innocuous as a dance. Then again, many a lady lost her heart—or her reputation through a seemingly innocent twirl about the room.

"Just what does Greyson think he is doing?" Anthony gnashed his teeth.

"I would say the allemande." Beaulieu sniffed. "Care for a refreshment?"

"No, I would not." When Greyson bent his head and whispered something to Arabella, she laughed, and Anthony envied the traumatized soldier in that moment, because he had never imparted anything witty enough to garner such a response from her. "What do you suppose they discuss? And why is Greyson here, when he hates crowds?"

"Well, I am not one to eavesdrop, and I would not hazard a guess at what flows through Greyson's mind. As for his attendance, he is here to support you." With a sly smile, Beaulieu nodded to a fetching young widow. Heralded as a war hero, for a storied charge that resulted in the capture of more than a hundred French troops, he never lacked for attention and expended little effort to fill his bed. Yet, Beaulieu never seemed happy. "The diversions are plentiful tonight."

"Is that all you ever think about?" The music ended, and Anthony waved to his lady. "There are other pursuits, you know."

"None that provide half so much pleasure." Beaulieu snickered, but his bawdy demeanor didn't fool Anthony for a second, and he wondered what his friend concealed behind the brash façade. Then again, didn't all veterans hide secrets? Did they not all tell lies to themselves, sometimes? "After the horrors of war, satisfaction is the only thing worth living for, and I have more than earned it."

"If you tell yourself that enough, you just might believe it, but I know better." Just when Arabella walked in Anthony's direction, a loud pop reverberated, and he jumped, as did Beaulieu.

"Do you think we will ever be as we were, before Waterloo?" White as a sheet, Beaulieu tugged at his cravat. "Will the day come when we no longer start at the slightest provocation?"

"I'm not sure." But Anthony was certain of the comfort he found in Arabella's company, and he wanted her with him, at his side, because her presence calmed him. "Still, as Lord Michael rightly argued, we owe it to those who did not come home to live to the fullest, to make the most of our good fortune."

"And if you tell yourself that enough, you just might believe it, but I know better." Beaulieu arched a brow. "The truth cuts both ways, old friend."

"Indeed, it does." Anthony patted Beaulieu on the back. "And we have seen each other through some difficulties, yet we persist. Given my father's hired men guard me, even now, despite the fact that my mother discharged them, I find sport in the irony. I am resolved to marry Lady Arabella in light of our talk. Thus he worries for naught."

"Sorry I am late, but I had a devil of a time negotiating the stairs." Hobbling on crutches, because he had yet to master a wooden limb, Lord Michael drew near and smiled. "You are singing a new tune, and

I am glad to hear it, because your fiancée approaches, and you don't want to insult her."

Gowned in emerald green, with her long brown locks arranged in a cascade of curls, she glided like an angel, and familiar warmth sashayed over his flesh, soothing charged nerves and quieting his unrest. She did that for him, when he could not help himself, and he desperately needed her.

"Good evening, Lord Rockingham." Given the announcement of their engagement, the crowd gawked when Arabella greeted him. "It is a lovely night, it is not?"

"A scarce minute ago, I would have disagreed, but it is much improved, now, Lady Arabella." To his delight, she blushed at his compliment, and he vowed to offer praise more often. He wanted to make her happy, given she settled for less than a man. "May I have—"

"Lady Arabella, I wonder if I might beg the honor of the contratems and rigadon?" Beaulieu extended an arm, which Lady Arabella clutched at the elbow, and Anthony wanted to scream. "And, perhaps, Rockingham might indulge Miss Wallace?"

"Oh—that would be such fun." Miss Wallace charged the fore, and it was then he noted her presence. "Shall we, Lord Rockingham?"

"Of course." To refuse would have been rude, but Anthony had no interest in Miss Wallace.

Cursing in silence, he did what any gentleman would do and led her to the dance floor. As they stepped in time with the music, he mulled Beaulieu's confusing behavior, which made no sense. Was Anthony not supposed to court his future wife? Was that not the scheme?

Yet, as the evening progressed, every time he tried to speak with Arabella, one of his fellow soldiers intruded. Just when he feared he could tolerate no more interference, Lord Greyson signaled Anthony.

"Care for a brandy?" Greyson glanced over his shoulder. "I have it on good authority that the study is vacant."

"I suppose." A quick check of the vicinity revealed Arabella in the company of Miss Wallace and Beaulieu, and Anthony shook his head. Were his friends not supposed to help him court his lady? "Because Beaulieu seems intent on keeping me from my fiancée."

"Then let us enjoy a quiet repast." Greyson rubbed the back of his neck. "Because I am not quite accustomed to the crowds."

"Why did you come here, tonight?" Weaving through the crush, they exited the ballroom and turned to the right. Anthony knew the location of the study, by heart, because he had seduced more than one lady in its dark, quiet confines. "You have not attended a single social event, save Vauxhall, since our return to London."

"I am here for you." Greyson navigated the small passage, until they came to a door on the left. Slowly, he twisted the knob and pushed open the oak panel. "I gave my word I would help you win Lady Arabella, in truth, and I will do so. Is there a more noble enterprise?"

As Anthony pondered his miserable start, he filled two glasses with brandy. "Only if we succeed."

"ARE YOU SURE this is the right course of action?" Arabella strolled the outer circle of the ballroom, with Patience and Lord Beaulieu, when she spotted Anthony with Lord Greyson, departing for the study, as prearranged. "What if Lord Rockingham changes his mind? What if he resists the marriage? What if—"

"What if you stop worrying and have faith in our fighting men, because they will not disappoint you?" Patience grabbed Arabella's hand and squeezed her fingers. "Besides, you want this. Don't try to deny it."

"I'm not denying it." Arabella bit her lip. "But I cannot pretend the situation is ideal."

"Don't fret, because our plan will work, Lady Arabella. Believe me, we need only put you in a room, alone, with Rockingham, and nature will take the reins. I gather he is raring to go after our shenanigans to keep you apart." Lord Beaulieu scanned the immediate vicinity. "That was my intent, but now we require a diversion if you are to escape without notice, because your presence attracts unwanted attention."

"What can we do about it?" Patience shifted close. "Even His Grace watches us."

"Relax, ladies." Lord Beaulieu nodded once. "I anticipated difficulties and planned, accordingly. My men will do their duty."

Tracking his gaze, Arabella discovered Lord Michael, lingering near the entrance to the dining room. Just as a manservant strolled past, carrying a tray overloaded with dishes, Lord Michael stuck out one of his crutches and tripped the unfortunate domestic, and a mighty crash echoed through the ballroom. While less than graceful, the scheme worked, and the disturbance garnered a collective of intrusive gazes.

"Go—now." Lord Beaulieu shoved Arabella into the hall. Then he drew Patience to his side, effectively shielding Arabella from sight.

Glancing left and then right, she clutched her throat and ran down the passage, until she arrived in the foyer. Recalling Lord Beaulieu's instructions, she followed a narrow corridor, until she stood before the requisite door.

So much weighed on her shoulders, and she shivered as her palm met the metal knob. Everything rested on her ability to convince Lord Rockingham that they had no other option than to obey his father. But there was more to her design, because she wanted a match based on friendship and respect, which she considered necessary for success, and she had to know that he believed it possible. That he was capable of such dedication.

Otherwise, they were doomed.

Still, she reminded herself that in life there were no guarantees, and a lady had no choice in the selection of her husband. Lord Rockingham presented the chance for something more. For something real. With him, there existed the hope for an equal partnership, and that was precisely what she wanted, so she would fight for him, regardless of previous reservations.

With that, Arabella opened the door.

In the study, Lord Rockingham and Lord Greyson occupied a matched pair of chairs before the hearth.

"Well, I believe that is my cue to depart." After setting a glass atop a small table, Lord Greyson stood and walked toward her. When she dawdled, her conspirator gave her a gentle nudge and secured the door behind her.

"My lord." Nervous, she curtseyed and prayed for the strength to persist, as her heart pounded in her chest. "It is remarkably pleasing to see you, again."

"And you, Lady Arabella." So resplendent in his black formal wear, he stretched tall to greet her. "I gather this was not your idea."

His was a statement, not a question.

"Not exactly, but neither did I protest." To her surprise, he expressed no anger. Instead, he extended a hand and flicked his fingers, and she stumbled forward. "Shall I join you?"

"For a brandy?" His eyes widened. "Do you favor it?"

"Actually, I have never tasted it." To foster amity, she stared at the glass he held in his grasp. Recalling Dr. Larrey's advice, she sought common ground to put Anthony at ease. If only she could put herself at ease. "May I sample yours?"

"Be my guest." Without hesitation, he passed her the elegant crystal balloon.

In her mind, she toasted to strong women everywhere and took a healthy gulp.

A wicked burning sensation stung her throat, searing a fiery path to her belly, and she yielded to a violent coughing fit. Tears streamed her cheeks, and she feared she might be ill. Laughing, Anthony patted her back. Just when she regained her composure, she surrendered to another embarrassing, unladylike bout of hacking.

"Are you all right?" To her chagrin, he chuckled. "You should not have tried to consume such a large amount in a single swallow, because brandy is to be sipped. It is to be savored."

"For heaven's sake, why didn't you warn me?" She set the offensive concoction on the table. "I would have followed your advice, had I known it could be so potent. I'm not daft."

"Lady Arabella, in some respects, you are the smartest person of my acquaintance, and you are blessed with an uncanny ability to offer comfort and support when I most need it." His kind words did much to alleviate her chagrin and trepidation. She still thought she might revisit her supper. "While I could have cautioned you, I must confess I wanted to see how you would handle it because, if you are to be my bride, you must possess an adventurous spirit."

"Am I to be your wife?" Of course, Lord Beaulieu proclaimed as much, that afternoon in the drawing room at her home, but she needed to hear the news from Anthony. "Because you made it clear you didn't welcome our union."

"My dear, if I may be so bold, I regret to inform you that my father learned of my plans to escape London, and he hired men to guard me, thus I am going nowhere, so I altered my position." He shifted his weight to face her. "But before you take insult, I should explain that I have other reasons for marrying you, none of which have anything to do with my father and everything to do with you."

"Oh?" It was the moment for which she waited, and the declaration, freely given, did much to allay her fears. "Might you clarify your statement?"

"It would be my pleasure." In that instant, he reached across the table and took her hand in his. "I practiced this discussion, yet I know not where to start."

"The beginning is usually best, in such circumstances." When he twined his fingers in hers, she relaxed. "Perhaps, you might describe how your father discovered your plan?"

"No." He shook his head. "I should start with Waterloo, although I have never told anyone what I endured, but I would share it with you, if you permit me."

"I should be honored to witness your account, my lord." Sitting upright, she mirrored his stance. "And I would have you know that I count myself most fortunate to be your fiancée."

"You might feel otherwise, after hearing my sad tale." When Arabella shook her head, Anthony smiled. "All right, little one. If you are so determined, I would describe the morning of the great battle, which commenced with my regular ration of stirabout—"

"What is that?" While she loathed interrupting his story, she wanted to understand him.

"It is what we call oatmeal and water, and it tastes as awful as it sounds." With his thumb, he traced circles on her palm. "After breaking our fast, the men prepared to fight, when Napoleon attacked Hougoumont and Wyndham's second battalion of Coldstream Guards. It was a diversion to draw Wellington's reserves to our right flank, but our artillery soundly defeated Baudin's brigade."

"Yes, I read the details in *The Times*." And what she recalled of the savagery chilled her blood. "Were you at Hougoumont?"

"No." Frowning, he averted his stare, but she recognized the familiar signs of distress. The rigidity in his posture. The clenched jaw. The rapid rise and fall of his chest. "I was camped at Le Haye Sainte, at the foot of the escarpment near Charleroi-Brussels road, where the fighting was by far the most intense, given we were woefully outnumbered. The bugles blared, heralding the charge, while squadron after squadron of Cuirassiers, Hussars, and Dragoons advanced, and we were overrun. Columns of infantry assailed us, and I led my men into the fray. From a distance, the *Marseillaise* played, as if to taunt us, and I drove for the enemy's heart, but...but..."

Anthony opened his mouth and closed it.

Then he bowed his head and shut tight his eyes.

Tension invested the study, and the silence only worsened her agitation, because he struggled with painful memories. Remembering the counsel detailed in Dr. Larrey's book, she steeled her nerves.

"It is all right, my lord." Arabella slid from the chair and knelt before him. "I'm here, and you are safe. I will never let anyone or anything hurt you."

Framing his face, she paused when he flinched. Embarking on her own campaign, of a sort, she revisited precious recollections of their evening at Vauxhall. Daring to venture beyond the guidance Larrey prescribed, she inclined her head and pressed her lips to Anthony's.

At first, he simply sat there, and she reconsidered her tack. But slowly, interminably slowly, he responded. Firm but gentle, he claimed her mouth, teasing her with flicks of his tongue, and she accepted his invitation to explore. Emboldened by a rush of power given his reaction, she gripped the hair at the nape of his neck and deepened the exchange, as a flurry of sensations, none of which she could master, traipsed her flesh. Just when she found her pace, to her disappointment, he broke the kiss. Her dismay was brief, given he wrapped his arm about her waist and lifted her into his lap.

"My lord, this is not proper behavior, for a lady." Even as she called for restraint, she embraced her man. Then again, she started them down the alluring path. "Is it wrong that I want to kiss you?"

"No. Rather, I think, for us, it is a very good thing, and I believe you know I cannot resist you, even though you distract me from my purpose. I can share the rest of my story with you, later." The strain in his expression eased, and he settled his palm to the curve of her hip, in a scandalous display of affection. "But I would know what ability you possess to calm me, when I am in the throes of hell on earth, because you, alone, influence me thus."

"If my mother could see me, she would be furious." Arabella rested her forehead to his and wondered if she should share the source of her altogether unique skill. "But I cannot bear your anguish, and I would comfort you, however I can, with any means at my disposal."

"Careful, dearest Arabella, because I might be tempted to take you up on your offer, and I would preserve your bride's prize, until we have taken the vows." At his pronouncement, she gulped, until again he brushed his lips to hers. "Even then, I would protect you, because I am damaged, and I would not harm you, for anything in the world. Would that I could spare you this union, because you deserve so much more, but I am powerless to stop what our parents have put in motion. And, heaven help me, I want you."

"Well, I will have no less than the very best of men, and that is you, my lord. So, I remain true to my principles." Caressing his cheek, she instigated the next kiss, and he nibbled the corner of her mouth, which sent delicious shivers spiraling through her. "Indeed, I will have no other."

"But you had no wish to take a husband." As he reclined in the high back chair, he studied her with unveiled interest. "In that respect, you were very clear when we met at your home, so I would settle our arrangement, once and for all. Are you positive you wish to marry me?"

"My lord, the new perspective is mine to own, because I admit I felt otherwise." In an attempt to amuse him, she cast the lethal pout her father could never resist, and Anthony rewarded her with a charming blush. She would store that information for future use, when dealing with her soon-to-be-husband. "However, it is a woman's prerogative to change her mind, is it not?"

"It is, indeed." Ah, now he favored her with a boyish grin. "But I would know why you wish to wed me. Indeed, I would know everything about you, just as I would have you know me, for good or ill, including the details of my war experience. In the end, if you have any reservations, I would know them."

"My lord, it is simple, really. And you must know I am in complete accordance with your position." She shrugged and tried but failed to ignore how he trailed his hand to her waist and higher, just shy of her bosom. "My standards remain the same. I am a woman of strong opinions, which I yield to no man. Yet, I am defined by a society that views me as less than a man, so I must marry. Why would it surprise you that I contemplated my choices and selected you, when we are well suited, and I consider myself your equal? I would be your partner, in every way, Lord Rockingham, if you will have me."

"Are you proposing to me, Lady Arabella?" When he poked her in the ribs, she yelped, and he arched a brow, as if to challenge her. "While I may not know much about marriage, and no woman has ever asked me to marry her, that sounded like a proposal."

"What if it is, my lord?" Indeed, she honored her beliefs and stood for her man. Not for an instant would she relent. "If I am so inclined, what say you?"

"All right." He nodded once. "I accept."

CHAPTER SEVEN

L IFE SEEMED SO much simpler, once Anthony consented to marry Arabella. After much consideration in the quiet hours, he resolved to embrace the fate his father planned, but Anthony would wed on his terms, which he intended to discuss with his bride-to-be that night.

No longer obsessed with clandestine dealings and escape, he skipped up the entrance stairs to his fiancée's home, for the heretofore agreed upon dinner. He made a quick check of his appearance and knocked on the door. Nervous, he rubbed his palm down a leg of his breeches. Juggling a bouquet of roses in the crook of his elbow, he swore to himself when he almost dropped a book of note, tucked under his arm, which he hoped would please his lady. When the butler set wide the oak panel, Anthony lifted his chin.

"Good evening." He crossed the threshold. "Lord Rockingham to see Lady Arabella."

"Indeed, my lord." The manservant bowed. "Lord Ainsworth expects you. If you will follow me."

As Anthony passed the hall mirror, he glanced at his reflection, cursed the sleeve pinned to his lapel, and his confidence flagged, because he still yearned for his old, whole self. An image of his bloody and mangled stump flashed before him, and he winced and shook his head. If only he could forget the past, he just might remember how to live in the present. Tension built in the pit of his belly, and he swallowed hard.

"Lord Rockingham, you are right on time." Stunning in a gown of ruby red, Arabella strode straight to him. "Oh, and you come bearing gifts. Dare I ask if they are for me?"

"They are, my lady." Every composed thought fled him in the face of her smile. He handed her the flowers, which she passed to the butler. "I hope they meet with your approval."

"Travers, have these put in a vase and placed on my bedside table." The grace and ease with which she conveyed her directive would serve Anthony well, and he envisioned her presiding over the casual dinner party for various members of Parliament, whereas the behavior she exhibited in the Netherton's study would keep him satisfied in their bed. "And what else have you brought?"

"Arabella, mind your manners." The Countess of Ainsworth wagged a finger. "Welcome, Lord Rockingham. We are so pleased you could join us for dinner."

"Indeed." Lord Ainsworth extended a hand in friendship, and they exchanged an awkward greeting, given Anthony fumbled with the book in his lone hand. "You do us a great honor."

"The honor is mine, Lord Ainsworth." Anthony noticed Arabella's interest fixed on the book, and he caught her stare and arched a brow. Her curious nature exercised his imagination. "I am grateful for the invitation and the opportunity to spend time with my future wife, because I would foster amity prior to our nuptials."

"Your motives are quite sound and do you great credit." Lord Ainsworth seemed cautious when he stepped back and assessed Anthony. What did Ainsworth mean by *quite sound*? "Lady Ainsworth and I partake of sherry. Would you care for a glass?"

"No, thank you." Anthony shrugged off his unease and told himself he was being overly sensitive on his first informal meeting with his future in-laws. "With your permission, I would speak with Lady Arabella."

"Of course." Lord Ainsworth nodded once. "Her ladyship and I will sit near the window, to offer you a measure of privacy."

"You are too generous." Yet, Anthony would prefer Arabella's company, unreservedly. Sitting at one end the sofa, he scooted to the edge of the cushion and handed her the old tome. "For my lady's pleasure."

"How kind you are to think of me." Biting her bottom lip, she perused the cover and came alert. When she met his gaze, he smiled. "*Thoughts on the Education of Daughters.* Is this a suggestion, or do you make sport of my predilection for Wollstonecraft?"

"I thought it might prove useful, someday." While she flipped through the pages, he availed himself of her distracted state and admired a single thick curl that dangled at her throat, along with the flirty layer of lace that called attention to her décolletage. Beaulieu described her bosom as wickedly tempting. In truth, she manifested an irresistible combination of virginal coquette and seductive siren. If not for the social Season, he would lock her in his bedchamber for a fortnight after their marriage. "Have you not read it?"

"Must confess I have not." Closing the book, she peered over her shoulder at her parents. Then she studied him and scooted closer. "How considerate is my fiancé, and I shall endeavor to express my gratitude at your earliest convenience."

"I like the sound of that." There it was again, the genial conversation and easy airs that typified their fledgling relationship, and he marveled at her ability to identify with him, when he struggled to find something to say to her. "I enjoyed our evening at Vauxhall and recall it with fondness."

"As do I." The charming blush that colored her cheeks declared she understood his meaning, because he referenced the tender kisses they shared along the serpentine. In the dark hours, he summoned a vision of that evening and slept in peace. "Perhaps, we might venture there after our wedding, that we might mark our brief courtship with equal affection."

"Excuse me, my lord." The butler cleared his throat. "Dinner is served."

"Let us adjourn to the dining room, because I'm famished." Lord Ainsworth stood and straightened his coat.

Trailing in Lord and Lady Ainsworth's wake, Anthony escorted Arabella. In that moment, he ached to kiss her, if only to savor the warmth of her mouth. But it was her comforting embrace he craved in the night, when he often woke to the brutal images of war. Yet, that happened less and less since they renewed their acquaintance.

"Lord Rockingham, if you will take the chair to my left, Arabella can assume the opposite position." After situating himself, Lord Ainsworth signaled the butler. "You may commence the service."

In silence, the servants moved into action with admirable precision, dishing portions of steak, mashed potatoes, and carrots. It was then Anthony panicked, because he could not cut his own food. At home, Walker performed the service. Anthony's heart pounded in his chest, his ears pealed, and he grew warm, because he anticipated disaster. Just when he was about to announce his deficiency and ask for assistance, a footman collected his empty plate and replaced it with another, which evidenced merciful intervention. To his surprise, the food had been sliced into perfect bites. When he glanced at Arabella, she winked.

He would kiss her silly at the first opportunity.

"Is there anything else we can do to make you comfortable, my lord?" So she had instructed the staff to accommodate him. Why was he not surprised? "Do you take wine?"

"Yes, and everything is perfect, Lady Arabella." A servant draped a napkin in Anthony's lap, as he picked up a fork and speared a tender morsel of meat. With no fanfare, he savored the quiet meal, yet his mind was anything but quiet, because he mulled the consideration his fiancée displayed on his behalf.

It was his first dinner taken outside his residence since his return to England, because he had not the courage to risk embarrassment in public when he often made a mess of things. Even at Vauxhall, he ignored his grumbling, empty belly and waited until he returned home to feast, by which time he was famished. That she went out of her way to oblige him, and address his needs, touched him in ways he had never experienced, and he would never forget her thoughtfulness.

Tomorrow, he would lavish upon her expensive gifts to show his appreciation of her efforts, and he would write more than his name on the accompanying cards. Indeed, he would compose something naughty, just to exercise her beautiful mind.

"I spoke with His Grace about the wedding breakfast." Lord Ainsworth eased back in his chair. "It is to be a small, private affair, with only family in attendance."

"Oh?" It irked Anthony that his father excluded him from the planning. Then again, some things never changed, because his father had been dictating Anthony's life from birth. "I expected him to invite all of London to witness the event."

"So did I, but I would not hazard to guess His Grace's motives." Lord Ainsworth pushed aside his now empty plate. "Shall we partake of brandy and cigars in my study?"

"No, Papa." Arabella opened and then closed her mouth. "Forgive my outburst, but you promised I could play cards with Lord Rockingham, and you could enjoy dessert in the drawing room, with Mama and I."

"Ah, yes." Lord Ainsworth waggled his brows. "Tonight, we indulge in a tasty syllabub with almond shortbread, my favorite."

"What say you, Lord Rockingham?" Like one of Botticelli's famous cherubs, Arabella inclined her head, and whatever she asked he would not refuse her. "I understand you are a past master at *vingt-et-un*."

"You have spent too much time with Lord Beaulieu." No doubt Beaulieu functioned as a veritable trove of information, which Arabella was smart enough to employ to her advantage. Yet, her intentions were honorable. But she did not anticipate the fact that Anthony's deficiency made him a poor player, given he could not hold his cards and draw from the deck, with only one hand. "Perhaps, we might sit by the fire and talk."

"But I did so wish to engage you in a simple game." In light of her frown, which cut through him like the sharpest knife, he could not deny her. "Please?"

"Of course, my dear." How easy she bended him to her will, but he would never admit it aloud. "Whatever you ask, I am your most devoted servant."

"Wonderful." In the blink of an eye, her demeanor transformed, and she bounced from her chair. "And I have a gift for you, too."

"You do?" When she settled her palm in the crook of his elbow, he lingered behind her parents. In a low voice, he said, "I thought you were my gift."

"Scandalous, Lord Rockingham." She clucked her tongue and grinned. "Now that is the charmer I have heard so much about but have scarcely seen, since our engagement. I thought it might have something to do with me and a lack of attraction."

"You think me indifferent?" In the foyer, he pulled her aside, while Lord and Lady Ainsworth settled in the drawing room, because he could not allow her to labor under a mistaken assumption. "Even after Vauxhall? Even after our delicious tryst in the Netherton's study?"

"You don't want to marry me." Craning her neck, she peered into the drawing room and then drew him toward a side passage. "Despite your acceptance of my clumsy proposal, do you deny your objections to our union?"

"You know, very well, my reservations have naught to do with you." Tempted by her full lips, he backed her into the wall. "While I concede, most regrettably, to opposing our nuptials, I must admit my hesitation was born of ignorance of your strength and character, which will serve me well when you stand as my wife. Where others would founder, you will succeed, and that is why I will have none but you."

Then he bent his head and kissed her. Summoning the finesse honed in the arms of some of the most seasoned widows and courtesans of London, he launched a full-scale seduction of his fiancée just feet from her father, which intensified the illicit rendezvous and drove him like a stallion with a burr under its saddle.

There was something about their intimacy that inspired unshakable confidence, which he craved, and he rode a wave of passion that harkened to the past. To his glory days, when he was whole, and nothing and no one frightened him. Somehow, Arabella restored his faith. She made him feel like his old self.

Like a man.

Reassured and emboldened, he suckled her little pink tongue, a pastime that quickly ranked as his favorite. No matter how much she yielded, he wanted more. When she yanked the hair at his nape, he pressed on her caresses meant to entice and arouse. No shrinking violet, she bit his flesh and scored her nails along the back of his neck. Hugging her about the waist, he thrust his hips to hers, and she gasped for breath. Desire surged and spiraled, and she opened to him as he loosened his reins, and he walked his fingers lower, to grip her bottom.

"Arabella, Lord Rockingham, are you there?" her father inquired from the drawing room.

Anthony started and came alert, and Arabella pressed a finger to his lips.

"Yes, I'm fine." With bright red cheeks he found rather arresting, Arabella blinked and squared her shoulders. "Er—Papa, I wanted to show Lord Rockingham the ermine muff you purchased for me. We will join you in a minute."

"I will not apologize for that," Anthony stated, in a low voice.

"I should be offended if you did." From his coat pocket, she retrieved his handkerchief. After daubing the corners of her mouth, she wiped his face, tidied his hair and cravat, and smoothed his lapels. "That should do it. How do I look?"

"Beautiful." In so many words, he wanted to tell her what she did for him, how she provided comfort when he most needed it. The way she silenced his demons. Yet he could not compose a single coherent sentence, so he said nothing more.

"Then let us play cards, given we have much to discuss, which is the reason I invited you to dinner." She took his hand in hers. "And I would have us plot a course to divert His Grace, because I will not let him commit you to an asylum."

THE SHOCK IN Anthony's expression stunned Arabella, and she realized he had no idea what His Grace had in store for his son, after the wedding. Her mind raced, and they strolled into the drawing room. She searched for a response to console and reassure him, because she would not surrender her husband without a fight.

But how could she stop His Grace?

Sitting opposite her fiancé, at a small square table suitable for the carefree exchange of gossip, she checked her parents. Noting their half-hearted efforts to ignore the young couple, she turned and met Anthony's turbulent gaze.

"I beg your pardon, my lord." She swallowed hard, when she noticed tears welling in his vivid blue eyes. If only she could hold him. "I thought you privy to His Grace's most foul scheme."

At first, he simply shook his head.

"I knew he plotted to secure an heir for the dukedom, but I knew naught of my fate." Then he leaned near. "Tell me everything you know."

So as not to arouse attention, in a quiet and calm tone she imparted the dastardly plot, and he grew paler by the second, with each successive revelation, such that she feared he might swoon. Stretching her arm, she grasped his hand and twined her fingers in his. At last, she recounted the settlement the duke pledged, as part of the marriage contract, if she fulfilled her duties to beget the all-important heir.

"I am so sorry, Lord Rockingham." She would have given anything to spare him the pain, but he had to know the truth, because he was in danger. "Indeed, I thought His Grace's ploy was your primary motivation for fleeing London, and it would make sense."

"I knew nothing of my planned commitment, but that is no surprise, given we rarely speak." He shivered, and she gave him a gentle squeeze. "But I never imagined this. *Commitment*, as if I am naught more than some embarrassing trifle to be locked away."

"I will not allow it." How she ached for Anthony, and she choked on overwhelming rage at his father. No matter what happened, she would not let a war hero end his days in an institution when there was nothing wrong with him, other than the fact that he was human. "I know not how, but I will save you. I will find a way—I swear it on our firstborn."

"You are fierce, Lady Arabella." For a brief moment, he smiled, but his good humor faded just as fast as it emerged. "I hesitate to point out you are just a woman. By law, you are but property, yet you know this, so what do you propose to do about my predicament when my father holds the power to destroy me, on a whim, and you scarcely exist in this world?"

"I don't pretend to possess all the answers to our quandary—and it is *our* quandary, my lord." When Papa cleared his throat, she grabbed the deck and dealt the cards. "But I cannot sit idly and let you be taken from me, so I will do something."

"Brave words for a little lady." He studied the cards and frowned. "While I hate to disappoint you, I must remind you that I have but one hand. How am I to hold my cards and play them, at the same time?"

"Oh, I forgot." She leapt from her chair and snatched a parcel from the mantelpiece. After returning to her seat, she presented the gift. "I had this commissioned for you, in preparation for our game, because I thought it might prove useful, and we should maintain the ruse for my parents."

"Of course." When Anthony fumbled with the bow, which she tied with care, she held still the box, and he tugged on the ribbon. He lifted the lid and arched a brow. "What is it?"

"It is my design, and I hope it suffices." From the bed of cotton, she removed the slender wooden platform and set it before him. "The slit is for your cards, so you may draw at your leisure, without showing your hand."

"Ingenious." Trailing a finger along the top of the platform, he smiled in earnest. "I know not how to thank you."

"But you will try." No, that was not a proper response for a lady of character, but she supposed it mattered not, given she teased her future husband. And she did so cherish his kisses.

"You may depend upon it." For a precious instant, Anthony held her stare, and what she glimpsed quite took her breath away. Bereft of the stress and anguish that often marked their interactions, she spied a rake of incomparable caliber, the sort young ladies spoke of when their mothers were not listening, and gooseflesh covered her from head to toe. "But I would have you answer a question."

"You may have anything you wish." When he arched a brow, she stiffened her spine. "I mean...that is to say, I am at your service, Lord Rockingham."

"You claim a desire to wed me, and your behavior at the ball convinced me to an extent, but I would know more about the reason for your change of heart. I wish to understand you." He shrugged and situated his cards. "Why me, when your father could secure a more advantageous match?"

"Because you need me." The instant she posited the bold statement, she cursed the burn of a blush. She didn't want to offend him.

"And because I think I need you, my lord."

Papa cleared his throat, and she almost jumped out of her skin. Smoothing her skirts, she bowed her head.

"How so?" Inclining his head, Anthony moved the deck to the center of the table and nodded once. "Your draw, my lady."

There was something in his voice, something primitive and possessive in the otherwise pedestrian salutation that bespoke fellow feeling and something more. A like-minded perspective. A cryptic attachment she did not quite fathom, but it was there, nonetheless.

"Thank you." She pulled the top card and assessed her hand. "Given you know of my affinity for Wollstonecraft, and my propensity for independent thought, I believe you are the perfect spouse for me, because you humor me, despite the fact that you do not share my views."

"I would not say that, but no man, sane or otherwise, would willingly proclaim he considers a woman his equal." His chuckle, a rich and throaty baritone, sent a rush of tremors pulsating through her. With care, he drew from the deck, exchanged a card, and placed it on the table. It should have been a simple game, yet there was more to it. In their own language, they made their pact, until, with a mischievous grin, he turned about the platform to display his hand. "I win."

He did, in more ways than one.

Just then, the butler rolled the tea trolley into the dining room.

"Ah, the dessert arrives." Papa clapped twice and stood. "Serve Lord Rockingham and Lady Arabella, first. And I will have a brandy."

"Yes, my lord." The butler set two glasses of syllabub and a plate of almond shortbread on the table.

"Feel free to dunk the shortbread in the syllabub." To set an example, and put Anthony at ease, Arabella did as she bade him. "It is delicious, is it not?"

"Indeed." When he leaned forward, she mimicked his movement. "But I prefer your sweet lips. Ah, you blush, and I adore that about you. Perhaps, now, you might tell me why your father stares at me as if I am a loose munition about to explode."

"My lord, you seek to shock me with your bold statements, when I invited you here to show my parents that you are not mad, so please behave." He halted mid-chew, and she gulped. "I do not mean to offend you, but should His Grace enact his dubious scheme, we may need my parents' support. Given His Grace told my father that you are mentally unsound, I must prove otherwise. They must see for themselves that you are no different than anyone else."

"And here I thought it was my estimable company you desired." The frown returned, and she bit her tongue, because she did not want to hurt him. "You should have told me I was to perform, tonight. Pray, how am I to acquit myself, Lady Arabella?"

"Act natural, and do not be vexed, my lord." She set down a piece of shortbread and reached across the table. To her relief, Anthony touched his fingers to hers. "Just be yourself, because your inclinations always do you credit, and we do this to ensure our future."

"I can manage that, and you are wise beyond your years." His professed confidence did not fool her for a second, given his pained countenance, and she longed to hug him. "But I submit this would be unnecessary if I still had my other arm. No one would question me. No one would view me as unfit, in any capacity. But because I am less than a man, I must be mad."

"My lord, you must stop looking to the past, because your history is written and cannot be changed, but that does not mean that your destiny is set in stone and you are done on this earth." Arabella chose her words carefully, because she honestly believed Anthony underestimated himself. "There is more to you than a single limb, and I would caution you not to define yourself by what you lack, because you are a better man than you realize. You need only stop looking over your shoulder and turn your eyes to the present and what looms on the horizon, to grasp the reins and charge forth."

"You expect me to forget what I was once, because you flatter me?" His scowl indicated she angered him, when that was not her aim, so she sought to soften her response, at the first opportunity. "I am to ignore the life I enjoyed before the war?"

"My lord, you mistake me, given I suggested no such thing." She quieted and smiled, when her father peered in her direction. For Anthony's sake, they had to maintain the image of a normal, happy couple. "Please, I would not set myself at odds with you, when I am not the enemy. If we are to defeat His Grace, we must combine our efforts. As a partner, you should know that I would never stop fighting for you, should His Grace take you from me. Regardless of what he promises, no fortune, townhouse, or rank will sway me from my purpose, which is to defend my husband and the family we create."

Again, he held her stare, and she could almost sense him tugging at her. Indeed, he wanted to hold her as she yearned to hold him.

"Formidable." Narrowing his gaze, he shook his head. "You are formidable, Lady Arabella. If only we had your fortitude in France, we might have been home much sooner."

"Do you mock me?" She was more than a little hurt at his perceived jest. "Because we are in serious trouble."

"I thought so, when I arrived this evening, and I apologize for that." Reaching for her, he toyed with her fingers. "But I am not so afraid, anymore. In fact, I believe we will be just fine."

"How can you say that, when you know what His Grace intends?" Surreptitiously, she glanced at her parents, but they were diverted by their dessert. "Must confess the situation keeps me up at night, and I am consumed with your wellbeing."

"Well, at least you are thinking of me, while you rest between the sheets." Anthony waggled his brows. "There is that. But you need not worry, because I will speak with my father and sort out the matter."

"How I wish I had known you, before the war." Once again, the invisible but nonetheless potent connection drew her to him, and she studied his blue eyes, the clarity of which never failed to steal her breath. "When I am alone, I imagine such grandiose notions of you, not that you are any less a man, now, because I would argue quite the opposite. I think you brave and strong, every bit as formidable as you believe me."

"Praise, indeed, my lady." The mantel clock chimed the hour, and he pushed back his chair and stood. "It is late, and I should depart."

"Must you?" She didn't want him to leave. She wanted him with her, so she could protect him. "But you didn't finish your syllabub, and you didn't take a brandy with Papa."

"I had quite enough, Lady Arabella." To Mama and Papa, Anthony said, "Thank you, so much, for a lovely evening. Indeed, I cannot recall enjoying such a pleasurable meal and most excellent company."

"We are honored you consented to join us." Papa crossed the room and shook Anthony's hand. "Your coach is parked at the curb, and I will see you to the door."

"Oh, no, Papa." Arabella shot to the fore. "Please, allow me to escort Lord Rockingham, given it is my duty."

"I can deny you nothing, my dear child." Papa chortled. "Perhaps, Lord Rockingham might accompany us to the Promenade, tomorrow."

"What a wonderful idea." Arabella bounced and peered at Anthony. "Say you will, my lord, else I shall be disappointed."

"What man could resist such a request from his beautiful betrothed?" She gripped his arm, and he clucked his tongue. "Of course, I shall be too happy to escort Lady Arabella."

"Then it is settled." She drew Anthony into the hall. "I shall return in a moment, Papa."

In the foyer, her fiancé glanced left and then right, before pulling her close. The kiss, hard and fast, did not appease her, and she held tight, while she made improper advances on his person. She didn't think he would complain, given his encouragement.

When he ended the glorious tryst, she clung to him. Shaken and vulnerable, she held tight to the lapels of his coat and gasped for breath, as did he.

"You know, I am beginning to wonder why I ever objected to our marriage." Anthony caressed her cheek with his thumb. "If I knew you could kiss like that, I should have insisted on hasty nuptials."

"My lord, I am a woman of many talents." She relaxed, when he claimed another kiss. "However, I never counted kissing among my abilities, due to my lack of experience, thus I wonder if it is to your expertise that you owe your thanks."

"I would argue my partner makes the difference." How his carefree demeanor worked on her, easing the tension of the evening, and she yielded to his infectious spirit. "Until tomorrow, lady mine."

"I'm yours, my lord." She opened the door. "Never forget that I am on your side, and we will triumph over His Grace."

"My dear, I don't want you to fret about my father." Anthony tapped her nose. "Because I promise I will speak with him before our wedding, and resolve our differences, so everything will be perfect for our special day. You have my word."

She perched on the first step, and he skipped to the sidewalk. "But, my lord—"

"It will be fine, my lady." After saluting, he boarded his equipage, and she backed into the house.

While Arabella didn't share Anthony's optimism, she could only hope he was right.

CHAPTER EIGHT

I T WAS LATE in the evening when Anthony walked into a private
room at White's, where the Mad Matchmakers, as Arabella called
his friends, waited. On normal occasions, such as those moments
when his father was not trying to commit Anthony to an asylum, the
gathering often devolved into a ribald but harmless contest of
recounted audacious seductions and exaggerated claims regarding the
length and inventive use of their most prominent protuberance.

Not so that night, given his reason for summoning them.

As expected, his fellow wounded veterans did not disappoint him,
and they lounged in a circle of high back chairs and quieted when he
entered. The collective of quizzical expressions gave him pause,
because he knew not where to begin his sad tale.

"Is it that bad?" Beaulieu inquired and shoved a crystal balloon of
brandy into Anthony's grasp. "You look like you could use a drink and,
please, don't tell me you changed your mind, and you intend to fight
the marriage after all our hard work to secure Lady Arabella's
submission. I am not half so sure we can find another impressionable
female to take you."

"In all honesty, I am not sure Lady Arabella submits to anything or
anyone." Smiling, Anthony reflected on their heated exchange at her
home, where she engaged him as an active participant in their games.
"In fact, she is no follower, because she keeps pace with me, better
than any woman of my acquaintance."

"Oh, I say." Greyson grimaced. "Not that I am shocked, but did we fail in our one and only attempt at making a match, when I thought it a triumph?"

"I told you we never should have got involved in the first place." Warrington shook his head. "Matchmaking is women's work, and we do not wear skirts. What is next, a trip to a modiste and a lesson in embroidery?"

"Come now. Why so cynical, when you have such lovely knees?" Ever the wit, Lord Michael snickered. "Indeed, I hope you will help me snare a bride, because I have always wanted to marry a charming debutante and raise a family, and who better to be involved in my selection than my lifelong friends?"

"I, too, shall take a wife, although not anytime soon." Beaulieu arched a brow. "Given I still reap the rewards of gallant service, I am in no rush to the altar. However, like Lord Michael, when the day of reckoning comes, I shall rely on my fellow soldiers to aid my connubial campaign, because I can think of no more qualified judges of character."

"Wait just a minute." With an owlish expression, Warrington wagged a finger. "I never agreed to enter into this folly in a permanent arrangement. We were only supposed to assist Rockingham."

"But you excel at it." Lord Michael snorted. "Want to take a turn at ribbons?"

"Don't be ridiculous." Greyson compressed his lips. "The mere suggestion gives me a vicious case of collywobbles."

"Serves you right, because you abandoned the right to protest, along with a great deal of pride, the moment you met with Lady Arabella and pledged your support." Anthony inclined his head, and he could not resist poking fun at his friends. Besides, the levity dispelled some of the stress inhabiting his shoulders. "Why stop now?"

"My friends, if we are honest with ourselves, we have been ridiculous from birth." Beaulieu appeared quite pleased with himself. "Some more than others."

"I resemble that remark and own it, with equal estimation." Lord Michael raised his glass of brandy, in toast. "Indeed, I am rather satisfied with our efforts."

"Speak for yourself." Greyson scowled. "I will take our machinations to my grave, where our embarrassing endeavors will surely haunt me for all eternity."

"Fear not, my friend." Beaulieu slapped Greyson on the back. "If you forget, I pledge to remind you, in the hereafter."

"Will you be serious?" Greyson smacked a fist to a palm.

"When have I ever been serious?" Beaulieu stuck his tongue in his cheek. "And I have no intention of changing my ways, now. By the by, it may interest you to know we may have another potential customer."

"Are you out of your mind?" Greyson echoed Anthony's thoughts. "Who, on earth, would be so foolish to trust us to secure him a wife?" Clearing his throat, Greyson peered at Anthony. "No offense."

"None taken," Anthony replied, although his self-esteem suffered a direct hit. Still, his fellow veterans worked on him like a tonic. "And need I remind you I never asked you to get involved in my personal affairs?"

"It appears I am the fool." Lord Michael propped an elbow on the armrest. "And you may mock me at your leisure, because I don't care. I welcome your assistance in securing a wife."

"You must be joking." Warrington blinked and paled, as if on the verge of an apoplectic fit. "You cannot be committed to such a wild undertaking."

"Let me assure you that I am in earnest, and I'm speaking for myself, because I am nothing if not brutally honest, but you know that." Lord Michael grinned. "And if you are equally frank, you will admit Beaulieu's idea has merit."

"Not that I concede your position, because I find this discussion one of sheer idiocy, but how so?" Dripping skepticism, Greyson folded his arms. "And explain it to me as you would a child, because I am well and truly lost."

"When have you not been lost?" Lord Michael narrowed his stare. "Consider a pedestrian query. Who would you prefer to find you a wife? Some shrewd, fortune-hunting, rank-seeking mama, who has, no doubt, stifled every natural, libidinous inclination her daughter might possess, or a man with similar reservations and objectives, as well as a keen sense of the sort of innate traits that could make a grown man cry in gratitude, regarding the female form, given we know what we want in the drawing room as well as the bedchamber?"

While the quirky cadre continued their debate on male matchmaking, Anthony stared at the sleeve pinned to the lapel of his coat and braced for the unavoidable reaction. Despite the passage of time, it surprised him how much it still hurt to recall his injury, and he wondered if he would ever get over the loss or if the wound would define him for the remains of his days. Then he remembered Arabella's words of encouragement and gained strength from her support, even in her absence.

"Gentlemen, while I am loath to encroach on your intellectual discourse regarding courtship, however entertaining I find it, I am in need of your assistance, and the situation is grave." Anthony pondered his failed attempt to meet with his father that morning and realized he had to ensure his future wife's safety, should his father enact his plan. "Indeed, I cannot revisit my quandary without suffering a shudder of terror and, in some respects, you are my only hope."

"You were not in jest." Beaulieu sobered and scooted to the edge of his seat. "What is it, Rockingham? What happened?"

"Betrayal, such as I have never known." Swallowing a healthy gulp of brandy, Anthony steeled his nerves. "Please, bear with me, and do not interrupt, else I might lose my courage and falter."

Recounting in order the villainous scheme devised by his own father, Anthony omitted no detail, however humiliating, because the veterans would understand. One by one, each soldier slumped in his seat, wearing the same revelatory mask of defeat. Although no one stated as much, each man could have walked in Anthony's boots, and he suspected that uncomfortable realization brought all levity to an end.

"Well?" Anthony nudged Beaulieu. "Have you no humorous reply to dispel the dour mood, as I could benefit from some of your aberrant quips right now?"

"My friend, I am more sorry than I can say." Given Beaulieu's morbid expression, Anthony's spirit plummeted to new depths. "How—and I ask this with all sincerity, but *how* can His Grace stoop so low as to condemn his own son to a lunatic asylum, when there is nothing wrong with you, aside from your missing arm, and then steal your heir? Must you yield even your firstborn? Have you not paid enough in the coin of flesh? Will His Grace take your dignity, too?"

"Valid queries for which I have no answer, my friend." Anthony shook his head. "And I am unutterably confused by my father's behavior. I knew he harbored reservations but not to this level of treachery."

"It is because they hate us." Greyson bit the fleshy underside of his thumb. "Did we not take the field? Did we not survive? Where is the disgrace in our service?"

"They don't hate us, Greyson." Anthony met his friend's troubled gaze. "Rather, they don't understand us. Unlike the dead, who were easily forgotten, and the whole, who simply returned to the ballrooms and blended into the crowd, we remind society of a debt they prefer to ignore. But our wounds mark us as something altogether different, and it is much easier to shove us aside, or pretend we don't exist, than face reality and the obligation we represent."

"So it is no small wonder they prefer to lock us away from sight, that they might abandon us, too." Beaulieu sneered. "But we will not go quietly into the night, and we will not be shunned, because I refuse to live in the shadows. Society waltzes through the *ton's* ballrooms, on the graves of those who gave all and on the backs of those who, albeit torn and tattered, made it home, and they will recognize and honor our sacrifice if I have to run naked down Park Lane to garner their attention."

"Well, that should provoke quite a response." Warrington scratched his cheek. "Although I am not sure it is the one you seek."

"Because then they will know we are crazy." Greyson sighed and bowed his head. "And that is the last thing we need."

"Have you a better suggestion?" Lord Michael arched a brow. "Is the sum of your contribution naught but complaints, or do you have anything constructive to add to our campaign?"

"Please, don't fight, because we are not the enemy." Their row brought Anthony so very low, and his spirits sank. If he couldn't inspire his friends, how could he move his father and save Arabella? "And I am not so worried about myself as I am for my bride-to-be and my future heir."

"Rockingham is right, and shame on us." With trembling fingers, Warrington fumbled for his glass. "A fellow soldier comes to us for help, and we waste time making petty jokes and arguing amongst ourselves."

"Shame on us, indeed." With a fist pressed to his chest, Beaulieu met Anthony's stare. "And you have my word, as a gentleman, that I shall defend Lady Arabella with my life if necessary."

"I must confess that is precisely what I want, because I may be in no position to protect her, should my father enact his plan." Contemplating his fate, he realized just how much he had to lose. "But what happens to me is of no account, given I am already scarred."

"Like bloody hell." As Anthony anticipated, Beaulieu protested. "What of friendship? What of the bonds of brotherhood, given all we have survived, together?"

"And over my dead body will I abandon you to some god-awful lunatic asylum. We defeated Boney, did we not?" Greyson snarled. "If His Grace thinks we will surrender you without a fight, he is mistaken."

"Indeed." Warrington slapped his thighs. "After all, we are soldiers, and we will beat His Grace at his own game." He opened and then closed his mouth. "At least, we will, somehow."

"One thing is certain." Lord Michael leaned back in his chair, folded his arms. "If we are to triumph, we must work as a single entity. Else, divided, we must surely fail."

"And we must strategize our response, because I am certain His Grace has done the same." Beaulieu seized control of the meeting, just as Anthony hoped, because he relied on his friend to protect Arabella in his absence. "Integral to victory or defeat is possession of Lady Arabella. Whoever holds the wife, and any issue, controls the engagement."

"Exactly," Anthony inserted into the conversation. It was Beaulieu that would save the day, although he didn't know it yet. "And in that respect, if you are willing to listen, I have a proposition."

THE SIDEWALKS OF Bond Street teemed with activity, as well-dressed Londoners patronized the exclusive boutiques that catered to society. While most young ladies lived in heightened anticipation of the opportunity to purchase new clothes, Arabella was not like most young ladies. Dragging her feet, because she detested all things frivolous and gratuitous, and shopping met those characterizations, in her estimation, Arabella followed her mother into the modiste's establishment.

"Mama, I do not understand why I require new gowns, when I am getting married and can take my things with me." Arabella huffed a breath, when her mother signaled the modiste. "The lavender will suffice for the ceremony, given we bought it last season, thus it remains relatively new since you refuse to permit me to wear black."

"Arabella Hortence, will you be serious?" Mama snapped her fingers. "You cannot wed Lord Rockingham garbed in mourning attire, and mind your manners, because we have little time to accomplish our objectives, before we return home."

"Oh, all right." While Arabella didn't seriously expect Mama to relent, she surrendered her position, because she had bigger battles to fight, on behalf of her fiancé. "What do you prefer, Mama? You know, in medieval England, brides wore blue, as a sign of purity."

"You shall marry in silver lamé." On her fingers, Mama ticked off a list. "With a mantua of silver tissue lined with white satin, trimmed with Brussels lace, and we must have embroidery."

"Is that not a tad presumptuous, Mama?" Arabella cringed, because she envisioned quite a spectacle. "I thought only royal brides wore silver."

"Nonsense." Mama lifted her chin. "You are to be the next Duchess of Swanborough, and only the finest will do for my daughter. Given I have long dreamed of this day, I want everything to be perfect."

"Of course, Mama." As usual, her mother observed the proprieties, thus Arabella resolved to cooperate. "I defer to your good judgment, in the matter, given I know naught of fashion."

For the next hour, she stood before a long mirror, while the designer measured, pinned, poked, and prodded Arabella, in an exercise she likened to torture. To endure the torment, she thought of Anthony and his father's nefarious scheme, but she fidgeted beneath the stress of the situation, so she cleared her mind. When she yawned, her mother frowned.

"Sorry, Mama." Arabella stretched long and winced from a pinprick. "How much longer must I persist in this manner?"

"My dear, quit complaining, because we have yet to visit the milliner or the hosiery." Mama folded her arms, in a familiar affectation of impatience. "Then we must order stationery and cards, with your new name and the Rockingham coat of arms." She tapped her chin. "And have you decided what you wish to give Lord Rockingham, as a small token of your esteem?"

"Not yet." At the moment, Arabella focused on the needles in the modiste's hands. "But I have some ideas."

"We can discuss it, later." From her reticule, Mama retrieved a piece of parchment, which she unfolded. "I almost forgot that we must have you fitted for new night rails and matching robes." To the modiste, Mama said, "Have you any chiffon in pale pink and, perhaps, a soft white?"

"I have some in the sewing room." The portly designer adjusted her spectacles and signaled a young seamstress. "Fetch the two bolts of chiffon, on the back table."

"Mama." Arabella huffed a breath. "You know my style, and I do not favor such fabrics. It is bad enough that you ordered lace for my wedding gown."

"The lady does not understand, *n'est-ce pas?*" The modiste tittered, as she draped a swath of emerald silk about Arabella's shoulders and then knelt to adjust a hem, and Mama smiled. "But she will, soon enough."

"What is it, Mama?" Confused, Arabella inclined her head. "What did I miss?"

"Perhaps, I should give you a moment." The modiste scrambled to her feet. "I have some lovely Swiss voile lace, upstairs. If you will excuse me, I will bring it for your inspection, Lady Ainsworth."

"Thank you." Mama sighed. "I will expound upon the topic this evening, because I have delayed long enough. But you must inspire Lord Rockingham, in order to produce an heir and satisfy His Grace's requirements, and your current nightwear is inadequate to the task."

"You refer to marital relations." Arabella gulped when she recalled the book, which featured detailed sketches of the human body, she hid beneath her pillow. Regardless of what the estimable author wrote, she thought the deed a physical impossibility. "And, more specifically, the wedding night."

"You know of such things?" Mama furrowed her brow, sobered, and then whispered, "Arabella, have you dallied with Lord Rockingham? Has he made improper advances on your person?"

"No." At least, she assumed he hadn't. "But I may have made improper advances on him." Biting her lip, she reflected on their sweet and oh-so-fascinating trysts. "How does one know what is and is not proper, when kissing one's fiancé, Mama?"

"*Arabella.*" Mama pressed a palm to her chest. "Upon my word, but you quite shock me." In that instant, the modiste returned, and Mama came alert. "Madame Clothilde, I am afraid we are called to another appointment, and I must reschedule."

"But, of course, Lady Ainsworth." The modiste bowed. "I am, as ever, at your ladyship's disposal, and I shall begin construction of Lady Arabella's gown, to your specifications, *tout suite.*" With care, Madame Clothilde removed the fabric from Arabella's shoulders. "And whenever you return, I shall make myself available."

"Thank you." Mama checked her appearance and clapped twice. "Come along, Arabella."

"Yes, Mama." With her mind racing, Arabella rushed to the sidewalk, where the family carriage parked. A footman held open the door, and she stepped into the elegant equipage, emblazoned with the Ainsworth coat of arms, which she always admired as a little girl. In a few days, the same conveyance would deliver her to the Duke of Swanborough's residence in Grosvenor Square for her wedding. When she settled into the squabs, opposite her mother, she reflected on her sweet exchanges with Anthony and wondered how anything that felt so good could be wrong.

"Around the park, until I say otherwise." Mama flung aside her reticule and smoothed a stray lock of hair. "All right, young lady. Out with it."

"Out with—what?" In light of her mother's disapproving stance, Arabella shifted in her seat and toyed with the hem of her sleeve. "Lord Rockingham is my betrothed, is he not? Why should we not kiss?" Yes, she omitted any mention of his risqué caresses of her breasts, because that behavior seemed a tad controversial. "Where is the harm?"

"Your questions evidence your naïveté, because most such exchanges do not end with a kiss, and you would do well to remember that, until you speak the vows." Mama shook her head. "Really, Arabella, how could you be so careless with your reputation? And I thought you were smarter than that, given all your intellectual books and erudite opinions."

"I beg your pardon?" She bristled at the criticism. "What do you mean, Mama?"

"Do you really think you fool me?" Her mother snickered. "Why do you believe I insisted on the best education, after your father agreed to send you to boarding school?"

"But, you protested, because you said highborn ladies had no need of knowledge." Indeed, Arabella committed Mama's argument to memory. "I distinctly recall your position, given it conflicted so completely with mine."

"Oh, my poor child." Mama smiled a sly smile, which Arabella could not quite decipher. "You may know much of science and literature, and you may be a strong supporter of female emancipation, but you remain ignorant in the ways of men and women. You should have guessed that I adopted the opposing perspective, of the hysterical woman, so your father might assume the posture of male superiority and overrule what he described as my 'unfounded fears brought about by my delicate nature.' Regardless of his incorrect supposition, I got what I wanted, just like you hid the medical treatise beneath that lowbrow novel and my cookbook, which I selected to distract your father."

"You knew about that?" Looking on her mother, as if for the first time, Arabella sank in the cushions. "You knew about everything?"

"Of course." Mama shrugged and arched a brow. "And you should know that the easiest way to maneuver a man, if you please, is to advocate against that which you desire. Believe me, it works with uncanny precision, because men cannot bring themselves to admit we know best, and they are honor-bound to dispute our judgment."

"That is why you objected to my private tutelage, when I returned home." When Mama nodded, Arabella gave vent to a strangled cry. "Why did you not tell me? All these years, I thought us at odds, Mama."

"Not so, anymore." Leaning forward, Mama reached for Arabella, and they clasped hands. "And I would have you seize the chance fate delivered to your feet, because Lord Rockingham is a man of honor, despite his impairment. You may even know love, Arabella."

"Love?" She laughed. "I do not believe in love, Mama. That emotion is naught but a fairy story contrived to oppress women, because they seek that which is unattainable." She lifted her chin. "I shall never fall prey to such fantasies."

"I caution you not to be too quick to discount what could be the greatest adventure of your life, my dear." Mama relaxed. "Because I assure you love exists."

"Mama, are you telling me that you love Papa?" Arabella considered the prospect but remained unconvinced. "Forgive me, but I never would have presumed it."

"No." Mama shook her head. "While I am quite fond of your father, love never entered the equation, given I married him out of duty, as was required of me." She sniffed. "But don't get me wrong, because we are friends, and he never hurt me. When he claimed my bride's prize, he was gentle, reassuring, and never rushed me. The years passed, and we grew as a couple. Unlike some society husbands, he never shamed me. When he took a mistress, he exercised discretion, and for that I am grateful, because not many so-called gentlemen concern themselves with their wife's social status."

"If you don't love Papa, how do you know there is such a thing?" To Arabella's surprise, Mama changed seats, and they clasped hands. "What is it? What do you hide?"

"I was in love, once, when I was but a girl of six and ten." Mama averted her stare. "His name was Nigel, and he was a stableman in service to my family."

"A stableman?" Stunned by the revelation, given Mama's usual stalwart demeanor, Arabella's heart raced. No matter how she approached the situation, she could not imagine her mother pining for a servant. "What happened to him, and why have I never heard of this story?"

"It is not the sort of thing one discusses, is it?" With her thumb, Mama drew imaginary circles in Arabella's palm. The habit harkened to her youth, when she fidgeted during church. "And it did not last long, because my father sent Nigel away. We never saw each other again, but Nigel is never far from my thoughts." With a wistful expression, she sighed. "So, tell me of Lord Rockingham. I promise, I will not be angry."

"Oh, Mama, he is not what I expected." Arabella envisioned her groom and grinned. "He talks to me, and he values my spirit, because he said as much."

"Then you are not afraid of him?" Mama tipped Arabella's chin. "Because His Grace is convinced of his son's mental infirmity."

"Mama, if I harbor any apprehension, it is the possibility that His Grace might succeed in committing Anthony—Lord Rockingham—to an asylum, because there is nothing wrong with him."

"But His Grace insists Lord Rockingham presents a viable danger to you and any prospective heir, which is why your father secured His Grace's pledge to shield you." When Arabella squeezed her mother's hands, Mama compressed her lips. "What occurred between you and Lord Rockingham, that you support his cause with such fortitude?"

"Not more than a few kisses, and while I do not understand His Grace's penchant for besmirching his son's sanity, I can assure you that Lord Rockingham is quite sane." Somehow, she had to convince her mother of the truth, so she related the information contained in Dr. Larrey's study, along with Anthony's symptoms, that she might secure an ally. "Mama, as God is my witness, I swear to you, if Lord Rockingham is guilty of anything, if he has any fault, it is that he is human. Given what he endured on the Continent, and the loss of his left hand, he is to be admired, not declared insane and imprisoned. If I am to be his wife, you should know I will fight His Grace with every fiber of my being. I will use any means at my disposal. I will give my life, if necessary, to protect my husband, before I allow anyone to take Lord Rockingham from me."

"You are that determined?" Mama asked with more than a little incredulity. "You believe in him that much?"

"I do, and Lord Rockingham needs me." It was not the first time Arabella realized she needed Anthony, because he functioned as her purpose, and hell would freeze before she let him down. With shoulders squared, she faced her mother, because she would leave no doubts regarding the constancy of her commitment. "The day may come when I must rely on your support, in order to protect Lord Rockingham, because I cannot do it alone. I would like to know I have your support, Mama."

"My dearest child, I have always been on your side." She cupped Arabella's cheek. "Never forget that, despite appearances, I have your best interests at heart, and I will assume a position to achieve your goal, even when it seems we are at odds."

"Oh, thank you, Mama." Indeed, Arabella needed her mother's

kindness just then. "Know that I will not involve you, unless it is absolutely necessary."

"Of course." Sitting erect, Mama wagged a finger. "Now, promise you will not kiss Lord Rockingham, again, until you are married."

CHAPTER NINE

TWO DAYS BEFORE his wedding, Anthony accompanied his parents to another in a long list of gross displays of opulence that characterized the *ton*. If not for his singular motive for joining the festivities, he would have stayed home. Garbed in the customary black formal wear, he stepped from the ducal coach. Tugging at his cravat, he glanced at the star-filled night sky and inhaled a deep breath.

Despite what he told Arabella, he had yet to set things right with his father, but he didn't want her to worry. Besides, he believed his fiancée's account may have been slightly exaggerated. At least, he hoped she exaggerated. Still, he needed to clear the matter with his father. At every opportunity, he tried to engage his father, but his endeavors went ignored for one reason or another.

"Anthony, stop delaying." Tapping his foot in an impatient rhythm, Father cleared his throat. "You are to make your final public appearance with Lady Arabella, prior to your nuptials, and you will not disappoint me, so you had better adopt a smile, now."

"Father, a moment, please." After several unsuccessful attempts to speak with his father, Anthony spied his chance. In the event he was wrong, and Arabella spoke the unvarnished truth, he had to intervene. Were he alone at risk, he would not protest, but he would do anything to protect Arabella, even if it meant playing the part of besotted groom, to appease his father. "I promise, it will take but a few minutes."

"All right." Father huffed and said to Mama, "Johanna, wait for us at the entry, and we will navigate the receiving line as a family."

"Of course." Mama nodded. "But don't tarry, and do not fight in the street like a couple of ruffians, else I shall be vexed with you."

"Worry not, Mama." Anthony waved to her. "And we shall soon follow."

"Well?" Father replied in a sharp tone and folded his arms. "Out with it, but if you wish to advance another objection to your impending union, then you waste your time, because I am done obliging you. You will do your duty, with or without your cooperation."

The declaration, unmistakable in its meaning, suggested Arabella didn't exaggerate.

Anthony was in trouble.

"You mistake my intent, because I have no desire to argue against my wedding." Nervous, he paused, recalled his purpose, and checked his tone. No matter what happened after the ceremony, his struggle was just beginning. "I simply wanted to say how grateful I am to have Lady Arabella for my future wife. Indeed, you were right about her. She is a very fine woman, and I am genuinely happy about the upcoming marriage."

"Really?" With a countenance of surprise, Father opened his mouth and then closed it. He arched his brows. "I am delighted to hear it, but why the change of heart, when you have done naught but protest?"

"I know my duty, and I will not fail you, but there is another reason for my new perspective." Squaring his shoulders, Anthony gained his footing. For a moment, he mulled his response and composed a few falsehoods he doubted he could deliver with any degree of sincerity. At last, he settled for the truth. "To be honest, I like Lady Arabella. She is beautiful, possessed of uncommon intelligence, and excellent company. So there is no need to worry, because I shall be a most attentive fiancé, this evening."

"Are you sure of what you claim?" Father held Anthony's stare, and he stood strong for himself and his lady. "And you don't conspire to fool me, while you prepare to leave England?"

"I deserve that, but it was a temporary lapse in judgment, of which I am embarrassed, and I apologize." Although Anthony believed otherwise, he had to yield the impetuous dreams born of fear, if only to spare Arabella a dreadful future with some ignorant dolt who would either abuse her, stifle her independent nature, or both. He told himself it was her fate that moved him to reconsider his position, and if he did that enough, he just might convince himself of the reality. "In that respect, I pondered my reasons for resisting the arrangement and decided I am better served, as is the dukedom, by acquiescing." He cursed his dry mouth. "Rather than oppose you, I would join you in celebrating my future."

"My son, you have made me very proud." Father moved to stand beside Anthony and rested a palm to his back. "Tomorrow, I shall dispatch the men I hired to guard you, and we will start anew, as if nothing happened."

"But, Mama terminated their employment almost a sennight, ago." Together, they strolled toward the sidewalk, where Mama waited. "And I have done nothing to merit such treatment, given I gave you my word I would not leave these shores."

"Blood under the bridge." Father chuckled. "But I could not be too careful, because I gave my friend my solemn pledge that we would unite our two houses. So, let us set aside any discord in favor of unity, and I look forward to the day we announce the joyous news of an impending addition to our family. Now, let us drink, dance, and make merry."

"Father, in that, we are one." They neared the entrance, and Anthony waved to his mother. His spirits lifted when she smiled. Clicking his heels, he stiffened his spine. "Come, Mama. Your son would like the pleasure of the allemande."

"Oh, he would?" She laughed and settled her palm in the crook of his elbow. "Well, it would be my honor to indulge him."

"And I shall claim the first waltz." Father hummed a ditty.

"You must be joking." Mama snorted and climbed the entrance stairs to the palatial Berkeley Square residence. "What is the occasion, Walter?"

"The answer is simple." Father crossed the threshold, glanced at Mama, and winked. "Tonight, the Bartletts mark the commencement of the union that shall produce the next generation, and we secure our legacy for the future. If that is not reason to dance a jig, then I am at a loss."

"All right." Mama smiled. "Who am I to say otherwise?"

In the foyer, Anthony exchanged pleasantries with Lord and Lady Howard, the hosts for the evening. And while he embraced an air of polite calm, he wanted nothing more than to locate his charming bride-to-be and make a few inappropriate encroachments on her feminine fields, if only to soothe the restless beast that threatened to charge forth and disrupt the party.

It was with that primary objective in mind he strolled down the hall and into the expansive ballroom. He veered left, right, and then left again, nodding acknowledgments of various members of society, until he neared the side interior wall.

A huge mural depicted, in violent detail, the Roman battle of Alesia. Often described as the crown jewel of Julius Caesar's campaign in Gaul, the brutal clash never meant much to Anthony, until he studied the tactics, an unparalleled example of siege warfare and investment, defined by the mass destruction of flesh and bone, in preparation for deployment. He must have looked upon the innocuous image countless times, through the years, but he had never really seen it until that moment.

At one end, in the bottom corner, a soldier rested on his back, an expression of horror, forever frozen, marring his face, while a Gallic warrior planted a *lancea* in the Roman's chest. In that instant, he closed his eyes, and a familiar drumbeat echoed in his ears. His pulse raced. He gasped for breath. His cravat seemed to choke him. Cries of men rose above the hum of idle gossip, and the refined ballroom yielded to visions of a bloody skirmish. The tattered remnants of a savage conflict flitted before him, when a woman's voice cut through the terror and uttered his name.

Pushing aside the ugliness of war, Arabella reached for him in a cherished reverie. In his thoughts, he clung to her, to the support she never failed to extend even in her absence. Little by little, his hammering heartbeat slowed. He rubbed the back of his neck and sighed, just when someone slapped him on the shoulder.

"Why so morose, my friend?" Beaulieu gave Anthony a playful jolt, yet he maintained the connection to the soldier's gaze, so blue, as if he glimpsed his reflection in a mirror. "Now this is a target-rich affair, and I intend to fire as many salvos as my Jolly Roger can withstand. My, my, but Lady Allen poses a most delicious dish."

"Just like old times." When the world was not so vile a place, and the *ton's* ballrooms presented nothing more than a forum for seduction. It struck him, then, that he could spend the rest of his days locked in the very same atrocity portrayed in the work of art, forever trapped in the past, or he could embrace life, like Arabella suggested. "Perhaps, not such a noble but certainly a worthwhile endeavor."

"There is the Rockingham I remember." Beaulieu elbowed Anthony. "Care to make a wager? See anything that tempts you? Are you feeling lucky?"

"But I am to be married." One lady held his attention, to the exclusion of all others, and he scanned the crowd for the slightest sign of her.

"All the more reason to take a turn at Bushy Park." Beaulieu smirked. "Besides, how long has it been, and do not lie to me?"

"That is none of your affair, but I would not give you the impression that I am ignorant of my predicament, because I thought about my situation, in the dark and quiet hours, and I learned something about myself. We engaged in war because we believed in something greater than ourselves, and we were willing to make the ultimate sacrifice, to uphold our convictions. We fought for England, to defend our homes and our way of life, to be free from tyranny, and we won the day, yet we gained naught for ourselves. While ours was an honorable cause, we have long since concluded our mission, and we reap no real rewards, because we remain rooted in bygone days."

Just then, he spotted Arabella, and soothing warmth enveloped him, despite the fact that he could not explain the effect she had on him, because he could not resist her. He knew not why he wanted her, but he would marry her, not of some vulgar, misplaced sense of duty.

Oh, no.

He would take her to wife because he needed her. Because she spoke to all that remained good within him.

"I am tired of this tedious existence—tired of fighting. Always fighting. Always hoping for something more, yet we languish in the violence and the horrors of yesteryear. While I did not see her coming, I cannot disregard the obvious conclusion, which is that Arabella offers a chance to escape this hellish prison that holds me captive, and I intend to seize her and all the beauty she brings to my world."

"Is that the way the wind blows?" With a countenance of surprise, Beaulieu narrowed his gaze. "Are you in love?"

"What is love, my friend?" Anthony snickered, because he did not believe in such nonsense. "Can you define it, because the singular emotion resists my efforts to identify it? Call it what you will, but I know how to make love and satisfy a woman, and I plan to deploy the finesse of a lifetime in her arms, on our wedding night. Indeed, I am bloody well going to enjoy a husbandly benefit even *I* cannot argue against, because this time I fight for myself."

"Oh, I say. There is my riding companion." Beaulieu chucked

Anthony's shoulder. "Now, let us mark our prey and savor a bit of salacious sport."

"No need to mark anything, because at present my quarry stands near the terrace doors, which would be perfect to sneak away, if not for Lady Ainsworth firmly anchored at my intended's side." Anthony scrutinized the noblewomen and swore under his breath. "Is it my imagination, or does the mother guard the daughter?"

"Unfortunately, I agree with your assumption, because that mama's stance boasts an intensity that would rival my best hound on the hunt." Folding his arms, Beaulieu shifted his weight and jutted his hip. "Lady Ainsworth searches for you. Do you think Lady Arabella would have been foolish enough to confide in her mother, given you have dallied with your fiancée on more than one occasion?"

"It is possible, although I hope not, but Arabella is incapable of duplicity, and she would answer honestly if questioned." Garbed in rich burgundy silk, with a low-cut that highlighted her ample décolletage, Arabella surveyed the throng, until she met his stare. Slowly, she smiled, and his loins went up in flames. "Beaulieu, I would never infringe on our longstanding camaraderie, but I am a desperate man, and right now I am in need of a diversion."

BENEATH THE SOFT glow of ormolu chandeliers, amid the crystal vases filled with hothouse blooms and the splendor of sixteenth century Italian embroideries, a sea of elegantly dressed ladies and gentlemen mingled in preparation for the ball. In the back corner, a quartet readied their instruments, sounding various notes. To the left, three sets of double doors opened to reveal a huge dining room, in which a collection of long tables festooned with green linens, polished silver, and Royal Worcester china encouraged revelers to savor a repast of mouthwatering dishes and tempting desserts. While the fare enticed the average guest, Arabella sought naught but her fiancé, because there was so much she needed to say, and she did not have far to look.

From across the room, in Beaulieu's company, Anthony peered in her direction, and his expression gave her gooseflesh. After a quick check of her appearance, she told herself she did not wear the new gown, with the bold neckline, to attract her man's attention, because she would never do anything so frivolous. But deep inside, where she was always honest with herself, she admitted she chose her attire for his delectation, because she wanted to be pretty for him. Wanted to make him proud.

"Arabella, stop fidgeting, because it is unbecoming a lady of your prestige." In a steady rhythm, Mama fanned herself in time with the repetitive tap of her foot. "And remember what I told you about Lord Rockingham. You are not to entertain him sans a chaperone, and if I am unavailable, Miss Wallace has offered to stand in my place."

"Of course, Mama." How Arabella rued her decision to confide in Mama, because the conversation led to an in-depth discussion of marital relations, which her mother described in terrifying detail, and what previously seemed a pedestrian act now shocked her. Science books made such intimate exercises seem simple and straightforward, so benign, if a tad messy, and she resolved to put the entire affair out of her mind. Still, when she assessed Anthony's rapid advance, something in his impassioned countenance suggested she would violate her mother's directive, that night, and Arabella would not protest. Slow and steady, he weaved through the crowd, his gaze never leaving hers, and she shivered, as naughty thoughts raced through her head. "Would you care for some ratafia?"

"I would rather drink dirty water from the mop bucket." Mama waved to a friend but remained rooted at Arabella's side. "The waiter brings champagne. Be a dear and fetch us a couple of glasses."

"Yes, Mama." Arabella flagged the servant and collected two portions of the bubbly confection, one of which she handed to her mother, just as Anthony and Lord Beaulieu emerged from the herd, and she mustered an air of calm. "Lord Rockingham, what a lovely surprise."

"Indeed, the pleasure is mine. Good evening, Lady Ainsworth and Lady Arabella." Clicking his heels, he bowed, and what she would have given to wipe the self-satisfied smirk from his face, before he clued her mother to his intent, which she guessed was anything but proper, even for her fiancé. "Shall we take a turn about the room, Lady Arabella?"

"I would love to, my lord." She stepped forward. "Perhaps, we can—"

"Lord Rockingham, we shall be too happy to accompany you on a brief tour." Mama nudged Arabella aside, to claim Anthony's outstretched arm. "After all, I should say hello to Lady Allen and Her Grace."

"Now that will not do, because I would beg Lady Ainsworth for the honor of a dance, given they play my favorite *chassé* step." Arching a brow, and clutching a fist to his chest, Lord Beaulieu placed himself in Mama's path. "What say you, my lady? Would you refuse a gallant war hero his humble request?"

"I beg your pardon, my lord." Given Beaulieu's boisterous tone, nearby attendees gawked, and Mama relinquished Anthony's escort, much to Arabella's relief and amusement. "I would never decline such a gracious invitation, and the honor is mine." To Arabella, Mama said, "Collect Miss Wallace, because she is your friend, and you should include her."

"We shall do so, at once." In the glare of Mama's piercing gaze, Arabella could not lie, so she rested her palm in the crook of Anthony's elbow and drew him in her friend's direction. "We must be careful, my lord. Mama watches our every move, tonight."

"I see that." Anthony tensed, and she squeezed his arm. "What did you tell her?"

"More than I should have, but in all fairness I could not deceive my mother, and she asked a direct question." Lines of strain about the corners of his eyes declared his unrest, and she tugged at him. "But we gained an ally, which I will explain when we are alone."

"Who said we are going to be alone?" Before she could answer, he came to a halt and sighed. "Miss Wallace, how are you this evening?"

"Lord Rockingham, Lady Arabella." Patience dipped her chin. "What is the plan, or do you have one, because I gather you seek an unimpeded audience?" Leaning forward, she whispered, "Lady Ainsworth charged me with your guardianship, and I would not fail in my duty, but neither would I interfere in your liaison."

"Good evening, Miss Wallace." On cue, Greyson appeared to the left. After a crisp bow, he extended a hand. "May I have this dance?"

"Of course, Lord Greyson." Patience grinned and partnered the veteran soldier. "Well, I suppose that solves my quandary."

"All right, my lord, where shall we rendezvous?" Arabella glanced at her brave soldier and hoped he would not be offended by recent developments, which she enacted on his behalf, and she needed to reveal her intentions. "The study or the garden?"

"The garden." Anthony led her toward the terrace doors. When he spotted His Grace and her father, her fiancé started and ducked behind a large bust of Sir Isaac Newton, which decorated a dark corner. "Bloody hell, if they find us, we are doomed."

"Then let us hide." They crouched in the shadows, and Arabella studied Anthony's profile, until he met her gaze. In close proximity, she inhaled his signature sandalwood scent and stifled a gasp, when he rubbed his nose to hers, and she ached to kiss him as she admired his beautiful mouth. "Are they gone?"

"Well, you certainly will not find them where you look." At his quip, she frowned, and he snickered. "Hurry, let us make our escape, because I am just as anxious to enjoy your unreserved company."

"Is it my fault I treasure your affection?" She twined her fingers in his, and they slinked along the wall. When she spied his mother, she pulled him behind a heavy velvet drape. "In light of my relative youth and inexperience, one might argue you took liberties, sir."

"Do you pose a complaint?" With the edge of the material drawn back, he checked the vicinity. "We remain undetected, but we must move quickly."

"No, I do not complain." Holding tight to his grip, she followed him, and they rushed to shelter behind the next drape. Just then, she noticed her mother, with Patience in tow, all but running toward the terrace. "Oh, no. We are discovered."

"Ye of little faith." Anthony pulled Arabella behind another drape. "Watch and learn, my dear, because the Mad Matchmakers know of my aim and will not fail us."

To her delight, Anthony's fellow Waterloo veterans surrounded Mama and Patience. While Greyson begged Mama for a dance, Beaulieu simply dragged Patience into the rotation.

"I will owe Patience an apology for that." Arabella bit her bottom lip and snorted with mirth. "But I wager Mama has never been favored with so much attention, and she laughs, my lord."

"Good. Now, let us away." In that instant, Anthony yanked hard, and they sprinted to the double doors, crossed the threshold, and burst into the garden. "If memory serves, there is an ideally placed gazebo that will suit our purpose."

"And how do you know of this gazebo?" Pebbles crunched beneath her feet, as they navigated the path that wound through the rose bushes, and in silence she reviewed her hastily composed arguments to defend her actions. "Or do I want to know the answer to my question?"

"Jealous?" Anthony chuckled.

"Don't be ridiculous." Yet, his characterization stated her emotions to perfection, much to her dismay, because she considered herself immune to such flightiness. "Who was she?"

"Does it matter, when she does not signify, because I am marrying you?" In the dark confines of the tiny structure, he pulled her close, held her tight about the waist, and kissed her. A tender and sweet expression, which ended far too soon for her liking. "I have been thinking of this moment, all day."

"Have you?" With a sigh of contentment, she rested her head to his chest, as he stroked the back of her neck, and it was time to speak her mind. "My lord, there is something I wish to tell you."

"How curious, because there are things I would say to you." Caressing the flesh at her nape, he nuzzled her. "Ladies first."

"Oh, no, after you." She swallowed hard, because her courage faltered, given she had never made such an important declaration, and she remained uncertain of his response, regarding the appointment she scheduled with a friend, a medical professional with ample experience treating wounded warriors. Would he welcome or reject her scheme to help him deal with the past? "I insist."

"All right." Shifting, he eased back and cupped her chin. "I spoke with my father, and all is well between us, so we have naught to worry about, from him." Anthony paused, as he caressed her cheek with his thumb. "You know, this is one of those instances when I truly regret that I have but one arm, because I would hold you, forever, if I could. But I want you to know that I want to wed you. Indeed, I cannot see myself, or my future, without you. I want to build a life, for us. I want to create a family, and spend my days in peace, fretting over naught more than crying babies, scraped knees, and our children's education."

"More's the pity." Grasping his wrist, she pressed her lips to his palm and then held his hand to her bosom. "Because I feel the same."

"Do you, little one?" Even in the dim light, Arabella detected a wistful tone to his voice. "Is it possible our desires are so fortuitously aligned?"

"Yes." On tiptoes, she kissed him. It was a quick affectation meant to reassure him. "I want to be your wife, to face the world at your side, and to make a home where we are safe to live as we choose, without fear of retribution. And if we never venture to London, I shall count myself quite satisfied to remain lost in the country, with you."

"Do you mean that?" None too gently, he hauled her against him. "Tell me the truth, and I will not be angry."

"My lord, I could not be more sincere." Hugging him about the waist, she held fast, and her spirits soared to new heights. "I know not how or why, and my attempts to comprehend it have failed, but you understand me better than those who have known me from birth." Something took root within her, in that instant, and she relished the sensation, as it unfurled and spread, suffusing her with renewed confidence. "You talk to me, and you listen when I speak, which is more than I ever thought I would find in a husband. With you, I found something I believed did not exist, and I embrace our union, despite past reservations, which I am convinced were unreasonable."

"I would laugh if this were not so incredible, but I could say the same of you." To her delight, Anthony trailed a series of kisses along the crest of her ear, and she hummed. "I know not how you managed it, but you understand me, in much the same fashion, and I am too smart to let you slip through my fingers, so we shall marry, my dear Arabella. And I engaged my solicitor to purchase a lovely cottage, on the beach, in Sussex, just east of Brighton, where we will spend our honeymoon, if you are amenable."

"Oh, I love the sound of that." The conversation with Mama echoed in Arabella's ears, and she cursed her burning cheeks, as unwanted images assailed her senses. "Because I prefer privacy when we consummate our vows, in the unlikely event I scream."

"I beg your pardon?" To her embarrassment, Anthony burst into laughter but quickly checked himself. "Are you so concerned, my dear, because I would never hurt you. On my honor, you have my solemn promise that we will take our time, because I will not rush you. Although I suspect you will have much to articulate, given your propensity for sharing your opinion, I will do my utmost to ensure you express naught but passion."

"My lord, it is not that I doubt you—what do you mean I will express naught but passion?" His bold statement startled her, because she feared the single most important part of his anatomy. "And my mother discussed the deed, thus I am hesitant, yet I will not fail you."

"Ah, Arabella, you make me happy." Again, he chuckled. "Have I told you as much?"

"More or less, but I never tire of it." Her mother beckoned from the terrace, and Arabella started and hunkered. "It is Mama. What shall we do, because she will raise quite a fuss if she finds us?"

"Shh." Anthony pulled her upright and licked her bottom lip, and she forgot the rest of her oratory. Indeed, everything yielded to the point of their delicious contact, and he playfully nipped her flesh, between words. "She will not find us, and we will return to the ball, in a moment, via the study door." He settled his hand to her hip, in a shocking display of familiarity. "For now, I would kiss you."

Several minutes passed before they dashed to the residence.

CHAPTER TEN

T HE DAY BEFORE Anthony's wedding dawned with a howling gale and a ferocious tempest, which was why the unexpected delivery of Arabella's summons surprised him, because he could not imagine any woman venturing forth in the storm. Then again, his fiancée did not fit the norm. Umbrella in hand, Walker shielded Anthony from the deluge, when he bounded down the entrance stairs and climbed into the coach. Secure in the squabs, he nodded once, and the butler retreated.

"Take Lord Rockingham to the corner of Upper Brook Street and North Audley, posthaste." After closing the door, Walker stood at attention, and the equipage lurched forward.

Curious about his bride-to-be's motives, Anthony tapped his fingers on his thigh. Then he brushed a speck of lint from his black wool breeches and considered the shine of his Hessians, during the short ride a mere couple of blocks to the prearranged meeting place. The rig slowed to a halt, and a footman leaped to the pavement and opened the door.

On the sidewalk, a cloaked figure shielded her face with an umbrella, but Anthony would have known Arabella anywhere. In a rush, she relayed an address to the footman. After closing her umbrella, she jumped into the coach, and eased to the bench opposite him, while he drew down the shades, to protect their privacy.

"The weather is dreadful, my lord." When she unbuttoned the

collar of her pelisse, he moved to sit beside her. "Anthony, just what are you about?"

"I thought it obvious, my dear Arabella." Cupping her chin, he moved to steal a quick kiss, but she rebuffed him with an upraised hand, and he groaned. "All right, why the secrecy, and why am I here, if we are not to re-enact last night's events in the gazebo?"

"My lord, you are a man of singular purpose, and I would oblige you, but there is a matter of importance I wish to discuss." To his dissatisfaction, she removed to the space he previously occupied. "And I would introduce you to a friend. If you cooperate, we might take a turn or two about the park, in the confines of your coach, before you return me to my home."

"How intriguing." But something in her demeanor struck him as odd. "Do your parents know of our rendezvous? Because I find it strange that you met me on the street and not at your doorstep. What did you tell them, and to what purpose?"

"That I am with Patience." Deploying a charming pout, she almost waylaid him, but he regrouped and gathered his wits.

"And what does Miss Wallace believe?" He compressed his lips and vowed not to fall prey to her considerable allure, which tempted him beyond reason.

"She knows I am with you." Averting her gaze, she furrowed her brow. "In regard to my purpose, I would wait until we arrive at our destination. Once I make the introductions, I will explain everything."

"How far must we travel?" When he posed the question, he peeked beyond the shade. To his surprise, the coachman drew to a halt. "Are we there, already?"

"I suspect so, because we do not venture beyond Mayfair." A footman opened the door. Arabella scooted to the edge of the bench and stepped to the sidewalk. "Come, my lord, and keep an open mind."

Curious, he did as she bade. When he exited the coach, he glanced about the immediate vicinity and discovered they journeyed to Albemarle Street. The nondescript residence, comprised of red brick with Portland stone trim, boasted a sign near the front window.

Anthony stopped in his tracks.

"Arabella, just what are you about?" His chest tingled, and his stomach rolled. "Why have you brought me to see Dr. Handley?"

"As I said, he is a friend, and he wants to help us." She tugged on his arm, but Anthony gnashed his teeth and remained rooted to the ground. "Please, do this for me. I beg you, do not refuse what could mark a new beginning for us."

"What does he plan to treat, given you have told me, time and again, there is nothing wrong with me, or do you claim some mysterious malady?" Anger mixed with fear, forming a formidable blockade, and he retreated a step. "Did you lie to gain my compliance? Did you conspire with my father to bring me here?"

"Never, and His Grace is no friend of mine." When she reached for his hand, he recoiled. "My lord, you must believe me, I would never betray your trust."

"Hello, Lady Arabella. You are prompt, as usual." A bespectacled gentleman loomed in the doorway, and he narrowed his stare when he looked at Anthony. "This must be Lord Rockingham. What an honor, sir." The stranger bowed. "Dr. Handley, at your service. Will you come inside, to get out of the rain, and enjoy a spot of tea?"

"I do not drink tea, sir." Shaking with irrepressible anxiety, Anthony knew not what to make of what he considered an unforgiveable betrayal. "There seems to be a misunderstanding, and I apologize for wasting your afternoon."

"Well, my wife is shopping, and the host provides brandy in lieu of tea." The doctor smiled. "If you decline my hospitality, I shall return to my study, smoke my pipe, and peruse the papers, so you see you keep me from nothing of importance."

"Anthony." Positioning herself opposite him, Arabella said in a low voice, "If you do this for me, I shall take a turn about the park with you, with the shades drawn, and I shall abide whatever you ask of me."

"Indeed?" Now that was enough to sway him, but he needed to dictate terms. "You give me your word, you will deny me nothing, regardless of what I require in recompense?"

"I will do anything." Clasping his hand, she gulped and twined her fingers in his. "If you indulge me, I shall return the favor, in equal measure. In fact, you need not even converse with Dr. Handley. Just hear what he has to say, but I wager you will like him." Again, she swallowed hard. "Thereafter, I am yours to command."

"All right, but I intend to collect on our bargain, in full." When she prompted, he followed her into the residence. "However, I do not appreciate being ambushed, and you will never do it again."

"Of course not." Glancing over her shoulder, she cast an expression of contrition. "But my cause is just, and I had to try, else I could not live with myself."

"It means that much to you?" He cursed himself when he spied tears in her blue eyes, because he did not want to hurt her.

"Yes." She nodded. Not for an instant did he doubt her.

"Why?" In the hall, after Anthony and Arabella shed their outerwear, the doctor motioned toward a modest but elegant drawing room, and Anthony strolled to the sofa. After he unbuttoned his coat, he sat. To his surprise, Arabella perched beside him and clasped his hand in hers.

"My lord, I cannot fail you." She scooted closer, while Handley poured a couple of glasses of brandy, one of which he sat on the table before Anthony. "As your wife, it is my duty to serve you."

"And that is what you are doing, now?" Confused and wounded by her breach of faith, he sighed and shook his head. He believed her incapable of dissemblance. "We are not yet wed, and you deceived me."

"I did no such thing." She squeezed his fingers. "In fact, I am here to reveal a simple truth, which you have inquired about on more than one occasion."

"What is that?" Reflecting on previous exchanges, he clung to the hope she had not fooled him, and somehow he misconstrued her scheme. "Because I recall nothing of the kind."

"My lord, often you have remarked on my ability to calm you, when you are out of sorts." When he blinked, she peered at Dr. Handley and then met Anthony's stare. "Like the afternoon in the park and the evening of my father's impromptu dinner. Do you remember?"

How could he forget?

"Then why did you not tell me, last night?" Releasing her hand, he cleared his throat and grabbed the balloon of brandy, the contents of which he downed in a single gulp, despite his trembling. "You could have warned me."

"I planned to do so." She opened her mouth and then closed it. "But you distracted me, in the gazebo."

Oh, he distracted her, all right. For several minutes. A series of salacious vignettes flashed in his brain, and familiar warmth spread from his center to his limbs. When his cheeks burned, he swore under his breath and shook himself alert.

"Lord Rockingham, I understand your hesitation, given the personal nature of the topic." Dr. Handley leaned forward in his chair. "But you are not alone. Indeed, many soldiers returned from the war as changed men, and I gather you are no different."

"What do you know of my plight?" Anthony responded, a little too defensively, and he checked himself. "I mean, do you presume to know me?"

"Ever struggle with night terrors, bouts of uncontrollable anxiety, intense excitement, fever, gastrointestinal discomfort, or feelings of hopelessness? Ever see or hear things that are not there? Perhaps a combination of symptoms?" Standing, Dr. Handley wrinkled his nose. "I beg your pardon, Lord Rockingham, but you are white as a sheet. Would you like to lie down?"

"No." Anthony pushed from the sofa and paced near the hearth. "I want to know what is wrong with me."

Leaning against the mantel, he gazed into the blaze, opened the door to his memory, and the drums signaled the battle commenced. The walls collapsed, and the floor pitched and rolled. How he wanted to run. When he closed his eyes, hoofbeats pounded in his ears, and his knees gave way, but he did not fall, because Dr. Handley and Arabella supported Anthony at either side.

"Can you hear me?" Arabella's plea came to him, as if from afar. "Anthony, you are safe. We are in London, and no one will hurt you."

"Lord Rockingham, come back and recline, please." The doctor draped an arm about Anthony's shoulders and situated a pillow. "Better?"

"Much, thank you." Weak, Anthony did not object when his fiancée sat at the edge of the sofa and wiped his brow with her handkerchief. "I am sorry if I frightened you."

"I am not afraid." With the backs of her knuckles, she caressed the curve of his jaw. "I am worried, and I want you to give Dr. Handley a chance to help you. If you will not do it for yourself, do it for me."

"If you wish." To his amazement, his lady bent and kissed him, despite the doctor's presence. "All right, I will cooperate. What do you require of me?"

"The answer is simple, really." Shifting his weight, Dr. Handley crossed his legs. "You need only talk, Lord Rockingham. Whatever comes to mind, share it with us. If you prefer, you may pretend I am not here, and speak directly to Lady Arabella."

"I am well-versed in that." Anthony half-chuckled and pondered the suggestion.

There was so much he wanted to say. So much he wanted to tell

Arabella of his former self, but he could not bear her rejection. Then again, she might not spurn him, and it was her idea.

Inhaling deeply, he relaxed and studied his beautiful fiancée, arresting in her morning gown of pale yellow. Reflecting on previous conversations, he told her of life in the camps. Of the long marches in the miserable heat. Of the trumpets blaring in the wee hours before dawn. Of the torrential downpours and the mud. Of the meager rations and the disappearing faces with each new battle.

Then he related the various aspects of war, including the telltale clash of metal against metal. The jarring blast of cannon fusillades. The crack of gunfire, which merged with the cries of the wounded to form a woeful requiem for the dead. The thunderous roar of advancing regiments. The sickeningly sweet smell of blood. The stench of damp earth mixed with munitions powder, and the often-mutilated bodies.

So many secrets fell from his lips, while Arabella gave him full attention, and he found himself, at last, describing the never-ending anxiety. The terror that twisted his insides, stretched his spine ramrod straight, and threatened to reduce him to a wailing babe. Worst of all, he lacked the ability to control any of it and seemed forever destined to live as a prisoner of the past.

Exhausted yet relieved, Anthony started when the mantel clock chimed, and he realized Arabella wept.

"My dear, please, do not cry for me." Sitting upright, he pulled a handkerchief from his coat pocket and dried her face. In that simple gesture, it dawned on him that he cared for her. He genuinely cared for her. Indeed, he could not envision himself without his lady at his side. "I can bear anything but your tears."

"Oh, Anthony, I once called you the bravest man of my acquaintance, but I am now convinced I grossly underestimated you." She sniffed. "Your courage knows no bounds, and I am truly honored to be your future wife."

"Darling, while I appreciate the compliment, mine are but the ravings of a coward and, I suspect, a lunatic." He glanced at Dr. Handley. "What say you, sir? Am I crazy?"

"I hate to disappoint you, Lord Rockingham, given you seem quite sure of your condition, but your diagnosis is incorrect." The doctor adjusted his spectacles. "Because only the sane react aberrantly to the aberrant. I assure you, there is nothing normal about war. Indeed, I would worry if you did not exhibit lingering signs of trauma, in light of what you survived, and you are to be admired. Not scorned."

"You must be joking." Anthony gave vent to a self-deprecating snort. "I did what I was ordered. Where is the valor in that?"

"You believe you had no choice to react otherwise?" Dr. Handley furrowed his brow. "Bless my soul, sir, but your actions in the heat of battle are nothing if not heroic, because you had an option, even though you do not recognize it. The decision you confronted was whether to fight or to flee, and you did your duty. Counter that point with me, if you can, Lord Rockingham."

For several minutes, Anthony tried but failed to compose a suitable rejoinder. Every possible argument he contrived came to naught, because the doctor's pronouncement offered immediate refutation, until he surrendered the cause.

"Not that I agree with your conclusion, but what do you recommend to cure me of my symptoms?" Anthony inquired. "Is there a tonic you can prescribe?"

"To be honest, there is no cure for what ails you, my lord, and you may struggle with the mental infirmities for the remains of your life." From a side table, Handley retrieved a piece of parchment, upon which Anthony noted a list. "However, you can manage the various maladies that typify what is referred to as 'nostalgia' or 'irritable heart.' In elementary terms, yours is but an attempt to deal with the abnormal events you witnessed, in highly irregular circumstances. It is doubtful you will ever forget what you met on the battlefield, but you can train yourself to cope with the discomfiting memories and mitigate your response."

"Interesting, because I did not think it possible." And reassuring, given Dr. Handley was a respectable physician with an estimable clientele. "What do you suggest?"

"There are many different methods of treatment, but I prefer the most basic." The doctor handed Anthony the paper. "Discussing the source of your distress, either with me, Lady Arabella, or another trusted confidante works best. I also encourage you to journal about your experiences. And Lady Arabella tells me you lost your horse at Waterloo. Forgive my indelicacy, but you need to get back in the saddle, my lord, the sooner the better. Experiment with the items I propose, and find what succeeds for you."

"I promise, I will support you." Arabella reviewed the inventory, and Anthony would have given anything to know her thoughts. "In fact, we can do it together, my lord."

"An excellent plan, my lady." And she was his lady, more than ever, though she knew it not. "For now, we must depart before your parents search for you, because we have been here for three hours."

Arabella stood, and he followed suit. Dr. Handley showed them to the door, and Anthony collected her pelisse, along with his greatcoat. When he peered down the hall, he was surprised to discover no butler or servant.

"For privacy and discretion, I relieve my staff when I see patients in my home, Lord Rockingham." Dr. Handley smiled and extended a hand, which Anthony accepted. "It has been a pleasure, and I am available, if you have need of me."

"I am grateful, sir. I cannot express that enough." With that, Anthony escorted Arabella to the coach. In the sky, the clouds parted. The sun cast its rays on the street, and he hoped for a future he never thought possible. Rolling his shoulders, he savored his tranquil and unencumbered state, the depths of which he had not enjoyed in years. To the coachman, Anthony said, "Deliver us to the corner of Upper

Brook Street and North Audley."

"Aye, sir." The driver nodded.

As he sat on the bench across from his fiancée, he glanced out the window, until Arabella lowered the shade and then plopped beside him. Before he could say anything, she framed his face and set her mouth to his, in an unutterably sweet demonstration of her devotion, which he returned, measure for measure.

Heat pooled in his loins and charged his nerves—and he broke the kiss. For the first time in a long time, he could think clearly. "Darling, you must take care, else you will lift your ankles for me, here and now, and I will not claim your bride's prize in my rig."

"I thought we were going to take a turn about the park?" She scooted closer, and he clenched his thighs. "Why did you change your mind? Did I do something wrong?"

"Sweetheart, today, you did everything right, and I owe you my thanks." He rested his forehead to hers and sighed in irrepressible contentment. "Whether or not you realize it, you lifted a great burden from my shoulders. It is as though Dr. Handley shone a light on my demons and banished them, and I no longer believe I am a danger to you. Indeed, I cannot wait to marry you, tomorrow."

STANDING BEFORE THE long mirror, Arabella admired the silver lamé wedding gown of Mama's design. Behind her, the lady's maid stowed the last of Arabella's clothing in a large trunk, to be transported to the duke's Grosvenor Square residence, because she and Anthony planned to depart for the coastal cottage after their wedding breakfast.

"Arabella, are you ready?" Papa called from her sitting room and knocked on the interior door, which sat ajar, to her bedchamber. When he spied her in her bridal finery, he sobered and splayed his arms, and she rushed into his waiting embrace. "My dear child, you are a vision."

"Thank you, Papa." Resting against his chest, she exhaled, and he hugged her. "I cannot believe I will soon be a married lady."

"And a marchioness, at that." Papa cradled her head. "You will outrank me, and I could not be prouder. While most expectant fathers live in hope of a male heir, with you I was never disappointed, and today you join two great houses and make me a most happy father. I only pray you can forgive me, someday, for forcing you to wed Lord Rockingham. But Swanborough pledged to protect you from his son, and I encourage you to provide the next in line to the dukedom, that you may be free of your obligation."

"Papa, I am not forced to the altar." As she retreated, she held her father's hands in hers. In light of the terms of endearment with which Anthony addressed her, yesterday, she anxiously anticipated her nuptials. "While I admit I harbored serious reservations, and I had no desire to wed, I have since come to know Lord Rockingham, and he is the best of men. Indeed, if my opinion holds any value, I promise I am in no danger from him, and I would have you know him, as do I, because he is the greatest man of my acquaintance, excepting you, of course. Despite what His Grace claims, Lord Rockingham is not insane. He is a brave war hero, and he is to be admired, not institutionalized."

"That is the second time you have insisted as much, and I would indulge in a debate, but I would not spoil your special day with talk of such unpleasant matters." Papa narrowed his stare, opened and closed his mouth. "You care for him."

"I do, Papa," she replied, without hesitation. Recalling tender kisses, she shivered, and gooseflesh covered her from top to toe. Then she blinked and laughed. "I do. I care for Lord Rockingham."

"And you do not fear him?" Papa shuffled his feet and consulted his timepiece. "I wish you had discussed this with me prior to now, because I would like to explore the topic, given I consider you an excellent judge of character, but at this moment we must away, else you may miss your wedding ceremony."

"Then let us depart, because I would not be late." At the threshold, she reminisced of nights spent on the floor, reading by candlelight, and afternoons filled with the study of plant life, as opposed to the usual ladylike pursuits of embroidery, painting tables, and covering screens, and then she bade a final farewell to her childhood room. Excited, she accepted her father's escort, and they strolled into the hall. "But you need not worry about me, Papa, because Lord Rockingham would never harm me."

"All right, my dear." Something in his expression gave her pause, when they descended the stairs and crossed the foyer. At the door, Papa took her pelisse from the butler and draped the outerwear about her shoulders. "That is quite enough, and I know everything will be fine."

"Oh, Papa, look at the brilliant blue sky. It is as if nature blesses my union." The sunlight blinded her, as she stepped outside, and she noted the empty coach parked at the curb. "Where is Mama?"

"She wanted to arrive early and visit with Her Grace." Papa handed Arabella into the elegant rig and then settled opposite her. "And you know your mother. She wanted to be sure everything was perfect."

As she smoothed the skirt of her gown, the coach pulled into the street and made a sharp turn. The short drive, which she could have walked had her father permitted it, from Upper Brooke Street to the Swanborough residence in Grosvenor Square took mere minutes. She barely relaxed when they passed through the wrought iron gates.

Beneath the porte cochère of the Corinthian-columned home, the Ainsworth coach drew to a halt, and liveried footmen sprang into action. Papa exited and turned to hand her to the pavement.

A cool breeze rustled her hair, and she ducked her head as she strode toward the side entrance. After skipping up the stairs, she lingered in a secondary foyer, where a very proper butler approached and bowed.

"Good morning, Lord Ainsworth and Lady Arabella." The stiff manservant extended an arm. "If you will follow me, I will direct you to the drawing room, where His Grace, Her Grace, and Lord Rockingham anticipate your arrival."

Trailing in the butler's wake, she admired the lush Rococo décor, which boasted mezzo-frescoes in the Carracci tradition, vivid pastorals, and gilt-bronze floor to ceiling mirrors framed with asymmetrical and abstract stuccowork. It dawned on her then that one day she would be mistress of all she surveyed, and it struck her as a daunting yet thrilling prospect.

At the end of the long corridor, they turned right. Standing near the fireplace, she spotted Anthony, resplendent in his regimentals, which she suspected he wore for her. When he met her gaze, from across the room, he smiled, and telltale warmth filled her cheeks.

"Ah, we are all in attendance." His Grace made what she considered an intrusive study of her person, and she shuffled her slippered feet. "Welcome, Ainsworth and Lady Arabella. Shall we commence the ceremony, because I am starved?"

"I thought we might visit, first." Her Grace drew near. "Lady Arabella, you look like a princess. Lady Ainsworth described your gown, but she did not do it justice."

"We can visit at the breakfast." His Grace pinched the bridge of his nose and pursed his lips. "Allow me to present the Archbishop of Canterbury, the Most Reverend and Right Honorable Charles Manners-Sutton. The Archbishop journeyed to London to officiate your wedding, expressly."

"It is an honor." Arabella curtseyed and then gave her attention to her groom. "Good morning, my lord."

"My lady." Bereft of the various signs of stress and anxiety that often marred his handsome features, Anthony bowed. Then he claimed her hand and pressed a chaste kiss to the back of her knuckles. In a quiet tone, he said, "That dress is inspiring."

"Oh?" In a whisper, she replied, "What does it inspire?"

"Minx." He winked. "You will regret that, later."

"Is that a promise?" Yes, she provoked her soon-to-be-husband, and it felt so good. "Because my imagination conjures all manner of delights."

"My dear, you may depend upon it." He waggled his brows.

"Let us take our respective positions." The archbishop moved to stand in the light of a large window. "Lord Rockingham, if you and Lady Arabella will join hands, we can begin." Holding the Book of Common Prayer, he waited until they did as he bade. "Dearly beloved family, we have come together in the presence of God to witness and bless the joining together of this man and this woman in Holy Matrimony. Therefore, marriage is not to be entered into unadvisedly or lightly, but reverently, deliberately, and in accordance with the purposes for which it was instituted by God."

The service progressed, and she held Anthony's stare, when she took her vows, reciting each word with care. To her amazement, the same mystical connection, an invisible but impenetrable bond impervious to the mortal constraints that distinguished and blessed their fledgling relationship, enveloped them in a glow of emotions she could not identify. Tears welled, when he pledged his troth, and his expression, filled with unmistakable if unspoken devotion, proclaimed he was not so immune to the moment.

At last, she made her final declaration, and her voice wavered, given the significance. "From this day forward you shall not walk alone. My heart will be your shelter, and my arms will be your home."

"Will all of you witnessing these promises do all in your power to uphold these two persons in their marriage?" The archbishop asked.

"We will," their parents responded, in unison.

"Grant that all married persons who have witnessed these vows may find their lives strengthened and their loyalties confirmed." The archbishop closed his book and smiled. "And now I pronounce you husband and wife. Lord Rockingham, you may kiss your bride."

Ah, the kiss.

Given the onlookers, she did not expect much. Oh, how wrong she had been, when Anthony wrapped his arm about her waist and covered her mouth with his.

In her mind, the ethereal communion of flesh commanded notice, and the moon and stars answered, as the tide halted, the birds quieted, the wind stilled, and the sun ceased its path, thus the world acknowledged the union of two souls so perfectly matched, to render the distinctions between them indiscernible. It was only when His Grace coughed, her father cleared his throat, and Her Grace and Mama giggled that Arabella and Anthony parted.

"I would say that bodes well for the union." The archbishop grinned. "Congratulations, Lord and Lady Rockingham."

"Thank you." Anthony shook hands with the archbishop. "On behalf of my bride, we are honored by your presence."

"Shall we adjourn to the dining room?" His Grace huffed. "I understand my son wishes to depart for Sussex, posthaste, and I would not delay the happy couple."

"Of course, Father." Anthony tugged Arabella's elbow. "Go ahead, and my new bride and I will join you, shortly, because I would like a brief word with her."

"All right." His Grace wagged a finger. "But do not take too long, because I am famished."

"We will be right there." The group disappeared down the hall, and Anthony cupped her cheek. To her surprise, he bent his head and bestowed upon her the sweetest kiss. "I wanted to tell you that I enjoyed an undisturbed sleep last night, for the first time since I lost my arm at Waterloo."

"Oh, how wonderful." Indeed, she could have cried. "I prayed you would welcome and employ Dr. Handley's advice, because he successfully treated several soldiers with similar symptoms."

"Must admit I was skeptical, but I cannot argue the results." Again, he claimed a kiss, and her knees buckled. "While I know I shall never be healed, I believe I can manage, as Handley suggested, and I know not how I will ever repay you."

"My lord, I require no recompense, because the look on your face, at this moment, is payment enough." But, in the spirit of their newly forged union, she indulged her reinvigorated playful side. "However, you may address me by a term of endearment, which I adore, and we shall call it even."

"You like that, darling?" He clucked his tongue, and she laughed. "Or do you prefer sweetheart? And here I thought I might be stepping on your independent toes."

"Not a chance, and I will take both, in equal measure." She toyed with a gold braid on his uniform. "If I have learned anything about our relationship, it is that I am stronger with you than without you, and I am so happy to be your wife."

"And I am your very fortunate husband, sweetheart." When she squealed in unmasked delight, he chuckled. "All right. Let us retire to the dining room, and I suggest you eat your fill, because I have quite an evening planned when we arrive in Sussex, and you will need your strength."

"I am uncontrollably excited." They strolled down the hall, and she feigned ignorance of his meaning, else she might swoon, not that he frightened her. "And I am at your service, unreservedly."

"Lady Rockingham, you are every husband's dream." Before she could reply, he swept her into the dining room, where the family and the archbishop waited. "Sorry to have kept you, but I needed to inform my wife of my plans following our celebratory meal."

"Ah, young love." His Grace snickered. "Well, we commenced breakfast without you. There are numerous selections on the sideboard, and you may help yourself."

"Here, my lord." Arabella collected two plates. "Let me assist you."

After dishing ample portions of eggs, kippers, and toast, she abided her husband's request and filled her belly. At the end of the meal, which she found rather dour and informal given the glorious occasion, His Grace extended an unremarkable toast. Then she removed to a guestroom, to change into a traveling gown of lavender wool.

Without fanfare, she accompanied her husband to the ducal coach, which His Grace insisted would make their journey more pleasant, and made her farewells to Mama and Papa. Shortly after pulling into the lane, she landed in Anthony's lap, in the privacy of the plush equipage, and they shared a heated interlude that seemed to last forever. Finally, he broke their kiss.

"Darling, once again, you tempt me, and if we continue on this path, I will take your maidenhead here and now, and that is not what I want for the consummation." With infinite care, Anthony set her aside and then moved to the opposite bench. "Promise me you will do nothing too accommodating for the remains of the trip, because there are limits to my self-control."

"Poor aggrieved husband." Imbued with newfound confidence, she inclined her head and bit her bottom lip. "I am quickly discovering there are other aspects to womanhood, which I grossly misconstrued, and I cannot wait to see our honeymoon cottage." She glanced toward the windows. "If you do not want to risk another tryst, why don't you raise the shades? No doubt, an audience will temper your enthusiasm."

"A great notion." Anthony wiped his brow, exhaled, and tried to lift the shade. "How odd. It appears to be stuck closed."

A grimace and a groan belied his difficulty, so she fumbled with the shade to her right.

"Mine will not budge." To her shock, after another failed attempt to loosen the shade, he ripped the fabric. Sunlight spilled into the compartment, and she shielded her eyes from the bright rays. She surveyed the passing landscape, and a heavy sensation settled in her stomach. "Where are we?"

"I am not sure, but this is not the road to Brighton." He peered at the terrain and pounded on the roof. "*Oy.* Driver, please, stop." The demand garnered no reply, and her heartbeat raced. "Hello. Driver, halt, at once." Given the lack of response, Anthony yanked on one door handle and then the other, to no avail. When he met Arabella's stare, she swallowed hard, and a dull ache nestled in the back of her throat. "My dear, it appears we are trapped."

CHAPTER ELEVEN

T HE WALLS OF the coach seemed to close in on him, creeping nearer, keeping time with the repetitive *clip-clop* hoofbeats of the six-horse team. Still, he summoned the resolve to persevere for his wife's sake, but the urge to take to his heels, unrelenting in its grip, seized Anthony by the gut. With each passing hour of their imprisonment, marked by the blazing path of the sun in the sky, he fought the urge to run amok, because he did not want to frighten Arabella. Yet, his outwardly relaxed demeanor did nothing to ease the anxiety clawing at his raw nerves.

"Anthony, are you all right?" Sitting across from him, his bride leaned forward and rested a palm to his knee. "You are pale, my lord."

"It is nothing." He ordered his thoughts and considered possible means of escape. In the distance, he noted an old barn, weathered and worn, marked by rotting wood and years of neglect. Stretched tall and craning his neck, he spotted an equally decrepit cabin, its inhabitants long since fled, along with the remnants of some broken down piece of farming equipment, another familiar sight that harkened to his youth. "I recognize the countryside. If I am correct in my deduction, we are bound for one of my father's properties in Surrey."

The revelation inspired naught but dread, because his father made his intentions known to Arabella's family, while Anthony believed they resolved their dispute in London. In truth, he should have known it was pointless to talk with someone who never listened. Someone who heard nothing but the sound of his own voice. There was no reasoning with the unreasonable, and the fate his father planned struck terror in his heart. The knowledge and betrayal hurt him more than he could say.

"But—why?" Pretty as a picture, she inclined her head. He knew the instant realization dawned, and she flinched. "Oh, no. It cannot be. You don't think he still intends to institutionalize you."

"I had hoped we settled our differences, but it appears I misjudged the situation, because I gather that is exactly where I am headed." Indeed, his father deceived him, which struck him as the only plausible conclusion. None-too-gently, he yanked at his cravat and unhooked the collar of his shirt. "I need air."

In the blink of an eye, the telltale *pa rum pum pum pum* matched the drumbeat of his heart, signaling the alarm of a fast-approaching mental thrashing, and he wiped perspiration from his brow. Steeling himself, he braced for the otherworldly plunge. When the macabre reverie materialized, intensifying in the confines of the coach, his throat tightened, and he gripped the seat cushion. As Dr. Handley instructed, Anthony tried to tell himself it was just an illusion, that it was not real, when *La Marsellaise* rose above the chaos of war, and he feared he might scream as imaginary French troops charged the line in his mind.

"Perhaps we can break the window." After shedding her pelisse, Arabella, blissfully unaware of his anguish, ripped the damaged shade from the frame, and he fought for calm. "Then we could jump."

"And risk breaking your lovely neck? Not a chance." Smothered beneath an avalanche of desolation, he gasped for breath and grasped for a diversion, because the delusory but nonetheless potent attack drew near. Why could he not resist the visions? Why could he not control his own thoughts? "Besides, I already contemplated that, and it would never work. At best, we would be walking a day or two to find assistance, and I wager they would discover our absence and run us aground. At worst, we could fracture something vital and be stranded in the middle of nowhere, left to die on our own. Neither sounds appealing or sane."

"What if you leapt to freedom, and I stayed here?" She tapped a finger to her chin and remained oblivious to his discomfit. "You could run for help and rescue me. Or I could come back for you, once I gain my liberty."

"Out of the question, because I will not leave you alone to face whatever is at the end of this drive." Anthony had thought of that, too, but immediately admonished himself, because he had only one arm, which presented a weakness he could neither ignore nor mitigate. Given their predicament, he would gladly trade all of his tomorrows for a single day as his former, whole self. A man with two arms. Old instincts tempted him, but he would not abandon his wife, and he covered her hand with his. "We are stronger, together, my dear."

"Then what do we do?" Her voice, imbued with a hint of distress, trembled. "How do we elude your father and save you from his ultimate scheme, because I will not let him take you from me. And I most certainly will not permit him to commit you to an asylum. I will fight him. I will fight with every inch of my being, if I must."

"You are formidable, Lady Rockingham." The coach pitched and rolled, and Anthony tumbled to the floor. When he righted himself, he eased into the squabs, beside his wife. She scooted close, and he wrapped his arm about her shoulders. "If it comes to that. If I am imprisoned, I imagine I may have to rely on your strength to save me, which is why I married you. Well, it is one of the reasons."

"Tell me more." Arabella nuzzled his chest and shifted to hug him about the waist. That was a new experience he savored. The intimacy of marriage. "Because I recall a time when you were set against me."

"I thought we moved past all that?" In the dark recesses of his mind, the hue and cry of battle combined with the thunderous reverberation of cannon fire. A vicious wave of nausea brought him low, and he swallowed. Somehow, he maintained a hair's breadth of composure.

"We did, but I require a distraction, and so do you," she said in a flirty tone. "Perhaps we can mutually divert each other."

"You are wise, as well as beautiful, my lady wife." He pressed his lips to her forehead, as he had done on occasions too numerous to count, seeking serenity in the otherwise mundane connection. "Well, I adore your curious nature, and your opinions, however misguided. But I truly admire your absolute insistence in your right to express your point of view." He chuckled when she wrinkled her nose. It was then he noticed her décolletage, given her position afforded him an excellent view. "To borrow from Beaulieu, though I would never tell him, he is correct in his assertion. You are blessed with a wickedly tempting bosom."

"My lord," Arabella declared in a high-pitched voice and shot upright. With a fist pressed to her chest, she narrowed her stare. "Are those the words of a gentleman?"

"No." He winked. "They are the words of a husband looking forward to his wedding night."

"Why, Lord Rockingham, you quite take my breath away." She hugged him tight and met his stare. Then her playful countenance changed into something not so impish. "Anthony, you are not all right." She cupped his cheek. "Why didn't you tell me you suffered?"

"What good would it do, other than to worry you?" He shrugged as the anxiety escalated, and the nonexistent savagery crept closer. Blurred vignettes mutated, forming razor-sharp glimpses of inexpressible barbarity that chilled him to the bone. Trapped in his own solitary nightmare, he reminded himself that none of the vivid representations were real. "Also, I am trying to rely on Dr. Handley's advice and muddle through the situation, myself."

"How are you managing?" she asked with a sly grin.

"Not very well, I'm afraid." In play, he chucked her chin, and she tsked. "But I am grateful you are here."

"I should hope so, because you are going to be with me for the rest of your life, despite your father's schemes. And while I admire your courage, you need not carry the burden alone." She shuffled and drew him into her arms, encouraging him to lean against her. With nimble fingers, she massaged the back of his neck, and magical relief flowed from her gentle kneading. "I am with you, and I will let nothing harm you. You have my solemn vow, which I meant when I proclaimed it, till death do us part."

"A beautiful declaration, but the symptoms honor no rules of engagement and extend no warning." A chorus of mournful cries echoed in his ears, and he shuddered. "If only I could dictate when I am assailed with memories, but every imaginary strike poses a lethal ambush I am powerless to resist."

"I am so sorry." She bent and kissed his temple, a soothing gesture that did much to comfort him. In a low voice, she said, "What if we try something new? What if you share your torment with me? Tell me what you see or hear. Describe it to me."

"You think that is a smashing idea, given our present circumstances?" The very notion inspired naught but skepticism. "I mean, do we truly need more misery, at the moment?"

"I think it an excellent idea, because of our present state of affairs." She rested her chin to his head. "Please, Anthony. Given we are alone, I might alleviate or even dispel your hardship, because I can assure you there is no one here but us."

"All right." With serious reservations, he gulped and stared at nothing, as he made the lonely journey back to the past. To the unchecked brutality of battle. To the bloody field at Waterloo, where he crawled in every wrong direction. Searching for salvation that eluded him, no matter how hard he grasped for it. "Faces. So many torturous faces. Men teeter at the final precipice, a mere step away from death, screaming for their mothers. And bodies, twisted and mangled, strewn about the ground like so much refuse. Scavengers pick at the corpses, stripping the dead of their trinkets and boots, along with their dignity. The heavy odor of gunpowder mingles with the pungent stench of rotting flesh so profound it taunts my nose even now."

"How awful." While she cast an air of imperturbable sangfroid, her muscles tensed, belying her outward, unruffled demeanor. "Is it always the same?"

"No." He crossed and uncrossed his legs. The gruesome scene mutated, and he glimpsed his reflection in the sea of faces. Thousands upon thousands of different versions of himself, lost souls, praying for salvation, locked in their own private hell from which there seemed no deliverance. "Although there are similarities."

"Such as—what?" she prompted.

"It always begins with a sound." He bowed his head, and a rush of emotions overtook him. "Hoofbeats hammer the earth." Gnashing his teeth, Anthony flinched and came alert. "Sometimes, I am startled by cannon fire. On other occasions, I've been haunted by the national anthem of France, to the extent I often hear it in my sleep."

"And then what happens?" Arabella bent and stole another kiss, which startled him given her tranquil manner.

Did she not comprehend what she did to him? Or the power she wielded over him? Of course, if she knew he could devour her in the wake of her innocent gesture, she might react otherwise.

"To be honest, I never know until I am confronted." And that most unnerved him, because he could never anticipate or guard against the shock. "Which makes it difficult to fight."

"Then why try?" She tightened her embrace, in another show of support. "I mean, if the memories are inevitable, if you cannot shield yourself, then why not oblige the remembrances? Accept them. Welcome them, if you must. Make them your own, as you see fit. Perhaps then you might dictate the content and its impact on your faculties."

"I had not thought of it that way." In truth, it never occurred to him. Pondering her suggestion, he sat up and scratched his cheek. "But your idea holds merit and fits with Dr. Handley's advice." The traveling coach jolted to a halt, and Anthony peered beyond the torn shade. "We have arrived."

"Oh?" She smoothed her skirt. "Where are we?"

"As I suspected, we venture to Sanderstead, my father's estate in Surrey." Summers spent at the property brought no fond recollections, given the duke merely deposited the family in the large, red brick house, while he dallied with his mistress, in London.

A footman, adorned in the ducal livery, fiddled with the handle, which Anthony discovered had been secured by a heavy, iron lock. At last, the footman freed Anthony and his wife. After he exited, he turned to hand Arabella down, and he noted a U-shaped hasp had been attached to the door.

Had he paid attention when they boarded, he could have protested. But his new bride captured his senses, unreservedly, and the modification escaped his notice.

"Welcome to Sanderstead, Lord and Lady Rockingham." Flanked by two large men, a bespectacled stranger garbed in less than elegant attire clasped his hands in front of him. With a beak of a nose and a narrow stare, he arched a brow as he assessed Anthony with a critical eye. "Will you not come inside and take refreshments?"

"Who are you?" Anthony inquired in a biting tone. "And why am I here?"

"I am Dr. Shaw, Lord Rockingham." The doctor had the good fortune to bow, else Anthony would have taken offense. "As to your second question, you have been remanded into my custody by order of His Grace, the Duke of Swanborough, for treatment of your mental infirmities and war injuries."

"I beg your pardon?" A dark sense of foreboding danced a merry jig down Anthony's spine, and he checked himself. There was no cause to be uncivil. "Dr. Shaw, I am no child, and I can assure you I have no *mental infirmities*, as you put it. In regard to my war injuries, my arm was removed, as you can see for yourself. Further, while I appreciate your interest, I have no need of your services and, thereby, you are dismissed. I am certain my father will compensate you adequately for your trouble."

"Lord Rockingham, you seem to be laboring under a misapprehension of the situation." Shaw snapped his fingers, and the two large men approached, assuming positions at either side of Anthony. "His Grace has charged me with your treatment, as I see fit to administer. Whether or not you comply is your choice. However, I believe you will fare much better if you cooperate, because I detest brute force but am not averse to using such tactics to achieve a successful outcome. Now, shall we go inside and discuss your course of therapy, or shall I have my men carry you?"

The threat, however unremarkably phrased, struck Anthony to his core.

"Anthony." Arabella took his arm. When he met her gaze, she tensed her fingers. "There is no cause to be disagreeable, and we are not heathens. Perhaps we should do as Dr. Shaw asks, given you did say you are quite famished after our journey. I'm sure he is a reasonable man." She leaned in and whispered, "Say nothing until we are alone." Then she continued in a normal tone, "Now, I should like to freshen up, if someone would be so kind as to show me to my quarters."

"Of course, my dear." Confused by her outward calm, but smart enough to understand she had a motive behind her request, Anthony offered his escort. Suppressing every natural instinct raging within him, he smiled. "Please, have a room prepared for Lady Rockingham."

BUILT IN THE Baroque style, in the seventeenth century, the manor house inspired a slew of dark thoughts, with nary a single happy ending, given it appeared all but abandoned. The Rococo décor boasted mezzo-frescoes in the Tiepolo tradition, along with vivid pastorals on the walls and the ceiling, framed with asymmetrical and abstract stuccowork. Despite the colorful artwork, the gold-laden structure conveyed an altogether dour impression. Oppressive as a tomb, with wall-to-wall wood paneling and crimson and black accents covering the maze of passageways, the cavernous estate extended as far as her eye could see. Putting one foot in front of the other, Arabella ignored her racing heartbeat, but her instincts screamed a warning.

Suppressing a shiver, she followed in Dr. Shaw's wake, with the two mountainous adjutants in the rear. As they wound their way deeper into their prison, she clung to Anthony and uttered a silent prayer for salvation. Again and again, she told herself someone would note their absence and search for them. Someone would raise an alarm. Yet, she doubted anyone would miss them until it was too late.

But too late for—what?

That was the worst part. Not knowing what fate awaited them.

"Ah, here we are." Dr. Shaw set wide an oak panel and stepped inside, before motioning to her. "Lady Rockingham, you will find all the basic necessities to perform your toilette, beyond the second portal, in the bedchamber. Know that we did our best to anticipate your every need. However, if we missed anything, you have but to ask. Remember, we are at your service, insofar as your requests do not exceed that which we are willing to give. Should you prefer a bath, you may ring for a footman, and I shall send up your lady's maid."

"Thank you." She bit her tongue and cursed herself. Although societal standing never impressed her, she just stopped herself from curtseying, because she outranked him, and she thought he would benefit from the reminder. To Anthony, she said, "My lord, permit me a moment to change out of my traveling gown, and I will join you in the drawing room, posthaste."

"Er, I beg your pardon, Lady Rockingham, but I must correct your presumption." The doctor nodded to the henchmen, who shoved Anthony, and he lost his balance and stumbled across the threshold. At once, she reached out to steady him. "Under the circumstances, and at His Grace's request, you will share accommodations with Lord Rockingham for the length of your visit."

Stupefied, given the odd arrangement, Arabella blinked and searched for a reply. Any reply. Yet, words eluded her.

The footmen carried in the trunks.

"You cannot be serious," Anthony declared with an expression of incredulity, as he righted his coat, and the servants vacated the immediate vicinity. "After all, this is my family home, and my usual rooms are located in the east wing."

"Not on this visit, I am afraid." Shaw lifted his chin and sniffed. "To foster a spirit of amity and encourage procreation, I recommended a different approach, which His Grace has seen fit to endorse, so you will both reside in a single chamber. Once Lady Rockingham is with child, we may revisit the subject of your private quarters."

"What on earth? Do you expect me to breed like a mare at Tattersalls?" Not that Arabella protested in regard to her husband, because she enjoyed Anthony's company, but the situation only affirmed her suspicions, and a chill ran through her blood. The duke intended to enact his plan, to the letter, which did not bode well for her or her tortured soldier. "Really, this is beyond the pale, and I warn you, Dr. Shaw, if your less than graceful associates so much as scowl at Lord Rockingham, much less put their hands on him, one more time, I shall be moved to violence. In the future, you will address his lordship with all due respect of his station and extend to his person the courtesy owed his rank, else I will fight you at every turn. Let us see how His Grace appreciates that when he has no heir beyond Lord Rockingham. Who do you think he will blame for your failure?"

"Apologies, Lady Rockingham, if I caused offense, because that was not my intent." Shaw snapped his fingers, and the pair of dolts returned to the hall. For good measure, she shook her fist in their wake. "Take a moment and settle your things, and when you are ready you may ring for an attendant to escort you to the drawing room, whereupon we will discuss the conditions for your impromptu holiday."

"Holiday? Is that what you call it?" Snorting, Anthony drew Arabella to his side, and she slipped her arm about his waist. "I consider it unlawful imprisonment, and I shall seek proper redress from the appropriate authorities, once I return to London. I promise, you will not get away with this, Shaw."

"Please, do not overreact, my lord." The doctor folded his arms and knitted his brows. "Then again, such drama is a symptom of your ailment, so I cannot hold you at fault. As I said, we can talk over the terms of your therapy, after you have tidied yourself and gathered your wits."

"My wits are gathered." Anthony stiffened, and she dug her fingers into his ribs. At once, he calmed. "And I promise, you will pay for this indignity."

"Have a light repast prepared to sustain us until dinner, given we were starved of food during our trip here. And I should like tea." Drawing herself up, she summoned every ounce of high dudgeon befitting a marchioness. "Now, you are excused."

With that, Arabella slammed shut the door.

Pressing a finger to her lips, she bade Anthony remain silent. When he nodded, she grabbed his arm and led him through the sitting room, into the bedchamber, and closed the heavy oak panels.

"Oh, Anthony, this is dreadful." She turned to face him and tried not to panic. Then she panicked and gripped the lapels of his coat. "Whatever are we to do?"

"What can we do?" He glanced about their quarters and splayed his arm. She threw herself into his embrace, and he kissed her forehead. In a low voice, he said, "Somehow, it will be all right, but until we identify a means of escape, we must comply. We must give every impression that we cooperate with and support Dr. Shaw in his mission. Whatever we do, we cannot give him any reason to separate us."

"You must be joking, because I am not sure I could survive a single night in this house of horrors, much less on my own. I should run amok." With a huff, she pushed free. To the rear of the elegant room, she located a large closet. In the opposite corner, behind an oriental screen, she found a washstand and a large tub. At the foot of a massive four-poster bed, she paused to contemplate their predicament. She snapped her fingers and gestured. "What about the window?"

"That was my first thought." Peering below, he shook his head. "We would never make it. There is no trellis, and the landscaping is too steep. I suspect we would break our necks were we to try."

"Oh." Perched on the edge of the bed, she slumped her shoulders. There had to be some way to break free of the evil doctor. She just needed to think. "What about the servants? Do you know any? Is there anyone in residence who might be sympathetic to our plight?"

"None of which I am aware." Anthony frowned. "It has been years since I spent any time here, and my nanny has long since been dispatched. The butler died last summer, and I am unfamiliar with the current staff, I suspect by design, so I am of no use to us there."

"That is too bad. There must be someone willing to provide assistance." Arabella tapped her chin. From every conceivable position, the situation seemed hopeless. Thus far, she had met only male domestics, and not a single one struck her as complaisant. "Although, I am not sure what anyone can do to help us."

"We do not need much." He surveyed the apartment and strode to a small desk, where he opened a drawer. "We have stationery and an inkwell. I can write a missive to your father, if only we have someone to dispatch the message. While it is a simple plan, we require no grandiose efforts. That is the beauty of it. We need but one person's assistance to succeed."

"My lord, you are brilliant." She shot from the mattress. "Surely, my father will save us, and he could be here in a day. He would never stand for his daughter being taken prisoner." She reflected on the possibilities and nursed a glimmer of hope. "I wager a pretty shilling the Earl of Ainsworth would show that Dr. Shaw a thing or two."

A knock at the door gave her pause, and her husband pressed a finger to his lips.

"Come," Anthony stated, as he turned toward the door.

"Beg your pardon, my lord, but I am sent to attend Lady Rocking-ham." A rather young maid offered a none too elegant curtsey. With her dark brown hair pulled taut beneath a crisp white mob cap, and round spectacles, she strode forward. To Arabella, the servant said, "My lady, my name is Emily. I am here to unpack your belongings and ensure your comfort. Shall I have the footmen prepare a bath?"

"Perhaps, after Lord Rockingham and I meet with Dr. Shaw, and hello, Emily." Arabella's thoughts ran wild, because she had just spied her target. If anyone could be coaxed into aiding their cause, it was the slightly awkward servant. Somehow, she had to win the maid's confidence, in order to persuade the girl to betray the doctor, and she had to work fast. "Why don't you have a seat, and tell me about yourself? If we are to be friends—and I do hope we can be friends—I should know something of your history."

"You wish to know me?" Emily blinked. "No one ever sees me, my lady. My mama says a good maid blends into the background from whichever angle you look at her."

"You can't be serious." Determined yet calm, Arabella cast a quick glance at Anthony, who nodded, and approached her prey. "Because I see you, and your mama is mistaken, if I may be so bold. I see a charming woman of refined carriage and discerning taste." She sat on a bench at the foot of the bed and patted the cushion beside her. "Please, have a seat, and let us enjoy a nice little chat. I do so hope we can be friends, given I am far removed from London and my usual acquaintances."

"You want to be friends, and you want me to with sit? And will you tell me of London, because I have never traveled to the city." Emily bit her bottom lip and shuffled her feet, as she wrung her fingers. "But Dr. Shaw told the staff that we were not to speak beyond that necessary to serve your ladyship."

"Oh, bother the doctor." Holding her belly, Arabella yielded to giddy laughter. "If you are to act as my lady's maid, then you know you must do as I say, and I require your friendship. Of course, if you do not wish to—"

"Oh, no, my lady." Emily sputtered. "I-I mean, yes, please. I should like, very much, to be your friend, because I have never known a fine lady like yourself." Then she peered toward the sitting room, where Anthony paced before a window, and plopped down. Leaning close, she whispered, "Is it true what they say? That Lord Rockingham is mad?"

"Oh, my dear, he is no such thing." Arabella should have guessed Shaw would have swayed the domestics to do his bidding. Still, she believed she could win Emily's confidence with the right appeal. "Indeed, we are not sure why the duke has taken such drastic measures to secure treatment for Lord Rockingham, when his lordship is already under the care of a very fine professional."

"Really?" With an expression of pure curiosity, Emily's eyes grew wide. "Dr. Shaw told us Lord Rockingham is dangerous, and you must be protected, at all costs." She clenched a fist to her chest. "Please, know that I will defend you with my life. Can you tell me what is wrong with his lordship?"

"Stuff and nonsense." Arabella waved dismissively. "I assure you, there is no reason to fear for my safety, because my husband is the last person who would ever hurt me. And there is naught wrong with Lord Rockingham, other than a missing arm. Since when is that a crime or a condition to strike terror in the heart of man? In fact, he is a brave war hero, but His Grace the Duke of Swanborough does not appreciate my husband's sacrifice. What manner of society disapproves of a man because he lacks a limb? Are we to institutionalize everyone in possession of a minor difference? Why, we should sooner imprison half our countrymen."

"Bloody hell, I should say so." Emily shrieked and bowed her head. She appeared on the verge of tears when she stated, "Forgive me, my lady. I am too forward for a proper lady's maid, and I spoke out of turn. I regret it has always been a fault of mine, which is why my mother says I have never been able to secure a long-term position. To put it simply, I talk too much."

"Posh." The scheme progressed perfectly, but Arabella suppressed her excitement. "Who am I to judge, given I have often been told I suffer the same affliction, so I can hardly complain of your behavior. In truth, I welcome your company."

"Really?" Emily smiled. "My lady, I should be honored to call you a friend."

"Then we are a pair." Spying an opening and an opportunity to foster fellow feeling, Arabella giggled and clasped Emily's hand. "And no one need know of our kinship. It will be our secret."

Chapter Twelve

THE EXPENSIVE WALL coverings stretched and swirled, manifesting a series of unforgiving spiderweb traps, and his throat constricted. Aubusson rugs shifted and lifted from the floors, forming ghostly figures, emitting a morose cacophony of hideous wails, and his insides tightened. Random trinkets and vases sprang to life, dancing a provoking jig, and he clenched his gut. From the shadows emerged imaginary combatants, the devil's army, to taunt Anthony as he navigated the maze of hallways, and he tensed his muscles. Doorway after doorway sank into a dark vortex, locking him in his own private hell, daring him to plunge into the abyss. To yield to the fright. To lose himself.

It was all in his mind.

Shaking himself alert, he reminded himself that the haunting visions were just that—visions.

They did not exist.

They could not hurt him.

Focused on the steady rhythm of his heartbeat, he descended the stairs. He sought solace in the constant *tick-tock* of the long case clock in the foyer, letting it guide him like a beacon to a place where safety and sanity dwelled, and slowly he emerged from the mental fog. Yet, hope for liberty diminished with each step, because he could not elude reality, and it was all he could manage to put one foot in front of the other, tramping to his doom.

With the burly escorts at either side, he clutched Arabella's hand and tried to ignore the usual inclinations. To panic. To shout a warning. But a warning of—what? A drop of perspiration traced a path down his temple, offering a mild distraction from the stress wreaking havoc within him, and he reminded himself to breathe. How he longed to scream in terror. To run from the house and never look back.

But Anthony would not abandon his bride.

Every seemingly innocuous piece of furniture morphed into an enemy soldier, advancing on his position, and his anxiety grew to epic heights. In his mind, duty waged war with fear, and fear seized the lead. Gasping for air, he craned his neck against his cravat and tripped.

"My lord, I apologize for trampling your foot." Of course, she did no such thing. Searching his eyes, no doubt seeing more than he wished to reveal, as was her way, Arabella grabbed his arm and then frowned. "In the future, I will take greater care to watch where I am going, so I do not injure you, but you knew I was clumsy when you married me."

"No apologies necessary, my lady." In the bright sunshine of her smile, he grinned and broke free of the illusive torment. "I believe I almost sent you for a tumble, after catching the toe of my boot on the rug."

"Then we are a fine pair." She giggled, but her attempt at levity didn't fool him. He detected the lines of strain at the corners of her mouth and the firm set of her jaw that belied her poised demeanor. She worried, too, and the knowledge only intensified his concern.

Together, they strolled into the drawing room, where Dr. Shaw loomed as a specter of doom before the hearth. "Ah, you are arrived." With brittle cordiality, Shaw extended an arm. "Please, be seated."

Anthony showed Arabella to an overstuffed chair, and he stood as sentry to her left. Simmering with unchecked agitation and ire, he longed to decry the unfairness of his predicament, but he recalled Dr.

Handley's advice and tamped his temper. He would give Shaw no reason to define him as mad. "I hope that now you will relate the details of our captivity, including the duration and scope of our stay, because we are eager to return to London and begin our married life."

"Indeed, we did not anticipate an impromptu visit to Surrey as part of our honeymoon, and I have previous engagements I must keep." Arabella folded her hands in her lap and inclined her head. "If I am to be inconvenienced, I should like to let my parents know of my whereabouts, else they will worry. I would allay their apprehension surrounding my unexplained absence."

"Lady Rockingham, there is no cause for concern." Shaw cast a brittle countenance laced with unveiled contempt. "It is my understanding that the Duke of Swanborough has apprised Lord and Lady Ainsworth of his plan and secured their agreement, so your alarm is unwarranted."

"W-what?" Her voice quivered, and Anthony rested his palm to her shoulder. She took a deep breath as she composed herself. "You mean my mother and father knew of the duke's intentions, including my imprisonment, prior to my wedding?"

"Indeed," Shaw replied with an air of superiority. "We all discussed it."

"I-I don't believe you." She half-whimpered and clenched a fist. "My parents would never support such nefarious enterprises, and I will not permit you to slander them in this fashion. My parents love me. They would not allow you to hold me against my will, so you must lie, sir."

"I can assure you, Lady Rockingham, that I act with the Earl of Ainsworth's blessing." With unveiled indifference and callous disregard for Arabella's feelings, Shaw assessed his fingernails and smirked. "As a matter of fact, the earl attended the last meeting with the Duke of Swanborough, shortly before your nuptials, wherein we finalized the details of Lord Rockingham's convalescence. Of course, securing an heir is of utmost importance, in the event Lord Rocking-ham cannot be rehabilitated to the extent he can perform his duties."

"What do you mean, 'In the event Lord Rockingham cannot be rehabilitated'? When has Lord Rockingham failed in his responsibilities? I challenge you to name one instance." Anthony adored her as she rose to his defense. "Who are you to judge anyone? What, exactly, are your credentials? And what authority do you possess to hold us, when we have committed no crime?"

How well he knew the expression on her face, because he'd spent months on the other side of it. The relentless bite of hurt. The unchecked ire. The utter devastation, black as a bottomless pit. When he rubbed the back of her neck, she jumped and then met his gaze, and he spied unshed tears. In silence, he cursed.

His world shifted in that moment, and he focused on her response and her needs, as he tried to comfort her in the midst of the harsh truth of their position. To his surprise, she brushed him aside and leaped from the chair. With no small hint of disdain, she charged the doctor.

"I demand you release us, at once." Toe to toe with Shaw, she squared her shoulders. "You cannot keep us here, forever. When I am free, I shall see to it you are severely punished for your illegal actions. I shall shout from the treetops in Hyde Park. I shall appeal to His Majesty for justice, if that is what it takes. Now, I say again, let us go."

For an instant, an eerie hush fell on the room, and Anthony braced.

Then, the doctor smiled a sickeningly sweet smile that did not inspire confidence, and Anthony flinched. Tension grew, and his gut wound tight as a clock spring. The floor beneath his feet seemed to pitch and roll.

"My dear Lady Rockingham, since you fail to comprehend the purpose and breadth behind His Grace's commands, permit me to explain, so there are no further misunderstandings between us. First, despite your forceful protestations, you are going nowhere until I allow it. Given you married Lord Rockingham, English law defines you as his property. Since Lord Rockingham has been deemed mentally incapacitated, his custody is remanded to his father, the Duke of Swanborough. I am tasked at His Grace's directive and act in accordance with his wishes." The villain counted on his hand. "Second, you are restricted to your quarters, and the doors will be locked at all times. If you wish to stroll the garden or peruse the library, you will do so under my supervision. Third, you are to produce an heir. Once the required child is conceived, Lady Rockingham will remain as a guest of His Grace until her confinement results in a healthy birth. Thereafter, she may return to London, leaving the babe in the care of those best equipped to prepare him for future duties. Finally, Lord Rockingham is to be placed in a medical facility, where I will direct his treatment, until I determine His Lordship is safe to resume his place in society. Now, are we clear?"

Panic surged to the fore, and Anthony yanked at his collar. Perspiration trickled down his cheek, and he suspected he might swoon. His stomach churned and he swayed. Just when he feared he would run amok; Arabella met and held his stare.

Then all hell broke loose.

"*How dare you!*" she screamed and slapped Dr. Shaw, leaving a telltale red print on his flesh. "I am the daughter of the Earl of Ainsworth. I am Lady Rockingham, peasant, and I will not be imprisoned by the likes of you." She grasped the lapels of his waistcoat, as Anthony's usual maladies disappeared in the face of her impressive outburst. "Hear me well, I rebuke your authority over me."

"Lady Rockingham, control yourself." Shaw clutched her forearms and set her back on her heels. "As you are a lady and a gentlewoman, I expect you to comport yourself appropriately."

"My dear, it will be all right." Stunned, Anthony caught her by the elbow and pulled her close to his side, even as she continued an incoherent rant at the top of her lungs. "My lady." He gave her a gentle tug. "Arabella, that is enough. Let us return to our chambers, where you might recover your wits." To Shaw, Anthony said, "Forgive her, as I believe the shock of the day's events are too much for her delicate senses. Remember, we traveled far and were denied an opportunity to break our journey for a brief respite. A hot meal and a good night's rest should do much to improve her spirits."

There would be hell to pay for that, he suspected, because there was nothing delicate about his wife, and she would take umbrage at his remarks.

"Of course, Lord Rockingham. Women are naturally predisposed to histrionics, so her ladyship's behavior is to be expected and pitied. Given her status, we will indulge her." The doctor dipped his chin, and his imperious demeanor rankled Anthony's last nerve, but he took no issue. His bride needed him just then, because Shaw's reply inspired another series of spectacular insults, and Anthony found himself fighting laughter. "Perhaps, you and I can continue our discussion tomorrow, in the study, my lord."

"I look forward to it, Dr. Shaw." Anthony pulled Arabella into the crook of his arm. "Come, my dear. Let us retire to the comfort of our quarters, for the evening. I will ring for your bath, and then we will dine in the quiet of our sitting room."

"I will summon the footman, posthaste, to heat the water, while you tend to her ladyship." Shaw righted his coat and tugged the bell pull. "You may send for dinner to be served, at your leisure, because we are not barbarians, here. We only wish to help."

"I suppose I should eat something, and I do need to wash off the road dust." Again, to his befuddlement, she leaned into him, and he steered her toward the door and into the hall, with the two stocky attendants in tow. His countess was anything but weak, and he wondered if the unpleasant developments had well and truly shocked her into hysteria. "You are wise, as well as thoughtful, my lord."

With care, he led her up the grand staircase, and on the landing he paused. Instinct told him there were games afoot, and he longed to inquire after her motives. Given their lack of privacy, he continued to navigate the passageways, until they arrived at the entrance to their rooms. One steward pulled a key from his pocket and unlocked the door, which he then set wide. Anthony drew Arabella across the threshold and strode straight to their inner bedchamber. The escort secured the door behind them.

"All right, what was that?" He narrowed his gaze, and she lifted her head and grinned. "You have never been given to such torrents of emotion, even when baited, and I should know. You are uncommonly calm under pressure, which is one of the many positive traits that draws me to you. Are you genuinely out of sorts, or is there another method to your madness?"

"Well, you appeared on the verge of an apoplectic fit, which I feared might lend credence to Dr. Shaw's assertion that you are unfit for your rank. I would not have him use your reaction to bolster his claims against your sanity." She furrowed her brow. "I had to do something, and hysteria proved the only weapon at my disposal. While I thought it a successful diversion, I apologize if I caused you distress, because that was not my aim."

"You are a remarkable woman, Lady Rockingham." Moved beyond words by her desire to protect him, he could have wept in gratitude. Instead, in a single swift sweep of his arm, he wound his fingers in the hair at her nape and pulled her near. Then he covered her mouth with his and kissed her hard and fast.

A knock at the door could not have come at a more inopportune moment.

Cursing audibly this time, he lifted his head and shouted, *"Come."*

Emily, the awkward maid, peered around the edge of the oak panel. "I beg your pardon, my lord, but Dr. Shaw ordered a bath for her ladyship. Since Lady Rockingham did not wash before your meeting with Dr. Shaw, I had water boiled, to service her ladyship without delay. Shall we set up the tub in the wash area?"

"Yes, of course. And that was very thoughtful of you, Emily." Anthony made no attempt to disguise the fact that he had been kissing his bride, because he bloody well enjoyed himself, and he loved the charming flush of Arabella's cheeks. He tugged her to one side, so the footmen could carry in buckets of steaming water. "Take your time and have a relaxing soak."

"What will you do, in the meantime?" she asked in a whisper. "Do you need my help formulating a plan?"

"Shh." He pressed a finger to her lips. "We will discuss it, later. Now, I will await your arrival in our sitting room, whereupon I shall take my turn and bathe, but do not hurry on my account."

"All right." Perched on tiptoes, she favored him with a feathery kiss. "I promise, I will not linger too long."

The look she gave him almost took him to his knees, and he cleared his throat.

The footmen exited the inner chamber, and he followed in their wake. When they marched across the sitting room and into the hall, Anthony eased into an overstuffed chair near the windows. In light of recent revelations, he realized he could not appeal to the earl of Ainsworth for assistance. Liberty would have to be secured elsewhere.

THE MANTEL CLOCK signaled the late hour, and Arabella stretched long and yawned. In the world beyond the windows, the sun had long since set, and she pondered ringing for Emily, but something odd left her rooted in place. Reclining on the *chaise*, and holding a book in her lap, she pretended to read. Pretended because she could not settle her thoughts. Instead, she studied her confusing husband.

For some reason she could not fathom, her once amiable and flirtatious spouse had become sullen and despondent. He barely said a word over dinner, despite her numerous attempts to discuss their situation. Yes, the conversation with Dr. Shaw did not yield the hoped-for results, because they remained where they started—in captivity. But she thought they would form a new plan, together.

"Shall I have the dishes cleared?" She sat upright. "Would you like more wine? I can refill your glass. Or I can pour you a brandy."

"Brandy, please." He nodded once and said naught more.

With a sigh, she scooted forward and dropped her feet to the floor. Standing, she rubbed the small of her back with her knuckles and walked to the tallboy. Reaching to the left, she yanked the bell pull. Then she lifted the heavy decanter and filled a crystal balloon with the amber liquor, which she delivered to her husband.

"What is wrong?" She perched on an ottoman near the chair he occupied, so he could not ignore her. "Aside from the obvious. You've hardly spoken to me. Have I done something wrong?"

"No." He took a healthy gulp and frowned. "But I am at a loss to discern a way out of this mess. I had thought we could rely on your father for assistance. In truth, we need his support. His complicity makes our predicament more dire."

"Well, I cannot argue with you there, because I never would have imagined Papa could betray me, but why should his involvement make our situation worse?" Cocking her head, she half chuckled. "Things are pretty bad, already, I suppose."

"My father can do with me as he wants. I am not concerned for myself, because I am not afraid of him or his doctor." Anthony compressed his lips and met her gaze, and the despondence she spied well-nigh punched her in the gut. "But your fate I cannot begin to contemplate without profound reservations."

"Fret not for me, because Dr. Shaw made it clear that I am to be returned to London." Yet, something dark and ominous stirred within her as she uttered the statement, and nagging doubts crept to the fore of her brain. He was right to worry. A light rap of the door signaled the maid's arrival, and Arabella whispered, "We will continue this discussion, later." Then she stated, "Come."

"Good evening, my lord and my lady." Emily curtseyed and approached. "Should I have the footmen remove the dishes?"

"Please, do so." Arabella dipped her chin and stood. "And I should dress for bed."

"Yes, my lady." Emily peered over her shoulder and waved to the footmen. With characteristic timidity, the maid bowed her head and walked with Arabella into the bedchamber. "I aired the white gown and the matching robe, as you requested. Shall I take down your hair?"

"Oh, indeed." She eased to the small, tufted seat at the vanity. As she reflected on what the night would hold, anticipation simmered beneath her flesh, and she smiled to herself. Tomorrow, she would be Anthony's wife in every way, and no one could change that.

"Are you nervous, my lady?" Emily gasped and covered her mouth with her hands. "I beg your pardon. I should not have asked such a personal question."

"That's all right." Arabella recalled she needed to grow closer to the servant. "Are we not friends?"

Emily nodded.

"Well, friends don't keep secrets from friends, do they?" Arabella asked, and the maid shook her head. "Precisely. And to answer your query, I am a little nervous, but I think that is probably natural for a new bride."

"I wouldn't know." Emily tugged several pins from Arabella's intricate coiffure. "My one and only beau married another girl from Weybridge, last year, and I suppose I will never find another suitor."

"Don't say that." Arabella grabbed her silver-backed brush. "There is always hope, and you never know what can happen. As a matter of fact, I never intended to take a husband."

"Really?" Surprise colored Emily's response. "But you wed a marquess."

"It was pure luck owing to birth on both our parts that we ended up together." Arabella turned to face the maid. "And, I should add, a dark twist of fate."

"I don't understand." The maid furrowed her brow. "Do you mean you were not destined to marry his lordship?"

"Yes and no." Arabella chuckled at Emily's perplexed expression. "You see, there existed a longstanding agreement, brokered before we were born, between our two families. Only, Lord Rockingham had an older brother who originally inherited the title. When John was killed at Waterloo, Anthony became the Marquess of Rockingham, assuming ownership of the title, the marquisate, and me, I suppose."

"How awful." Emily picked up a comb and worked to untangle a knotted curl. "Did you love the first Lord Rockingham?"

"What a curious question, given love rarely enters the equation when it comes to marriage." Arabella considered the two men and wondered how different her life would have been with the elder Bartlett son. "To be perfectly frank, I never had the opportunity to know John. He sent the occasional gift, and we spoke briefly, when I was very young. Beyond that, I seldom heard from him."

"Well, at least for you, love didn't matter, but I could not take a husband who did not claim my heart," Emily replied in a melancholy tone. Arabella almost challenged the servant's assertion but held her tongue, because she needed an ally. "I used to envy what I thought were the delights of London, including the balls and socials. You get to wear such lovely clothes and eat some of the most delicious food. You attend the theater and Vauxhall. It sounds so exciting. Yet, I would not trade places with you, because if I wed, it will be to a man of my choosing. I suppose that is a concession of poverty."

"It does seem rather dreadful when you put it that way." Indeed, never had Arabella pondered that perspective. After assessing her hair in the mirror, she stood and gave her back to the maid. As Emily unlaced Arabella's gown, she reminisced of her brief courtship with her injured hero. "Still, if I had a choice, I would have set my cap for Lord Rockingham."

"Who wouldn't?" Emily snorted and tugged the dress from Arabella's shoulders. "He is a wealthy marquess, heir to a dukedom, and, if you don't mind my saying, a vast deal more than a little in twig."

Together, they giggled. From beyond the doors, Anthony cleared his throat, and Arabella came alert.

"We should be about our business, because my groom awaits." Steadying herself with the maid's support, she stepped free of the gown. "But I would not have you linger under the impression that I do not care for Lord Rockingham, because the truth is, I am quite fond of him."

"That's right." Emily whisked Arabella's chemise over her head. "If I remember correctly, you called him a war hero."

"Yes, but he is so much more than that." She sat at the edge of the bed and unhooked her garters. "Lord Rockingham is the kindest, gentlest, and best of men. He has a particular partiality for *neige de pistachio* ice, and he is blessed with a boyish innocence that quite slays my defenses, despite what he endured in France. Although the duke does not recognize it, his son possesses uncommon courage. Where others might never overcome the loss of an arm, Lord Rockingham greets every day with newfound strength and optimism, and I hold him in great esteem. Indeed, I could not have hoped for a better husband."

"Begging your pardon, my lady, but you speak like a woman in love." Emily picked up the diaphanous night rail Arabella selected for her wedding night. When she prepared to drape it over Arabella's figure, she flinched and came to a halt. "Oh, dear. I did it again. I said something wrong. Please, forgive me."

"No." Arabella blinked, as her world seemed to spin out of control. "There is naught to forgive, because you put into words what I did not see until now. Until just this moment." Resting her palms to her thighs, she inhaled a deep breath. "I knew I harbored an attachment for him, but I never explored the depth of my emotions. Yet, I cannot deny what I feel." She gave vent to nervous laughter. "You are correct. I love Lord Rockingham. I know not when or how it happened, but I love him. Regardless of what the Duke of Swanborough or Dr. Shaw claim, his lordship is not mentally infirm. Indeed, I find the mere suggestion abhorrent. More than that, it is false, and I will defend my husband with my life, if I must."

"My lady, if you believe in Lord Rockingham, then I believe in Lord Rockingham." The maid enveloped Arabella in the sheer robe, more an afterthought than a practical garment, letting the delicate folds fall into place. Then Emily secured the single mother-of-pearl button at Arabella's throat. "There. Oh, my lady, you are a vision. Daresay Lord Rockingham counts himself the most fortunate of men, tonight."

"Thank you, Emily." Arabella eased into her slippers and told herself everything would be fine, even as butterflies fluttered in her belly. "If you will put away my things, you may retire for the night."

"Yes, ma'am." Emily scurried about, tidying the room. She hung the discarded clothes on a peg in the armoire and turned down the bed. After one last survey of the area, she curtseyed and cast an impish grin. "Sleep well, my lady."

Alone, Arabella walked to the long mirror and studied her appearance. Cupping her chin, she glanced from side to side. What she spied in her reflection stole her breath. Her eyes filled with newfound spirit, and her face presented a canvas colored with emotion. A warm, vibrant fire burned within her, and she could not deny the truth.

How had she missed the obvious development?

How had she yielded her heart and not known it?

She was a woman in love.

The answer to the mystery proved simple. While she studied all manner of intellectual topics, often conducting her own experiments, she never explored the passionate complexities of the male-female relationship. To that day, the connection bewildered her, because she never bothered to examine it. She used women's novels to conceal what she considered more serious books, when she patronized the booksellers with her father. Perhaps, she shouldn't have been so quick to discount what she deemed a frivolous waste of time. Were she as smart as she presumed, she should have investigated sentimental attachments before she married. Now, everything seemed muddled except for a single nagging prospect that consumed her thoughts. Which begged the question: Did Anthony share her attachment?

Determined to find the answer, Arabella marched to the double door portal and turned the cool metal knob. With the heavy oak panel set wide, she thrust herself into the fray. Seated where she left him, Anthony did not acknowledge her dramatic entrance or her presence, much to her disappointment.

"My lord, are you unwell?" she prompted, hoping for some recognition of her provocative attire. After all, she dressed for his delectation. "Is there something I can do for you?"

"Hmm?" He faced her, and his expression sobered, as he scrutinized her appearance from top to toe. Slowly, he stood. "My lady wife, you are more beautiful than I can say."

"Thank you." Steeling her nerves, she walked to him, her eyes never leaving his. "Shall I refill your brandy?"

"No." He shook his head and furrowed his brow. Something sinister and foreboding danced in his troubled gaze. "I've had enough." He pulled her close. "Come and sit, because we need to talk."

"Of course, I am at your service." His reaction was not what she anticipated. Given the sheer material that did little to conceal her body, she had prepared to be ravished. At the very least, she expected him to kiss her. Still, she did as he bade. "What do you wish to discuss?"

"Well, since our original plan involved an appeal to your father, and we now know he is a willing accomplice in our abduction, we must alter our tack." Ah, he ogled her breasts, just visible and posing a tantalizing temptation, meaning he was not so immune to her enticing turnout as he pretended. "I have been thinking about our situation and of those in a position to assist us. The solution is obvious. We must appeal to Beaulieu and the Mad Matchmakers, but first we must make contact. How far have you progressed with the maid?"

"As well as can be expected, under the circumstances." Arabella snapped her fingers. "But I may have had a breakthrough, today."

"Oh?" He reached for her hand and stroked her palm with his thumb. The gentle sashay gave her gooseflesh. "Tell me."

"She asked about you. I believe she is naturally curious, given what Dr. Shaw told her and my characterizations to the contrary." For some reason, she didn't feel comfortable sharing the news of her affection, because she sensed he would not welcome the development. "In fact, she declared that if I have faith in you, so does she. That must count for something."

"That is good to hear." It was a fortunate turn of events, yet he did not seem pleased.

"My lord—Anthony, what is wrong?" If only he would kiss her. She could sit and listen to him for hours, if only he would kiss her. "You seem out of sorts. Have I done something to upset you?"

"My dear, you are blameless. I could not fault you for our current predicament, if I tried." He shifted and faced her. In a low voice, he said, "Escape is not our only concern. The danger is two-fold."

"How so?" she inquired, puzzled by his somber demeanor.

"According to Dr. Shaw, my father's plan alters once I get you with child. At that point, they will separate us." Anthony gazed into the hearth and swallowed hard. "I care not what happens to me, but I cannot countenance the thought of you in Shaw's custody. I don't trust the man. And even more loathsome is his stated intent to take possession of our babe. That I cannot abide."

"Neither can I, so what do you recommend?" She squeezed his fingers. "Also, I would have you know that I care what happens to you, but you know I am with you, come what may, so how do we defeat Shaw?"

"There is only one solution, and it requires great sacrifice on both our parts. We must not make love." He met her stare and frowned, and her stomach plummeted. "Not yet. Not until we are free of this place. Only then will it be safe for us to consummate our vows."

CHAPTER THIRTEEN

S UNLIGHT PEEKED THROUGH the heavy velvet drapes, rousing Anthony from a deep sleep, and he rubbed his eyes. Sitting upright, he grimaced and kneaded the nagging ache in the small of his back, which bore the brunt of his decision to use the *chaise* as a makeshift bed for the past fortnight. Across the chamber, tucked in the huge four-poster, Arabella had not roused. How he envied her insouciant slumber, something that eluded him since their arrival, yet he had no one to blame but himself, because it was his grand idea to forgo consummation of their vows.

Although Dr. Shaw did naught but hold them captive, his simple plan proved brilliant. Throwing Anthony and Arabella together, all day and night, in close quarters with few if any distractions, posed an enticing situation that yearned to take its natural course. While they learned each other's predilections and habits, adapting whenever conflict emerged, they nurtured an immeasurable, abiding devotion he could neither ignore nor resist. In short, he desperately desired his wife, but he could not have her. Not yet.

Blessed with a host of physical attributes that could drive a sane man mad as a March hare, coupled with the unimpeachable innocence of a virgin, she posed an intoxicating, irresistible allurement. Under different circumstances, he would gladly commit himself to getting her with child, but he would not cooperate with his father's scheme. To do so could only result in ruination and misery. They would have to wait, but he feared he might be hard until the new year.

On the heels of the thought, the other persistent ache, the fully loaded cannon in his crotch, reliable as ever, beckoned, as it did every single morning without fail, and he collapsed on his pillow. Staring at the intricately moulded ceiling, he wagered that if the relentless nightmares didn't drive him insane, forced celibacy in her continued presence would send him straight to the nearest asylum.

Desperate for relief, he checked to be sure she had not stirred, because he wanted no witness to an act he had not performed since his randy days at Eton, when he still wore shortcoats, knew nothing of women, and discovered a new use for soap. But he had to do something—anything—to ease his hunger. Rolling onto his side, he bit back a groan. Then he eased his hand beneath the blanket. Since Arabella often woke late, he always doffed his nightshirt after she dozed, preferring to retire in the nude, because he knew no man who enjoyed sleeping in a cotton gown.

With a firm grip of his Jolly Roger, which was wildly jolly and only too ready to raid the bride's prize nestled between Arabella's legs, he worked himself in a repetitive motion. Staring at nothing, he relaxed and exhaled. In his mind, he conjured prurient images of her performing the deed with her nimble fingers and with her beautiful mouth, along with a host of erotic fantasies that well-nigh sent him over the edge. Each vision more salacious. Again and again, he pleasured himself, flexing his muscles in time with his movements, and he gritted his teeth.

"My lord, are you all right?" Arabella asked in an urgent tone.

Anthony deuced near jumped out of his skin, and his momentary loss of control unleashed a torrent of unspent passion, as his loins erupted. Before he could respond, he let fly a rapid salvo, and wave upon wave of unrestrained relief washed over him. Powerless to fight the involuntary contractions or the accompanying grunts of sensual gratification, he yielded.

"Oh, dear, you look quite fitful. Are you ill?" Through a haze of uncontrollable delight, in the throes of which he could not suppress a grin, he spied his wife as she threw aside her covers, flew from her bed, and rushed to tend him, sans her robe. "Shall I call for assistance? Do you want me to summon the doctor?"

"No," he barely managed to utter. Through the sheer material that did nothing to hide her from his open admiration, he stared at her lovely breasts and their rosy tips. When she turned to sit at the edge of the *chaise*, he ogled the cleft of her round derriere. What he would do to that succulent bottom when he enjoyed free reign to ravish his lady. Propped on his elbow, he lifted his chin and kissed her. Unhurried yet unrestrained. To her credit, she did not reject him. At length, he savored her soft lips and her warmth. So much warmth. While he could not hold her, she compensated by wrapping her arms about him.

He needed that just then. He needed her. Needed to know she still desired him as he desperately desired her. Needed her to validate the fact that he was a human being minus a limb, and no more or less, if only to remind himself that he was a man and not some demented monster, as his father and Dr. Shaw would have Anthony believe.

And Arabella fed him. Strength. Confidence. A resurgence of his former self.

At last, when they parted, they were both breathless.

"Good morning, my lord." With a charming blush, she smiled her impish smile and averted her gaze. Despite all that happened, she remained the virginal coquette, innocent in body and spirit, and he adored her for it. "I feared you suffered some strange malady, but your behavior suggests otherwise. Shall I ring for breakfast?"

"Yes, please." When he sat upright, she peered at his bare chest and gasped. Again, the inexperienced society maiden surfaced, and he ached for either a cold bath or a long ride. "Er, I got hot during the night. Would you be so kind as to hand me my robe?"

"Certainly." She reached for the black silk garment, even as she continued to stare, transfixed, at his body. "Do you often sleep without benefit of clothing?"

"Sometimes." He suppressed a snort of laughter, because he would not stifle what he considered her healthy curiosity for anything in the world. "Does that bother you?"

"Who—me?" she inquired in an unusually high pitch. Never had he seen her so discomposed, and he liked it. "Oh, no. You are free to retire however you choose." She bit her lower lip. "But, is it done? I mean, is it proper?"

"Probably not, but we won't let that stop us, will we, darling?" Anthony waited with baited breath for her response.

"Us?" Her nervous titter did naught but increase his interest. Seducing his own wife presented heretofore uncharted territory he ached to explore at his leisure. "I never heard of such a thing. And I supposed we would occupy separate chambers, as is customary in most marriages."

"Well, we can always store our personal belongings in our respective quarters, and you may birth our babes in your room." Never had a woman in his company flushed beetroot red from top to toe, and he savored the moment and pondered his next move. "But you will spend your nights in my bed."

"I will?" She gulped. "Am I to forgo clothing, too?"

"I hope so." He waggled his brows. "Else I am not doing a proper job of seducing my wife."

"And will you seduce me?" In the blink of an eye, she checked her demeanor but failed to conceal her interest. "I mean, when we consummate our vows?"

"I may do so before then." He winked and relished the thrill of the chase. It had been a long time since he flirted with a woman, in pursuit of a singular delicious goal, and it was as if he reclaimed another part of his old self. "You know, it is possible to satisfy you without actually taking your maidenhead."

"Really?" He didn't know if it was his imagination or just wishful thinking, not that he cared, but she appeared enrapt by the suggestion. "How is that possible?" Just as quick, she flinched and bowed her head. "Never mind. Forget I asked, because such conduct is not permissible for a lady of character."

"You little hypocrite." He chuckled. "Admit it, you want to know what I can do for you. In fact, I will go a step further and assert you want me to pleasure you. Your inquisitive mind demands it. You want to know how it feels to soar beyond the earthly plane to the place where ecstasy prevails above all else."

"I should summon Emily." To his infinite disappointment, his suddenly reticent bride gave him her back. When she yanked on the bellpull, he realized he had erred in pressing his suit. "I'm sure Cook has our meal prepared, and I would like to break our fast while the food is still warm, if that is all right with you."

"Arabella, wait." Although she had already summoned the maid, he needed to apologize, because husbands did not proposition their wives like some dockside doxy or three-penny upright. "I apologize if I offended you, because that was not my intent."

"No apology necessary, my lord." Her downcast expression declared otherwise. "I assure you I am not offended. To be honest, I share your desire for intimacy, however inappropriate it might be for me to express it, aloud. Often, I have dreamed of such tantalizing assignations, wondering if I can fulfill your expectations. Given the books I have read, I understand how our bodies work to achieve the physical connection, but the emotional bond defies my attempts to study it. It is my greatest regret that our present circumstances prevent us from exploring our potential as a married couple, because I had such high hopes. However, I look forward to the day we are free to seal our vows and live as we choose."

"Now, you shame me." In a single sweep, he draped his robe about his shoulders. After fumbling with the belt, he secured the garment and stood. "Know this, my dear. You have my solemn promise that day will come, and we will spend the rest of our lives satisfying mutual desires."

"You feel it, too?" She halted before the door to their sitting room. "You share my struggle?"

"Aye." Clutching the soiled blanket, he walked to her. "More than you know."

"Oh, Anthony." To his surprise, she flung herself at him. With her arms wrapped about his waist, she rested her head to his chest. "I thought I suffered, alone. While I would not see you distressed, I am somewhat mollified by the revelation."

"Misery loves company, sweet Arabella." He kissed her hair. "While our situation is dire, all is not lost. We may yet defeat my father and Dr. Shaw. What we require is naught but unyielding discipline and a degree of intrepidity to survive."

"And we must not allow them to separate us." She lifted her chin and pressed her lips to his. "I will fight to my death before I surrender you to Shaw."

"You are formidable, Lady Rockingham." When she loosened her grip, he retreated a step. "The morning meal will soon arrive, and I should wash before I join you. Shall I bring your serviceable robe?"

"How very thoughtful of you, my lord." With that, she curtseyed and strode into the sitting room.

In her absence, he strolled behind the small screen that shielded the bathing area. He dropped the blanket and lifted the pitcher on the washstand. After filling the basin, he scrubbed his face and brushed his teeth. From the closet, he retrieved his silk trousers and a clean shirt and dressed himself.

At the opposite side of the small enclosure, his wife's items had been neatly folded and stacked on a bench. Wall pegs held her gowns and various accoutrements. When he located the item she required, he yanked the robe and knocked over some of her belongings. A stack of books tumbled to the floor, and he bent to retrieve them.

It was then a curious title snared his attention. *Soldier's Nostalgia and Other Battlefield Maladies,* by Dominique Jean Larrey. He recognized the name of Napoleon's personal physician. Fighting nausea, Anthony sank to the floor and opened the leatherbound tome. As he flipped through the pages, for how long he knew not, digesting bits of information, something inside him fractured. Unspeakable treachery, relentlessly painful, wreaked havoc in his gut, twisting his insides into knots, and he gagged on the revelation that his wife betrayed his trust.

He thought she believed in him.

After composing himself, and it wasn't easy, he flung her robe over his shoulder and shuffled the heavy book into the crook of his arm. Struggling to remain calm, because he knew there had to be a reasonable explanation for her choice in reading material, at least, he prayed there was, as he crossed the bedchamber and walked into the sitting room.

Near the large windows that overlooked the topiary garden, Arabella arranged covered dishes on the small table where they took their meals. When he approached, she smiled.

"I hope you don't mind, but I dismissed Emily." His cherubic bride collected her robe and shrugged into the garment. "We are more than capable of serving ourselves, and I enjoy my time in your company, unreservedly."

"Do you?" Unspeakable anguish nestled in the back of his throat, and he coughed. "You are not afraid of me?"

"Good heavens, no." When he thrust the book onto the table, toppling a cup and rattling the china and silverware, she jumped. "My lord, where did you find that?"

"It was hidden among your things." He knew not to make of her countenance, which wavered somewhere between guilt and innocence. "Including your lady's novels, which I believe you intended to use as cover, to deter me from discovering your dirty little secret.

Have I miscalculated? Am I wrong? Do I owe you an apology?" Her silence only inflamed his ire. "Answer me."

"You are not wrong, although I have realized the sentimental genre has much to teach me of the relationship between men and women, and it was unmitigated arrogance to dismiss it." Wringing her fingers, Arabella inhaled a shivery breath. "As for Larrey's work, I admit I sought it to help me understand you."

"Are you making a study of me?" So it was true. His wife betrayed him. Gritting his teeth, he gave vent to an unholy howl of misery. "Do you think me mad?"

"No." In a fit of insanity or just plain courage, she marched straight to him and stood toe to toe, in the face of his rage. Again, to his shock, she framed his cheeks with her delicate hands. "I would never presume to study you, given I am no professional. When we first met, you were naught to me but a stranger in pain. Where no one seemed interested in understanding you, I wanted only to grasp your suffering and find a way to allay it. Books have taught me a lot about life, and in my quest to comfort you, I sought knowledge in the one place I've always found it."

"You make yourself sound rather noble." He narrowed his stare. "If you had nothing to hide, why conceal the truth? Why not simply share what you learned? You've had ample opportunities."

"Because I feared your reaction, and we were just becoming acquainted." With her thumb, she caressed his bottom lip. "Think back to our first meeting. You did not wish to marry me, and you resisted all my attempts to offer succor. Even a blind person could see you were hurting, and I couldn't bear it, so I looked to Larrey's work to guide me, that I might be of use. If that is a crime, then I am culpable."

"Then it is true. You think me insane, just like my father." Railing against the realization, he flung the book to the floor. "Do you not see that I needed you to believe in me? Without your faith, I am left to wonder if everyone around me is right, and I am mad."

"No." Despite his outburst, she held fast. He expected procrastination and subterfuge, as she composed a sufficient excuse. She might even cry. Instead, she shed nary a tear. "I have naught in common with the duke, and you are not mentally unsound, my lord. Rather, you are human." Not what he expected her to say. "The symptoms you exhibit are merely manifestations of your exposure to the horrors of war. I should be concerned if you did *not* display evidence of the trauma you survived. That would be sufficient cause to suspect you were unhinged. Conversely, any normal, sane person who witnessed the savagery of battle would be affected by it." Now she made sense, as she refused to yield. "That is what Larrey's writings taught me. But don't take my word for it. Read it, yourself, and tell me you do not relate to his analysis and conclusion."

"My lady wife, I will do just that, and we shall see."

THE MANTEL CLOCK chimed twelve times, marking the midnight hour. Beyond the windows, a rumble of thunder and a howling wind heralded the arrival of a wicked tempest. A flash of lightning illuminated the bedchamber, while rain played a frantic drumbeat on the glass, and Arabella stirred and rolled onto her side. She punched her pillow and sighed as she tried to find a comfortable position, but the source of her unrest had nothing to do with the mattress or the storm and everything to do with her reserved husband.

Sitting upright, she yawned and stretched her arms over her head. A sliver of yellow light glowed beneath the closed doors to the sitting room, and she glanced at the empty *chaise*. Anthony never came to bed, and it appeared he still lingered over Larrey's book. Indeed, he'd spent the entire day engrossed in the seminal treatise on what many professionals referred to as nostalgia or irritable heart. She wasn't sure whether or not that was a good sign.

"Ho-hum." She patted her mouth.

After he discovered the work, and accused her of duplicity and betrayal, she'd made her stand, hoping to persuade him that her motives were pure and to give the teachings a chance. Yes, she should have told him the source of what he deemed her uncanny ability to soothe his troubled soul, but she suspected he would reject Larrey's ideas simply because the doctor was French. It seemed a reasonable conclusion. Hoping for an opportune moment, when her husband would be more receptive, to share the innovative perspective, she delayed. However well-intentioned, that had been a huge miscalculation on her part. One she feared he might never forgive.

Following their row, while she broke her fast, he sat on the settee, flipping through the pages. He took his lunch from a tray perched beside him. He ate dinner in the same place. Nary a word passed between them for the remains of the day, much to her chagrin, because she would have loved to examine Larrey's deductions through her husband's perspective.

Another thunderous roar shook the house, and she thought she heard Anthony shout. In a rush, she flung back the covers and dropped her legs over the edge of the bed. Then she paused. What if she overreacted? What if naught were amiss? Another cry caught her ear. Standing, she eased her feet into her slippers and grabbed her robe.

Again, her tormented soldier bellowed.

"I'm coming, my lord." She ran to the doors and flung open a single oak panel. In the sitting room, she spotted him, slumped to the right and still hugging the book. As she tugged on the heavy tome, he rolled his head from side to side and muttered incoherent gibberish. "Shh, my darling, else Shaw's henchmen may assail us."

"The cannons. They attack the center. They attack the center." He winced and flinched, and his agony, so apparent, gnawed at her gut. "Boney advances on the crest of Mont Saint Jean. We are too close. Too close."

"No, my lord," she stated in a soft voice, in an attempt to calm. To soothe. She wiped his damp brow and tried to hush him, as she whispered reassurances. "There are no cannons here, and you are fine. Are you chilled? Shall I stoke the embers?"

"We must retrench. We must fall back to the line and gather what survives of our forces, else we will lose the day." Ignoring her pleas, he gave vent to an unrecognizable exclamation, something almost inhuman remarkably timed with another resounding crash of thunder. "Lively, men. Make haste. Make haste to La Haye Sainte, else we are doomed."

"Anthony, please, you must be quiet." His trauma, almost palpable, spoke to her on an elementary but nonetheless powerful level she could not quite identify. Desperate and unable to free him from his imaginary prison, she shook him hard, and at last he opened his eyes and searched her face. "It is me, Arabella, and you are safe. We remain locked in our bedchamber, in your father's house."

"Can you not hear the gunfire and the mournful cries?" He grabbed her by the forearm and wrenched her close, so he could hug her about the waist. "Do you not smell the smoke?" He sucked in a breath and nodded toward the overstuffed chair near the window. "Look there. Do you not see the enemy hides in the shadows, waiting to attack? We are surrounded, and we are routed, but we cannot yield."

"No, my lord, there is no enemy here, and there are no guns. What you hear is a storm. Mother Nature throws quite a row, tonight. That is all." She cradled his cheeks and held his turbulent gaze. "I, alone, am with you, and I will never leave you."

Just when she thought she reached him, he released her and retreated. With his hand covering his eyes, he groaned. Thunder rattled the windows, and Anthony reverted to his fitful state. Clenching his teeth, he scrunched his face and emitted a spine-chilling growl that gave her gooseflesh.

"Make it stop," he begged and thrashed with his arm. "Please, by all that is holy, make it stop, as I can bear no more."

"Tell me what to do, and I will do it." Her mind raced in all directions, and she recounted Larrey's methods for calming an agitated veteran. In rapid succession, she recalled the various suggestions. Seizing on a course of action, she grasped her husband by his shoulders and jolted him. "My lord, focus on my voice. Listen to the words I speak, and breathe. Inhale and exhale. Do you hear me? Can you do as I ask?"

"Aye." He nodded once and compressed his lips. "I will try."

"Do you know who I am?" she inquired and uttered a silent prayer that he answered in the affirmative, because she knew not what to do otherwise. "Do you recognize me?"

"Of course, I do." He sighed, a mournful, heavy expression she felt down to her toes, and she resolved to support him, come what may. A moment passed. It seemed like a lifetime until he, at last, replied, "You are Arabella, my wife."

"Yes." Perched on tiptoes, she massaged his temples, and he moaned an approval. "Where are we, at present?"

"Surrey." He swallowed, and she coveted a small victory. "At one of my father's estates."

"Are there any French soldiers here?" Beneath her fingertips, he tensed, and she kneaded her way along the sides of his neck. "Do the cannons still fire?"

Just as she posed her query, an ear-splitting thunderclap rocked the house, bathing the sitting room in blinding staccato bursts of silvery light. A cheerful pastorale painting dislodged from its hook on the wall and landed with a muffled thud on the Aubusson rug, and a book fell from a side table. Trinkets clinked atop the escritoire, and under her feet the floor tremored.

When Anthony lunged, she braced to extend or withstand whatever remedy he required to endure his latest episode of nostalgia, and she vowed not to fail him. The first touch gave her little warning of the incoming tide of emotion he unleashed on her, reminiscent of their heated, impromptu interlude the night her father announced the engagement. Then, it had been quite a shock, because she had never been kissed. But her husband had long ago schooled her in the art of ravishment, so she responded in a manner sure to ease his pain, as she unwittingly did in her father's study.

In short, Arabella kissed him.

Wrapping her arms about his neck, she met him measure for measure, as he set his mouth to hers. Her thighs erupted in flames, searing a path to her belly, and desire rode hard in its wake. There was nothing reserved or refined in his approach, when he flicked his tongue to hers and squeezed her bottom. As usual, he charged with unfettered passion she could neither contain nor control, and his lone hand proved no real obstacle, because he caressed her everywhere with the gentlest strokes.

While outside, a violent deluge pounded the roof, inside a torrent of another sort intensified. Resolved to ride the wave of pleasure he provoked; Arabella denied him nothing. Unswerving in his advance, he whirled her about and backed her against the wall, but she feared him not, because he would never hurt her. Unshakeable trust in her instincts bolstered her confidence, so she let go the reins and rode hell bent for leather with her man into uncharted territory.

At some point, he drew her into the bedchamber, and the backs of her knees connected with the footboard of the large four-poster. Unbalanced, she waved her arms wildly in the air before toppling onto the mattress. Whereas she expected Anthony to help her upright, instead, he covered her.

The decadent slip and slide, an intoxicating and new sensation, overwhelmed her, and she knew not how to respond. No doubt, he expected her to assert herself, as an active participant. Her book knowledge offered no real strategy, but her hesitance mattered not, because it became clear her husband had a plan.

Again, he claimed her mouth, bruising her lips as he moved on her. The urgency. The raw hunger beckoned, and she answered the summons. Together, in a clumsy dance, they scooted toward the pillows. When he became tangled in his coat, she helped him shuffle free and then removed his waistcoat, cravat, and fine muslin shirt. To her shock, he made quick work of her robe and nightgown, exposing her, unimpeded, for his enjoyment.

She should have maintained her modesty. Should have shown self-restraint. Instead, she extended her hands and flicked her fingers in an unmistakable invitation. To her relief and benefit, he accepted.

As the storm escalated, so did their heated tryst. With her palms pressed to his bare chest, she lifted her chin, and he trailed feathery kisses along the curve of her neck and lower. Reclining amid the soft sheets and the plush counterpane, she stared, unseeing, at the rich velvet canopy, as her husband licked one breast and then the other, and fire scorched a path across her flesh. Charged her nerves. To her inexpressible delight, he lingered, suckling gently and grazing his teeth playfully to her nipples, and she struggled with a heretofore-unknown ache. Sensations foreign yet unutterably seductive.

He pressed on her caresses meant to entice. To arouse. And she followed his lead. Denied him nothing, even as a warning flashed in the dark recesses of her brain. Not that he did anything wrong or that he forced himself on her. Oh, no. She desired her husband. There was something about duty and producing an heir, but all of that flew out of her mind when he parted her legs and rested his hips to hers.

"Lift your heels, my dear." With patience, he showed her how to hug him with her thighs.

"Like this?" She did as he bade, knowing full well what was about to happen.

"Yesss."

After fumbling with the placket of his breeches, he gave her his weight, and pressure built at her core, as he pushed forward. Their bodies merged, such that she knew not where she ended and he began. The first thrust threatened to tear her in two, as Anthony gave her no time to adjust to his intimate invasion. And it was intimate. Profoundly personal. Unlike anything she had ever experienced and certainly nothing for which a book could have prepared her. Indeed, practical knowledge had much to recommend it.

Despite the initial discomfort, she found her rhythm and matched his, as he set a frenetic pace. Wave upon wave of pure, unadulterated bliss blanketed her, and her insides twisted and turned in anticipation, to accommodate him. Glorious warmth coiled in her loins, spreading throughout her limbs, pervading every part of her. On wings of ecstasy, she soared ever higher, to a place where she existed as something more than herself. Teetering on the brink of a precipice, she held her breath and tensed.

It was then her husband groaned and stretched taut, well-nigh scaring her to death. The elusive peak vanished, shattered by his vociferous expression, even as she reached for release, and how she grasped for the intangible yet enthralling summit. In that moment, he collapsed atop her, and everything came to an abrupt and frustrating halt, leaving her yearning for what she knew not.

For a while, she remained rooted beneath him, his flesh still buried deep within hers, fearing she might startle him and trigger another episode of nostalgia. She whispered encouragement and walked her fingers along his beautiful back. Flexing her thighs, she held him close, long after the torrent passed. At last, he turned his head. She expected him to say something. Anything about what just occurred between them, because she wanted to talk.

Instead, he wept.

CHAPTER FOURTEEN

B IRDS CHIRPED A lilting singsong, and the sun filtered through a water-speckled window, casting a mosaic of light on the floor, signaling that little remained of the storm, as Anthony squirmed in the bedside chair and guarded his sleeping bride. Clothed in naught but his silk robe, he closed his eyes and revisited the events of the night, which saw him abandoning his heretofore-vaunted self-control and thoroughly seducing his wife. He could only imagine what she thought of him, in the wake of his rakish behavior, and he vowed to endure, without complaint, whatever redress she delivered. Just then, Arabella roused, and he girded himself to withstand the consequences of his actions, which he more than deserved.

"Hmm." Her eyelids fluttered and lifted. When she spotted him, she smiled. She smiled. "Good morning, my lord," she said in a breathy voice that set him on his heels, because he expected hysterics. Recriminations. A candlestick lobbed at his head. "How are you on this glorious day?"

"Er—fine." Of course, he was better than fine after a night spent in her arms, but hers was not the reaction he anticipated. Still, he tensed and prepared to pose a question guaranteed to incite his lady, and it was nothing less than he deserved, given his bawdy conduct. "And you?"

"I'm wonderful." Her reply came to him, as if from afar, and echoed in his ears. Yet, she showed no hint of fear or anger. Rather, his bride appeared…euphoric. That couldn't have been right. He must've been mistaken, and he believed that, until she patted the space beside her and pouted. "What are you doing over there, my lord? It is chilly, and we could be so much warmer, together, beneath the covers. Will you not cuddle with me?"

"Are you sure you are well?" He scratched the back of his neck and shook his head. Then he glanced about the room, to be sure he was cognizant of the situation. "Given what occurred, I thought you might be quite put out, and I would understand, because I did not behave as would a gentleman. I brought shame to myself and my family, and I am so sorry, Arabella. I have no excuse, but I promise I will make amends."

"Why should I be put out? And amends for—what?" She giggled. She actually giggled and wagged a finger. "My lord, you were incapacitated. It is true, you were no gentleman, but neither were you yourself, and I believe the state of our affairs necessitated something else, entirely. Oh, you were a naughty boy."

"Precisely." It must have been shock, because he took a gently bred virgin like a seasoned courtesan, and that was no way to ease an unbroken mare into harness. He acted in a reprehensible manner, and he owed her an apology and so much more. "I took liberties."

"How so, when we are married? Are our actions not government sanctioned?" Clutching the sheet to her bosom, she closed her eyes and dropped back her head. "Besides, you were overwrought. The storm triggered another episode, and I needed to calm you."

"Ah, yes. I remember naught but bits and pieces." Memories flooded his mind, and salacious images flashed before him. Tangled legs. Breathy sighs. Tender kisses. Despite his efforts to manage his arousal, his body ached for her. "That is no excuse."

"It is to me." She sat upright and met his stare. "You were hurting, and I will not stand idly by while you suffer. Not now. Not ever. It was within my means to provide relief, as would any wife, and it is not as if you forced me to do something against my will. I assure you, I gave myself to you of my own volition. Indeed, I provoked you, on purpose. I would argue it was my duty to submit, to consummate our union as well as offer comfort, but it was also my pleasure."

"Your pleasure?" Again, she stunned him, and he blinked. "You mean to say you enjoyed it?"

"Well, it was a tad rough the first time—"

"The *first* time?" He sifted through the remnants of his memories from last night, much of which remained a haze. "We did it more than once?"

"Oh, I should say so, my wicked lord, but it is disappointing that you do not recall it, because it was unforgettable for me." She shrugged and hummed a flirty ditty. "And you more than redeemed yourself on the second and third rounds of coitus. I may require a nap, today, because I slept little thanks to your connubial games, although that is not a complaint."

"Indeed?" She could have knocked him over with a feather, and he wondered if he was locked in a dream. A crazed but fanciful dream no sane husband would ever conjure. "So, you liked it?"

"More than liked it." The expression on her face left him in no doubt of her sincerity. "It far surpassed my expectations, which I thought reasonable and sound, because I based my suppositions on what I read about physical intimacy. But I am convinced the so-called experts pose ill-informed conclusions based on little if any practical knowledge."

Anthony could only laugh at her charming assertions, however naïve.

"Then you are not traumatized, and I am forgiven?" He pondered the circumstances and sighed. "Even though we should have waited?"

"I am not traumatized, and there is nothing to forgive." Arabella tucked a wisp of hair behind her ear and furrowed her brow. "Whether or not you realize it, you are not to blame for what happened, because I could have stopped you, but I didn't want to stop you. I could not bear your suffering, and I needed to be close to you. If you recall, my efforts proved efficient in Papa's study, the night our engagement was announced."

"Yes, but I didn't claim your bride's prize then." Yet, it was too late to undo his actions, but he suspected there would be hell to pay, in the end. "Regardless of intent, we may have given my father exactly what he wants."

"Then the fault is mine to own, because you were not fully *compos mentis*." She frowned. "I had to do something, given your shouts of alarm, which could have summoned Shaw and his villains. We know not how they would have responded to your episode of nostalgia, although I'd wager it would not have been good, and I was not willing to take that chance."

"Nostalgia." He mulled Larrey's book and rubbed his chin. "A fascinating treatise I was ready to discount, but I am grateful I listened to you."

"I am so glad you think so, because I see so much of you in his words." After fluffing her pillows, she settled amid the down. "While I know it is a sensitive topic, which I more than understand, I only wanted to help."

"I know that." He nodded once. "Like you, I saw myself on every page. Between the lines in each paragraph. It was if he knew me."

"And what did you learn?"

"That I am not insane." He exhaled and savored the liberating declaration. "That thousands of soldiers, regardless of rank, disability, or background, suffer the same symptoms, and it is an enormous relief to know that I am not an oddity. I am not alone." Anthony leaned forward and rested his elbow to his knee. "Until yesterday, when I examined Larrey's deductions, there was always the smallest amount of uncertainty, given I assessed myself. Since my father seemed so insistent, I presumed there could be a kernel of truth to his position.

That I might just be unhinged, but now I know he is mistaken."

"You are not mad, my lord. Although you are a vast deal more than a little ardent in your affections, but that is an observation, and your lack of a limb does not impair you, in that respect, as I well learned last night." She folded her arms, adopting an authoritative posture that might have worked had she not dropped the sheet and bared a single, rosy nipple. "In regard to your injury and what you witnessed in battle, you are misunderstood, and I will defend you, no matter what the world throws at us. Just let your father try to separate us. There will be a fine wake in this house."

"From the start, you believed in me, even when I didn't believe in myself. You supported me." He inclined his head and studied her delicate features. "Instead of giving up on me, you sought knowledge to understand me. Had the storm not triggered a response, I may have been able to practice Larrey's suggestions on managing my symptoms. However, I would have remained oblivious to his solutions had you not brought them to my attention, and I am forever in your debt, but I may have something to offer in modest repayment, compared to your priceless gift, if you will wait here."

"Anthony, you owe me nothing." She reached for her robe. "I promise, I enjoyed last night. Indeed, I shall never forget it."

"Stay where you are." He snatched the garment from her grip. "And don't get dressed."

"But Emily should be here, in an hour or so, with our morning meal." She cast a lopsided grin. "Would you have me break my fast sans clothing?"

"Of course not." Halfway to the armoire, he halted. "But let us not entirely abandon the idea."

"Scandalous," she replied.

"And yet you appear interested." He chuckled. After turning the key, he opened one side of the hand-carved chest and drew a velvet covered box from between a stack of neatly folded shirts. "I was saving this to commemorate the night we consummated our vows. I had no inkling it would occur under such inauspicious circumstances."

"Don't say that, because it was truly memorable for me." She scooted to the center of the bed, and he perched at the edge of the mattress and handed her the parcel. "Whatever it is, I love it, already."

"I hope so." Tension built in the pit of his belly. "Because I moved heaven and earth to purchase it for you."

"You are thoughtful." She lifted the lid and gasped. "Oh, Anthony. It is magnificent. Never have I seen anything so beautiful."

"They are but fancy baubles." He traced the curve of her cheek with his finger. "You are beautiful."

"You are too kind, my lord, but I am not sure I can accept something so extravagant." From a bed of cotton, Arabella retrieved a necklace, the centerpiece of a parure comprised of a matching bracelet, earrings, brooch, stomacher, ring, and diadem boasting large, oval faceted sapphires accented by green chrysoberyl and diamonds set in precious gold filigree. "And you have me at a disadvantage, because I have naught to give you."

"My dear, you gave me your most precious gift, and you gave me peace of mind. Also, it is my duty, as your husband, to dress and adorn you." He longed to kiss her, even as he cautioned himself against getting her with child. "I am told the jewels were once worn by Grand Duchess Anna Petrovna of Russia."

"They are magnificent." The look with which she favored him almost brought him to tears. "I shall treasure them, always."

"I am pleased they meet with your approval."

"Does this mean you are no longer vexed with me?" she asked in a small voice. "I am forgiven for hiding Larrey's book from you?"

"My sweet wife, I admit I was disappointed—"

"You were furious with me."

"I concede that point, and I regret it. Perhaps I overreacted. If I may, permit me to explain." He scooted closer, so he could hold her hand. "From the moment we met, you have planted your loyalties firmly in my favor. I knew it when you stood in the window of the drawing room in your family's home, after I rudely walked out on you. When you stared at me through the glass, my insides stirred. You touched me without actually touching me, and I found that infinitely more unnerving than our forced engagement. I suppose I knew then that there was something between us, even though I tried to deny it."

"I felt it, too." She nodded. "And that belief set my course, from the start."

"Because you had faith in me, I had faith in you." He squeezed her fingers. "That you kept a secret, however well-intended, from me hurt more than you realize. I need you in my corner, because often it seems as though you are the only person on which I can depend. I count on you for the unvarnished truth, in all enterprises."

"That has never changed, and you have my solemn assurance that I shall never again conceal anything from you. I am truly sorry I disappointed you." A tear trickled down her cheek, and he cursed himself. "However, you are mistaken, because I am not your lone supporter. The Mad Matchmakers champion your cause, too. They would follow you, anywhere."

"I will not dispute that, but no one knows me like you know me. After last night, and the intimacy we shared, that is doubly so." She choked on a sob and bowed her head, but he cupped her chin and held her gaze. "Now I've made you cry." A knock at the door halted his attempt to make amends, but he would not be deterred. "Hell and the Reaper, can we not enjoy an uninterrupted interlude? Who is it?" he barked with unveiled impatience.

"It is Emily, my lord," the maid called from the sitting room, and he rained silent invective on her person. "Breakfast is served. Shall I pour her ladyship a cup of tea?"

"Her timing is perfect," he said to Arabella. "No, thank you," he responded to Emily. "We will tend ourselves and ring to have the dishes cleared. You are dismissed."

"Yes, my lord." Faint footfalls signaled the maid's exit, and he stood.

"My lord, there is something I must tell you." His bride inhaled a shaky breath. She opened her mouth and then closed it. "I care for you."

"I know you do." He mulled putting into words what she did for him. How and what she made him feel.

Reflecting on the current circumstances, and what passed between them, they had to reaffirm their commitment to each other. He needed it, and so did she, and he knew of no better way to show her what she meant to him. After tugging on the belt of his robe, he shrugged free of the swath of black silk. With a delightful blush coloring her face, she peered at him.

"Anthony, what are you about?" she asked in a whisper.

"Correcting a gross miscarriage of husbandly duty, enchanting Arabella." Lifting the covers, he eased beside her, balancing on his elbow, and she rested her palms to his shoulders. "Now I am going to make love to you as I should have, as it should have been for your first time."

A GENTLE SUMMER breeze whistled and thrummed through the thorny hedges, as Arabella clutched Anthony's arm. On that glorious morning, they strolled through the maze, sharing ideas or assessments of Larrey's work, as had become their routine after breaking their fast. Given their confinement, they spent every moment of every day, together, and she loved it.

"I was wondering what you thought of Larrey's argument that men suffering from nostalgia are neither homesick nor malingerers." Her husband peered over his shoulder, at Emily and one of Shaw's henchmen, who followed at a discreet distance. There were others nearby, waiting to pounce if Anthony or Arabella took a single wrong step, so they stayed on the path. "We are not mentally infirm or weak-willed milquetoasts. And I take offense to the universal assumption that we are afflicted with lifelong character defects or, worse, cowardice."

"Never thought that for an instant, and you are no coward," she assured him. It was to their good fortune that they were quite thrown together, because such proximity fostered a spirit of fellow feeling they might never have otherwise experienced in the beginning of their marriage. "To have survived the horrors of war, you would have to be uncommonly strong. I suspect it is ignorance of the lingering effects of continuous battle, which is an important distinction, and how to treat our fighting men, that leads to such impractical therapy and medicaments. It makes no sense to drown a tormented soldier in laudanum."

"Or to administer regular beatings." He winced. "To inflict physical pain strikes me as the cruelest blow, which would only intensify the associative agony. Instead, Larrey recommends regular rotation of troops, to avoid constant exposure to military action. I'm not sure how that would work, in a practical sense, but it is worth a try, if only to spare the wounded additional torment."

"When we return to London, you should meet with someone in the Ministry of Defense or the Royal Academy." An unforgiving wave of nausea rose in the back of her throat, and she halted. Covering her mouth with her hand, she closed her eyes and inhaled deeply through her nose. "Oh, dear."

"Again?" Anthony inquired with an undercurrent of concern. How she adored his expressions of solicitude. In the darkness, while he slept, she told herself he cared for her, even though he neglected to say as much. "Perhaps, we should return to the house."

"No." She swallowed hard, and the world tilted. Spreading her legs, she splayed her arms to avoid falling flat on her bottom. "It will pass."

"We have walked long enough, and I am not willing to risk your health for a bit of fresh air." When he tried to turn her toward the back parlor, from whence they exited the main residence, she resisted. "Maybe we should ask Dr. Shaw to examine you. What if you are ill?"

"I would sooner trust a chimney sweep to perform surgery." That reply garnered a healthy laugh from her husband, and how she loved the carefree sound. So much had changed in his demeanor since their arrival at Sanderstead that she almost felt a sense of gratitude toward his father. Almost. "But I would sit on the stone bench overlooking the fountain, if you are amenable."

"Lady Rockingham, I am at your service." Despite his claim, he seemed preoccupied, because he didn't look at her. When they navigated the hedgerow arch, shielding them from the ever-present guards, she expected him to sneak a quick kiss, but he escorted her straight to the flagstone walkway. "Is it possible that last night proved too much for you? I mean, I was deuced rough. Did I hurt you?"

"I beg your pardon?" She knew exactly to what he referred, and nothing about it injured her. "Apart from my initial hesitance, because I never conceived of any such position, and nary a book mentioned it, you gave me naught but pleasure, as always. Had I experienced any discomfit, or had I not wanted to participate in what you must admit is one of your more inventive maneuvers, I would have declared such reservation. However, after you explained your objective, and we cushioned my knees with a pillow, I was quite comfortable. While I do not believe the table was ever intended for that purpose, you are nothing if not resourceful, because you have transformed every unexceptionable piece of furniture in our chamber into a means to demonstrate your ingenuity and virility."

"Is that a compliment?" He led her to the bench, where she sat and smoothed the skirt of her sprig muslin dress. "Not that I require any."

"Liar." She giggled and admired his sun-kissed brown hair, which harkened a comparison with his evening brandy, which he took after dinner, sitting beside the hearth, with her firmly planted in his lap. "But I wish you would cease your attempts at abstinence, however noble, because I cannot sleep due to your tossing and turning when you forgo intimacy, and then I get no rest when you resume physical relations."

"I am trying to do right by you and thwart my father, but you are impossible to resist." Anthony rolled his eyes and groaned. "And that nightgown you wore to bed, last night, should come with a warning. How am I supposed to restrain myself when you dangle such delectable bait?"

"Well, what do you expect?" She shrugged and laughed, as she recalled his reaction when she emerged from behind the screen. "You schooled me in the ways of desire, such that I wager I could teach my mother a thing or two, and I'm supposed to stand as the chaste debutante? It had been almost a sennight. Who is the past master and who is the pupil, my naughty lord?"

"You have me there." He motioned with his head. "Emily approaches."

"Oh?" Arabella glanced toward the house and waved a greeting. "She and I are becoming fast friends, but I have not brought up the prospect of dispatching a letter since last month. I don't want to rouse suspicion or, worse, alienate her."

Indeed, she extended considerable effort getting to know the reserved but affable servant. A good-natured soul, Emily was loyal to a fault. While Arabella needed the shy domestic's help, she genuinely liked the provincial ragamuffin. When the ordeal ended, she planned to take Emily to London, so the maid would avoid any retribution and an unknown fate.

"My lord. My lady." Emily curtseyed. "Cook asks me to inform you that the noon meal is prepared. Dr. Shaw says you may dine on the terrace, if you prefer." Then she glanced from side to side and stepped closer. In a hoarse tone, she said, "But I suggest you remove to your chambers, so I can assess the torn hem you mentioned yesterday."

"A torn—oh, yes. The hem." Something was wrong, because Arabella required no seamstress, and she peered at Anthony. "My lord, the sun is rather warm today. If it is all right with you, I prefer to return to our quarters."

"Of course." He furrowed his brow and patted the back of her hand. "Shall we, my dear?"

In silence, they strolled through the topiary garden, posing as a besotted couple, to the terrace door. Yet, she was wound tight as a clock spring. Inside, they crossed the parlor and walked into the hall. In the foyer, they turned left, just as the long case clock chimed its dulcet melody, and ascended the stairs.

A footman rounded a corner, and Emily said, "Their lordships will take the noon meal in their sitting room. Please, tell Cook."

"Yes, ma'am." The footman bowed and rushed to the landing.

At the entrance to their private apartment, a guard sat in a chair. As Anthony and Arabella neared, the henchman stood and opened the door. She never acknowledged her jailer, because he deserved no notice or respect.

After navigating the sitting room, Emily waved Anthony and Arabella into the inner chamber. At last, the maid faced them.

"My lord and my lady, I have given much thought to your confinement and your wish to contact your family, and if you write a letter, now, I shall collect it after you take lunch and post it, myself, in the morning." Emily bit her bottom lip and shuffled her feet. "I believe it best for you to leave Sanderstead, as soon as possible, and I am willing to help you escape."

"You are scared." Arabella glanced at her husband and then back to the servant. "What has happened to frighten you?"

"It is Dr. Shaw." The maid wrung her fingers, and Arabella's thoughts raced. "He does not have your best interests at heart, and he has the morals of a gotch-gutted toss pot." The maid shrieked and covered her mouth. "I beg your pardon, your lordships."

"It is all right, Emily." Anthony pulled Arabella into the crook of his arm. "Pray, continue."

"While I knew of his plans for Lord Rockingham, and I do not support Dr. Shaw's conclusions, it is what he intends for Lady Rockingham that most concerns me. I cannot, in good conscience, live with myself if I allow him to succeed." The footman entered the sitting room, and Emily stretched tall. "Leave the tray on the table, and I shall serve their lordships."

"As you wish." The footman bowed and retraced his steps.

"My lady, forgive my indelicacy, but Dr. Shaw asks every month if you bleed, and he tracks your habits." When Arabella gasped, Emily blinked, and her fingers shook as she smoothed her hair and straightened her white cap. "Worry not, because I told him you have, even though you have not used the rags in more than a month."

The world tilted in that moment, and Arabella's ears rang like the bells in a Wren steeple. At her side, Anthony tensed. In her mind, she counted the weeks, and her knees buckled. The upset stomach. The nausea. The general feeling of weakness in the morning. It all made sense in light of Emily's observation.

"You are with child." Anthony put Arabella's immediate thoughts into words. "That is why you fell ill."

"Did it not occur to you?" Emily asked in an unnaturally high pitch. She bowed her head and cleared her throat. "Again, forgive my discourtesy, my lady."

"To be honest, no." But she should have known, given Anthony's nocturnal games, and it wasn't as though she knew nothing of the consequences of their behavior. "I presumed we were safe, because we were not consistent in our...*activities.*"

"My lady, I change your linens." Emily averted her stare and said in a low voice, "I knew it was a possibility."

"Oh, good heavens, how could I have missed it." Well, it was no great mystery. Although Arabella could count, she focused her attentions on her husband in the months since they were confined at Sanderstead. Her days were spent either perusing the library or reviewing Larrey's book. She never spared a second thought for the unused strips of fabric. "What can we do?"

"Wait, because there is more." Anthony rested his hand on his hip. "Emily, you mentioned that Shaw has plans for Lady Rockingham. What can you tell us?"

"Well, one of my duties is dusting the library and the study, and what falls under my eyes falls under my eyes, if you take my meaning." The maid checked over her shoulder and then looked at Arabella. "I found a letter from Dr. Shaw to His Grace. In it, he advised His Grace of a new plan. After Lord Rockingham is locked away in an asylum, and Lady Rockingham increases, Dr. Shaw intends to supervise Lady Rockingham's confinement and the babe's birth. Her ladyship will not be returning to London, even after providing an heir."

The room seemed to spin out of control, and Arabella feared she might swoon.

"Bastard," Anthony muttered under his breath and supported her. "This cannot happen. I will never allow that blackguard to put his hands on you."

"Neither will I, Lord Rockingham." Emily folded her arms. "Since you came to Sanderstead, your lordships have been naught but kind to me. You speak to me like a grown person and not a child, and for that I am grateful. But Lady Rockingham has bestowed upon me the honor of her friendship, and I could not call myself a friend if I stood by and let Dr. Shaw have his way."

"Thank you, Emily." Moved by the lofty speech, Arabella fought tears and guilt, because she deliberately manipulated the young woman. "You are a right and true friend. What do you recommend?"

"First, you must write your letter." Emily squared her shoulders. "There is only one problem. The post could take a sennight to deliver the correspondence to your family, but a messenger could take it straightaway."

"Then we use a messenger," Anthony replied. "Do you know someone?"

"I do, my lord." Emily compressed her lips, and again Arabella sensed a problem. "Mr. Parker, the local merchant who supplies the estate. He rides to London, every sennight, to purchase excess goods and produce on the docks, but he requires payment."

"How much?" Arabella asked.

"My dear, I apologize, but I haven't dealt in coin since before the war." Anthony rubbed his chin and paced the length of the hearth. "But we must reach Beaulieu if we are to have any chance of success."

"My lord, my mother taught me never to leave the house without money to pay for a hack, in the event I needed to make my own way home, and I am always prepared." Arabella turned to Emily. "What is the messenger's price?"

"A guinea, my lady," the maid replied. "No more or less."

"Where is my reticule?" Arabella tapped her cheek. "The one with the seed pearls and embroidered lace?"

"The top drawer of the tallboy, my lady. Permit me to fetch it for you." The maid strode to the mahogany dresser and retrieved the item in question. As she handed Arabella the frilly indispensable, Emily said, "Have the letter ready when I return to clear the dishes from your noon meal. I will meet with Mr. Parker, tonight, and he departs on the morrow."

"I know there is one here, somewhere." Arabella sifted through the coins and located a shiny, gold guinea, which she passed to Emily. "This should satisfy Mr. Parker."

"With any luck, the missive should reach the city in the afternoon." Anthony frowned. "Now, how are we to escape? And where do we go?"

"Well, as with any cobbled together plan, we require a little luck, but I know the guards' schedule. The one named Fergus is grimy and shiftless, and he often falls asleep when he is on duty. He will be watching your door, overnight, Thursday next." Emily neared. "That is when we make our break for Weybridge, where we might meet your rescuers."

"And you will come with us, to London." Arabella clutched Emily's hands. "I will not leave you to face the consequences, when you have done us such a service."

"Thank you, my lady." The maid sniffed. "You should eat, because the food gets cold, and you must keep up your strength."

"I will." Arabella pressed a chaste kiss to Emily's cheek. "I am in your debit, my friend. And I will repay you."

"Live free and take care of your babe, and that is repayment enough, my lady." Emily curtseyed and said aloud, "Ring when you are ready for me to clear the dishes."

Too anxious to even think about eating, Arabella sat at the small table and lifted the silver cover from her plate. A healthy portion of bread, a thick slab of cold ham, a square of cheese, and grapes left her wrinkling her nose, as her belly rebelled. "I am not sure this is a good idea."

"Darling, consider our child." Anthony tugged a single grape from the bunch, bit off half and fed her the rest. "I will write to Beaulieu and have him gather the Mad Matchmakers. If necessary, we make our stand for freedom, in Weybridge."

CHAPTER FIFTEEN

T HE PROSPECT OF failure had a way of forcing a man to face his own mortality, to confront past regrets. To ponder his priorities and rank each item according to that without which he could not live, emphasizing the importance of family and love. Ah, love. It posited a curious emotion, two-fold in its power, manifesting unfathomable strength and incapacitating weakness at the same time.

At war, he knew no such impediments, because he had no wife or child. No rosy future of which to dream. Unencumbered by husbandly responsibilities, he charged the field, indifferent to the potential consequences. Never considering the cost. Unafraid of death. Death. A prospect he defied countless times. But all that changed, because Arabella's demise he could not begin to contemplate. To succeed in making his escape and ensuring Arabella and his babe's safety, Anthony held tight to the strength. Coveted it. Let it bolster his courage as they prepared to flee Sanderstead.

"She is late." His bride, bedecked in a traveling gown of lavender wool, sat on the sofa. She slapped her thighs twice and stood. Before the hearth, she paced. Then she walked to the windows and gazed at the night sky. She stopped and hugged herself. "What if something happened? What if Shaw discovered our plan? What if—"

"What if you take your ease in my lap and calm your nerves? We will be much more comfortable, together." He told himself she worried for naught, and Emily would be along, soon. They just had to be patient, although patience was a scarce commodity, at the moment. "Perhaps a sip of brandy will help?"

"It burns my nose." She wrinkled her adorable appendage, and he chuckled. He needed a distraction, and she always proved most capable at diverting his torments. "But I will take you up on your first offer, because if we delay much longer, I shall scream."

He understood the anxiety. The bone-gnawing agitation ever present. Like an old friend, the battlefield reflections flashed before him, and he closed his eyes against the barbarity. The blood. The bodies.

"Well, that will certainly garner unwanted attention." He patted his leg, and she stepped about his knees and complied with his suggestion. Soft and feminine, she was his balm. His sanctuary. His voice of reason amid the chaos that loomed in the fringes of his mind. Watching. Waiting for a moment of vulnerability to strike. "I just wish we heard something from Beaulieu. Of course, he may not have been able to send word."

"Emily said Mr. Parker assured her that he gave the letter into Beaulieu's hand, so we must believe the Mad Matchmakers ride for Weybridge, as we speak. They will not disappoint us. They will be there." How he envied her faith. Unshakeable. She rested her head to his shoulder and sighed. "Anthony, I'm frightened."

"As am I, darling." He gave her a gentle nudge and kissed her forehead. "But we must have courage. At the very least, Beaulieu knows our location and the details of our imprisonment. While I wish we had time to formulate a more reliable stratagem, wherein my friends could ride to our rescue, here, I suspect we would be grossly outnumbered, and Shaw would hold the advantage. With no reinforcements, it is likely our little rebellion would fail, so we stick with our plan."

"I know, but—oh, where is she?" Arabella bit the fleshy base of her thumb. "Talk to me. Tell me something. Anything to divert me, I beg you."

"As you wish." He glanced at the book that occupied most of their days. "Did you know Larrey saved General Blücher's son, after he was taken prisoner by the French, near Dresden?"

"Indeed?" She pressed her lips to his neck, and his senses awakened.

"Aye." He set his crystal brandy balloon on the side table and cupped her bottom. "At Waterloo, Wellington ordered our men not to fire on Larrey, because of the uncommon bravery he showed as he treated the wounded. Later, the Prussians captured him near the border, and they wanted to execute him, but a German doctor recognized Larrey. Blücher invited Larrey to dinner, gave him money, and released him."

"The man sounds too good to be true, does he not?" She ran her tongue along his jawline, and every fiber of his being honed in on her.

"He is a genuine humanitarian." Anthony caressed the crest of her ear with the tip of his nose, and she shivered. "When I found the book, I was prepared to dismiss Larrey's conclusions, because of his nationality. Given what I've read, I could not have been more wrong."

"What matters is that you know you are not infirm." She placed a series of feathery kisses along the curve of his cheek, until she hovered within striking distance. "You may be different, but you are the best of men."

With that, she claimed his mouth in a searing affirmation of her desire. She pressed on him sweet caresses and whispered words of encouragement. She told him what he did to her. How he made her feel, and he reveled in every moment of it. Delighted in her show of passion, leaving him in no doubt of her ardent admiration.

Until they were rudely interrupted.

The wrought iron bolt clicked, and they parted. The hinges creaked, as Emily pushed open the door. With care, she secured the heavy oak panel and tiptoed into the sitting room.

"Your lordships, we must go, now, without delay." The maid

waved at them. "The house is abed, and Fergus sleeps."

"You do not think we will rouse him?" Anthony asked, as he stood, carrying Arabella with him. Every nerve charged with palpable agitation, and his muscles tensed. "What if he wakes and shouts an alarm?"

"I doubt it, my lord." Emily grinned. "I laced his ale with laudanum, and the man is a pig. He snores like my grandfather, after he's had too much rum."

"Then let us away." Arabella pulled on her gloves and grabbed the bundle of items she refused to leave at Sanderstead. As they spent the day preparing for departure, it became painfully clear she did not doubt, for an instant, they would succeed. It never occurred to her that their grand scheme could founder, potentially leaving them in a far more dangerous situation. Oh, no. Not his resourceful bride. She set her mind to do something and assumed she would achieve her goal. He prayed he didn't destroy her optimism, because he dearly cherished that part of her character. "It is past due to put this dreadful affair behind us."

"All right." Emily lowered her voice. "We must take the servants' stairs to avoid discovery, because Shaw refuses to use them. He does not view himself as a member of the below stairs staff. I asked the stablemaster to prepare the wagon, because I needed to pick up Cook's order from the grocer. I have done this, before, on many occasions, so I should not have aroused suspicion."

"You are wise, as well as loyal, my friend." Arabella grasped Anthony's hand and squeezed his fingers, and it was an endearing habit he had come to rely upon and expect. "We are fortunate to have you, and we are with you. We shall take orders from you."

The maid turned the knob and slowly opened the door. She peered into the hall and glanced left and then right. After a quick nod, she led them into the wide passage. Sitting in a chair, with his arms folded and his chin resting to his chest, Fergus rattled the rooftops with an unusual, three-syllable exclamation.

Following in Emily's wake, Anthony brought up the rear, as they navigated the house in the dark. They wound their way through a maze of corridors, some faintly illuminated by wall sconces. At one point, the maid halted, and Arabella followed suit, which caused him to bump into her. She gasped, and he slipped his arm about her waist and kissed the back of her neck.

Again, Emily waved for them to trace her path.

Old demons haunted and taunted him, faceless figures emerged from various doorways, and he told himself he imagined the enemies crouching in the shadows. The urge to run proved a potent intoxicant, as familiar torments echoed in his ears, provoking and terrifying him, and he longed to flee. The only thing that stopped him was the constant thought of his wife and child. They captured his attention to the detriment of all else, and that, alone, helped him control his otherworldly urges.

In a dimly lit corner, the maid paused.

"These are the servants' stairs," Emily whispered. "There are four and ten steps, so take care not to fall."

Anthony and Arabella nodded, in unison.

With caution, they descended to the first floor, the wood boards creaking beneath their feet. As they stepped into the candlelit servants' sitting room, Anthony detected hushed voices coming from the dining area. Emily halted them with an upraised palm. Slowly, she walked the length of the hall and peered around the corner at the other end. Then she waved, frantically. Anthony scooted Arabella forward, and they continued into the kitchen.

"Over there." Emily pointed. "Through the butler's pantry, there is another hallway that leads to the servants' entrance. The wagon should be waiting, there. We will depart at a slow pace, so we do not attract attention. You must hide beneath a burlap blanket, in the back, so you are not spotted."

"We understand," Anthony replied.

Moving swift and sure, they all but ran to exit the main residence. Outside, he inhaled a deep breath and peered at the stars that twinkled like a field of diamonds in the night sky, which reminded him of the predawn hours, as he camped at Le Haye Sainte and prepared for battle. They were not free, but they were closer to their goal.

The farm wagon, hitched to a lone horse, had been parked on the pebble drive, and as Emily ran around to the opposite side to climb into the high back seat, he lifted Arabella into the box. The tattered blanket, which smelled of damp earth, had seen better years, but he was not about to complain, as his wife reclined, and he pulled her into the crook of his arm.

Tension built, and the cavalry bugle blared in his brain. In his mind, the infantry drummer beat the *pa rum pum pum pum*, and the troops formed the line. Cannons fired a rapid salvo, the explosions ripping open large gashes in the ground. Reducing men to naught but unrecognizable bits and pieces of flesh and bone.

It wasn't real.

It was a symptom of the horrors he witnessed. He knew that. He understood that. Shaking himself, he blinked a few times and flexed his jaw. Again and again, he told himself he was safe. He was with his marchioness, and they drove for Weybridge.

The big guns silenced. The mortars vanished. The drums faded. The soldiers disappeared.

"Stay down." Facing forward, Emily clucked her tongue and flicked the reins. The wagon lurched forward and rocked in a repetitive rhythm. "We are rounding the side of the house."

"Do you see anyone," he asked, as Arabella clung to him. He stole a quick kiss.

"No, my lord." The maid glanced at them. "We approach the hedges, which provide some shelter, but I suggest you remain where you are until we have cleared the gates."

"Of course." He shifted, and Arabella drew him near and kissed him.

"Better?" she inquired with a knowing smile. "You know I am with you."

"I know." While she said naught, she knew the agony he fought. He bent his head and claimed another kiss, because he needed her. "And you? Are you anxious to get home?"

"What do you mean?" Arabella rubbed her nose to his and caressed his cheek. "Wherever we are together, that is home, my lord."

"Even here?" He chuckled, and the last of the harbingers dissipated. "Huddled in the back of a farm wagon, beneath a smelly burlap blanket?"

"Even here, my darling husband." With her teeth, she grazed his chin. "But worry not, because it will all be over soon. And one day, we will tell our children of our adventure and laugh about it, I promise."

He hadn't the heart to dispel her notion or disillusion her. He could only hope she was right.

"Your lordships, we have passed the gates." Emily urged the horse into a canter. "If only we make it to Weybridge."

ARABELLA ROLLED ONTO her back and rubbed her eyes. When she reached for Anthony, she grasped nothing. Alert in an instant, she lurched upright and discovered the wagon parked before a quaint building marked with a sign that read: Weybridge Inn. They made it. They found their freedom in the town where old tradition claimed Julius Caesar crossed the Thames.

"Are you all right, my lady?" Emily asked, as she still perched in the high back seat. "Is there anything I can do for you?"

"I'm fine." Arabella yawned. "Where is his lordship?"

"He went to find a friend." The maid stretched tall. "And he bade me not disturb your slumber, given your condition."

"Emily, I am with child. I am not dying." Arabella craned her neck and peered over the edge of the box. There was no sign of her husband. "How long has he been gone? It will be dawn, soon."

"Do not fret, my lady." Emily glanced over her shoulder, as if she were on guard for a sudden attack. "I am sure we will evade Shaw and his men, should they pursue us. They would have had to navigate the same muddy roads that slowed our progress."

"True." Still Arabella could not escape the feeling that they remained vulnerable to discovery and recapture. That prospect she could not abide, as it was doubtful the doctor would keep his prisoners together. Once Shaw discovered she increased, he would send Anthony to an asylum, and she might never see him again. She could not allow that to happen. "But I would just as soon depart for London, even if we must journey in the wagon."

"My lady, I understand your hurry, but it would be a difficult trip in the best of circumstances." Emily took Arabella's hand, as she climbed up to sit beside the servant in the high back seat. "The wagon is no place for you, right now. An extended trip could harm the baby."

"You are right." Arabella massaged her sore neck. "I am anxious to get home, to safety. If we can reach the city, we can fight the duke. He detests malicious gossip, and I would grant interviews to every newspaper and scandal sheet in town to protect Lord Rockingham."

"My lady, look." Emily pointed toward the mews. "Is that not his lordship and another gentleman coming this way?"

"It is Beaulieu." Arabella breathed a sigh of relief and waved a welcome. For the first time since they departed Sanderstead, she coveted a small glimmer of hope. "He is here. We will succeed in our escape."

"Lady Rockingham." Beaulieu bowed with his customary exaggerated flourish. "And who is the dove at your side?"

"This is Emily, my lady's maid, and you will mind your manners,

Lord Beaulieu," Arabella warned him. To Anthony, she asked, "Where were you? I woke, and you were not here."

"It is all right, darling. I was not sure where to find Beaulieu, but luck is on our side, because Weybridge has but one inn. However, it took me a while to wake him, along with his coachman and footmen, and then we had to fetch the stablemaster to hitch the horses to the traveling coach." To Beaulieu, he said, "Can you help her down?"

"Of course." Beaulieu stretched his arms and flicked his fingers. Arabella scooted toward him, and he lifted her to the walk, where she sheltered at Anthony's side. "I understand felicitations are in order."

"Thank you. I am uncontrollably excited." Instinctively, she hugged her belly as she scanned the immediate vicinity. "Where are the other Mad Matchmakers?"

"Indisposed, I am afraid." He frowned. "Greyson resides at his beach cottage. Lord Michael and Lord Warrington remain in the country. It was a stroke of good fortune that I was in London, overseeing the renovations of my new townhouse. Otherwise, your letter would not have reached me. Given the pressing nature of your situation, I thought it best to depart for Weybridge, immediately. However, I did post correspondence to the others, asking them to journey to London, prior to taking my leave of the city. Since I decamped four days ago, they should be there, when we arrive."

"That is most welcome news." A stiff breeze rustled her hair, and she shivered. "It is quite chilly tonight."

"I think it is almost morning." Anthony took her by the elbow. "Let us wait inside the inn, where it is warm. The stablemaster will bring the coach around when it is ready."

The care with which her husband tended her did much to calm her nerves, and she accepted his proffered escort. Telling herself they would make their break, she believed they would find safe haven in London, where they would challenge the Duke of Swanborough's actions.

Inside the charming inn, an innkeeper stood behind a tidy counter. He smiled and dipped his chin, as they crossed the foyer and walked into a small sitting room, where a fire burned in the large hearth, and Anthony led her to an overstuffed chair. From a well-used sofa, he drew a lap blanket, which he tucked about her legs. Then he bent and kissed her forehead.

"Thank you, my lord." He winked, and she noted the lines of strain about his eyes. She wished she could spare him the stress of their misadventure, but his father left them no choice. In silence, she vowed the duke would pay for his affront. She didn't know when or how, but she would exact recompense for the suffering he caused Anthony.

Beaulieu rested his elbow atop the mantel and motioned for Anthony to join him. Together, they huddled, whispering and gesturing about what she did not know, and she strained to hear them. At the front window, Emily perched, watching for the coachman.

"Would the lady like a refreshment?" the kindly innkeeper asked. "We have ale, or I can have my wife prepare a pot of tea."

"I appreciate the offer, but I am quite content," Arabella replied with a smile. "You have a delightful establishment, sir."

"Thank you, my lady." He bowed. "But I am Jones. If there is anything you require, you have but to ask."

Quiet fell on the pleasant inn, save the tick-tock of a clock on the wall. The constant rhythm lulled her into a dreamlike state. Arabella stretched out her hands and warmed them before the roaring blaze, and once again sleep beckoned. Relaxing, she closed her eyes and sighed.

"Lord Rockingham, there are men on horseback, riding down the lane" Emily shouted. "I recognize them. They are Shaw's men."

Arabella came alert and flew upright, and her heart hammered in her chest. Fear traipsed her spine, and she tossed aside the blanket. As Anthony and Beaulieu rushed to the window, Arabella leaped from the chair.

"Bloody hell, it is the dastardly cavalry." Anthony cast a worried glance in her direction. "And there are too many to fend off."

"Look there." Beaulieu pointed. "A rig joins them."

Arabella fought fast rising nausea and clutched her throat. They had not traveled so far and risked so much to lose the fight, and she would not cede the battle. Resolved not to panic, she gathered her wits and searched her mind for a solution, one that would see them safely beyond Shaw's influence.

"It is Shaw." Anthony gritted his teeth. "We are heavily outnumbered." To the innkeeper, her husband asked, "Is there a servants' entrance?"

"Aye, my lord." Jones stepped aside and extended his arm. "Past the kitchen and through the storeroom."

"If anyone asks, we were never here," Anthony asserted. "I shall see you are handsomely rewarded for your assistance."

"I heard nothing." Jones averted his gaze. "And no reward is necessary, my lord."

With that, Anthony grabbed Arabella by the hand and rushed past the counter. They walked through the somewhat rustic kitchen and into the crowded pantry, which was stacked high with crates and barrels. A small door opened into the mews, where the stablemaster brought a third horse to harness. When he spied them, he tipped his hat.

"Almost done, Lord Beaulieu." The stablemaster adjusted a leather strap.

"An additional crown is yours, if you can finish the job in half the time." Beaulieu tossed a coin into the air. "I must away, now."

"Aye, sir." The stablemaster ran back into the stable.

"Beaulieu, you have to admit we cannot outrun men on horseback, and Shaw drives a curricle." Anthony pulled her into the crook of his arm, and she leaned against him. "They would easily overtake your heavier traveling coach, and what chance would we stand against their number?"

Arabella didn't like the sound of that. Something in his voice gave her a sense of foreboding, and she tried to ignore what her instincts all but screamed.

"Are you serious about this, major?" Beaulieu addressed Anthony by his military rank, and it was not lost on her. "I thought your plan a contingency, in the event of an emergency."

"This is an emergency, and I know of no other way." With his thumb, he caressed her cheek. "My wife and unborn child take precedence, but I fear Shaw may still catch you, unless you divert and take an alternate route to the city."

Puzzled by the curious conversation, Arabella tried to discern her husband's meaning. After all, he was a priority for her.

"Are you unwell, my lady?" Emily inquired, but Arabella ignored the maid.

"Let us ask the stablemaster." Beaulieu flagged the grey-haired, bespectacled groom. "I say, is there another path to London that does not involve the turnpike or traverse Shepperton? Perhaps, a small town to the west?"

"Aye, sir." The stablemaster tightened the bellyband on the fourth and final horse. "You can take the road at the opposite end of the alley, which leads southeast, to Hersham. It will add about a half a day to your journey, though."

"There is our advantage." Anthony compressed his lips. "You must push for Hersham, while Shaw and his men will undoubtedly take the turnpike, north, to Shepperton. By the time they realize their mistake, you should be out of danger."

"And what of you?" Beaulieu grimaced and shifted his weight. "You are a brilliant military strategist, and I submit this is war, albeit of a different sort. Is there not another option?"

"No." Anthony stiffened and her suspicions roused. "If Shaw takes my wife, he holds the power, and I would submit to anything to protect her and my heir. We may as well yield the field, and I cannot allow that, when I might forestall catastrophe."

Thoroughly confused, Arabella watched the events before her play like a scene at a theatre on Drury Lane, and none of it inspired confidence. Why did Anthony speak as though he wouldn't be traveling with her?

"My lord, you frighten me, and before I leap to unsupported conclusions weaved of whole cloth, I would have you explain yourself." She shifted so she could hug him about the waist. "You are going with us, so there is no cause for alarm. Shaw cannot harm me when I have you to defend me. Is that not what you mean?"

"My sweet girl." His grip tightened, but it did little to calm her nerves. "We cannot let you fall into Shaw's clutch else he holds all the cards. No matter what happens, if one of us escapes, we can ultimately defeat Shaw and my father, because I know you would fight for me."

"To my last breath," she replied without hesitation. "I would move heaven and earth for you, my lord."

"Oh, I'm counting you." He smiled. "Because you are quite the *force majeure* when you are determined, and no one knows better than I. I wager you will give my father quite a thrashing."

"It would be my pleasure, but it will not come to that, because we depart Weybridge, together." She clung to him in desperation, because her instincts told her she would soon lose his company. "You worry for naught, my lord." To Beaulieu, she said, "Pray, tell him." The usually boisterous Lord Beaulieu replied not, and the hair at the back of Arabella's neck stood on end. She met her husband's stare, and the resolve in his eyes proclaimed a terrible truth. In a bare whisper, she uttered his name, "*Anthony.*"

"Darling, we cannot escape Shaw's men without a diversion. Someone must distract them." He rested his chin to the crown of her head, and she fought tears. "If I lure them in one direction, you can flee in the other, and it would be too late when they discovered their mistake. You would be free and halfway to London, well beyond their reach."

"No." She gripped the lapels of his coat. "I will not let you go. I will not let you sacrifice yourself for me."

"I do it for you and the babe that grows in your belly." He kissed her forehead. "I'm afraid we have no choice in the matter. It is that or we return to Sanderstead, where Shaw is sure to separate us once your pregnancy becomes apparent. And we know not what Shaw's henchmen would do to Emily and Lord Beaulieu. There is too much at stake, and I will not risk their lives when they are imperiled because they helped us."

"I do not accept that surrendering yourself is the only answer to our quandary." She yanked hard to draw him closer. "What if we—"

"My lord, your rig is hitched," the stablemaster called, as the coachman and footmen joined their party.

"Rockingham, if we are going to make a run, we must go, now," Beaulieu stated, and she rained all manner of invective on his miserable hide. To the coachman, he hollered, "We drive south, to Hersham, and you will stop for no one."

"Aye, sir." The coachman climbed atop the seat.

"My lady, and you are my lady, you must have faith that we will meet again." Anthony nudged her with his nose, and again she met his gaze. "You have courage. And spirit. And charm. And passion such as I have never known. I want you to know something, before we part. The months I spent locked in a room with you were the happiest of my life, and you must know how ardently I love you. Indeed, I am in love with you. I have loved you since you stood in the window at your parents' house, watching me on the street. You saw something me, and you said as much. Well, I saw something in you, too. My only regret is that I did not make my declaration sooner. I should have told you, every day we were together."

"Oh, Anthony, I love you, too." Now the unchecked tears flowed.

"Like you, I felt a connection. I knew it then, even though I claimed the opposite. That is why I supported you."

"I know, my love." He brushed his lips to hers. "Because you are my brave, brilliant marchioness." Then he mingled his tongue with hers, and she opened to him. Welcomed him. Scored her nails to his neck and savored the warmth that pervaded her flesh. Anything to delay their separation.

Bereft of reticence or apprehension, he favored her with a soul-stealing kiss. And then she detected an altogether different emotion. Elusive and foreign. She licked and suckled his beautiful mouth, and then she identified the unwanted expression. It was a farewell. In that moment, Anthony lifted his head and set her at arm's length, as she mustered a protest that died in her throat.

"I love you, Arabella, Marchioness of Rockingham. Never forget that." He tucked a stray wisp of hair behind her ear. Before she could respond, he lowered his chin, and his features hardened. "Take her."

Lord Beaulieu lifted her from her feet and covered her mouth with his hand, when she screamed. With both hands, she reached for Anthony, but he retreated beyond her grasp. Emily pushed aside a footman and held open the coach door, and Beaulieu shoved Arabella into the squabs.

"Drive on, and make haste." Beaulieu caught Arabella about the waist when she tried to escape. "Don't even try it. I promised the major I would guard you with my life, and I will do so, whether you like it or not."

"How could you let him do it?" she asked, as she pressed her face to the window. Anthony sprinted down the alley, the distance between them increasing with each successive step. Was there anything so sad as watching someone she loved run away from her? "They will hurt him."

"Not without you they won't." Beaulieu drew down the shade and pulled a flintlock pistol from his coat pocket. "Without you, they cannot touch him." The stress of the day caught up with her, wreaking havoc on her faculties, and she collapsed against his shoulder, in a fit of tears. "What is this? I thought you a woman of uncommon strength, not given to flaps or starts. Was I wrong?"

"What?" She sniffed, as everything inside her rebelled against reality. "What did you say?"

"Rockingham sings your praises, and you even had me convinced that you possess rare sagacity for the female sex." Beaulieu inclined his head and smirked. "Was I mistaken, given your predictable but woefully disappointing hysteria?"

"How dare you." She righted her skirts and moved to the opposite bench, to sit beside Emily, who clutched her hand, and rage charged the fore. "Who are you to lecture me, when my husband has been stolen from me?"

"Which is why you should be focused on how we will get him back, instead of blubbering like a child." The cocky earl snorted. "Of course, you probably have no idea where to begin, so I shall end up devising a plan, as per usual. Men are far more rational than women."

"Rot you, Beaulieu. I know precisely where to commence the fight." With renewed purpose, Arabella collected her thoughts and plotted her bearing with lethal precision. She would retrench. She would strategize. And she would win the day. "Well, that is if I can convince my parents of Shaw's ultimate goal, because Swanborough told my father I would be permitted to return to the city, after giving birth. Without proof, he might never believe his friend deceived him."

"My lady, I have Dr. Shaw's letter." From a small haversack, Emily produced an envelope. "When he asked about it, I explained that I threw several ruined sheets of stationery in the refuse, when I cleared the blotter, and I must have tossed his correspondence, by mistake."

"Oh, Emily, I could kiss you." Arabella unfolded the crisp parchment, and her skin crawled when she read Shaw's intentions. "Heed my words, Lord Beaulieu. This travesty will not stand. I shall bring down hellfire and brimstone on the Duke of Swanborough, the likes of which he has never known, and he will rue the day he took my husband from me. I swear on the life of my unborn child, I will win justice for Anthony." Lowering her chin, she inhaled a deep breath. "When I am done, the whole of London will know my wrath."

CHAPTER SIXTEEN

A DULL ACHE throbbed in Anthony's head, as he stirred and opened his eyes. Resting on his back, he gazed at the ceiling and noted cracked and chipped plaster. Confused, he clung to remnants of his memories, which came to him in bits and pieces that made no sense. The imprisonment at Sanderstead. The nefarious Dr. Shaw. The hard drive to Weybridge. The agony in Arabella's expression, when he bade her farewell. Images flooded his consciousness, and he sat upright and surveyed his surroundings.

Once white walls now sported countless yellow stains and marks. A rustic, stone floor covered in muck provided the source of a stomach-turning stench. Wrought iron bars blocked the window and reinforced the door. Eerie screams echoed from beyond his room. One thing was certain. He was no longer confined at Sanderstead.

After Beaulieu departed with Arabella and Emily, Anthony confronted Shaw and his men. It went about as well as he expected. For a while, he led them on a merry chase throughout Weybridge, given he could sprint and dart, on foot, between buildings. Eventually, the villains ran him aground and took him prisoner.

While Shaw demanded Anthony reveal Arabella's whereabouts, he refused, and the doctor did exactly as Anthony predicted. Shaw ordered his men to pursue Beaulieu's rig on the road to Shepperton. And then someone struck Anthony from behind, and his world collapsed into a black vortex.

He could only pray his wife made it to London, safely.

When he tried to move, an odd heaviness pinned his ankle, which had been shackled to the wood frame of a rudimentary bed. There were four, in total, all of which bore a single occupant. The men appeared to sleep, and he stilled to avoid disturbing his neighbors, because he knew not whether they were friend or foe. He scooted to the edge of the mattress, and the hefty chain scraped and clanked.

"You are awake." The party in the next bunk rolled onto his side, the worn structure creaking beneath his weight. With visible injuries in various states of healing about his face, the stranger saluted. "Welcome to hell. I am Charles Lumley, fifty-second Light Infantry. A mortar blast took both my legs at Waterloo."

"Henry Whetham, thirty-second Foot," stated the wounded individual directly across from Anthony. Like Charles, Henry evidenced signs of abuse. "Lost my leg at Quatre Bras."

"Thomas Pulteney, twelfth Light Dragoons." He dipped his chin, and Anthony noted the black eye. "Although I am physically hale and whole, I am told I suffer brain fever from prolonged exposure to battle."

"So what brings you to Little Bethlam?" asked Charles. "Or should I inquire after who brings you to the British Army's dirty secret?"

"Little Bethlam?" Anthony reflected on the name but could recall no past reference. However, he knew of its namesake, a notorious asylum built atop a sewer that often overflowed into the building. The patients confined in squalor, provided naught but piss-pots and left to wallow in their own excreta, with no suitable food or clothing. Doctors who traded in lunacy to amass a small fortune, never helping anyone but themselves. "I have never heard of such a place."

"That is because the only ones familiar with it are those locked within its walls." Henry snorted and rolled his eyes. "As well as our jailers and the blackguard that has the nerve to call himself a doctor, George Shaw. From what I have learned, Shaw has the favor of some powerful lords with deep pockets. He holds us prisoner and drains our families of their money, promising we are much improved but not quite well enough to rejoin society. If only our relations pay for additional therapy, he guarantees he can cure us of our ailments."

"The man ought to be charged with crimes against humanity." Anthony pondered Shaw's arrogance and temper. "I have no doubt he is dangerous, and one of the first actions I will take when I am free of this place is to see him brought to justice."

"Watch yourself with Shaw, because he has gained formidable power. The Parliamentary Committee on Madhouses entrusted him with both quiescent and severely disturbed patients during the rebuild of Bethlam." Thomas shivered and hugged himself. "He loves his water torments, and he has a real taste for them. I believe hurting others gives him pleasure. Rumor has it he killed three soldiers in the lily pond, in the garden, but no one cares about us. Underestimate him at your own peril."

"We have met, and I do not doubt you." Anthony cursed the villain. "He convinced my father that I needed to be institutionalized, and he may have been persuaded by Shaw's manipulations. Following my recent marriage, Shaw took my wife and I hostage, with my father's blessing. It was only by a stroke of good fortune she was able to escape. Must confess I may have made it easy for my father to be prevailed upon by an unscrupulous doctor. I should have shared my experiences with my family. I should have told them what I witnessed and how the recollections impacted me. Instead, I shut them out, but I have to believe my father's intentions were honorable. At least, I would like to think my father acted in good faith."

"I am in a similar position." Thomas averted his stare. "I was engaged, and my fiancée and I planned to wed this Autumn. But the visions that plagued me frightened my lady, and her father reneged on our contract. After that, my grandfather had me committed."

"I am more sorry than I can say." Anthony had much in common with his bunk mates. The violent representations he could not control. The imaginary enemy waiting to pounce. The nightmares. The cold sweats. "I know what it is like to be suspected of madness. To be punished for that against which you cannot defend yourself. To be called other, because you lack, when your only fault is that you answered the call of duty."

"So, you served?" When Anthony nodded the affirmative, Henry arched a brow. "Therein lies part of the problem. Shaw did not, and he hates us for it. He punishes us for our principles and his lack thereof. The man is more brutal than any officer of my acquaintance, and I knew Picton."

"When His Majesty issued the war cry, I purchased a commission. I rode with the fifth Cavalry Brigade, seventh Hussars." Anthony glanced at his stump and frowned. "Lost my arm at Waterloo."

"The Hussars?" Charles whistled in monotone. "You must be well-connected. What is your name?"

"I am Lord Anthony, Marquess of Rockingham." The three patients glanced at each other, surprise marking their expressions, and in concert returned their scrutiny to Anthony. It was then he realized he was garbed only in a dingy cotton gown, the same as the others, and his state of undress must have undermined his credibility. "I concede it appears I am not so well-connected as you believe. What happened to my clothes?"

"They take them." Henry smacked a fist to a palm. "When I was admitted, I was stripped of all personal items. Just as they take everything from us. Our dignity. Our freedom. Our humanity."

"Your belongings will probably be sold. Shaw is a greedy bastard, and he will do whatever he can to make your confinement as miserable as possible." Thomas inclined his head. "I beg your pardon, but are you really a nobleman?"

"He is, indeed," Charles answered and smiled. "Must admit I didn't recognize you, at first, Major Bartlett. In here, we all begin to look

241

alike. That was a devil of a charge at La Haye Sainte. But I thought your elder brother held the title."

"He did." The tattered red coat, riddled with holes and singe marks, the mangled remains, almost unrecognizable, flashed before his eyes. Anthony shuddered and blinked. "John was killed at Waterloo. And the fifty-second's rout of the *Garde* should go down in history, although Wellington did not give you proper credit."

"Commiserations and my thanks. There is enough glory to go around, and Wellington's oversight in his report does not negate what we accomplished." Charles arched a brow. "I beg your pardon, but how did you end up here? That is to say, you were born into wealth and privilege. You are heir to the dukedom of Swanborough. Your family can afford the best medical professionals and treatment. Why, on earth, would they deliver you into Little Bethlam, where no one knows we exist? Where there is no salvation. There is no hope. There is only never-ending pain."

"It is doubtful your families know what you endure. I suspect they wanted to help you. In that respect, I suppose my story is much like any other." Anthony shrugged, even as Charles's words cut him to the marrow. "My father thinks me mad, because I am often beset, through no fault of my own, by nightmares and assailed by unpredictable images of battle. In hindsight, I never welcomed his support. In my struggles with memories of the carnage, I shut him out. I excluded everyone, preferring to suffer in silence."

Yet Arabella forced her way into his heart and soul, offering unfailing strength and understanding. He envisioned her, as she slept in the early morning hours, so cherubic in slumber. The way she splayed her arms, welcoming him when he made love to her. And her kisses. Ah, her kisses, which could banish the darkest thoughts from the deepest crevices of his mind.

"Who is not after surviving war." Henry punched his pillow. "Despite what Shaw claims, I submit we are not mad. We evidence symptoms of army life. We spent years on guard for enemy combatants hell bent on trying to kill us. We subsisted on meals comprised of fare no sane person would call food. We left our loved ones and all that was familiar to us to journey to the Continent, where we camped in conditions unfit for man and beast, fighting on lands that were not ours to own. And we are blamed because we exhibit lingering effects of the horrors we witnessed."

"In that I cannot argue." In that moment, Anthony remembered he was not alone. "You remind me of my friends." He sat upright. "I know you have no reason to believe me, but I promise you ours is not a lost cause. Even now, there are those working to free us, and I will not leave here without you. This I pledge on my honor as a gentleman."

"I would have it on your word, as a soldier." Thomas narrowed his gaze. "I have known no gentleman with honor."

"You have me there." Anthony chuckled.

The rasp of keys had everyone looking toward the door.

"Lively, men." Charles plopped on his pillow, and the others followed suit, so Anthony took their lead. "No matter what happens, remember, it will go better for you if you yield. If you resist, Shaw will exact blood in recompense."

The door opened to reveal two burly attendants garbed in white shirts and trousers. From a pocket, one guard produced a large key. He walked straight to Anthony's bed and unlocked the shackle.

"Dr. Shaw wishes to speak to you." None-too-gently, the surly ruffian grabbed Anthony by the back of the neck and threw him to the floor. "Get a move on, fancy pants."

"There are no ranks, here." The second thug kicked Anthony in the ribs. "We hold the advantage."

Given Charles's warning, Anthony held his tongue and scrambled to his bare feet. There would be time enough for retribution, after he was liberated. With a custodian at either side, he marched into the wide but dark hall. Screams emanated from all directions, inspiring a host of familiar vignettes.

His heart raced, and his ears rang with cannon fire. Enemy soldiers, bearing rifles and swords, emerged from the walls. Panic rose in his throat, choking him. In silence, he reminded himself that none of the images were real. They were a figment of his tortured imagination.

To fight the torments, he summoned Arabella's angelic face. He envisioned the subtle bounce of her breasts as he took her. He savored the taste of her lush lips. Then she was there, by his side. Bolstering his courage. Calming his frazzled nerves. Banishing his demons.

Slowly, he emerged from the disturbing reverie and focused on breathing. On the simple act of inhaling and exhaling in a relaxed rhythm.

"This way." The first guard struck Anthony upside the head. "If you give me any trouble, you will be lucky if you live to regret it."

At a double door entry, the blackguard pushed open a single oak panel and shoved Anthony over the threshold. In contrast with the sparse, dirty asylum, the well-appointed office boasted rich carpets and damask wall coverings, in indigo. A hand-tooled desk held pride of place between two huge windows sans bars. At right, a side table held a crystal decanter, filled with amber liquid, and six brandy balloons. At left, bookcases spanned from end to end.

"Welcome to my lair, Lord Rockingham." A leather high-back chair rotated to reveal Shaw. With his elbows perched on the armrests, he steepled his hands and sneered. "Have a seat."

"I would thank you, but I doubt I could do so with conviction." Anthony eased into one of the two matching, shield-backed Hepple-white chairs. He shifted his weight and noted a slight tic at the corner of Shaw's mouth. Resting his hand in his lap, he rolled his shoulders. "Perhaps you can tell me how long I am to be a guest in your dubious facility?"

Shaw nodded once, and a guard slapped Anthony across the face.

"You do not ask questions, Lord Rockingham." Shaw glowered. "You do as I say, when I say, or you will know my wrath." He lurched forward and slammed a fist to the blotter. "Where is Lady Rockingham? What have you done with her?"

"She is far beyond your reach, in the safety of friends who would give their life to defend her." Anthony smiled. "You may do what you wish with me, but you should know those same friends will come for me."

"You should hope you live that long." Shaw threw back his head and cackled, and gooseflesh covered Anthony. Then the doctor quieted and caught Anthony in a lethal glare. "No one makes me look like a fool. The Duke of Swanborough is not privy to Lady Rockingham's escape, and you had better pray he never discovers her little mutiny. Now, where is she?" Again, he pounded the desktop. "Answer me. Answer me, or so help me before I am done with you, you will wish you were never born."

Anthony lifted his chin but said naught.

Shaw waved.

The first blow landed to Anthony's stomach. The second caught him in the jaw and sent him flying from the chair. The taste of blood filled his mouth, as both attendants kicked him repeatedly. Relentlessly. Someone lifted him from the floor, only to knock him to the rug. His vision blurred, and the sound of rushing water filled his ears. At last, he drifted into merciful unconsciousness.

TRADESMEN AND MILKMAIDS hurried about their business. Light spilled from the windows of a bakery, the smell of fresh bread wafting in the air, and a young man drove his paper delivery cart, as the coach steered through the sleepy, pre-dawn heart of the British Empire. On the sidewalk, laborers collected discarded refuse, and stray dogs foraged for food.

To evade Shaw and his men, they drove northeast from Hersham, until they reached the turnpike and the Mile End toll gate. With her nose pressed to the glass, Arabella reflected on various appeals, to sway her father, because she would need his help to free Anthony. Her heart beat in time with the steady clip-clop of the horses, and she wrung her fingers in her lap. Then she plopped into the squabs, and at her side Emily stirred.

"Are you certain your father will be in town?" Beaulieu checked his timepiece and yawned. "Most members of the *ton* remain in the country until October."

"My father journeys to the city at the end of summer, without fail." She settled her skirts and worried her bottom lip. She crossed and uncrossed her legs. She shifted her weight. "He prefers to visit his tailor and plan his agenda for the upcoming parliamentary session, without the crowds associated with the Little Season. He will be here."

"Then let us hope he will hear our side." Beaulieu glanced at the passing storefronts, as they navigated Cheapside, and frowned. "We will need Lord Ainsworth's support, if we have any chance of succeeding. It is doubtful Swanborough will grant us an audience, but I wager he will listen to his lifelong friend. Their comradeship is the stuff of legend, and from whatever angle I approach our situation, your father is the only person with legal standing to protest Swanborough's actions. With Rockingham institutionalized, your custody should revert to your father, per the marriage contract, but he will have to challenge the duke, in court, or so I suspect. My solicitor will have more to say on the matter."

"Papa will not fail me." If she said that enough she just might believe it. Old alliances died hard, and her father often toed the line, especially when Swanborough wanted something. And the duke wanted her. "After all, his blood runs in my veins."

When the luxurious equipage turned onto Oxford Street, she

stretched her legs and tugged the hem of her sleeves. Still wearing the lavender wool traveling gown, she tucked a lock of hair behind her ear. She would have preferred to change into something more suitable to greet her parents, but Beaulieu refused to stop except for necessary conveniences.

The coach traversed Grosvenor Square and veered onto Upper Brook Street. With palms resting on her thighs, she inhaled a deep breath. She revisited her well-rehearsed lines and methodically arranged her arguments. The rig slowed to a halt before her family home, and a footman placed a stool and tugged the latch.

She should have waited for assistance, as would a proper lady. Instead, she hiked her skirts, in a scandalous display of her calves, and leaped to the sidewalk, leaving Beaulieu and Emily in her wake. She ran up the entrance stairs and knocked on the door. When no one answered, she gritted her teeth and pounded her clenched fist on the oak panel, which at last opened.

"My lady." A bleary-eyed Travers responded, as he pulled on his black jacket. "Pray, come inside."

"Where are my parents?" She pushed past him and stomped into the foyer. "Are they awake?"

"Arabella?" Mama peered from the landing and belted her robe. "What are you doing here? Is Lord Rockingham with you?"

"You do not know?" Tears welled, and Arabella sniffed. She did not want to cry. "Have you not heard, or did Papa lie to you, too?"

"I beg your pardon?" Papa appeared, just behind Mama, and they descended to the first floor. "What is the meaning of this? Why have you brought Lord Beaulieu and a stranger into our home at this hour?"

Well-composed charges and rebuttals, based in logic, always her ally, traipsed her tongue. Instead, she marched to her father and pummeled him. She beat her father for the husband she loved. She fought for her unborn babe. More than anything, she let her fists speak for her, pouring all the fear and anger from her hands, that he might know how much he hurt her.

"Arabella, control yourself." Papa caught her by her wrists, so she resorted to kicking his shins. "Will you cease your outlandish behavior, and tell me why you behave like a berserk mare."

"How could you do it?" She wrenched free. "How could you betray me, so completely?"

"I don't understand." Papa motioned to Travers. "Wake the household and prepare tea, in the drawing room."

"Oh, no." Arabella shook her head and bared her teeth. "You will not negotiate your way out of this, Father. After what I have endured in these last months, you will face me and the consequences you wrought."

"Arabella, calm yourself." Her father raked his fingers through his hair. Once her hero, her champion, he seemed so small in the cold light of day. "Sit down and tell me of what you believe I am guilty."

"You greet me with easy smiles and polite hospitality." When Beaulieu tried to draw her to the sofa, she shrugged from his grip. "Are you so certain of your innocence? You knew of Swanborough's plan for his son. You told me of it, prior to the engagement."

"Of course, I did." Papa eased into an overstuffed chair. "I would never lie to you. And, as far as I know, the terms have not changed. Lord Rockingham is to receive the best of care, and you are to be housed, as befits a marchioness, in London."

"Anthony spoke with his father prior to our marriage. They settled their disagreements, or so we thought." She paced before the windows overlooking North Audley. So many times, they gathered in the comfortably appointed room, she could navigate it with her eyes closed. The soft scent of lilac, which her mother favored, teased her nose. She admired the *chaise* upon which her father sat and read many a Christmastide story. Everything evoked fond memories, but she found no comfort. "En route to our honeymoon, we were taken captive by a disreputable doctor named Shaw."

"*What?*" Mama rushed to Arabella's side. Taking her by the hands, Mama met her stare. "I thought you were in Brighton." To Papa, Mama said, "My lord, did you know of this?"

"I was assured that my own father supported Swanborough's scheme." Arabella narrowed her stare. "What say you, Papa? Did you or did you not consent to my imprisonment?"

"I...I—that is to say, I'm not sure." Papa opened his mouth and closed it. Then he stood and glanced at Emily. "Who is this person you have brought into my house?"

"She is Emily, my lady's maid." Arabella flicked her fingers, and the dutiful servant came to stand beside her. "She has proof of Swanborough's nefarious plot." She accepted the letter from the maid. "In this correspondence, written in Shaw's own hand, he confirms the duke's intent that I remain at Sanderstead, even after delivering a child. There was to be no London residence. And my husband has been taken I know not where."

"There must be some mistake." Papa blinked like an owl. He paced and then halted. He pointed and then waved at no one. "Swanborough is my oldest and dearest friend. He has been a brother to me from the cradle. He would never deceive me."

"Swanborough is the worst of libertines." Beaulieu squared his shoulders. "He must tell us what he has done with Rockingham."

"Beggin' your pardon, my lord." Emily curtseyed. "But I know people, and Shaw is a no-good silk snatcher."

"Please, one at a time." Papa rubbed his eyes. "I am scarcely awake, and I will not have you besmirch the name of my friend, when he has done naught wrong."

"But he has, Papa. Do not take my word for it." Arabella offered the correspondence, which he accepted. "Read it for yourself."

Her father unfolded the parchment and moved near a candlestick bearing a single taper, and Mama peered over his shoulder. As he perused the missive, he squinted. When he furrowed his brow, she stepped forward.

"It is all there for you to see." She fought a lump in her throat, and the blasted tears resurfaced. Her chest tightened, as her heart bled for her father, because she never wanted to hurt him, but she had to save Anthony. "Do you deny involvement in this dastardly enterprise?"

"I deny nothing and own to nothing." Papa pressed the backs of his knuckles to his mouth. Again, he scanned the dispatch, his gaze darting back and forth. "Yet, I cannot reconcile the instructions documented herein with what I was told."

"Do you suspect me?" Arabella held a clenched fist to her bosom. "Do you accuse me of falsehood, Papa?"

"N-no. That is to say—I don't know what to think." Transfixed, he wiped his furrowed brow and licked his lips. For a pregnant moment, quiet fell on the impromptu gathering, but the tension grew thick as the London fog. "I would speak with my daughter, in private."

"Lady Rockingham, please, check your temper," Beaulieu whispered and cupped her elbow. "I know you are upset, and you have every right to be, but we need your father's support, if we are to get Rockingham back."

With nary a reply, she nodded.

Mama stepped forward. "But I want—"

"Am I not the master of this household? I said I will speak with my daughter, *alone*." With a flushed face, Papa grabbed Arabella by the arm and stomped to his study. With a swift push, he thrust her across the threshold and slammed the door shut behind him. When a reproduction of an oil portrait of Hans Holbein fell from its mount, she started. Papa eased into his high back chair and sighed. "All right, my girl. Out with it, and I will have the whole, ugly truth, no matter how unsavory."

"Papa, what I detailed in the drawing room is what happened." She neared the large desk, where her father always meted punishments, when she was a child, and perched on the corner. It was a familiar position, designed to grant her the advantage, because her father could never discipline her. "We were ambushed in our traveling coach. En route to Brighton, we discovered the doors were locked. The rig delivered us into the custody of Dr. Shaw, where we have been held, all these months."

"Why didn't you write me?" Papa tapped his fingers to the blotter. "I could have traveled to meet you and provided reassurance."

"Are you not listening to me?" She smacked her open palm to the desktop. "We were denied contact with everyone. We were locked in our bedchamber, under guard, unable to move about as we pleased." Again, she slapped the desktop. "Did you know of the duke's plan? Were you privy to his double-dealings?"

"I swear to you, I did not know of any endeavor that involved kidnapping my own daughter, else I never would have agreed to the marriage." Papa reached for her, but she withdrew. He winced and sucked in a breath. Then he pushed from the desk and stood. He walked to the window and flung back the heavy drapes. For a while, he gazed at the sky, a watercolor of vivid blue, pink, and yellow, signaling the dawn. "But I *was* aware of Swanborough's intent to remove his son to an asylum, for treatment. It was for his own good, or so I was told, and I had to protect you."

"Papa, you hosted Lord Rockingham in our home." She tugged on the sleeve of his robe, but he steadfastly refused to look at her. "He shared our dinner table. We broke bread together. Did he strike you as mad?"

Again, unending silence.

"No, he did not." Papa turned and searched her face. With his finger he traced the curve of her jaw. "You have grown into a woman, overnight, but I recall, with fondness, so many afternoons spent in reflection about some trivial scientific discovery. It has been my honor to nurture your inquisitive spirit. I should like, very much, to hear your assessment of Lord Rockingham. If I trust anyone's judgement in regard to the man's character, it is yours."

"You wish me to plead on his behalf?" When Papa indicated the affirmative, she steeled her spine and swallowed hard. "Lord Rockingham is the kindest, gentlest man of my acquaintance. I had not known him more than an hour when I determined he needed my support. He convinced me, during our courtship and brief engagement, that he suffered no mental defect. Indeed, he is human, Papa. He witnessed unspeakable horrors, at war. I submit, only an insane person could be exposed to such carnage and remain untouched. Unfeeling. It is the very symptoms upon which the Duke of Swanborough casts aspersions that mark Lord Rockingham as sane."

"You care for him." Mouth agape, Papa recoiled. "You have formed an attachment with Lord Rockingham."

"I love him, Papa. He owns me, body and soul, and there is more." She pressed a hand to her belly. "I carry his heir, and I shall go to my grave before I allow the Duke of Swanborough to take my babe from me."

Papa stumbled backward and fell into a chair. Resting elbows to knees, he cradled his head. With no acknowledgement of her, he stood and strode to his desk. From a drawer he pulled a few sheets of stationery. He snatched the pen from the inkwell and scribbled a note, which she couldn't read.

The stress of the escape, Anthony's capture, and the argument with her father stretched taut her nerves, and she broke. Arabella bent forward and sobbed.

"None of that, now." Papa rushed to provide support. To her relief, he enfolded her in his warm embrace. "None of that, my girl. It will be all right, I promise."

Still, she could not stop crying. She wept for her husband. She wept for her unborn child. She wept for the future she desperately desired.

"Oh, Papa, what am I going to do if I cannot find Anthony?" Again, she wailed, and her father stroked her hair. "I cannot abandon him to Swanborough's clutches."

"And we will not." Papa fumbled with his robe, and stuck his hands in his pockets. "Well, given I am not properly dressed to receive company, I have no handkerchief to offer you. Perhaps, it is time to rejoin the others."

"Papa, what are you going to do?" She sniffed.

"Let us discuss our next move, with our guests." Papa led her back to the drawing room, where the butler served tea. Her father thrust a letter into the manservant's grasp. "Travers, have the missive delivered into the hands of the Duke of Swanborough's solicitor. Send a footman for my representative, and have another footman fetch Dr. Handley. Tell him Lady Rockingham is indisposed and requires his services."

"Right away, my lord." Travers bowed.

Beaulieu and Emily stood and cast a glance at Arabella. She shrugged.

"And one more thing." Papa raised a finger. "Have footmen posted at all doors. No one is to enter this house without my expressed permission, and no one is to be granted an audience with Lady Rockingham, unless either myself or Lord Beaulieu is present."

"Very good, my lord." The butler hurried into the hallway.

In a short span, Ainsworth House morphed into a beehive of activity, as maids and footmen rushed in all directions. Arabella met her father's stare, and he winked. In that instant, she knew she was not alone.

"My lord, what is happening?" Mama came to stand beside Arabella. "Why do you reassign the staff?"

"Because we are going to war, my lady wife." Papa lifted his chin. "We challenge the Duke of Swanborough."

CHAPTER SEVENTEEN

A DELIGHTFUL CHERUB flitted above him, sprinkling him with gold dust. Dancing and prancing through the air, in seraph form Arabella soared. Her smile, stretched across her face, fed his soul and soothed his nerves. Her effusive laugh, bubbling with joy, filled his ears, and Anthony relaxed and sank into the mattress of his filthy bed. When his wife splayed her arms in welcome, he reached for her, and the treasured vision dissipated.

"How are you this morning, Rockingham?" Charles glanced at Anthony, winced, and quickly averted his gaze. Yes, he required no mirror to know he looked bad after Shaw's henchmen practiced their pugilist skills on his face. "This cannot be allowed to continue. You will not survive much more of Shaw's torture."

"We must get you out of here." Thomas scooted to the end of his bed and hefted the chain attached to the shackle on his ankle. "I would gladly take another beating for you, today, but that is no real solution. If we do not liberate you, and soon, Shaw will kill you."

"That will not happen." Anthony choked and sputtered, and he bit back the searing agony in his ribs. Thanks to Thomas, who intervened when Shaw's men arrived to take Anthony for more therapy, he enjoyed a brief respite the previous day. "Lady Rockingham will find me. She will find me and free us all. Just wait, and you will see."

"It has been a fortnight." Head bowed, Henry sighed and punched his pillow. "Surely, they would have found you, by now. And Shaw starves you. You grow weaker with each successive day, and you are powerless to defend yourself. How much more can you—can any man withstand? And what did you do that he attacks you so? I have never seen him assault a patient with such ferocity and ruthless abandon. If necessary, I will take your *treatment*, today."

"No." Anthony shook his head and sucked in a breath. His eyes watered, and the room spun out of control. "I cannot, in good conscience, permit that. I will take whatever Shaw metes out, and I will prevail." He swallowed hard. "With my wife as a shield, he cannot touch me."

"Despite evidence to the contrary." Charles snorted. "You look like you've been trampled by a herd of elephants, and they focused particular attention on your face. And your wife is not here."

"Thanks, ever so much, and she will come for me." Anthony's stomach growled, and he ignored the hunger gnawing at his insides. At one point, out of sheer desperation, he envisioned some of his favorite foods, like Yorkshire pie, a savory ragout of beef, and onion soup. The images, so vivid in detail, he could almost taste them. "I beg your pardon, but I am so famished I may eat my pillow."

The telltale scrape of the keys heralded the arrival of the morning meal, and he rolled onto his side and sat upright. Two guards entered the chamber and set a tray at the foot of each man's bed. Whereas the other veterans were given a bowl of porridge, a large chunk of bread, and a cup of tea, Anthony received naught but a meager crust and a small glass of water.

"Eat your food, and be quick about it." The larger attendant, a beast of a fellow with a half-moon scar from his mouth to his chin, scowled and waved a fist. "Else I will shove it down your throat, and I would enjoy it."

Shivering, Anthony blanched at his paltry fare, but he had to keep up his strength, if only to stay alive until Arabella saved him. And she would save him. He would believe in her to his last breath. Just as he retrieved the crust, Charles tossed a portion of his bread.

"You cannot subsist on that, soldier." The infantryman grinned. "Besides, I have more than enough to satisfy me."

Henry and Thomas followed suit.

Their generosity touched him more than he could say.

"Gentlemen, I will never forget your kindness." His mouth watered, as he claimed a warm morsel. "When we are liberated, I shall see you rewarded for your benevolence."

"No reward necessary, major." Henry dipped his chin and compressed his lips. "We are all but marking time, and we support you. Never doubt that."

In silence, Anthony inhaled the scant portion and gulped the water. With his finger, he caught every crumb, yet his belly grumbled. He developed a newfound respect for cooks and vowed to pay his chef double the usual salary upon his return to London. As he pushed aside the empty tray, the guards reappeared.

While two attendants collected the dishes, two additional keepers made straight for Anthony. He sat poised and sedate to meet his fate. The schedule remained the same, and he admired the rolling hills and lush greenery while an escort removed the shackle.

"Come along, Rockingham." With customary benignity, the scoundrel grabbed Anthony by the back of his gown and threw him to the floor. When he didn't move fast enough, the guard kicked Anthony in the arse. "Get a move on, fancy pants. I haven't all day, and Dr. Shaw awaits your presence."

So many recriminations danced at the tip of Anthony's tongue, but he said nothing. Instead, he tucked his legs beneath him and scrambled to his feet. Thomas met Anthony's gaze, and he cast a warning glance, but Charles shuffled to the end of his mattress.

"Now, see here." The infantryman frowned and pointed for emphasis. "Your methods are cruel, and Lord Rockingham should be shown the deference owed to a member of the aristocracy."

"Aw, what have we here?" The beast struck Charles across the face. "I will be sure to tell Dr. Shaw how Lord Rockingham has incited rebellion in our ranks. You just earned your friend additional therapy."

How Anthony longed to protest, but he knew he would only make the situation worse. Anxiety wrapped like a vise about his throat, and he concentrated his attention on the dirty floor. He imagined strange shapes transforming into various depictions of his bride and clung to her likeness.

The usual combatants surfaced, crouching in dark spaces, waiting to pounce. The drummer's *rat-a-tat-tat* played in rhythm with his pulse, and he ached to scream and run amok, but Arabella anchored him to reality. When the cannons fired, he flinched, but he blinked and centered her image, a cherished reverie, before him.

From the moment he met her, he thought her the handsomest woman of his acquaintance. And the most talkative. He adored her sweet nose and her impish grin. The little pink tongue he loved to suckle. Her heart-shaped face and her patrician features any debutante would kill to possess. But her best quality was that which he could not see. It was her capacity for compassion.

Anthony tripped, and a blackguard smacked the back of his head.

"Watch your step, fancy pants."

At the door to Shaw's office, the larger brute pounded on the oak panel, before pushing it open and shoving Anthony over the threshold. Perched behind his desk, Shaw smiled his sickening smile, and Anthony braced himself to endure another session of treatment in the form of unmitigated violence.

"Lord Rockingham, my favorite prize. We have no one with such estimable lineage in our facility, so I consider you my most valuable patient." With a sneer, Shaw closed a ledger and rested his hands atop the blotter. He appeared calm. Too calm. "Please, have a seat."

The room, decorated in various shades of blue, with mahogany accents and an ever-present hint of cigar smoke, struck Anthony as far too refined for its occupant, given what often occurred there. Without complaint or comment, he plopped into one of the Hepplewhite chairs.

"What, nothing to say, today?" Of course, Anthony wouldn't reply, because whatever he might have said would have only garnered him more pain. Shaw laughed and drew a book from a drawer. He flipped through the pages and furrowed his brow. "I thought we might work on your attitude, because you cannot improve until you accept that you are very ill. You do understand that, do you not? That battle has perverted your character and damaged your sanity?" When Anthony refused to respond, Shaw pounded a fist to the desktop. "Answer me."

"No, I do not accept your assessment of my mental health." Given Arabella's counsel, and Larrey's work, Anthony knew there was naught wrong with him. He inhaled a deep breath and repeated a single phrase in his mind: *I am not alone.*

"Your continued refusal to acknowledge your infirmity validates my conclusion and your need of further treatment, as I recommend. I shall compose a letter to the duke, informing him of your deteriorating condition and ongoing descent into madness." Shaw snatched his pen from the inkwell and scribbled on a piece of parchment. "By the by, you should know we recovered Lady Rockingham, along with the maid, Emily, and Lord Beaulieu."

"That is not possible." Anthony's hand shook, and a chill slithered down his spine. His heart raced, and his nerves tightened. "You lie."

"Ah, now I have your attention." Shaw leveled his gaze, pinning Anthony on the spot. "But it is true. My men ran them aground, just outside the London environs, and Lady Rockingham again resides at Sanderstead, under my supervision."

"And what of Beaulieu and the servant?" Anthony swallowed hard. "What have you done with them?"

"Why, I have done nothing to them, Lord Rockingham." Shaw

inclined his head. "I have no intentions of harming your allies, unless you refuse to cooperate. Don't you want to get well? Don't you want to return to your home and your position in society?"

"I think we both know that will never happen, if you have your way." Anthony shifted his weight and ordered his thoughts. "You are not interested in helping me, or anyone, for that matter. You want money."

"Oh, I want more. You know, in your absence, Lady Rockingham and I have become fast friends." Shaw sniffed and assessed his nails. "Indeed, we have grown quite close, and I believe she has grown rather fond of me. She is a beauty, and it would seem she prefers my company to yours."

Shaw's ploy might have worked, had Arabella not made her declaration the night they parted in Weybridge. She loved Anthony, and no one could convince him otherwise.

The absurdity. The outright preposterousness of the suggestion reduced Anthony to unhinged mirth he could not control. It began with a chuckle that soon grew into a full-blown belly laugh. He convulsed and howled, uncontrollably. And with each successive peal of mirth, Shaw grew more flushed.

"Lord Rockingham, how you do go on about nothing. Now, you will be silent. Silence, I say." Shaw shouted and snapped his fingers. "Bind him."

From behind, two guards yanked Anthony from his chair. Crouched on the floor, they thrust a wrought iron ring about his neck and fastened it with a rivet. Attached to the collar, a heavy, thick chain dangled. About his waist, they fastened an iron bar, with two rings affixed at either side. In one of the rings, they pinioned his arm. Additionally, two iron bars, which were connected by double links to the neck ring, passed over his shoulders and were riveted to the bar at his waist, both in front and in back.

With Anthony confined, the attendants dragged him to his feet.

"Look at you." Shaw smirked and slapped his thighs. "All trussed up like a Christmas goose, but you have yourself to blame for that. I would have preferred other methods to cure your dementedness, but you resist my efforts, so you leave me no choice." To the guards, he said, "Bring him to the pond."

Carried on his side into the garden, Anthony prayed for the courage to face whatever abuse Shaw dealt, but the makeshift cage provoked the usual torments, and he moaned when the first enemy combatant lurched from behind a thorny hedge. He jerked, and an attendant struck Anthony in the back of the head with the chain.

Many afternoons, he stared out the window at the little lily pond, with the stone statue of Venus at center, and noticed the tall, iron pole at the far end. He often wondered after its use, and now he realized it held a sinister purpose. Stifling a cry of alarm, he started as he plunged into the cold water, the shock stealing his breath, and the level of which stopped just below his chin. A blackguard affixed the chain at his neck to the pole.

"There, now." With hands on hips, Shaw curled his lip. "Let us see if that improves your disposition and responsiveness to our therapy."

"Dr. Shaw, are you sure about this?" the brutish attendant asked. "The last time you employed the water punishment, the soldier died."

"When I want your opinion, I will give it to you." Shaw folded his arms. "Lord Rockingham, you will remain in the pond for a few hours, at which time I shall send my men to retrieve you. What say we try, again, tomorrow, to work on your impairments?"

"I-It will b-be my p-pleasure." Submerged for only a few minutes, and already he could not hold still.

With the guards in tow, Shaw walked back to the main building, halting briefly to pluck a rose from a bush. Subtle hints of lilac and lavender teased his nose, and he recalled his wife's fondness for lavender water. For a moment, he studied the bright clusters of zinnia and petunias, bordering white daisies. It was an odd contradiction. So much agony amid nature's splendor.

After a while, he could no longer feel his feet or his legs. Instinctively, he flexed his fingers but could move nothing else. The biting cold set his flesh alight, and his teeth chattered. Resolved to endure the pain, he opened the door to his memory and let recollections of Arabella warm him.

A FORTNIGHT HAD passed since Arabella bade farewell to her husband and boarded a coach that would part them for what felt like forever. Ensconced in the back parlor of her family home, she reclined on the *chaise* and stared out the window at the blue sky, her thoughts filled with harrowing assumptions of what Anthony suffered in Dr. Shaw's clutches. In the wake of their separation, she realized her imagination could conjure such fanciful dreams and the most wretched nightmares, all of which centered on her tortured soldier.

Did he think of her? Did he suffer? Did he lose faith?

"Would you care for more tea?" Patience asked. The perfect picture of feminine deportment, she lifted the pot with the grace of a delicate swan. "And you should try not to worry. It is not good for the babe."

"Oh, Patience, I miss him." Arabella rolled onto her side and hugged a pillow to her belly. Many a holiday was celebrated in that very room, with its pale blue wall coverings, oak paneling, navy upholstery, cream-colored draperies, and a renowned frieze depicting the fateful lovers, Orpheus and Eurydice. Mama always kept fresh, long-stemmed lilies on the sofa table, and the familiar scent comforted her, but nothing could replace Anthony's embrace. "I want him home, with me."

"You really do love him." It was a statement, not a question. Patience, always poised, scooted to the edge of the sofa and bounced like a giddy debutante. "Lord Rockingham, I mean."

"I do, more than I ever thought possible." Arabella sat upright and tossed the pillow to the floor. "When I married Anthony, I hoped we might become good friends. It never occurred to me that I would fall in love. That I would commit my heart, body, and soul, to my husband. But I will neither deny nor hide my feelings."

"To be honest, I am not surprised." Leaning forward, Patience folded her arms and rested elbows to knees. "You do nothing halfway." She stretched her feet and stared at her slippers. "What will you do if the duke does not answer the summons your father dispatched? After all, it has been more than a sennight, and you've had no word."

"Papa had his solicitor draw up papers, accusing Swanborough of breaching the marital contract." It had been a difficult decision on Papa's part, owing to his longstanding friendship, but he pledged to protect Arabella, and footmen continued to guard the house. "Even now, he meets with his advisor, concerning the return of my dowry."

"Then he means to go through with it?" Patience's mouth fell agape, and she blinked. "He will sue for dissolution of the union?" When Arabella nodded, Patience gasped. "Then Lord Ainsworth will take the duke to court?"

"It is the only way to bring Swanborough to heel and negotiate Anthony's release." Arabella pushed from the *chaise* and stood before the window. "Given the law defines me as chattel, I have no standing to pursue legal remedies to rectify the absence of my lawful husband. My father must take action, on my behalf."

"What happens if the duke counters your father's suit?" Patience inclined her head. "Where does that leave you?"

"I'm not sure." And the answer to that question kept Arabella awake most nights, pondering life without Anthony. "However, I will not surrender without a fight, and neither will I simply go along with whatever Swanborough wants. I will see my husband freed, or I will not yield."

"That is wise." Patience tapped a finger to her cheek. "In reality, you hold the power, because you carry the babe. While it is not the most reputable defense, it is the most logical, and I would argue you have no choice. Lord Rockingham's heir is the key to your success or failure. To secure your future happiness, you must avail yourself of every advantage. After all, you said it yourself, you are but property, with no standing."

"Which is why I must bargain with Swanborough for my husband's salvation." Arabella worried her lower lip and pondered Anthony's location. Where could his father have sent him? "Thus far, we have heard nothing. Papa awaits a letter or some response from his friend. I would prefer the duke make his case, in person, because—"

The door opened to reveal Lord Beaulieu. As his gaze lit on Patience, his expression morphed into something almost wolfish.

"Good afternoon, Lady Rockingham." He saluted Arabella and marched straight to Patience, where he took her hands in his and kissed the backs of her bare knuckles. "Miss Wallace, always a pleasure to see you. And how is your father?"

"He is well, Lord Beaulieu. I shall tell him you remembered him." Cheeks flushed, Patience dipped her chin in deference, given he outranked her. "And your parents?"

"Quite well, thank you." To Arabella's shock, the bold lord plopped beside Patience, on the sofa. Then he splayed an arm, to drape it along her shoulders, in an outrageous display of familiarity, and Patience slowly inched to the end of the cushion. Arabella bit her tongue against laughter but made a mental note to monitor the situation. "I thought you might like to know the results of my man's search for the major."

"Do tell, my lord." Arabella came alert and returned to sit on the *chaise*. "What did he learn?"

"Not much, I am afraid." Beaulieu extended a leg and scrutinized his polished Hessian. "He made a thorough investigation but discovered no hint of Rockingham's whereabouts. After canvassing Weybridge, he interviewed the innkeeper, who stated the major made a decent run of it, after our departure, but in the end Shaw's men, in too great a number, overcame Rockingham. Beyond that, we discovered nothing new. I am so sorry."

"Thank you, for looking for him." Crestfallen, Arabella slumped and considered her next move. "Any news of Swanborough? I had thought we would have heard something by now."

"I have it on good authority that he is en route to the city." Although he focused his gaze on Arabella, Beaulieu shifted and moved closer to Patience. "And he has engaged his solicitor. I expect we will know something, sooner than later, which bodes well for the major. Also, it should please you to know the remaining Mad Matchmakers arrived, last night, so we are all in attendance."

"That is a most welcome development." Arabella cautioned herself not to overstimulate herself. Then something occurred to her. A mystery she had longed to solve. "Lord Beaulieu, forgive my impertinence, if I give offense, but I would pose a personal question, if I may."

"By all means, Lady Arabella. I have no secrets." When he sidled nearer still, Patience jumped from the sofa, but Beaulieu caught a fistful of her skirt and held fast. "Where are you going, Miss Wallace?"

"Unhand me, sir." Patience tried to wrench loose, but Beaulieu refused to relent. "You are no gentleman, and you take liberties that are not yours to own."

"Did I ever claim to be anything so noble?" He snorted and tugged Patience back to her seat. "Now then, where were we? Ah, yes. Lady Arabella's query. Suffice it to say, I address my friend by his military rank, as opposed to his title, as a sign of respect, given the one he inherited by birth and the other he earned."

"You say you are no gentleman, but those are pretty words for a rake." Arabella knew not what to make of the one-eyed earl. "And I warn you, Lord Beaulieu, do not accost my friend, or you will deal with me, and I am in no mood to be trifled with. Do so at your peril."

"A thousand apologies, Lady Rockingham, if I injured the delicate flower." Beaulieu chuckled.

"Delicate flower, indeed." Patience drew herself up with high dudgeon. "I would have you know I am a vast deal stronger than I look, and you would do well to remember that, sir."

"Delighted to hear it, as you do not disappoint, Miss Wallace." To Arabella, Beaulieu said, "It has nothing to do with polite decorum, my lady." He averted his stare and sighed. "It is a sign of deep and abiding admiration for a man I consider family. We served in the trenches. We witnessed war, we faced death, and we survived, together. Before that, he supported me during numerous adversities, most of my own making, almost from the cradle. Believe me when I say I would give my life to preserve his."

"I do believe you." A knock at the door brought her up short. "Come."

"I beg your pardon, my lady." Travers held wide the oak panel. "Lord Greyson, Lord Warrington, and Lord Michael Donithorn are just arrived. I installed them in the drawing room, your ladyship."

"Excellent." Arabella stood. "Let us join them and strategize, because I shall go mad if left to my own devices."

"Perhaps, we could consider sending the Mad Matchmakers to make a thorough survey of the areas surrounding Weybridge." Patience attempted to take Arabella's escort, but Beaulieu shamelessly anchored the general's daughter at his side. "Lord Beaulieu, I am quite capable of walking on my own accord. I assure you; I have been doing it for years."

"An interesting proposition, but I am left to wonder how much of your suggestion is rooted in a desire to rid yourself of my company." Beaulieu steered Patience into the hall, and Arabella led them into the foyer. "However, I am honor-bound to guard Lady Rockingham, so you must learn to tolerate my presence or devise another scheme to rid yourself of my much in demand companionship. Who knows, you might enjoy my special attention, which I am more than willing to bestow."

"Silly, ridiculous cretin." Patience humphed, and Beaulieu burst into laughter.

"That is quite enough, you two." Arabella rotated on a heel and folded her arms. "Lord Beaulieu, you test the limits of my charity and forbearance. Patience, I dearly love you, but you must not take the bait, because his lordship is a past master at trickery and temptation. Now, I have no time or inclination to arbitrate your association, so I expect you to behave as befits your station."

"I'm sorry." With her head bowed, Patience at least had the sense to appear contrite.

"I will not apologize." Beaulieu lifted his chin. "I shall be hanged if I do."

"Patience is right." Arabella stomped a foot. "You are a silly, ridiculous cretin."

"Well, at least we understand each other." Beaulieu arched a brow and clucked his tongue.

"What is going on out here?" Looming in the doorway of the drawing room, Greyson rested fists on hips. "Lady Rockingham, commiserations and felicitations are both in order, I am sad to admit."

"Unfortunately, you are correct." She extended a hand, and he placed a chaste kiss to her knuckles. In turn, Lord Michael and Lord Warrington made similar greetings. "We eagerly anticipate the Duke of Swanborough's acknowledgement of my father's letter, which challenged the validity of the marriage contract and rightful custody of my person, given Lord Rockingham's admittance to an asylum. Of course, my husband's location is merely speculation, as we have had no word from him."

"I have a man surveilling Swanborough's residence, and I am told the duke emerged from his traveling coach, in the forecourt, early this morning." Warrington scratched his chin. "We thought it best to journey here, given we are all charged with preserving your safety."

As if on cue, someone pounded on the front door.

Arabella hugged her belly and her insides tightened.

The tension in the room weighed heavy, as Travers crossed the foyer, and all eyes focused on the main entry.

"Hold hard, Travers." Papa strode forth. "I shall see who pays call."

"Of course, my lord." The butler bowed and stepped aside.

Again, the unknown visitor pummeled the door.

Papa turned the latch in the bolt and swung wide the thick, oak panel, to reveal the Duke of Swanborough, along with two liveried footmen.

"Ainsworth, what is this meaning of this?" A vein pulsing in his temple, and his face flushed beetroot red, the duke stormed over the threshold, waving an unfolded piece of paper in his upraised fist. Then he spied Arabella and narrowed his stare. "You are to come with me, this instant."

"I don't think so." Lord Beaulieu drew her to stand behind him. "If you want Lady Rockingham, you will have to get through me."

"And me." Lord Warrington stepped forward.

"And me." Lord Greyson stood tall.

"And me." Lord Michael squared his shoulders."

"And what of you, old friend?" Swanborough bared his teeth. "Am I thus hailed?"

"I would ask the same of you, *old friend*." Papa moved to confront the duke, toe-to-toe, and Arabella clutched her throat, else she might scream. "You invoke our lifetime allegiance, as you threaten my only child. I would submit you drew the first sword. I merely meet your challenge. What have you to say for yourself?"

"What do you mean?" Swanborough shrank and retreated. "You knew of my plan and my justification. Now you pretend a slight? Who is the disingenuous party?"

"You never mentioned anything about kidnapping my daughter." From his coat pocket, Papa produced Shaw's letter and thrust it at Swanborough. Arabella swayed, but Patience provided unshakeable support. "And I never agreed that she should be imprisoned under the supervision of a so-called doctor whose credentials breach the limits of any semblance of probity."

"Shaw's methods may not be the most popular, but he has un-matched success." Swanborough licked his lips. "As to Lady Rockingham's confinement, I reneged in the best interests of my son, as I saw fit. I am convinced Shaw is the best possible hope my son has of resuming a normal life."

"A normal life?" Arabella pushed forward, with Beaulieu and Patience perched at either side. "Do you even know your son? Do you not recognize that he suffers lingering effects of battle and naught more? Lord Rockingham is not mad. He is human. Yes, he lost an arm. He is different, in that I will not argue. But that does not mean he is less than you or any man. He is merely unique."

"Lady Arabella, you do great credit to your family, as well as Lord Rockingham. However, you are but a woman, driven by obstreperous emotions, incapable of understanding such intricacies of the mind." Swanborough shook his head, and something within her snapped. "I demand that you return to Sanderstead, at once, in fulfillment of the marriage contract."

"How dare you patronize me." Her jaw set, she could abide by the rules of polite decorum no longer. With the wind of conviction in her sails, she advanced, evading her father's attempt to stay her, and grasped the duke by the lapels of his coat. "Have you any idea what your ignorance of Lord Rockingham's state may have wrought? You may have done more damage to his overall health than the war ever could have."

"While I appreciate your loyalty to Lord Rockingham, I must let knowledge and reason guide my actions, given I must preserve the dukedom." Swanborough grabbed her by the forearms. "Now, you will come with me."

"As you were." Beaulieu drew a flintlock pistol and took careful aim. "Else I will put a lead shot between your eyes, rank be damned. Although I am partial to my life of relative comfort, I will not hesitate to pull the trigger, so you will stand down, or you will die."

All hell broke loose in the foyer, and the gathering descended into chaos, as her father shouted recriminations, and the Ainsworth staff challenged the duke's personnel. Beaulieu thrust Patience to the rear, and the Mad Matchmakers surrounded Swanborough and Arabella.

"Wait." Arabella wrenched from the duke's hold and took a position to Lord Beaulieu's right. "Pray, let me speak."

"I will hear you." Swanborough shifted his weight and jutted his hip. "But I will not forget this, Ainsworth."

"Neither will I, Swanborough," Papa replied between gritted teeth.

"Gentlemen, please." Arabella stood in the middle of the fray, and it dawned on her there was only one option. As her Anthony sacrificed himself for her, she had to sacrifice herself for him. Then she faced the duke. "I will make you an honest bargain. If you allow me to see Lord Rockingham, for myself, I will return to Sanderstead, without protest."

"That is out of the question." The duke narrowed his gaze. "An asylum is no place for a lady."

"What about Lady Rockingham's appointed representatives, given I agree with your assertion?" Still bearing the weapon, Beaulieu inched forward. "Lord Greyson and I can journey with you, to Lord Rockingham's location, and verify he is in good health, as you claim."

Infuriating silence fell on the foyer, and the duke stared at the floor.

"No." He shook his head. "I fear any disruption could impair his treatment."

"Your Grace, I carry Lord Rockingham's heir." At Arabella's proclamation, the duke stumbled back and his mouth fell agape. "If you wish to see the babe, you must yield to my demand, and I beg you to listen to reason. Yours is not a *fait accompli*. You can alter your course. If Anthony approves of your tack, I will not protest."

"Y-you are with c-child?" he sputtered. When she nodded, he pressed a fist to his mouth, and his gaze darted, back and forth. Then he pinned her with a lethal stare. "I accept your offer, and we depart at once." To Beaulieu and Greyson, the duke said, "Gentlemen, let us away."

Beaulieu pocketed his pistol and turned to her. Taking her hands in his, he lowered his chin. "On my life, we will not return without Rockingham."

CHAPTER EIGHTEEN

S UNLIGHT FILTERED THROUGH the bars on the window, casting peculiar shadows on the floor. Outside, a bird swooped and soared in the cloudless, azure sky. The pond that once served to soothe his troubled soul now inspired naught but terror. Propped in a corner, and chained in a chair, Anthony stirred from a much-cherished dream and clung to the vision of Arabella as his only salvation.

In the days since he was enclosed in the makeshift cage that confined him, he had not eaten. Shaw ordered that Anthony was to have no food, in further punishment of his refusal to admit he was insane and to submit to the doctor's therapy. But temptation beckoned with each passing hour, and he grew weary of the pain.

Left to wallow in his own waste, moved only to be plunged into the cold waters of the lily pond, he began to question his own humanity. Violent hallucinations filled his mind, conjuring all manner of vengeful fates he would exact on Shaw, inflicting agony without mercy. That might have been the most impactful result of Shaw's torture, the disturbing images and the lust for blood, and Anthony wondered if he would ever find peace, again.

Just when he feared he had reached the limits of his sanity, just when he prepared to yield, Arabella saved him. She may not have been present in person, but she was with him in spirit, and he never lost hope. With renewed courage, he prepared for the daily sessions that devolved, without fail, into unqualified savagery.

And Shaw accused *Anthony* of lunacy.

"Rockingham, how do you fare?" Thomas asked with a sad smile.

"As well as can be expected, I suppose." Anthony cleared his sore throat. Dying of thirst, he resorted to drinking some of the foul pond water and retched uncontrollably the previous day. Of course, since he'd had nothing to eat, there was nothing to vomit. "But I believe I am becoming accustomed to sleeping upright. It is rather convenient, because you expend no energy getting out of bed. You should try it, sometime."

He chuckled, which reduced him to a coughing fit.

"Easy, major." Charles stretched upright and yawned. With his brow a mass of furrows, the infantryman frowned. "While I am relieved to see you are still alive, you cannot continue on this path, and I am prepared to rebel, whatever the cost."

"No." Given the iron collar about his neck, Anthony could not even shake his head to discourage his newfound friends. "Pray, I beg you, do nothing, else I will pay for it. We must have faith in my wife. She will come for me, and I will see you released and Shaw punished. I swear it on my firstborn."

"Major, I know you want to believe that we will be rescued, but it is not going to happen." Henry stared at his hands. "No one is coming for us, because no one cares about us."

"Don't say that. Don't even think that." Anthony struggled in vain against his cage. "You have to have faith, or Shaw wins."

"That is the problem." Henry wiped his eyes. "I have no faith, major. I have only despair and the realization that we are never leaving this place. If I had any shred of hope, it vanished when the guards carried you in here, imprisoned in that hellish contraption. Now, all I feel is fear. Deep-seated dread."

"Please, for my sake, do not give up." Anthony stretched out his dirty feet and licked his lips, when he spied a morsel of bread, which Thomas had attempted to toss into Anthony's mouth at dinner, yesterday. "We must hold the line, for a little longer."

"The major is right," Charles said with a curt nod. "We ought to be ashamed of ourselves. If he believes we will be liberated, despite being locked in cage, unable to recline, eat, or relieve himself in the piss-pot, should we not support him?"

"Perhaps, we delay the inevitable." Thomas sighed. "Sooner or later, Rockingham will have to come to terms with reality. He must face facts."

"I'm sorry, Thomas, but you are wrong." Anthony sought pretty words and phrases to reassure the wounded veterans. "Every day you spend above ground is cause to hope."

"What makes you so certain?" asked Henry. "How do you know you are not mistaken?"

"Because I know my bride." Anthony recalled Arabella's declaration, freely given, that sorrowful night in Weybridge. "She loves me. She told me so, when last we met, and nothing will stop her from finding me."

The telltale rasp of the keys signaled the arrival of the morning meal.

The usual two guards entered the chamber, carrying three trays. The larger brute, who often expressed enjoyment of Anthony's pain, placed the customary bowl of porridge and hunk of bread at the foot of Henry's bunk.

Instead of collecting the food, Henry scooted toward the end of the bed, picked up the tray, and swung at the attendant's head. Charles followed suit, striking the hulk of a man just under his chin. A melee ensued, with Thomas employing the chain that secured him to choke the thug.

The smaller fiend shouted the alarm, and two additional henchmen charged the fray. An aide punched Henry, rendering him unconscious. Another villain slammed Charles's head into the floor, and he collapsed. The first blackguard strangled Thomas, until the wounded warrior fainted.

"Grab fancy pants." The scoundrel slapped Anthony, hard. "Shaw has something special planned for him."

The chain at his neck loosened, and Anthony stood. Steeling himself for another session of torture, he marched alongside his captors, in silence. At the painfully familiar door to Shaw's office, Anthony stepped aside, and the guard turned the knob and pushed open the oak panel. Inside, Shaw sat at the front edge of his desk.

To the right, a new addition to the room brought Anthony to a halt, but the sizable swine shoved him to stand at center. A long, narrow table hugged the wall, and a latch and panel marked one end, with a bucket situated beneath, on the carpet. He had seen something similar employed, in the torture rooms, by counterintelligence officers, and suspected he might not live till dusk.

"I see you are interested in my recent acquisition." Shaw pushed from the desk and neared. "It is so rare to find a remnant of war that I can implement in my work, and I am most anxious to give it a try. What say you, Lord Rockingham? You never cry out when I administer treatment. You never make a sound, and I consider you a most unique challenge. Eventually, you will give me what I want. I wonder if that will happen, today." To the attendants, he said, "Put him on the table."

Anthony stared at the ceiling, tracing the cracks in the plaster with his eyes. It was a mundane task, but it kept him calm. The bastards tied down his legs with leather straps at the ankles and another belt across his torso, despite the fact he remained locked in the makeshift cage that kept him immobilized. An additional binding stretched across his forehead, pinning his head in place.

"So, who is going to run the buckets?" Shaw inquired of his henchmen. "I will require a steady supply of water."

"I'll do it." The diminutive guard raised a hand. "I have no stomach for this."

"All right." Shaw doffed his coat and rolled up his sleeves. Then he hovered over Anthony. "Comfortable, Lord Rockingham?"

Anthony kept his gaze transfixed, overhead.

"Still no comment." Shaw tsked. "Let us see if I can loosen your tongue."

The evil doctor fiddled with a latch, and a panel dropped at an angle. Shaw covered Anthony's face with a cloth, and then there was water. A deluge that filled his nose and mouth, and he fought to breathe.

"Ah, at last, we provoke a reaction." Shaw chuckled. "You fight against your restraints but do not favor me with plea for mercy. What a pity."

Another torrent threatened to drown Anthony, but he refused to yield. When Shaw snatched the cloth from Anthony's face, he spat at his tormentor.

"That was unwise, Lord Rockingham." Shaw leaned over and whispered in Anthony's ear, "You will scream, or you will die."

"Go to the devil," he replied, knowing it could mean his doom.

Shaw resituated the cloth, and a veritable flood engulfed Anthony. He struggled to no avail, gasping for air, but he only swallowed more water. When he thought it a lost cause, that he would perish and never see his beloved Arabella again, the flow suddenly ceased.

With his face uncovered, he coughed and sputtered, vomiting water, as the belt at his legs loosened. Dazed, he could scarcely make out a silhouette, and the unknown individual helped Anthony sit upright. He blinked his eyes, and then it was as if he was thrown into the present, and he thought he imagined his father, upbraiding Shaw. At last, Anthony's vision cleared, and he discovered Beaulieu and Greyson supported him.

"I must be dead." Anthony convulsed and regurgitated water. "I prayed for an angel and I got you two. Tell me, are you really here, or am I dreaming?"

"Dreaming of me?" Beaulieu chucked Anthony's chin. "You must be mad, and I am relieved to see your sense of humor survived, unscathed." Beaulieu's expression sobered, and he half-hugged Anthony. "Thank god, we found you."

"Your bride will be happy to see you." Greyson grinned. "She put up quite a fight and challenged your father, on your behalf."

"Of course, she did." Anthony laughed.

"What is the meaning of this affront?" Holding a handkerchief to his nose, Anthony's father wagged a finger at Shaw. "You were supposed to help my son, not kill him."

"Your Grace, my methods may be crude, but they are effective." Shaw shuffled his feet. "With a little more time—"

"Are you out of your mind?" Father glanced at Anthony and winced. "I wouldn't house my best hound in this facility. Gather my son's belongings and give him a bath. I am taking him home."

"Father, they sold my personal effects." Anthony sat still, while Beaulieu and Greyson unfastened the rivets and iron bars. "And they stole my signet ring."

"Is this true?" Father lowered his chin and favored Shaw with a look that reduced many a man to a shuddering mass of flesh, and the doctor fared no better. When Shaw nodded the affirmative, Father narrowed his gaze. "Where is the ring?"

"Actually, Your Grace, it is a simple misunderstanding." Shaw retreated and then ran to his desk. From a drawer, he produced the item in question. "Here it is, safe and sound. I thought to preserve it for Lord Rockingham."

"Dr. Shaw, although I doubt you are an actual doctor, I was wrong to think so highly of you, and that is a mistake that ends here." Father snapped his fingers, and his footmen stood at attention. "I hereby withdraw all financial support, and I shall report you to the proper authorities when I return to London. But until that time, I demand you terminate patient therapy until further notice, when qualified specialists can assess those still housed within these walls. For now, your services are no longer needed."

"Wait." Exhausted, Anthony dropped to his knees, on the floor, and Beaulieu and Greyson lifted Anthony to one of the Hepplewhite chairs. "I cannot depart without freeing my friends, and they require medical attention, after they intervened on my behalf. We must help them."

"We will do so." Greyson brushed hair from Anthony's face. "Right now, you are our primary concern. Have you looked in a mirror, of late?"

"No." Anthony examined his bruised wrist. "And neither have I eaten in two days. As of this moment, I could feast on my own toenails."

"How appetizing." Beaulieu wrinkled his nose. "First, you require a bath and a fresh set of clothes. We cannot take you to your wife in this condition."

"Promise me something." Anthony studied the countless cuts and scrapes to his legs. "Do not allow Arabella to see me like this. I would not traumatize her, given her delicate condition."

"I would argue there is nothing delicate about your bride." Beaulieu snickered. "Now, let us get you into a tub of hot water, and then we journey to London."

"To London." Anthony anticipated a heartfelt reunion, but he would delay until the majority of his wounds healed and he regained some weight. "Take me away, my friends."

With that, he stood—and promptly fainted.

DARKNESS FILLED THE drawing room, and a maid lit a candelabrum, illuminating the chamber in a soft, saffron glow, as the sun set on the day after the terse exchange with the Duke of Swanborough, and

Beaulieu and Greyson departed, in search of Anthony. On the sidewalk, Londoners scurried in all directions, carrying packages and going about their business, blissfully unaware of the dark cloud that enshrouded her home.

With Warrington acting as a disinterested arbiter, Patience played cards with Lord Michael, Papa sat in his comfy chair and perused the latest copy of *The Times*, and Mama embroidered. Stationed at the window, where she lingered for the past three hours, Arabella remained on guard for any sign of the ducal traveling coach, her hopes dashed every time a hack or a town carriage drove past.

"My dear, please, sit down." Mama patted the empty space beside her, on the *chaise*. "You will wear yourself out, and that is not good for the babe. Worrying will not make them magically appear."

"Mama, if I do not stand, I fear I shall explode, because the suspense is killing me." Arabella paced and hugged her belly. Countless possibilities haunted her waking hours, and she had to do something to expend the nervous energy that threatened to rip her in two. "I must know what happened to Anthony, and I cannot rest until I am apprised of his fate."

"What if he is content in his position?" Papa inquired in a soft tone. "What if Dr. Shaw is not the villain you portray? Have you considered that?"

"I have, Papa." In reality, she had thought of little else, but she trusted her instincts, and she knew, without doubt, that Shaw was the most heinous libertine. "If Lord Rockingham is convinced he is where he belongs, if he is happy, I will not interfere. But I will accept no one's word but Lord Rockingham's."

"And what of the bargain you struck with Swanborough?" Papa lowered the paper and frowned. "Do you intend to honor your promise, because I am not sure I can allow it."

"I suppose I shall decide when it is time." She reflected on the possibilities and resolved that, no matter what, she would never permit Shaw anywhere near her or her child. Indeed, she would renegotiate the terms of her agreement with the duke. "But you have my solemn vow, I will not bring disgrace on our family."

"Arabella, you are a Gibbs, and we are made of sterner stuff. Swanborough can go to the devil before I surrender you on the altar of genteel protocol." Papa scooted from his chair and stood. She faced him and he caressed her cheek with his thumb. "We will weather whatever scandal erupts from this ordeal, because I am disinclined to relinquish you to Swanborough, so the choice is not necessarily yours. You should know I shall carry many regrets to my grave, but the disservice I did to you and Lord Rockingham will haunt me into the hereafter. I should have trusted you. Worse, I should have trusted my own instincts, because I knew, deep down, there was nothing wrong with Rockingham."

"Oh, Papa, I do love you." Choking on tears, Arabella sobbed and wrapped her arms about his waist, and he drew her into his comforting embrace. "You could not have known what the duke intended, given he deceived you, too."

"There, there. It will be all right, girl." He stroked her hair as she wept. "We have not yet ceded the fight, and I believe we will prevail, in the end."

"It must be so, Papa." In that instant, she detected the steady clip-clop of horses, and she lifted her head. "Do you hear that?"

"I do." Lord Michael dropped his cards atop the table and hobbled on his crutch toward the foyer, with Patience escorting Warrington. "I think it is them."

"I will get the door." Papa strode forth and waved off Travers. When he opened the oak panel and peered outside, he flinched and shouted over his shoulder, "Summon the footmen—*now*. And send someone to fetch Dr. Handley."

"Aye, sir." Travers bowed.

"Papa, what is it?" Arabella perched on tiptoes. "Is it Anthony? Do you see him? Is he with them?"

"It is, my dear." Papa rubbed the back of his neck and stayed her with an upraised palm. "Clear the area and make way."

As she hugged the wall, two ducal footmen ascended the entry stairs. Behind them, Beaulieu and Greyson carried Anthony, who appeared unconscious. His head listed from side to side and suddenly dropped back, and she shrieked in horror at his gaunt visage. With a black eye and a horribly disfigured and bruised cheek, he hung limp.

"Follow me." In a flurry of activity, she grabbed a candlestick from the foyer table, hiked her skirt, and sprinted to the second floor. "We have a room prepared." She hurried into the chamber next to hers, an arrangement she insisted on, so she could guard her husband, and lit several tapers placed about the spacious accommodation. "Put him in the bed."

With care, Beaulieu and Greyson navigated the huge four-poster, settling Anthony in the center. A muffled moan snared her ear, and she set the candlestick on the tallboy. Easing to the edge of the mattress, she brushed a lock of hair from Anthony's forehead, and then she bent and kissed him. To her relief, he stirred. For a moment, he simply stared at her. All of a sudden, he scrunched his face and turned away from her.

It was not the reconciliation for which she prayed.

"Get out." He rolled on his side, and she sobbed. "Get her out of here."

"Anthony, it is me." Certain he had to have been confused, given his disheveled state, she reached for him, but he shook free. "It is Arabella, and you are safe."

"I said *get out*." Again and again, he repeated the same words. "Do not let her see me in this condition."

"Lady Rockingham, perhaps it is best if you wait downstairs with the others." Beaulieu lifted her from the bed and escorted her to the exit. "He has endured a terrible shock, and it is not wise to agitate him." When she hesitated, he stated, "I promise, I will come to you after Dr. Handley completes an examination, and I have news to share. I shall give you a full report."

"All right." A tear traveled a path to her chin, and she dried her face on her sleeve. A cold chill settled in her chest, as she dutifully withdrew from Anthony's quarters. She dragged her feet, straining for the slightest summons. At the landing, she prayed her husband would call her, but quiet fell on the household.

Halfway down the stairs, she paused, when a footman arrived with Dr. Handley, bearing his black bag. Setting aside her heartache, she continued to the first floor.

"Thank you for coming on such short notice." She extended a hand in welcome. "Lord Rockingham is installed in the third room on the left. Lord Beaulieu and Lord Greyson are with him, and he seems quite out of sorts."

"That is to be expected, Lady Rockingham, and I have been at the ready since I received Lord Ainsworth's note yesterday. Must confess I was glad to receive it, but I lament the circumstances." The affable medical professional adjusted his spectacles on his nose and smiled. "I know you are concerned, but I caution you not to panic. We do not yet know the details of what he endured, but Lord Rockingham is strong. He will get through this with your love and understanding. Now, if you will excuse me, I must assess my patient."

"Of course." She dipped her chin and lingered until he disappeared from sight. Bowing her head, she walked into the drawing room and collapsed onto the sofa. "He does not know me. He banishes me from his presence. My god, what did they do to him?"

"I have never seen anything so medieval." The duke snapped his fingers, and Travers lifted a decanter from the tea trolley and filled a brandy balloon. "They caged my son like an animal. Can you believe it? To treat a marquess, and the heir to the dukedom of Swanborough, with such barbarity?"

"What?" Drowning amid an ocean of frightful images, she snapped to attention. "What did you say?"

"They restrained Lord Rockingham in a device such as I have never seen." Swanborough took a healthy gulp of the amber intoxicant. "Shaw stripped my son of any semblance of humanity, sold his clothes, and stole his signet ring. They commenced to beat my issue without compunction. If it is the last thing I do, I shall bring Shaw and his men to justice, for the affront to my estimable ancestry, and I will see that asylum razed."

"*Justice?*" Wound tight as a clock spring, everything inside her railed, and she leaped to her feet. "You dare speak of justice, after you put Anthony in Shaw's care? And you would have done the same to me and your future grandchild, had we not rebelled."

"I rescued him, did I not?" The duke averted his stare. "I would argue I am owed a measure of gratitude and recognition of my efforts to liberate Lord Rockingham."

"He would not have required rescuing had you not committed him, in the first place." She marched to his chair and slapped the crystal glass from his grip. "I said it before, and it bears repeating. Your son lost his arm, not his mind, but you equate one with the other, and your mistake almost killed him. I neither acknowledge your attempt to make amends nor congratulate you on saving him from your worst proclivities, because you are deserving of naught but a swift kick in the arse."

"I am insulted, and I demand an apology." The duke slowly stood and rotated to glance at her father. "Ainsworth, are you going to permit your daughter to accost me thus under your roof?"

"Aye." With unimpaired aplomb, Papa cast a stoic expression. "She states the truth in much prettier language than I would employ, were I in her position. If you don't like it, you may leave my humble abode."

The duke's mouth fell agape. "Well, I never—"

"But you did, and therein lies the problem." Riding a crest of fury, Arabella backed the duke into the foyer. "You adopted an unscrupulous enterprise, soliciting my father's unwitting cooperation based on deception. You entrusted the care of your son to an unprincipled charlatan, the consequences of which now rest, battered and bruised, in a guest room. And now you laud your actions as worthy of acknowledgement and a sense of obligation?"

"I corrected the situation." Swanborough retreated a step. "What else would you ask of me?"

"I want you to suffer." She inched forward, and Travers, stationed near the main entry, opened the door. "I want you to bleed as Anthony bled, until you know what it is to be cast out. To be rejected. To be abandoned by those you love and have naught but yourself to provide succor."

"That is not very charitable, Lady Rockingham." The duke withdrew, looming at the threshold. "I made you an honest bargain, and I upheld our arrangement. I, too, was fooled by Shaw. You cannot fault me for that."

"But I do blame you." Again, she advanced. "I had spent a mere handful of minutes in Shaw's company when I knew him to be the most dastardly, immoral villain of my acquaintance."

"Pray, some of us are not so observant, Lady Rockingham." Ignorant of his precarious perch, the duke alighted on the first step. "But I expect you to honor our agreement, as befits a woman of your station, and I will call on you, tomorrow."

"Of course, you would insist that I adhere to the social dictates that govern our set, even while you flout them. And why wouldn't you, when you think yourself above such scruples." Arabella dismissed the butler with a wave of her hand. "Permit me to speak in a language that is familiar to you and borrow a page from your stratagem, so we understand each other. In short, I renege."

"But—you cannot do that." The duke planted his feet wide, and his nostrils flared. "I am the Duke of Swanborough."

"Oh, yes, I can." Arabella shook her fist. "For I am the whirlwind, and you shall reap it."

With that, she slammed the door in his face.

CHAPTER NINETEEN

I T WAS LATE when Anthony jolted awake. He reached for Arabella but found nothing, because he had not shared his bed with her in the fortnight since his liberation. Sitting upright, he glanced about the chamber of his London townhouse, but all remained quiet save the crackling logs in the fireplace. After reassuring himself that he remained safe, he punched his pillow, rolled onto his side, and stretched long.

"*Anthony.*"

In an instant, he came alert, when Arabella beckoned in a shrill exclamation. He tossed aside the covers and scooted to the edge of the mattress. Standing, he shrugged into his robe and fumbled with the belt. At the hearth, he lit a single taper, grabbed the candlestick, and rushed into the little corridor that joined their rooms. As he entered her suite, she called to him, again, and gave vent to a strangled cry.

Tossing and turning amid the sheets, she whimpered, and he recognized the fitful slumber he knew all too well. At the bed, he sat the candlestick on a table and eased to her side, and she flinched and mumbled his name. With care not to startle her, he rubbed her cheek.

"Arabella." When she did not rouse, he gave her a gentle nudge. "Darling, I am here."

With a shriek and gasping for breath, she opened her eyes and flinched. When she noted his presence, she lurched and flung herself at him. Bursting into tears, she clutched fistfuls of his silk robe.

"You were gone. You were gone. I searched for you, but you were gone," she said, between mournful sobs that tore at his gut. "Everywhere I looked, you were not there, and I was alone. So very alone."

"Sweetheart, it is all right, and you are safe." He hugged her about the waist and kissed her hair, and she buried her face in his chest. "And I am here, so you are not alone. I will always anchor at your side, and I will never leave you, so you worry for naught."

It dawned on him, then, that he used the same words to reassure her that she often used to comfort him. With their roles reversed, it fell to him to support her, and never had he felt more a man than in that heartbreaking moment, while his wife trembled in his embrace and relied on him for succor.

"But you were gone." She fought for breath and clung to him. "You were gone, and I could not find you."

For a while, he simply held her, and she shivered and wept. Her distress, painfully familiar in its intensity, shredded his heart.

"Darling, you need not seek what sits before you, what resides within you, now and forever." Shuffling her in his hold, he drew her with him and stood. "Come with me, and let us return to my bed."

"No." With an abrupt sniff, she shook her head and tried to push free. "I know you no longer want me there, and I'm fine—really, I am." Ah, he knew that sharp tone. Not for a minute did he believe her, as she wiped her nose. "I apologize for disturbing you, my lord. If you wish, I can move to a room at the other end of the hall, so I will not interrupt your rest, in the future."

"Like bloody hell." In that instant, he realized his mistake in dealing with his bride, and he should have known better. Clutching her wrist, and determined to set things right, he dragged her back to his apartment. "How long have you suffered the night terrors?"

"Since you were taken from me." Of course, he should have known of her discomfit. Should have recognized the signs, so evident now that he opened his eyes, to see beyond his own angst. In his room, she again tried to wrench loose, but he tightened his grip. "Anthony, this is not necessary. I am quite content in my own accommodation, because I would not impede your recovery. Indeed, in your absence, I have grown quite accustomed to sleeping by myself."

"Really?" At his four-poster, he led her to sit. After pulling back the covers, he patted the mattress. She nodded and bit her bottom lip. Then shook her head, and he laughed. "Neither have I, now take off that ridiculous nightgown, because you know I prefer you naked."

"In my defense, I am cold when we do not share a bed." Without hesitation, she stripped from the fine lawn garment and flung it on the floor. Pouting, she climbed between the sheets. After doffing his robe, which exposed his healthy erection, he joined her, and she nestled at his side. "I missed you."

"I missed you, too. And tell me, my dear, whatever gave you the impression I no longer want you?" Inching closer, she eased her head to his shoulder, and he speared his fingers in her long brown hair, to massage her scalp. "Why would you ever think such a thing, when my body provides ample evidence to the contrary, even now?"

"Because you close yourself off from me," she replied, in a small voice, and he exhaled in disgust with himself. "And I am not welcome in your meetings with Dr. Handley, when there was a time when you would not venture to the doctor without me. And you stopped talking to me, when conversation once manifested the sum of our relationship." He could have kicked himself in the arse, because he hurt his wife. "Indeed, we share nothing but this house since you returned. Yet I cannot be angry with you, given I failed you. Now I must accept what has become of us. It is only right that you are cross with me, when I broke my promise, and I'm sorry, but I tried everything to find you and bring you home."

"Wait—what?" In shock, he shoved her onto her back and propped on his elbow, so he could look directly into her eyes. What he spied in her tormented gaze ravaged his conscience. "What do you mean? Just how did you fail me, when I am here, as you see, owing to your efforts?"

"My lord, I am confused." She blinked. "If you are not at odds with me, why do you deny me, when I need you as you once needed me?"

"Oh, my darling, I have neglected you, and that shame is mine to own, but it ends, here and now." He bent his head and offered an olive branch in a kiss. At once, she opened to him, displaying the characteristic raw hunger for which he adored her. She yanked his hair and mingled her tongue with his. She dug her fingernails into his shoulders. Then she broke. "Shh, sweetheart. This is my fault, and I will make amends, until first light and beyond, if that is what it takes to prove you are still my most desired lady."

With his knee, he spread her legs, which she immediately wrapped about his hips, and in a flex of his spine, he merged their bodies. To his unutterable delight, she exhaled a shivery breath and wrapped her arms about him, supporting him as he commenced the delicate dance.

It was a deed as old as humanity, yet for him it represented a rebirth.

In the gentle slip and slide, he found unshakeable validation, and Arabella declared her love, twofold. The incomparable connection, irrefutable in its meaning, carried him to new heights of pleasure and reassurance, when she gripped his arse and hastened his rhythm. Thus, he whispered fervent declarations, for her ears only, proclaiming what she did for him and how she brought him alive, when so many conspired to destroy him.

Given their time apart, he gritted his teeth, and completion beckoned. In silence, he vowed to delay until she found release. Just as he thought he could withstand no more, she gave vent to a heartrendingly sweet cry, and he let fly his seed, deep within her.

Some moments later, he floated back to the mortal plane. As usual, she embraced him, stroking his back until the passionate storm passed, and he turned his head to press his lips to hers.

"My darling, I am home, at last." He rubbed the tip of his nose to hers. "Because, when we are one, this is home, and I love you."

"If that is how you feel, why have you ignored me?" A single tear streamed her temple, and he realized he had work to do, to restore his lady's faith. "Don't you understand that I need you? That I love you, too? And it hurts me when you exclude me from your life. Indeed, I cannot bear it, given the pain is such that I falter beneath the burden of my loneliness."

"Sweetheart, that was never my intent." With a sigh, he withdrew from her, fluffed a pillow, and reclined. As before, she sidled next to him, and he rested his palm to her hip. "Rather, I hoped to spare you the details of my brief imprisonment. It is difficult to explain, but they treated me less than a man and more like an animal, and it was humiliating. But I would have you know that I survived because of you."

"Oh?" With a finger, she toyed with the hair on his chest. "How so?"

"When I arrived at the asylum, they chained me to a bed and beat me." Recalling the horrible night, when he feared he might never see her again, he shuddered, and she kissed him. "And that is what helped me endure. To escape the pain, I conjured visions of you, of your tempting lips, of your glorious face, of your warm embrace, and of your affirmations, in the most grievous situations. No matter how hard they tried, they could not touch me. So, you did not fail me, because regardless of their ruthless endeavors to break me, in my darkest moments, when I needed you most, you were there, and you saved me."

In her continued silence, he sensed a request, and he submitted to his wife's unspoken demand.

For the next hour, he detailed the length of his confinement, omitting nothing, however seemingly insignificant, and Arabella cried for him, as he expected and once thought to avoid. Incomparably strong, his lady stood for him, and in her tears he found something powerful and curative. She wept for them, both. And in her tender expression, he found restorative healing and peaceful calm.

"You know, on more than one occasion, I have declared you the bravest man of my acquaintance, because you survived what no man should have had to endure." Dragging the backs of her knuckles across her face, she sat upright. "But that description does not do justice to your character, and words are grossly inadequate to convey the depth of my sincere admiration, so I am left to find some way to pay tribute to your remarkable courage."

"Am I that worthy?" With his hand, he caressed her breast, and she sighed and favored him with her singular shy smile. "Are you not recompense enough for my travails, because I consider myself a most fortunate man, to be Lady Arabella's husband?"

"I thought I was Lord Anthony's wife." She bit her bottom lip and closed her eyes, when he flicked a taut nipple with his thumb. "And I am content to exist as such."

"But you are so much more, Arabella." When she brushed aside the sheet and straddled his hips, he groaned and relaxed atop the down mattress. Sighing in unutterable contentment, he admired the subtle bounce of her breasts as she moved on him. "While I never lived for anyone or anything, I live for you and our babe. Indeed, you are everything, and I should declare my appreciation, that you may never doubt my devotion."

"My lord, that is lovely, and I should be delighted to hear it, in the morning, but no more talking, for now." As she rocked her hips, she closed her eyes, dropped back her head, and gave vent to a soft moan. "I wish to make love to my man."

HUMMING HER CUSTOMARY flirty little ditty, Arabella strolled down the hall and walked straight into the study, where Anthony, fully recovered from the ghastly confinement at the asylum, held court with the Mad Matchmakers, while they plotted their next successful, if less than elegant, courtship. While he included her in every aspect of his business, she preferred to forgo the meetings with his friends, which often devolved into boisterous, altogether humorous discussions unfit for a lady of character.

"Ah, there is my beautiful bride." Anthony's expression lit up, as it always did when he met her gaze, and he his patted his thigh. "Join us, my darling, because we decide which of my fellow soldiers should benefit from our matchmaking skills, and I would have your input."

"Must we choose now?" Beaulieu crossed and then uncrossed his legs, in unveiled discomfort, and she bit her tongue against laughter. "Can we not wait, and just see what develops?"

"I, for one, volunteer." Lord Michael perched on the edge of his seat. "Because I am more than ready to marry and start a family."

"I second Lord Michael as our next groom, because you need not put yourself out on my account, given I have no intention of taking a wife." Warrington folded his arms in unmasked disdain, which did not quite convince her of his position. "I am here for moral support and to provide assistance, as needed, but naught more."

"And I am not sure I am meant for that sort of happiness." Greyson rubbed his chin. "Indeed, I am not half so confident as the rest of you, so we may begin with Lord Michael, because he is amenable, and we have much to learn of the shark infested waters known as courtship."

"I concur." Beaulieu nodded, yet Arabella reflected on her husband's half-smile. Something in his expression gave her pause. Indeed, Anthony had other plans, and he flicked his fingers in a telltale sign of unrest. She would give anything to know his thoughts, which she expected he would share, later. "But I don't understand why some refer to the marriage mart as a game of love, when it is truly war unlike any other, and those who stir the pot should know what they cook, else they might get burned."

"I agree." Warrington arched a brow, when Arabella crossed the room and planted herself firmly in Anthony's lap. "Lord Michael should offer much easier sport, given we have an obliging candidate."

Anthony wrapped his arm about her waist and anchored her firmly in his grasp. When he pressed a chaste kiss to her cheek, Beaulieu cleared his throat.

"Are we delaying something of importance?" Beaulieu stood and stretched. "If you wish, we can continue strategizing Lord Michael's courtship and potential targets—er, I meant brides, tomorrow."

"Actually, I have an urgent engagement with my wife." When she met Anthony's gaze, he winked, and she understood too well the so-called engagement he referenced, because he made no secret of his preferred pastime, which involved the inventive exercise of his tongue and her body. "Shall we, my dear?"

"What about our guests?" She peered at her co-conspirators, and they feigned ignorance, because once again they extended their aid in a noble mission. "I would not ignore the Mad Matchmakers, given the aid they offered me, in your absence."

"Oh, I say, we can manage without you for, what does it take Rockingham, ten or fifteen minutes? Hardly enough time to enjoy a brandy." Beaulieu snickered, and he ushered the Mad Matchmakers from the study. "Besides, I believe I need to relieve Greyson of more of his inheritance, and we never finished our card game, last night."

"Very funny," Greyson replied, from the hall.

"What?" Chuckling, Beaulieu exited the study. "I am nothing if not brutally honest."

The house quieted, and Arabella prepared to launch her scheme.

"Alone, at last, Lady Rockingham." As she anticipated, Anthony initiated the prelude of his favored activity, and he trailed his tongue along the curve of her jaw. "Shall we adjourn to our chamber?"

"My lord, that sounds lovely, but I have a surprise for you." She gasped when he squeezed her bottom, leaving her in no doubt of his intentions. "Perhaps, I might persuade you to accompany me to the courtyard, before we retire for the afternoon, because I have a gift for you?"

"I have a gift for you, too." He nuzzled her neck, drew her closer, and tempted her with his tender touch. "And it is ready to burst for want of you."

"*Anthony*, you are insatiable." Determined not to encourage him, she brushed aside his hand and eased from his lap. Soon, he would understand. "And I shall be too happy to accommodate you, if you indulge me."

"Now?" He pouted, and she almost relented. "Can it not wait until I have expressed my appreciation of your most delectable bottom?"

"My lord, you do that every morning and night, such that I am assured of your unwavering dedication to my posterior." With fists on hips, she inclined her head. "But if it will sway you to do my bidding, I shall permit you free reign of my person, to your heart's content, for the remainder of the day, *if* you will accompany me to the courtyard this instant."

"Without benefit of clothing?" Anthony narrowed his stare, and she giggled at the burn of a blush, as she indicated the affirmative. "Until dinner and, possibly, beyond, because I am quite aroused, in light of your oh so delicious offer."

"So I gather." She bit her lip, when he stood and buttoned his coat, to conceal the evidence of his desire.

"All right. I bend to your will, Lady Rockingham, but I warn you I shall exact recompense in equal measure."

"Is that a promise?" She took his arm in hers. "Because I shall be vexed if you disappoint me."

"Indeed, my cherished bride." Together, they strolled into the hall.

"What say we have dinner served in our sitting room?"

"But we host the Mad Matchmakers, and it would be the height of rudeness were we to abandon our guests." All manner of mischief flitted through her brain, and she would never hear the end of it if they did not make an appearance, given the eccentric veterans had become like brothers to her. "And I suspect you enacted that brilliant flanking maneuver between the sheets in the wee hours, for their benefit, because I could not contain my response. I suspect I woke the entire household with my roof-rattling approbation of your ravishment."

"In truth, I did, and I shall do it again, tonight," Anthony responded, with a self-satisfied smirk to which she would have taken exception if she did not require his cooperation. "While you are the queen of the house, and no one disputes your reign, it is good to remind my friends that I am the king, and the men can entertain themselves, this evening."

"Then I shall occupy you, my lord and master." In the foyer, they turned left, where the butler lingered, and the manservant set wide the double doors. The sun spilled into the entry, and Anthony let go her arm and shielded his eyes.

She clutched his elbow and led him down the stairs, and the gravel crunched beneath his boots, as they crossed the courtyard. A telltale nicker caught his attention, and he came to an abrupt halt, when he spied her present.

That was the moment she had to stand for him, once again.

"No." Standing ramrod straight, he shook his head. "Arabella, what have you done?"

"I beg you, my lord, do not deny me." When he tried to pull free, she held fast, because he could not run from his fears. "I selected a white Andalusian, because I would never try to replace Hesperus. This resplendent creature is sweet-tempered and eager to make your acquaintance. Will you not come and meet him? Will you not give him a chance?"

"My angel, I know what you want, but I cannot do this." When he closed his eyes, she brushed a lock of hair from his forehead. While she hated causing him unrest, he could not spend his life forever longing for his past self. He had to look to the future. "Please, ask anything of me, but do not ask this."

"Trust me, you can do it, my darling." Framing his face, she pressed her lips to his, ever so briefly. "Anthony, I know you are afraid. I do so wish you could see yourself as I see you, because you are the strongest, bravest man of my acquaintance, and I shall go to my grave, declaring it for all to hear." With care, she slipped her arms about his waist and hugged him. "You have endured and survived unspeakable horrors, yet you remain the gentlest soul, unspoiled by the cruelties inflicted upon you. You work to ensure those about you are protected, without concern for yourself, and you are generous, to a fault. Will you not let me do something for you? Will you not let me help ease your last gaping wound?" Again, she kissed him. "Please, my love. If he does not suit you, we can return him to Tattersalls, but I ask that you give him a chance. Just come and meet him. If you will not do it for yourself, do it for me and our unborn child."

A war of emotions invested his handsome visage, and she bit her tongue against further encouragement. He had to make the decision for himself. To her relief, when he noted the presence of his friends, he advanced two steps.

"Major." Beaulieu held the lead of the impressive stallion she purchased for her husband. "We stand at the ready, sir."

"You conspired with my men?" Anthony turned to her, and she could not miss the hurt in his expression. "Why did you not discuss your plan with me, because you know how I feel?"

"It is because I know of your affliction that I did not consult you." Little by little, she coaxed him, with a caress here and a gentle nudge there, and he did not resist her. Slowly, the lines of strain about his mouth relaxed, and he exhaled audibly. "But you cannot let your fears keep you from moving forward, my love. For good or ill, you must get back on a horse, else you risk remaining a prisoner to the past, and I will not allow that."

"What if I am not ready to let go? What if I need my pain?" When her husband spoke, the beautiful steed flicked his ears and peered in Anthony's direction. "Well, hello there." He paused just at the stallion's head. "Do you have a name?"

"I suppose I should leave that to you, if you keep him." Arabella anchored at his side. "But I thought we might select something Greek, in keeping with our tradition."

"Our tradition?" Anthony blinked. "Ah, yes. You have Astraea."

When she dipped her chin, Beaulieu pried open the creature's lips, that Anthony might inspect the teeth. For a while, her courageous soldier simply stood there. Then, to her surprise, Anthony bent and ran his hand down the cannon bones, one after the other.

"What solid, sturdy legs you have." Anthony chuckled and rubbed the back of his neck, and the horse whinnied a reply. Arabella uttered a prayer. "You have a muscular chest, too, and a chiseled jaw, with wide-set, intelligent eyes, which I would do well to heed, I suspect. I should give you free rein at my own peril." He continued his inspection, running his palm along the prominent withers, the strong back, and the powerful haunches. "He is blessed with a perfectly balanced conformation. Superb, Arabella. I could not have chosen a better specimen."

"I did so wish to please you." She caught Beaulieu's stare, and he signaled the stable hand, who saddled the stallion. "Shall we venture into the north field?"

"I am not sure." Anthony retreated and stiffened. "What if it rains?"

"My lord, there is not a cloud in the sky." After waving to the stablemaster, who brought forth Astraea, Arabella tugged on her kidskin gloves. "If it makes you feel better, we need not ride far.

Please, Anthony." Leaning forward, on tiptoes, she whispered in his ear, "I will do anything."

"I will hold you to it," he replied, in a low voice. "If I am to make a fool of myself, I expect a reward. Now then, let us get this insanity over with, because I would not waste my time on useless endeavors."

Moving slow and steady, and with Beaulieu's assistance, Anthony grasped the reins and eased his left foot into the stirrup. With a half-hearted leap, he tried to gain the saddle. On his first attempt, he tripped and almost fell flat on his arse. His second try landed Anthony in Beaulieu's arms, and she swallowed a snort of laughter. For the third effort, the stable hand set a mounting block on the ground and gave Anthony a boost.

With her man secure in the saddle, Beaulieu lifted Arabella atop Astraea and urged the elegant mare into an easy trot. Following in her wake, in a less than inspiring sight, Anthony bobbled and bounced, and she feared her grand scheme just might break something of importance. Or worse, widow her. Still, she persevered.

Trailing the path, they cleared the formal grounds, and her husband pulled beside her. Together, they proceeded to the lea and veered into the verdant meadow dotted with clusters of wildflowers. In an encouraging sign, he rode past her, and she urged Astraea into a gallop.

Faster and faster, they drove their mounts, and her heart raced, as the wind whispered and thrummed in her hair. Charging a rise, her husband exhibited confidence, yet she checked her enthusiasm. He sped forth and drew back, and she followed his lead.

And then it happened.

In the wide, open space of flat earth, Anthony let go the reins. Closing his eyes, he flung back his head, and splayed his arm. In that instant, she steered Astraea to the shadows of a crescent of mighty oaks, where they stopped, because she would not intrude on the intimate moment.

It was a rare bit of magic, when the immediate surroundings faded to black, and horse and rider merged into complete oneness. The birds ceased their lilting singsong and the breeze stilled, as all of nature roused to attention, to witness the great beast yielding to human fragility. Man and horse moved as one, such that the distinctions between them all but disappeared, and they soared across the land with speed and precision. The delicate ballet, unique in its combination of incomparable grace and raw power, posed an awe-inspiring sight to behold, and she would not have missed it for the world.

At the verge, Anthony reined in and walked the stallion in a straight line. Then he cantered in circles to the left and the right, taking the horse through its paces. It was more than she could have hoped for, and she wiped more than a few happy tears from her cheeks.

After a few additional turns, he glanced over his shoulder and searched for her. When he spied her, she smiled, and he waved. In play, she blew him a kiss, which he pretended to catch. At last, he urged the horse into a trot and joined her, near a copse of trees.

"I have given some thought to a name." Anthony leaned forward and patted the horse. "How does Aeolus strike you?"

"Well, that depends." She shrugged and struggled to contain her excitement mixed with reticence. Her belly flip-flopped, and she swallowed the lump in her throat. "Does he resemble the god of the winds and air?"

"In truth, he rides like the wind." Her husband chuckled but then sobered, and he studied her. "What troubles you, my darling, when this is a glorious day?"

"You are not angry with me?" It was then she realized she had been holding her breath. "You are not vexed that I purchased the stallion without consulting you?" she blurted.

"No." He shook his head. "To be honest, I never would have done it, had you left the decision to me, so it appears I am in your debt, again."

"My lord, you are absolutely resplendent, and you belong on a horse." She raised a hand. "Before you protest, I am not just saying that because you are my cherished husband, and you owe me nothing. Indeed, you were to the saddle born."

Yet, there was something else that caught her attention. A miraculous transformation overtook her husband, and she admired the playful dance of mischief in his beautiful blue eyes and his carefree expression.

"Thank you, love." Grasping the reins, he clucked his tongue and drew Aeolus near, and Astraea shifted but displayed no apprehension. With telltale hunger dancing in his gaze, Anthony beckoned, and she met him halfway. The first touch of their lips ignited her flesh, and she nibbled playfully at his tongue. When Aeolus nickered, Anthony and Arabella parted. "I believe you promised me a boon, Lady Rockingham."

"I did." She sat upright and cast him a come-hither glance. "And I fully intend to honor the bargain, to equal benefit, Lord Rockingham."

"You pledged anything I require. What say we place another wager?" His voice grew husky with the promise of unspoken pleasures, when he narrowed his stare and waggled his brows. "First one to the stable gets to undress the other."

"My lord, let us race." With a nudge, she set a blazing pace but tempered Astraea's gallop. In a mere flash, Anthony sped past, and she laughed in his wake.

Of course, she would ensure her man won the contest, and she would savor his prize.

EPILOGUE

S UNLIGHT KISSED THE earth, bathing the lush gardens of Glenden-ning in a blanket of gold. In the sky, nary a cloud marred the vibrant blue tapestry. In the distance, a lone tern swooped and soared, dancing on the wind. Standing before the window in his study, Anthony smiled and reflected on the simple pleasures of life, which he relished in the quiet moments of his peaceful existence.

After the birth of his heir, a proud moment that would sustain him to the grave, and an extended period of recovery under Dr. Handley's astute care, Anthony and Arabella remained at the ancestral seat of the marquisate. There, they focused on strengthening their relationship, and they planned their child's future. And he paid particular attention to the conception of more babes, every morning, noon, and night, much to the expressed appreciation of his spirited bride.

"Darling, I am sorry to intrude, but His Grace is just arrived." Ah, how he loved when she addressed him thus. When he faced his wife, she frowned. "Shall I prepare the guillotine?"

"You would do that." He chuckled and strolled to sit behind his desk, in a position of power. "I do not doubt you for an instant, because you are formidable, Lady Rockingham."

"Why should you? And you knew that before you married me." She shrugged, then furrowed her brow. "Do you really believe this is a good idea? While he is your father, I don't trust him."

"Neither do I," Beaulieu added, as he entered the study. "And Lady

Rockingham is an uncommonly wise woman, though I am loath to admit it."

"We second and third that." Lord Greyson followed with Lord Warrington, who nodded, and they occupied positions near the hearth.

"I concur," replied Lord Michael, and he perched like a sentry near the door. "While I support you, and always will, I have no faith in His Grace. He merits none, based on past actions, but I defer to your judgment and follow your lead."

A knock preceded his father's entrance, and Anthony steeled his nerves. With a deep breath, he rolled his shoulders and motioned to Arabella. Without hesitation, she assumed her place at his side.

"Anthony." Father dipped his chin. "You are looking quite well."

"No thanks to you," Arabella responded with a sharp tongue. When he gripped her hand, she quieted but scowled, and how he adored her temper.

"You requested this meeting." Despite an overwhelming desire to rail at the injustice of his imprisonment, Anthony mustered an air of unimpaired aplomb, but anger simmered just below the surface. "What brings you to Sussex?"

"I came to apologize." With an expression of contrition, the once mighty duke appeared a mere shadow of his former self. A pale complexion emphasized dark circles beneath his eyes, and he had lost weight. When he sat before Anthony's desk, he fidgeted and adjusted the hem of his sleeve. "But my intentions were honorable. I only wanted to help you, and what is my reward? I have lost my duchess and my closest friend."

"You think yourself deserving of recompense for almost getting Anthony killed? The only reason he survived is because I challenged you." Arabella clenched a fist, and never was a husband prouder of his bride. He would express his appreciation of her defense, later. "If it is a reward you seek, I shall be too happy to give you—"

"It is all right, darling." Biting his tongue against laughter, because he could only imagine what his fiery hellion might say next, Anthony stretched upright, and she quieted. Oh, he would put all that energy to use, that afternoon. Then he gave his attention to his father. "I have no business interfering in your quarrel with Lord Ainsworth, so I advise you to take it up with him. As for my mother, she is here at my invitation, visiting her grandson."

"A right I am owed but denied." Father sniffed. "Am I to be forever punished for a minor mistake?"

"A *minor* mistake?" Arabella shot from her chair. Just as quick, Anthony tugged her skirt, and she reclaimed her seat. "The only thing we owe you is a sound horse whipping and a swift kick in the arse."

The Mad Matchmakers chuckled in concert.

Fighting for control of his emotions, Anthony remained stock-still. After a moment of reflection, during which he carefully considered his words, he inhaled a deep, calming breath.

"You know what you did, and it was rather more than you imply." A series of brutal images flashed before him, and he reached for his wife. At once, she twined her fingers in his. "However, the birth of my heir softens my position in your favor, and I am prepared to be charitable where you are concerned, although I am not certain you deserve such consideration."

"Anthony, as God is my witness, I thought I was doing right by you." Father splayed his arms in contrition. "I was led to believe you would receive proper care and treatment. Never did I suspect nefarious motives, else I never would have placed you in the asylum. Please, forgive me."

Silence blanketed the room, and he mulled his father's request. The hurt and the pain of the previous summer resurfaced, and he closed his eyes against the vivid memories. The bugle sounded, horse's hooves thundered, and Napoleon's men charged, executing a perfect flanking *manoeuvre sur derri res*, Boney's favorite tactic.

Arabella caressed his hand.

In an instant, his wife's face, and that of his newborn son, came to him. Their smiles, their joy trounced the angst, brushing aside the agony. It was then he realized he had to forgive his father or risk forever being tied to the horrors of his past. He shook himself alert.

"You wish to see your grandson. A reasonable request I am inclined to allow. You may even speak with Mama, provided she is amenable." Anthony pointed for emphasis. "But I will have you thrown out of this house, head over heels, if you upset her. Is that clear?"

"Yes." Father slumped forward.

"And I would have your word, as a gentleman, that you will make no attempt to take custody of my son." Anthony pounded his fist on the desk. "On that I will not relent, and you may leave, at once."

"I say, that is wholly unfair, and I am offended by the mere suggestion." Father thrust his chin and glanced at Arabella. Beneath her scowl, the duke shrank. "Be that as it may, know that you have my word, as a gentleman, I will not infringe upon your duties as primary caregiver for your heir, in any capacity."

In rigid motion, which underscored her displeasure with his actions, Arabella reached behind her and tugged the bellpull. When the butler appeared, she huffed. "Merriweather, show His Grace to the nursery."

The butler bowed. "This way, Your Grace."

When Father stood, Arabella snapped her fingers, and the Mad Matchmakers surrounded the duke. Anthony narrowed his stare and studied his beloved bride.

"Is this necessary?" Father asked with more than a little incredulity.

"It is if you wish to see my son." She folded her arms, and how he loved her stubborn streak. Anthony would put *that* to good use, too. "Lord Rockingham may forgive you, but he is a better man than most. I, on the other hand, know no such affinity." To Beaulieu, she said, "If

His Grace makes one false move, shoot him."

"Aye, Lady Rockingham." Beaulieu clicked his heels and saluted. Then he gave the duke a none-too-gentle shove. "Move, Your Grace."

The awkward party departed, with Arabella trailing in their footsteps. At the door, she secured the oak panel and set the latch. A particularly protuberant part of his anatomy roused to attention, especially when she turned and bit her bottom lip.

"Are you vexed with me?" Ah, she deployed the charming pout he could never resist. When he slapped his thigh, she walked to him. After stepping about his knees, she eased to his lap and rested her head to his chest. "I'm sorry, my love, but I may never forgive your father."

"It is all right, sweetheart. Your loyalty does you great credit." With his nose, he gave her a gentle nudge. To his delight, she threw her arms about his shoulders and claimed his mouth with her usual fervor. After a few groping, heated, achingly desperate minutes, he broke their kiss. "I needed that."

"Oh?" She nipped his chin and wiggled her bottom. "I never would have guessed."

"You tempt me, Lady Rockingham." Anthony pressed his palm to her hip, leaving her in no doubt of his desire. "You may regret it when we adjourn to our chambers, shortly."

"Is that a promise?" Arabella scored her nails across the nape of his neck and nibbled the curve of his jaw. "Or do you require additional encouragement?"

"You are in a mood, and I like it." He bent his head and suckled her lips. "What got into you?"

"Well, I was thinking of Lord Michael." That was like a splash of cold water, and he eased back in his chair. "I rather fancy the idea of finding his true love, given the success of our union. Indeed, I want to see all the Mad Matchmakers similarly situated."

"Then why do I detect a note of hesitation?" Anthony squeezed her derrière, and she squirmed. "Has he spoken to you about a possible candidate? Has a particular lady caught his eye?"

"No, he has said nothing, and it's not that." Once again, she reclined against his chest and sighed. "Please, don't be angry with me, but I suspect one of your friends presents far greater need at this time, although he would never admit it. Therein is where we should focus our efforts."

"Someone who helped us, when we most needed him." He smiled when she shuffled to meet his gaze. "While they all deserve love, and I vow to find each one of my fellow soldiers a wife, this particular individual is in immediate peril, and we must act, now, if we are to save him."

"Do you know what haunts him? He often rattled the rooftops, late at night, while guarding me in your absence." Arabella framed his face with her delicate hands. "Have you any idea what chases him in the wee hours?"

"Aye, but it is not my story to tell, because he is unaware that I know the truth." And it was a tragic tale, but he would take his friend's story to the grave. "So, have you a target bride, in mind?"

"I do." With a mischievous grin, she nodded. "And I believe she could be his salvation, with his cooperation."

"I wager an afternoon of delight that I can guess your mark." Anthony waggled his brows and stood, carrying her with him. He extended his arm, which she accepted. "As for his cooperation, I predict his courtship will be about as easy as peeling a turtle."

Together, they strolled from the study and down the hall. In the foyer, they turned right and ascended the stairs. At the landing, they continued through the gallery to their private quarters. When they neared the double-doored entry, Arabella inclined her head.

"Then we are agreed?" she asked.

"Indubitably."

"Our next Mad Matchmaker to marry will be..."

Anthony paused to usher his delectable bride into their domain, and he handed her over the threshold. In their sitting room, where they often took their meals, where they discussed their future, where they shared a book, and where he made love to her in every conceivable position and place, she stopped and squared her shoulders. He mimicked her stance and caught her stare. In unison, they smiled and said, "Beaulieu."

About the Author

A proud Latina, *USA Today* bestselling, Amazon All-Star author Barbara Devlin was born a storyteller, but it was a weeklong vacation to Bethany Beach, Delaware that forever changed her life. The little house her parents rented had a collection of books by Kathleen Woodiwiss, which exposed Barbara to the world of romance, and *Shanna* remains a personal favorite.

Barbara writes heartfelt historical romances that feature not so perfect heroes who may know how to seduce a woman but know nothing of marriage. And she prefers feisty but smart heroines who sometimes save the hero before they find their happily ever after.

Barbara is a disabled-in-the-line-of-duty retired police officer. She earned an MA in English and continued a course of study for a Doctorate in Literature and Rhetoric. She happily considered herself an exceedingly eccentric English professor, until success in Indie publishing lured her into writing, full-time, featuring her fictional knighthood, the Brethren of the Coast.

Connect with Barbara Devlin at BarbaraDevlin.com, where you can sign up for her newsletter, The Knightly News.

Barbara Devlin Website: barbaradevlin.com
Facebook: BarbaraDevlinAuthor
Twitter: @barbara_devlin
BookBub: bookbub.com/authors/barbara-devlin
Goodreads: goodreads.com/author/show/6462331.Barbara_Devlin
Pinterest: bdevlinauthor
Instagram: barbara.devlin